Praise for

the novels of the Nine Kingdoms

Princess of the Sword

"Beautifully written, with an intricately detailed society born of Ms. Kurland's remarkable imagination, this is an extraordinary tale for fantasy readers as well as those who just want to read a good love story."
—*Romance Reviews Today*

"An excellent finish to a great romantic quest fantasy . . . Readers will relish Ms. Kurland's superb trilogy." —*Genre Go Round Reviews*

"An intelligent, involving tale full of love and adventure . . . If you enjoy vast worlds, quiet love stories, and especially fantasy, I would suggest you give this trilogy a try." —*All About Romance*

The Mage's Daughter

"Engaging characters—family, friends, and enemies—keep the story hopping along with readers relishing every word and hungering for the next installment. [A] perfect ten." —*Romance Reviews Today*

"Lynn Kurland has become one of my favorite fantasy authors; I can hardly wait to see what happens next." —*Huntress Reviews*

"*The Mage's Daughter*, like its predecessor, *Star of the Morning*, is the best work Lynn Kurland has ever done. I can't recommend this book highly enough." —*Fresh Fiction*

"I couldn't put the book down . . . I highly recommend this book, the series, and all of Ms. Kurland's other works. Brilliant!"
—*ParaNormal Romance Reviews*

"This is a terrific romantic fantasy. Lynn Kurland provides a fabulous . . . tale that sets the stage for an incredible finish." —*Midwest Book Review*

continued . . .

From This Moment On

"A disarming blend of romance, suspense, and heartwarming humor, this book is romantic comedy at its best." —*Publishers Weekly*

"A deftly plotted delight." —*Booklist*

My Heart Stood Still

"The essence of pure romance. Sweet, poignant, and truly magical, this is a rare treat." —*Booklist*

If I Had You

"Kurland brings history to life . . . in this tender medieval romance." —*Booklist*

The More I See You

"Blends history with spellbinding passion and impressive characterization, not to mention a magnificent plot." —*Rendezvous*

Another Chance to Dream

"Kurland creates a special romance." —*Publishers Weekly*

The Very Thought of You

"[A] masterpiece . . . This fabulous tale will enchant anyone who reads it." —*Painted Rock Reviews*

This Is All I Ask

"Both powerful and sensitive . . . A wonderfully rich and rewarding book." —Susan Wiggs

A Dance Through Time

"An irresistibly fast and funny romp across time." —Stella Cameron

Lynn Kurland

A Tapestry of Spells

BERKLEY SENSATION, NEW YORK

THE BERKLEY PUBLISHING GROUP
Published by the Penguin Group
Penguin Group (USA) Inc.
375 Hudson Street, New York, New York 10014, USA
Penguin Group (Canada), 90 Eglinton Avenue East, Suite 700, Toronto, Ontario M4P 2Y3, Canada
(a division of Pearson Penguin Canada Inc.)
Penguin Books Ltd., 80 Strand, London WC2R 0RL, England
Penguin Group Ireland, 25 St. Stephen's Green, Dublin 2, Ireland (a division of Penguin Books Ltd.)
Penguin Group (Australia), 250 Camberwell Road, Camberwell, Victoria 3124, Australia
(a division of Pearson Australia Group Pty. Ltd.)
Penguin Books India Pvt. Ltd., 11 Community Centre, Panchsheel Park, New Delhi—110 017, India
Penguin Group (NZ), 67 Apollo Drive, Rosedale, North Shore 0632, New Zealand
(a division of Pearson New Zealand Ltd.)
Penguin Books (South Africa) (Pty.) Ltd., 24 Sturdee Avenue, Rosebank, Johannesburg 2196,
South Africa

Penguin Books Ltd., Registered Offices: 80 Strand, London WC2R 0RL, England

This book is an original publication of The Berkley Publishing Group.

This is a work of fiction. Names, characters, places, and incidents either are the product of the author's imagination or are used fictitiously, and any resemblance to actual persons, living or dead, business establishments, events, or locales is entirely coincidental. The publisher does not have any control over and does not assume any responsibility for author or third-party websites or their content.

PRINTING HISTORY
Berkley Sensation trade paperback edition / January 2010

Library of Congress Cataloging-in-Publication Data

Kurland, Lynn.
   A tapestry of spells / Lynn Kurland.—Berkley Sensation trade pbk. ed.
      p.   cm.
   ISBN 978-0-425-23213-2
   1. Magic—Fiction.   I. Title.
   PS3561.U645T37 2010
   813'.54—dc22   2009038221

PRINTED IN THE UNITED STATES OF AMERICA

10   9   8   7   6   5   4   3   2   1

Prologue

*T*he evil leapt up like a geyser, cascaded down, and washed the boy away
with it.

It wasn't unexpected, that eruption from the well, but it was terrifying in
its quickness and horrifying in its ferocity. The lad would have stopped that
spewing, or mitigated its effects, or reached out but a moment sooner to take
his younger sister's hand if he could have managed it, but events happened too
quickly for him to do aught but struggle frantically to find his footing on top
of that wave so he wasn't pulled beneath it and drowned.

Yet even with all his efforts, he was sent tumbling over and over again
through the forest until, bruised and battered, he came to rest against a
mighty oak.

Time passed without his having any sense of it until he came to himself
and realized he was alive. He pushed himself up to his knees but could rise no
farther. After many moments of simply trying to gain his bearings, he managed to turn and crawl painfully back through the trees, back the way he'd

come. He knelt at the edge of a particular glade and looked at what another might have considered to be the remains of a great battle.

He knew better.

It had been a slaughter, a hopeless, unforgiving slaughter. He sought frantically for signs of life, but saw none. No doubt the force of the eruption had been enough to wash away all the others—save his mother who was still there, lying motionless by the well. He watched her for several minutes, hoping beyond hope that . . .

He looked away quickly. Obviously, he was the only one left alive. He pulled himself up by means of an obliging tree, then staggered from trunk to trunk, forcing himself to scour the surrounding area for any sign that he had judged amiss. But nay, there was none moving save him. He realized suddenly, with a certainty that left him cold, that he would join the slain if he didn't flee.

The evil was still there, alive and seeking.

The thought of leaving his kin behind was a hot dagger thrust without mercy into his chest, so painful that he could hardly bear it, but he knew he would die if he didn't run, so run he would have to. He had failed that day to stop the destruction, but if he could stay alive long enough to regroup to fight another day, to avenge his mother, and his brothers, and his wee sister . . .

He turned and staggered away. He managed to keep his feet for perhaps half a league before the effort became too much. He fell to his hands and knees in dirt that would have been tolerable before but was now full of the marshy, putrid leavings of what had recently washed over it. He ignored the foulness. He had to get away and there was no other direction but forward.

Time continued to stretch, from minutes to hours to days. He continued to creep along, stopping to rest only when he couldn't manage another step. The ground eventually became rugged paths through mountains, then well-worn tracks over inhospitable plains, and then unpleasant slogs through muddy farmland.

It was then that he began to notice the magic.

At first he saw it only out of the corner of his eye. He turned aside several *times to reach for it, only to have it disappear. He began to suspect it was nothing more than a cruel trick played on his weary mind until one particular moment on that interminable journey through his dreams. He saw a piece of magic lying on the ground in the shape of a page from a book. He stumbled over to it, then reached out to touch it.*

The spell reached up, took hold of him, and pulled him down into itself . . .

Ruith of nowhere in particular found himself on his feet in front of his own hearth without knowing quite how he'd gotten there. He was breathing harshly, as if he'd run for leagues without pause. He'd done that regularly over the course of his thirty winters, so he felt fairly safe in comparing the two. He leaned over and put his hands on the long table there, sucking in desperately needed breaths until he thought he could manage a few normal ones without feeling as if he were drowning.

He didn't dream often. In fact, he had spent more of his youth than he should have not sleeping in an effort to avoid dreaming. In time, he had learned to simply sleep dreamlessly.

It had taken years, but he had also eventually learned not to remember how he'd managed to crawl up the rugged path to what had turned out to be an empty house, bury his magic deep inside himself with a single, powerful spell, then surrender to the weariness he had no longer been able to fight. He rarely thought about how he'd woken later in front of a stone-cold hearth only to find wood chopped and ready for his use, food preserved and set aside to keep him from starving that first winter, and a library large enough to engage his ten-year-old's curiosity.

Eventually, he had settled quite comfortably into an existence that was physically and mentally demanding in a strictly pedestrian sort of way. If he could sense the spells that surrounded his house and protected him, or if he sometimes amused himself by thinking on ways they could have been fashioned differently, or if he now and again found himself tempted to add something extra to the local alemaster's latest offering, well, those were things that other men thought on without incident.

Surely.

He hadn't used a single word of magic in a score of years, not since that last spell he'd woven, a dwarvish spell of concealment. He was, for all intents and purposes, just a man—or, rather, a man pretending to be a mage whom the nearby villagers feared too greatly to approach. He sometimes wondered what he would have done had one of them dared beg for a decent piece of magic to be wrought on their behalf, but that never required much thought.

He wouldn't have used magic if his life had depended on it.

He straightened, took another deep, cleansing breath, then turned and walked back into his bedchamber. He pulled on boots and a heavy tunic, then walked back to his front door. He snatched up a brace of hunting knives and strapped them to his back. He might have been out merely for a run, but he was also not fool enough to leave the safety of his house without some sort of weapon to hand.

He buckled the belt for his sheathed knives and winced at the pain in his hand. He looked down at that hand and frowned. There was nothing to be seen, of course, but he felt the remains of his dream wrapped around his arm, from his wrist up past his elbow. He clenched and unclenched his fist, then purposely ignored the discomfort. Overindulgence in Master Franciscus's finest pale ale, no doubt. Spending the better part of the morning running would be penance enough, perhaps.

It was odd, though. He hadn't had dreams of that sort in at least a decade. He'd all but forgotten that he'd ever had them.

He pulled his door shut behind him, then loped off down the path. Dawn was still an hour off, but the darkness didn't deter him.

He had run through the woods surrounding his mountain for so long, he likely could have run them with his eyes closed—

Which at the moment might not have been such a wise thing to do. He was almost on top of a man strolling through the woods before he realized it. He supposed 'twas a fortunate thing he was as light-footed as he was, or he might have had a battle on his hands he didn't particularly want to fight. He drew back and waited until the man continued on past him, walking without haste, apparently oblivious to what was in the woods around him. Ruith watched him go, then shook his head. The fool would likely end up in a ditch somewhere, dead and missing not only his very fine cloak but his boots as well.

He consigned the almost-encounter to the list of rather odd things that had happened to him in the past several hours, then decided that perhaps he should make a vow to swear off more than a single glass of ale at a sitting. Perhaps Master Franciscus's brew was more potent than he'd led himself to believe all these years.

He considered the direction the man was taking, then frowned. He had no stomach for conversation and now south was apparently denied him. He muttered a curse, then put his head down and took a direction he hadn't intended to take.

And he ignored the pain in his arm that had nothing to do with a visible wound.

One

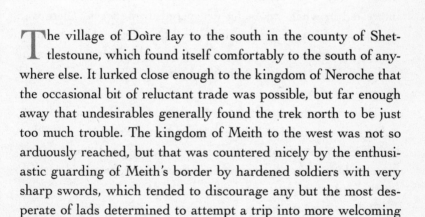

The village of Doìre lay to the south in the county of Shettlestoune, which found itself comfortably to the south of anywhere else. It lurked close enough to the kingdom of Neroche that the occasional bit of reluctant trade was possible, but far enough away that undesirables generally found the trek north to be just too much trouble. The kingdom of Meith to the west was not so arduously reached, but that was countered nicely by the enthusiastic guarding of Meith's border by hardened soldiers with very sharp swords, which tended to discourage any but the most desperate of lads determined to attempt a trip into more welcoming territory.

Shettlestoune was a place where men with secrets went to hide and women with aspirations of a decent future tried to escape as soon as possible. Villages were few and far between, taverns were rough, and local constabularies more than willing to find the relentlessly sunny skies more interesting than whatever mischief might have been going on under their noses.

It was also quite possibly the most unrelentingly bland landscape in all of the Nine Kingdoms.

Urchaid of too many places to name acknowledged the truth of that as he eyed with disfavor the flora and fauna, such as it was, that huddled nervously beyond the boundaries of the one-street village he was wandering in. Traveling in the south was always tedious, but he'd found himself, against all sense, blown down from more civilized countries on an ill wind that seemed reluctant to let him go.

He checked his sleeves briefly, tugged at a bit of lace that had somehow become tucked where it couldn't be seen, then smoothed his hair back from his face. At least it could be said that no matter where he went, he traveled there well dressed. Perhaps he should have continued on a bit longer on wing, as it were, and spared himself even a few hours' worth of travel stains, but he'd been interested in what was being whispered in the trees. There was something afoot, something untoward. Given that the only thing that intrigued him more than a well-stocked haberdasher was an evil spell, it had been worth the trouble to settle back into his usual form before dawn.

There were those, he had to admit, who found his magical preferences distasteful, but fortunately for him those lads were either locked up in the schools of wizardry or doing good whilst sitting on some kingly throne or another in countries he tried his damndest to avoid.

He hated do-gooders.

He tried to counter their efforts as often as possible, though he couldn't say his current journey had anything to do with that. It had merely been the result of nothing more villainous than a bit of eavesdropping. He'd heard rumors of magic, magic he hadn't heard discussed in years, springing up in unexpected places. What else could he do but see for himself if those rumors were true?

He walked into the only pub in town, a decent-looking place as far as rustic pubs in the midst of hell went, then found a relatively comfortable seat by the fire and waited patiently for someone to come take his order.

He waited without success until he realized he was still wearing a spell of invisibility. He frowned and removed it with a snap of his fingers, which had the added benefit of drawing the attention of the lone barmaid. She looked every bit as wholesome and well fed as he'd expected a local country miss might. Whatever else they did in the south, they certainly didn't forget to eat. At least she was quick about her business and remembered to deliver exactly what he'd ordered.

He sipped his ale hesitantly, then found to his great surprise that it was eminently drinkable. He sat back in his chair, stretched his long legs out and crossed his feet at the ankles, then amused himself by looking at the patrons who had wandered in for an early-morning constitutional.

Thieves, liars, cheaters—and those were the more upstanding souls gathered there. The few honest ones stood out like gold nuggets lying in the sun on dark soil. The wench who had served him was one of those, as was the master brewer who had come in from his workroom, but the barkeep didn't qualify, nor did most of the patrons. Well, save that gawky farmhand who had stumbled into the pub and was asking for watered-down ale, if the barkeep wouldn't mind seeing to it for him.

The alemaster elbowed the barkeep aside and saw to the deed himself. Urchaid frowned thoughtfully. The man pushing the glass across the wood seemed familiar, though he couldn't fathom why. He considered a bit longer, then shrugged. Perhaps he had frequented so many pubs in a search for something decent to drink that all the alemasters had begun to look alike. Such was the hazard of a very, very long life, apparently.

The alemaster waited until the boy was well watered, then slid a jug across the counter to him.

"Best hurry home, Ned, lad. I heard tell that Lady Higgleton is off to see your mistress this morn."

The lad looked nervously over his shoulder out the window, as if he fully expected to see a legion of black mages clustered there with his death on their minds. "She wants a spell, do you think?"

"What I think, lad," the alemaster said with a wry smile, "isn't fit for speaking most of the time." He started to say something else, then looked up and stiffened. He reached out and pulled the boy around the counter. "Go out the back, Ned, and run home. Keep Sarah safe."

The lad clutched his jug of ale and did as he was told without hesitation.

Urchaid turned to see what had spurred the alemaster into such abrupt action. A man stood in the doorway, clutching it as if it were all that held him up.

He lurched inside and stumbled over to a table where he cast himself down into a chair for only so long as it took him to rid himself of his cloak. He bounced back up as if he was simply too full of energy to sit. He walked over to the bar and demanded a meal first from the alemaster, who merely favored him with a sour look and turned away, then from the barkeep, who apparently had a stronger stomach. That, or the barkeep had noted the fatness of the restless one's purse, a purse that made a copious noise when he moved.

Urchaid caught the elbow of his serving maid the next time she passed by him. "Who is that lad eating as if he hasn't in a fortnight?" he asked casually.

Her gaze flicked to the man and back quickly, then she hesitated. Urchaid fished a gold sovereign out of his purse and laid it on the table. There was no use in being frugal when information was to be had.

"He's the brother of the village witch up the way," she said promptly. She leaned over and wiped the table with her cloth, deftly scooping the coin into her hand at the same time. "He's an unpleasant sort."

"He certainly seems to be," Urchaid said, depositing more money onto the table. "Does he weave spells, or is it just his sister with all the common magic?"

"Oh, he wouldn't bother with useful spells," she said, pocketing the new offering with alacrity. "'Tis beneath him."

"Is he so powerful, then?" Urchaid asked, tracing his finger idly around the rim of his glass.

"So he says, though I wouldn't know." She shivered. "Thought we were rid of him."

She turned and headed without hesitation to the back of the pub. Urchaid looked at the local witch's brother and decided that perhaps he could pass a bit of time in conversation with the lad—just for the sake of being polite, of course.

Urchaid rose and picked up his ale. He nodded at the barkeep on his way across the room, then sat himself down at the table next to the newcomer's. He wasn't one for seeing things, but he could certainly smell them. A stench clung to the man, much like the smell of charred meat that lingered in the house even after it had been thrown to the pigs.

The smell of something the lad before him definitely shouldn't have been up to.

Curious.

The barkeep himself arrived with another pint of ale. Urchaid casually gestured with his pointer finger toward the man sitting at the table next to his. The barkeep set down the second glass in front of the witchwoman's brother.

"With his compliments," the barkeep said, nodding in Urchaid's direction.

"Thank you," the man said, reaching for the glass and downing the contents in one long, ungainly pull. He belched loudly and dragged his sleeve across his mouth.

Urchaid lifted an eyebrow, then nodded to the barkeep again.

It took half an hour before the man had surrendered his name, which Urchaid already knew, and his business, which was apparently large, important pieces of magic that were bound to garner the notice of equally important people. Urchaid leaned one elbow on the table and his chin on his fist as he listened in fascination to the spewings of an utter neophyte. He could bring to mind without effort a dozen mages who would have had his naive companion for breakfast accompanied by a fine, dry sherry.

"I didn't succeed the first time," Daniel said, his eyes full of terrible things he likely wished he hadn't seen, "but I will this time."

Urchaid smiled pleasantly. "Of course you will, my lad."

Daniel looked about himself blearily, as if he couldn't quite remember how he'd gotten to be where he was, then he turned back to Urchaid. A shuttered look came over his face, something profoundly unpleasant and cruel. That was, Urchaid suspected, a fair sight closer to who he truly was than was the persona of a happy drunk. Daniel looked down his nose coldly.

"I thank you for the ale. I'll remember it and show you mercy when the time comes."

Urchaid sat back, thoroughly enjoying the display he was witnessing. "Off to do foul deeds, are you?"

Daniel leaned close and looked at him with dark, fathomless eyes. "I am. And I believe, friend, that you would be wise to be very far away when they're wrought."

Urchaid suppressed the urge to laugh out loud. What a ridiculous boy, to be so completely unaware of whom he was dealing with. He managed a solemn nod, then watched Daniel stride off toward the doorway with the sudden soberness of a man truly off to do something truly vile. Urchaid finished his drink in a leisurely fashion and considered what he'd heard. It was tempting to dismiss the lad's ramblings as those of one who'd had too much hard ale to accompany his eggs, but there had been something in the lad's eye.

Something as intriguing as that faint hint of magic clinging to him.

He pushed his cup away and decided it would be rather interesting to follow Daniel of Doìre for a bit, just to see where he led. With any luck at all, the direction would be *out of Shettlestoune*. He looked around the pub again, shaking his head. To be trapped in such a place without any hope of escape. Very unpleasant. Even the barkeep looked miserable. The alemaster looked less miserable than calculating, standing there suddenly as he was with his arms folded over his chest and an unwelcoming look on his face.

Urchaid supposed that was his cue to exit stage left before he drew more attention to himself than he cared to have. He rose, nodded to the alemaster and barkeep both, then left the pub without haste. He stopped in the shadows of the building and looked up into the bright morning sky. The world trembled, as if it held its breath for a mighty change. There were things afoot in Neroche, of course, but this . . . this was different. More wrenching. More dangerous.

Quite a bit more interesting.

He looked to his right, saw the path in the distance that led through yet more profoundly unattractive clutches of scrub oak, then sighed. He could hear the faint sound of Daniel's cursing from that path. Perhaps the lad had decided that a quick visit home would be useful before he trotted off to see to his villainous business.

Urchaid began to whistle softly as he walked toward the mouth of that path. He would follow and see if Daniel of Doìre's sister was as full of inadequate magic as her brother was. For all he knew, he might find the girl more powerful than Shettlestoune merited.

Though he sincerely doubted it.

Two

❧

Sarah of Doìre watched a cauldron that bubbled ominously over a substantial fire and supposed that, given who she was, she should have been stirring some sort of potent witch's brew. Unfortunately, all that found home in her pot that morning were unremarkable, unmagical skeins of wool.

She blew her hair out of her eyes, then walked away. She was too restless to give her dyeing the attention it needed, too restless to sit, too restless to even stand still and accept events as they came her way. She had known for years that she wouldn't spend the rest of her life in Doìre, for more reasons than just the landscape and the inhabitants. She had a secret that would spell her end if it was known, a secret she had kept uneasily her whole life. In truth, 'twas a miracle her brother hadn't blurted it out in some drunken stupor. Fortunately for her, he'd been gone for the past two months, so she'd slept a bit easier at night. She didn't have much hope the reprieve would last.

She walked along the edge of the glade, touching the trees as she passed them. She didn't allow herself to look past them to the spots where she'd been burying gold for the past fifteen years, from the moment she'd realized that it would take more than a few coins to get past Shettlestoune's gnarled reach. She'd covered the hiding places with clutches of nettles and carefully transplanted clusters of poisonous mushrooms. That blended in nicely with the rest of the untamed forest surrounding her mother's house and assured her that her coins would be there when she needed them.

She almost had enough. She had supposed that five hundred gold sovereigns would, if she were very careful, finance her journey and buy her either a modest house or a very small shop when she reached the right place to land. She lacked only a handful more gold to reach that tally, though business hadn't been precisely brisk of late. The odd silver coin, the occasional chicken plucked and ready for her stewpot, and the customary loaf of bread and jug of ale were lovely gifts, true, but they wouldn't see her over the mountains or into a new life.

Nay, an infusion of coin of the realm it would have to be.

She walked back to her pot, picked up a stick, and lifted a skein up to study. The wool was an unremarkable, unmagical shade of greyish green that would, by evening, deepen into a much darker hue. She would dry it, then weave it into a cloak that would hide her and a blanket that would hide her horse as they both disappeared into the surrounding woods.

Actually escaping Shettlestoune was the last part of the plan she had woven in secret for months, patiently, carefully, waiting for the right threads to find themselves under her hands. She had a means of travel in the person of Castân, her faithful chestnut steed who snorted when he saw her and would have walked through fire for the love of her. She would earn her future bread by the spinning wheel she had sawed into as many pieces as she'd dared, then hidden in two saddlebags buried under piles of hay along with the other, smaller tools of her handworking trade. Once she had her cloth woven, she would take Castân and be off—

"Mistress Sarah!"

Sarah spun around, the knife she kept in the back of her belt ready in her hand. Her mother's farm boy stood ten paces away, suddenly frozen in place. A jug fell from his hands and shattered on the stone at his feet.

" 'Tis only me," he squeaked. "And Lady Higgleton. She's coming with her daughter, and oy, she's in a tearing hurry. I just saw 'em a hundred paces down the path."

Sarah closed her eyes briefly. Lady Dorcas Higgleton's purse was every bit as ample as she was. She wasn't a generous woman with her servants, but she was willing to pay a fair price for magic to solve her problems. Obviously, she was ready to open her purse today.

Sarah abandoned her wool to its fate without hesitation and walked briskly toward the house, stepping over the shards Ned had created, then continuing on, wishing she looked less like a sweaty stable hand in need of a wash and more like a self-possessed, slightly mysterious brewer of potions. She snuck around the corner and into her house, trusting she hadn't been seen. She looked quickly around her, relieved there was no last-minute hiding of household clutter to be done.

Her loom was pushed into a corner, sporting a half-woven blanket on its substantial frame. Baskets of wool in rainbow hues were tucked tidily underneath it. Hearth, shelves with bowls and platters, her own sleeping nook with its curtain drawn discreetly across it: everything was in order. She glanced at the only door inside the house, but turned away just as quickly. That was her brother's bedchamber, a place she never approached for reasons she didn't care to examine too closely at present.

She snatched up a skirt from off the back of a chair and yanked it down over her tunic and leggings. She scarcely had time to tie a clean apron around her waist and pin her braid around her head in some organized fashion before she heard the imperious tones of the alderman's wife wafting into her home with all the delicacy of a woodsman's axe.

"Witch! Witch, where are you?"

Sarah hastened to the door and stood there, attempting a pose that hinted at no haste whatsoever. She looked down at her hands, green from her morning's work, and quickly put them behind her. She fixed a slightly aloof expression on her face and watched a potentially quite hefty infusion of gold approach.

Lady Higgleton and her daughter were, as Ned had said, marching furiously up the path toward her. Or, rather, Lady Higgleton was. Prunella was being pulled along behind her mother like a recalcitrant dinghy. Sarah half wondered how Dorcas Higgleton managed the path and her daughter at the same time. The way up from town was not particularly steep, but it was full of twists, turns, and uneven places that discouraged all but the most determined. Those who came were ones who either didn't want to pay the wizard over the mountain in Bruaih his substantial fee, or didn't care about the handblown vials or embroidered silken sachets that could be purchased from the sorceress over the river to the south. They wanted spells, at a decent price, provided with a minimum of fuss and a great deal of secrecy. Her mother's stock in trade, as it happened.

"She makes me nervous."

Sarah glanced over her shoulder. Ned, whom she had inherited along with half her mother's house and the entirety of her dam's workroom upon her mother's death, was never anything but nervous. Why her mother had taken him in the first place, then kept him on in spite of his lack of usefulness, was something Sarah had never understood. An uncharacteristic burst of charity, no doubt.

Ned gulped, then suddenly dashed for the corner of the house.

"I'll fetch wood," came floating back on the breeze he'd created with his haste.

Sarah didn't begrudge him his flight. The sight of the terrible storm sweeping up the path, dressed in purple silks and sporting a spray of feathers on her hat that would have put the finest of Isean of Eunadan's menagerie to shame, was enough to make all but the most strong-stomached—or desperate—take a step backward. Sarah was no weak-kneed maid, though, so she waited where she was without moving.

Lady Higgleton stopped just short of the doorway and put her hands on her substantial hips.

"There is a ball tonight," she announced in stentorian tones. "Prunella is not ready."

Sarah didn't need to look at Prunella Higgleton to know that such was the case. The girl was plain, true, but what she suffered from primarily was a visible desire to fade into the background and leave her overbearing parents out in front where they preferred to be. But lessons on the benefits of standing up straight and not hiding behind her hair were not what her mother had come for. A potion it would have to be and a strong one by necessity to repair hair that had been chewed on when the fingers had become too raw to endure the travail.

"Of course I have just the thing," Sarah said, stepping back and beckoning for her guests to enter. "But first, let me bring you refreshments. The journey from the village is a long and difficult one."

Lady Dorcas harrumphed in pleasure and went to seat herself at the little table in front of a lovely fire Ned had started earlier. Sarah fetched cakes she hadn't baked herself and served them with as much tea and ceremony as necessary. Her mother would never have offered refreshments. Her wares, as she had said on more than one occasion, were all the villagers were buying. If they wanted dainty baked goods, they could splash out for them elsewhere.

But Sarah had her own reasons for wanting her customers to feel as if they'd gotten their money's worth, so she offered tasty edibles whenever possible.

She left Lady Higgleton chewing on cake whilst Prunella chewed on her thumb, and walked into her mother's workroom, pulling the curtain across the doorway behind her. There was a worktable there under the window, flanked by thin shelves resting on long nails hammered into the wall. Scores of bottles stood on those shelves, bottles that had been full of tinctures that Sarah had brewed and her mother had enspelled. After her mother had fallen ill a year ago, the number of filled bottles had decreased. The supply had not been added to after her mother's passing. Sarah hadn't dared cut what had been left with things of her own make. She'd simply made do and put aside as many coins as possible against the day when the magic would run out.

That day, she supposed, would be today, for she had one last bottle of enspelled tincture. With any luck at all, Lady Higgleton would buy the entire thing.

She walked to the shelves on her left and reached up to pull down a cobalt bottle from off the topmost shelf. She held it up to the window to see how close to the cork the liquid might find itself so she might judge just how much she could charge for it—

But there was no line visible.

Something settled in her stomach. It might have been dread, or perhaps something amiss with her breakfast. Given that she'd cooked the latter herself, she supposed quivering eggs were potentially to blame. She pulled the cork free with her teeth, then stuck her wee finger into the bottle only to draw it back completely dry. She rubbed her eyes, on the off chance they were deceiving her, then gingerly tipped the bottle's mouth toward her hand. When that produced nothing, she upended the bloody thing and shook it vigorously.

It was empty.

"Witch! Witch, make haste!"

"I'm coming!" Sarah called, hoping she sounded less frantic than she felt.

She pulled the stool out from under the table and shoved it toward the shelves to her right. Several bottles protested the bump, and she managed to catch the two that fell only because she'd been doing the like since childhood. She opened every cobalt bottle on the highest shelf, on the off chance she'd moved her tincture without remembering it, but they were all as empty as the first. It wasn't possible that she had used up the last of her goods without knowing it.

She stepped down heavily to the floor and looked up at the shelves in astonishment. She hadn't miscalculated, she was sure of that. It also wasn't possible that Ned had been in her mother's workroom. He never went near the place if he could help it. There had to be some other explanation—

Her eyes narrowed. She leaned up on her toes suddenly and looked closely at something she hadn't noticed before. It was very faint, almost more of a hint of something than something in truth, but she had to believe what she could almost see.

A single thread of spell that had become snagged on a rough piece of wood.

She reached up to touch it, but there was nothing there. Indeed, she might have thought she was imagining the entire thing, but that wasn't the first time she'd thought she'd seen an echo of a spell where it shouldn't have been.

She had the feeling she knew who had woven that spell.

Damnation, but that missing bottle was full of her mother's last, best bit of magic, something Sarah had held in reserve for the right customer with the deepest pockets. And if she didn't have that to sell, she wouldn't have that last bit of gold she needed. If she couldn't get well past the Cairngorm Mountains into more friendly territory, she might as well remain where she was and hope she saw a score and ten. Most didn't. Witches' get with secrets had an even poorer chance of survival than that.

She muttered vile things about her brother under her breath, then picked up the first bottle she'd reached for. Now that she looked more closely, she realized it wasn't the bottle she'd been looking for. The one she sought had a flaw that looked like a drip of water running down the side of the glass, as if it had come from a well that had overflowed its bounds—

"Make *haste*, gel!"

She glanced at the window and cursed her mother for never having put in a back door. *Keeps me customers from runnin' out with me wares* had been her mother's reasoning. Sarah had never once considered that she might come to regret the fact that whilst no back exit had been good for her mother's business, it was rather inconvenient when the former village witch's daughter might want to make a hasty getaway.

She was halfway to heaving a chair through the window when something occurred to her. If Daniel had poached her vial merely to vex her, perhaps its hiding place wasn't as far away as she might have feared.

She took a deep, calming breath, then turned and walked back into the great room. "I'm not finding exactly what I want in the back," she said with an ease she most certainly didn't feel. "Let me fetch what I reserve for only the most discriminating customers."

Lady Higgleton chortled in pleasure, but that could have been over finding something chocolate under a stack of mince tarts. Prunella turned her attentions to one of her pointer fingers and twirled her hair with the other.

Sarah lit a candle in the fire, then walked confidently over to her brother's door. She steeled herself for potentially unpleasant things, then took hold of the latch and opened the door.

Invisible spiderwebs fell over her face as she crossed the threshold, almost suffocating her. Spells, obviously, and not very nice ones. She dragged her sleeve across her eyes to dislodge them and looked inside the chamber. She wasn't sure what she had expected, given that Daniel had banned both her and their mother from entering his chamber years ago, and she wasn't disappointed. Along with the clutter, there were hints of unpleasant, unfinished spells hiding in the corners and tossed carelessly about the place like so many soiled clothes.

Unfortunately, there were no bottles tossed about equally as carelessly.

She set her candle down on the worktable in the middle of the chamber and cursed silently. Lady Dorcas had a patience Sarah knew she couldn't outlast, and an ability to spread gossip with a speed that rivaled a brushfire on a windy day. The woman would wait all day, eating, until she had what she'd come for. If she left disappointed, she would tell everyone she knew that the witch up the way had failed her.

And then things would go very ill for Sarah indeed.

She looked at the stacks of books cluttering up her brother's table and straightened them absently. There was nothing useful . . . She paused, for she realized that books were not the only thing on that table. She swept her hand over it, clearing away the hints of magic she couldn't quite see.

And then she saw what she hadn't before.

A single sheaf of parchment lay there, tattered and scorched on its edges. Actually, it wasn't even an entire page. Just half of one page, looking as if it had been fought over and torn asunder as a result. She couldn't imagine why anyone would have bothered, for it looked perfectly unremarkable to her. She reached out to pick it up—

Magic leapt up from the page and wrapped itself around her wrist, slithering up to her elbow before she could think to cry out.

"What are *you* doing in here?"

Sarah ripped her arm away from the spell, ignoring the white-hot pain that flashed up her arm as a result, then whirled around to see her brother standing in his doorway. She was very surprised to see him when she'd sincerely hoped she never would again. Obviously, this was not going to be one of her better days.

Her brother was naught but darkness, but she was certain that had less to do with his sorry self and more to do with his being silhouetted by the light from the great room's fire. She was surprisingly reassured that there was a knife in the belt of her apron. She had never used it for anything more lethal than forcing a chicken to meet its end in her stewpot, but she supposed there was a first time for everything.

She put her burning hand behind her back, conveniently close to her blade, and looked at her brother coolly.

"I'm looking for something that went missing."

He walked unsteadily into the chamber and threw his cloak onto his table, almost extinguishing her candle. "And why would I stir myself to take something of yours?"

"You left a fragment of spell hanging from a shelf in Mother's workroom," she said. "Near my last bottle of potion."

He drew his hand over the table, disturbing other spells she hadn't seen. And there, next to her candle, sat a cobalt blue bottle with the tear running down its side to pool at the bottom. She reached out to take hold of it, but Daniel caught her by the wrist before she could.

Her skin burned like hellfire.

"I know your secret," he said in a low voice, "and I plan to tell anyone who'll listen."

"Surely you didn't come home just to do that," she said, trying to ignore the pain that crawled up her arm and almost felled her where she stood. Of course, she knew exactly what he was talking about, but she would be damned if she would admit it.

He released her and turned to look at his table. He started to speak, then apparently caught sight of the torn page. He went very still, as if it were so mesmerizing that he simply couldn't look away. Or perhaps he'd had one too many glasses of ale down at the pub and had lost all sense. Given the smell of his breath, she suspected the latter was indeed the case.

She decided very quickly that she didn't care why he was home, what mischief he was combining, or why he'd seemingly forgotten she was standing next to him. The sooner she was out of his sights, the better off she would be. She picked up her bottle and slipped from his bedchamber with as little fuss as possible, closing the door softly behind her and ignoring the spiderwebs that again fell against her face. She brushed them aside quickly, then walked over to Lady Higgleton and presented the bottle to her with a flourish.

"Prunella Higgleton will be the most enchantingly beautiful lass in all of Shettlestoune," she said. And if she wasn't, Sarah fully intended to be too far away to hear about it.

Lady Higgleton clutched the bottle to her ample bosom. "I'm counting on that."

Sarah accepted a handful of coins without counting them, then stood back and waited as Lady Higgleton rose and swept past her. She reached out and caught Prunella by the arm before she could escape.

"Stand up straight," she said very quietly, "and for pity's sake, stop chewing on yourself unless you'd rather live under your mother's thumb for the rest of your days."

Prunella shot her a look from under her hair, but said nothing. She started to put her hand to her mouth, looked at it for a long moment in silence, and then trotted off along after her mother.

Sarah followed them outside. She took a deep breath of sweet, crisp air as she watched Prunella march along behind her mother with her hands clasped behind her back and with a bit more vigor in her step than usual. Sarah smiled, then looked down at the coins in her hand. They weren't what she'd expected, but she would just make do. She would wait until her brother had gone, then quickly weave her cloak and be on her way herself.

She felt a chill wash over her and looked back to see that Daniel had come out of the door. His cloak was draped around him and a pack was slung over his shoulder.

"Off on another journey?" she asked brightly. *Now, damn you, don't say you're taking the same path I'm intending to take.*

He looked at her with disgust. "Do you actually think I want to stay here in this pitiful house with that pitiful village down the way for the rest of my life?"

She didn't imagine he was interested in her answer, and nay, she had never imagined he would stay. She was only surprised that he hadn't left the day their mother had died instead of waiting a month to go. At the time, she'd supposed laziness had been the reason. Now, she suspected he'd been plotting something and it had taken a bit to come to fruition. She hadn't cared for the look in his eye as he'd left, and she liked even less the reek of magic he now carried with him, obviously acquired on his jaunt to points unknown.

"What are you going to do?" she asked, because she apparently couldn't stop a last attempt to be polite to her only sibling.

He picked a speck of lint off his black cloak, then looked at her. "I am off," he said, with no inflection at all to his words, "to destroy the world."

She blinked in surprise, then laughed before she could stop herself. "Don't be ridiculous—"

The change in his mien was swift and terrifying. She watched as the darkness that surrounded him rose up and rushed toward her.

"I *will* do it, but before I do, I'll make a brief stop in the village where I'll tell everyone what I know about you. Be grateful. At least that way you won't be alive to see what I do to the rest of the Nine Kingdoms."

Sarah watched, openmouthed, as darkness loomed over her.

It was full of terrible things that she had only half imagined in nightmares, though she would be the first to admit that there were a few pockets of light where she supposed Daniel's spell hadn't been woven very well. She stared at those holes and looked absently at the bits of scenery she could see through them. Shettlestoune as a county was not a pretty place, and Doìre was surely the ugliest part of it. She had hoped she wouldn't have to look at it much longer.

She hadn't intended that to be because she was dead.

She felt herself falling. She supposed she should have said something to Daniel about that shadow she saw lurking in a scraggly bit of scrub oak behind him, but before she managed to open her mouth to say anything, she blinked and the shadow was gone. She frowned. Did figments of her frenzied imagination have lace at their wrists, or had Daniel woven a better spell than she'd given him credit for and she was now losing her mind as a precursor to losing her life?

She felt her head crack against her mother's threshold with a sickening crunch before she could decide.

She felt darkness descend and knew no more.

Three

Sarah dreamt that snow was falling. It wasn't an unpleasant sort of dream, except for the chill, but it did nothing for her arm, which she could see was burning with a fire that no amount of snow could quench. The snow soon became bits of fire that fell onto her face. She opened her eyes, intending to brush the ashes aside, then came fully out of her dream with a squeak.

Ned stood over her with a dripping stewpot of something that he was apparently poised to upend onto her face.

She rolled out from under whatever spell her brother had cast over her—grateful he hadn't managed to do her in completely—and staggered to her feet only to find that she couldn't see for the stars that suddenly swirled around her head. She felt for something solid, found her mother's house, then leaned against it heavily.

"Mistress Sarah, are you unwell?"

She didn't bother to answer. She felt as if she'd spent a solid se'nnight eating vile, rotted things only to have them strike her down all at once and leave her too ill to even begin to retch. She couldn't do anything but hold her hand over her eyes and pray that the scenery around her would cease spinning sooner rather than later.

She listened to Ned make little noises of distress for several minutes until she managed the question that concerned her most.

"Where's Dan?"

"He took himself off toward the village awhiles back. Don't know what he intended."

Sarah knew exactly what her brother intended, but she didn't bother to enlighten Ned. The only question left was how soon it would take the villagers to round up torches and pitchforks so they could come fetch her. Better to be off sooner than later. She turned and felt her way into her house to fetch her gear—

Only to walk into a marshy, reeking swamp of spells.

She looked in horror at the inside of her mother's house. Evil coming from under her brother's door had already covered most of the floor, slithered up three out of four walls, and crawled up the curtain that covered the nook where she slept. The only thing still untouched was her weaving, but the spells were gathering there as well. She supposed it was just a matter of time before they managed to overcome their revulsion of something beautiful to smother it along with the rest.

I am off to destroy the world.

Daniel's words came back to her with unpleasant clarity. She couldn't imagine he had the power to do that, but she couldn't deny that he'd certainly wreaked a fine bit of havoc in front of her. No doubt he'd been happy to add to that by stirring up trouble in the village. Perhaps the villagers were already on their way—

She turned away from the doorway and walked into an immovable object. She jumped back with a shriek, then realized it was merely Lord Higgleton standing there, smiling. Before she could ask him his business, he had enveloped her hand in his beefy paws and begun to shake it vigorously.

"I'm here to thank ye, Mistress Sarah," he said happily. "Already we've seen a great difference in the lass."

"Oh," Sarah said, feeling light-headed all over again. "How lovely."

Lord Higgleton reached not for his rather substantial dagger tucked into his belt—it was Shettlestoune, after all, and even an alderman wasn't above dispatching the odd vagrant or villain himself when necessary—but for his equally substantial purse. He opened it, fished about in it with a pudgy finger, then pulled the drawstrings shut. He handed the entire thing over with another smile.

"I would have thanked your brother on your behalf," he said, "but he seemed particularly determined to closet himself with the constable and I didn't want to disturb. Mage's business, as you well know, is always carried on more successfully without unnecessary distractions."

Heaven help her. "Indeed, it is," she agreed. "And how long ago was it that you saw my brother about his goodly work?"

Lord Higgleton looked thoughtfully up at the sky. "An hour, perhaps, no longer. Shall I hasten back to the village and have him fetched for you?"

"Nay," Sarah said, her mouth rather dry all of a sudden. "Nay, though I thank you for the thought. And I wish Prunella every success tonight."

"Her mother is forcing her to wear perfume-scented gloves to keep her from chewing on her hands," Lord Higgleton admitted, "but we have great hopes that she'll keep her hair out of her mouth on her own."

Sarah managed a smile, accepted another round of profuse thanks, then forced herself to wait until Lord Higgleton was out of sight before she pulled on the drawstrings of his purse and peered inside. There was less gold than silver, but when added to what his wife had already given her, it would be enough to see her over the mountains and well on her way to somewhere else. She would have indulged in a well-deserved swoon, but she didn't have time. Perhaps later, when she was certain she would get out of Doìre without any other visitors. She silently wished Prunella Higgleton a very happy match and turned to her own plans.

Ned was peeking around the corner. She walked over to him and handed him two silver coins. It was likely more than she should have given him, but he had served her mother for years and stayed on quite happily after her passing. She could do no less.

"Thank you, Ned," she said honestly, "for your service to me and my mother."

He blinked in surprise. "What do ye mean, mistress?"

"I'm off on an adventure," she said, putting on a confident smile.

"Mage's business?" he asked, in hushed tones.

"Of course." And that was true, especially if that business included being as far away from mages as possible. "I think I must be off on it posthaste. I'm sure your father will be glad to have you back."

Ned didn't look as if he thought so, but he went because she gave him a push to start him in the right direction, then another pair of them to keep him headed that way. He looked over his shoulder, once, then frowned in a baffled sort of way before he turned and shuffled off reluctantly toward home.

Sarah abandoned any hope of going inside the house for gear or waiting to weave a cloak. She would just make do with what she'd hidden away in the barn. If she hurried, she might manage to be deep in the mountains by sunset. She walked quickly around the house, then winced as she grazed her wrist accidentlly against the wall. She paused and looked down at the wound she'd earned in her brother's bedchamber by touching that scorched book.

... Destroy the world ...

She tried to laugh that off silently, but it suddenly didn't seem very amusing. He couldn't be serious.

Could he?

An unsettling feeling snuck up on her from behind, a little niggling something that suggested that she pay attention to what he'd said.

She considered, then shook her head. Daniel was seven kinds of fool and would destroy himself long before he managed to destroy anything else. She put her shoulders back, took a firmer grip on her rampaging imagination, and turned to the task at hand.

She walked swiftly into the trees, found a particular one, then turned and looked down at the ground as she counted the paces to the first of her hidden caches of gold.

Only to realize that no counting had been necessary.

She came to an abrupt halt and gaped at the hole at her feet. It had been neatly dug, she could say that much. Neatly and thoroughly and obviously quite carefully, for there was a pile of nettles laid tidily to one side. She dropped to her knees and reached down into the hole on the off chance that her eyes were deceiving her.

It was empty.

She would have said it was impossible, but she could see the pilfering of her funds was all too possible. She pushed herself up to her feet, then strode off to see if her next hiding spot had suffered the same fate. She looked, but she could hardly believe her eyes.

Obviously, the mushrooms hadn't been deterrent to whomever had stolen her future.

A quick, furious search proved that every last bloody one of her stashes of gold had been discovered and plundered. Magic had obviously been brought to bear in a foul way.

She would have made a very long list of why magic vexed her and added this latest insult to the list, but she was too angry. She had gone to ridiculous lengths to make sure that her future had remained hidden. She had never talked about her plans with her mother or Ned—and certainly not her brother. She had never even hinted that she might want to live anywhere but where she lived. She likely should have left home at ten-and-five and chanced a village on the other side of the mountains, but she'd remained another ten very *long* years simply to make certain that when she left, she would leave with enough to begin a successful, respectable life somewhere else.

If someone else didn't manage it first, she was going to find her brother—who she was certain was responsible for her loss—and kill him.

That, or perhaps she would slip up behind him, clunk him over the head, then tie him up until he could be delivered to some sort of mage-ish tribunal where they would surely sentence him to some sort of disgusting labor as punishment for his vile self simply drawing breath. She kicked a tidy pile of dirt back into its hole, then stomped out into the glade. She paused by her cauldron, saw the remains of her fire that had long since ceased to be of any use, then peered inside the pot. The contents were a vile, putrid sort of green.

Unsurprising.

She was revisiting the thought of going after her brother to do him bodily harm when she became distracted by a noise that wasn't quite audible coming from her mother's house. She looked up to see a thin stream of something coming out of the chimney, something that wasn't smoke. As she watched, the house trembled for a moment or two, then with an enormous rumble, collapsed onto itself. Only part of one wall remained, the wall that supported the bulk of her mother's bottles. There were a few of them left sitting on the windowsill, their colors rather pretty in the faint winter sunlight, all things considered.

She gaped at the ruin, then shut her mouth with a snap. Perhaps Daniel had more magic than she had supposed. And if that was the case, the farther away from him she was, the better. And the sooner she was about that, even with the pitiful coins she had in her hand currently, the safer she would be. She crossed the glade, then walked into the barn and whistled for her horse, fully expecting to see him poke his nose immediately over his stall door.

But he didn't.

She walked over to his stall, then looked inside. There in front of her stood not a chestnut gelding, but rather a chestnut dog. A big dog, actually, that drooled. A big dog with hooves the size of halved melons.

"Castân?" she said in astonishment.

He whinnied at her.

Sarah could hardly believe her eyes. Daniel again at his work, apparently. She would have cursed him for it a bit longer, but the barn had begun to creak in a very unwholesome way. She jerked open the stall door, snatched up a blanket and a feed bag, then bolted for the open door, leaving her horse—er, her onetime horse, rather—to follow, which he did with just as much enthusiasm as he always had. He came to a skidding stop in the middle of the glade, then turned and leaned against her leg as she watched the barn collapse just as the house had. Sarah let her gear slide from her fingers, wrapped the blanket around herself, then looked at her . . . dog. She took a deep breath.

"We have problems."

He seemed to agree. Silently.

"The first of which being that I don't have a way to fix you."

He only looked up at her with sad brown eyes.

She couldn't fix any of the rest of it either. She looked around herself in silent wonder at the ruin that had become her life. Almost all of her gold was gone, her home was gone, her future buried under bits of barn it would take her a week to clear away, and her brother was no doubt currently telling the villagers a secret that would have them up in arms the moment they heard it.

Then that brother would be off to raze the world with his very vile magic.

She was slightly disconcerted by the last, but she gave herself a hard shake to rid herself of any undue concern. She didn't care what Daniel did with his unpleasant gifts. As her mother always said, when faced with difficulties, the only sensible thing for a body to do was look out for himself and leave the heroics to the Heroes. A very wise woman, her mother. Sarah started across the glade, with a spring to her step, fully prepared to take that advice as her battle plan. She had places to go, things to do, more gold to earn. Just because she was the only one alive who knew what Daniel intended didn't mean she had to do anything about it.

It didn't.

She realized, after a bit, that she was no longer walking. She would have preferred to blame her lack of forward progress on a dastardly spell, but she couldn't. It was just her damnable sense of do-gooding rearing its ugly head and befouling her well-laid plans. She looked away from it, tried to ignore it, cursed it, and hoped it would go away.

To no avail, unfortunately. Her better self was obviously determined to outlast her.

She gritted her teeth and sidestepped anything to do with magic, mages, or tasks that were far too large for her. There was doing good, of course, and then there was being stupid. She didn't lack courage, of course, or the stamina to endure a long, arduous quest, but even Heroes had to take stock of their weapons, didn't they? She might have had the desire to stop her brother, but the truth was she didn't possess anything equal to fighting what he could do.

Besides, she wanted a peaceful, safe house where she could sleep for hours at a stretch without a very large knife in her hand. She didn't want peril she couldn't see coming wrought by men with power she couldn't fight. Surely there were lads enough left in the world to attend to her particular sort of difficulty. The task didn't have to fall to her.

She stood there for several minutes, unable to go either forward or backward. Finally, she looked over her shoulder. Only now it wasn't the ruins of her mother's house that lay there, it was a vision of her own little yet-to-be-built cabin on the edge of a perfectly pristine lake surrounded by beautiful mountains. That once-safe, peaceful place was overrun by the evil she'd seen seeping out from under her brother's door, that twisting, serpentine magic that had spread over the floor and slithered up and over everything—

The last wall of her mother's house suddenly trembled, then fell onto the rest of the rubble with a tremendous crash.

Sarah turned away. She stood there and simply breathed, in and out. She didn't want any of it. Not the darkness. Not the ruin. Not the magic she couldn't hope to best—

But if not you, then who?

She wasn't terribly fond of that voice in her head that echoed in her heart and always seemed to put her in Fate's sights. It was the second time she'd heard it that day and that was two times too many. She was a village witch's daughter, not a mage, nor a court wizard swathed in velvet robes and wearing a hat whose height was commensurate with his power and stature.

She cast about promptly for some pointy-hatted lad who might be willing to take on such a task. The wizard of Bruaih was three days' journey to the northeast through mountains she would have to cross eventually anyway, true, but rumor had it he was an unpleasant and unhelpful sort, persuaded to extend his services only if a great amount of gold was exchanged. The sorceress to the south of Shettlestoune was equally skilled, but also notoriously unwilling to work for less than her full fee. There wasn't another mage within a hundred leagues . . .

She paused.

That wasn't exactly true.

She lifted her eyes to the northwest. The western arm of the Cairngorm Mountains stood there, an impenetrable barrier between the bulk of Shettlestoune and Neroche, the city of Istaur, and the province of Meith. Rumor had it that those mountains were more unfriendly if possible than the ones to her right that separated her from the rest of the Nine Kingdoms. The forests to her left were full of ruffians and wild beasts.

And a mage.

That mage had lived there for centuries, or so it was hinted at gingerly, surrounding himself with spells and reputation and the bodies of those he'd slain for irritating him. No one braved the inhospitable path that led up to his house, at least no one she knew. Any who might have certainly never lived to tell the tale. That mage there was ancient, foul-tempered, and reclusive.

And quite possibly just the sort of man who might be bothered by the thought of her brother ruining his view.

She stood there for far longer than she should have with Castân leaning hard against her hip and the wind beginning to whisper unpleasantly through the surrounding forest of scraggly scrub oak. She didn't want to have anything to do with mages or magic or hiring the former to see to the latter.

But, again, if not her, then who?

And if not the mage on the hill, then who else?

She took a deep breath and started up that path before she could think on it overmuch. She did look up, once, because the afternoon was waning, leaving not only the path but the lee of the mountain in shadow. She shivered in spite of herself. She wasn't one to give credence to foolish tales told down at the pub, but she also couldn't deny that there was nothing at all welcoming about either the mountain before her or the path that led to it.

There were other paths that led through the mountains to the northwest of Shettlestoune, but none so faintly worn as the one she stumbled along. Obviously, she wasn't the only one who found other things to do besides visiting a mage who reputedly wanted his entire mountain to himself.

She rubbed her arms as she walked along, avoiding her right forearm and wrist. Perhaps the man could be bought. She obviously couldn't give him everything she had, but perhaps a bit of gold along with an appeal to his sense of decency might do.

Though he was certain to have no decency. She supposed she would be fortunate to state her request before he attempted to silence her with some sort of dastardly spell.

She walked until the sun began to set, continuing up that faint path, continually brushing aside things that caught her across the face, spiderwebs of magic that she thankfully couldn't see. Given that the mage had had centuries to perfect his spells of concealment and protection, 'twas a wonder she hadn't run into a more impenetrable bit of business. Perhaps he saved that for those who had the cheek to actually brave his front door.

It took her less time than she wanted to reach his house, which was easily as frightful-looking as she'd imagined it might be—even in the deep shadows of sunset. It looked as if it had simply grown out of the rock behind it. What wasn't cut from stone was built up with brick and impossibly weathered wood. Smoke from the fireplace curled upward into the frigid evening air. That should have been a good sign, but Sarah realized only then how badly she had hoped the wizard wouldn't be at home.

She put her shoulders back and lifted her chin, refusing to entertain any more of those sorts of thoughts. She had a goodly work for the man in front of her, her coin while not much was sufficient, and she had other things to be doing. She would bring all of her powers of persuasion—and a fair amount of guilt, if necessary—to bear on the man and simply leave him no choice but to accept her quest.

She strode up the remainder of the rough-hewn path to the stout wooden door with its crude knocker. She reached out to lift it only to catch sight of her arm. The sinewy trail left by the spell had already stained the cloth of her sleeve, leaving a black spiral around her wrist and up to her elbow. She put that hand behind her back and knocked vigorously with the other.

No one answered.

She knocked again, then continued to knock until the door was wrenched open.

Darkness stood there in the doorway. Her mouth went completely dry despite her command that it not. She wasn't one to cower, and she was unfortunately not unaccustomed to inventing reasonable-sounding tales on the spur of the moment to cover whatever exigency she might have been laboring under, but she found herself presently without a single useful thing to say.

The darkness didn't move. It only stood there, filling the doorway and drawing all the light available into itself.

Or at least it did for a moment or two. Then it receded and revealed a simple man—if a mage could ever be called that. He wore a cloak with the hood pulled forward to cover his face. Perhaps his visage was ruined, or terribly wrinkled, or so fierce that he thought to spare anyone the ordeal of looking at it.

Then again, given that he was likely more interested in frightening off any potential visitors than sparing them discomfort, perhaps he was simply cold, or had just come in from a lengthy bout of terrifying his neighbors and hadn't had the time to hang up his gear.

"Well?" he demanded, his voice rough, as if he didn't use it very often. "What do you want?"

"I need aid," she said quickly. "With magic."

He stood there for another moment or two in silence, then slammed his door shut in her face.

She wasn't quite sure what she had expected, but it wasn't that. She looked at that rough-hewn door for a moment or two, then knocked again. And again. She knocked until she was pounding on the wood.

The mage jerked the door open again suddenly. "Woman, if you don't stop that, I'll make it so you can't knock again."

His threats were nothing worse than she'd heard from her brother and his tone nothing worse than she'd been accustomed to from her mother, so she stuck her foot in the doorway so he would have to shut her in the door before he might shut her out, and quickly got down to business.

"I need your services," she said frankly. "I can pay you."

He folded his arms over his chest. "I don't need gold."

"Good, for I have very little to give you."

He seemed to consider for a moment or two, then cursed as he turned and walked across his great room. Sarah was surprised to find he didn't move as an old man might have, but perhaps his magic rendered him eternally young. He cast himself down into a chair by a table, his hood still shadowing his face. Sarah didn't particularly want to come inside his house, but if that was what was required, then that was what she would do. She left Castân sitting on the path outside, then started across the threshold. There were spells there, but they were merely fierce, not evil, so she parted them as she might have a curtain and passed through. She continued on until she stood next to the mage's table.

'Twas obvious he lived alone. The floor wasn't disgustingly filthy, but it hadn't been swept recently either. Books littered the table in front of her, along with plates needing a wash and a collection of cups that begged for the same attention. She started to straighten a pile of manuscripts, but stopped when she remembered what had happened the last time she'd touched something on a mage's table.

She hazarded a glance at the mage in question, but he sat with his head bowed, studying his fingers steepled together in front of his face. She took the opportunity to dust a little and stack a plate or two whilst making certain out of the corner of her eye that he wasn't reaching for a wand of any sort.

He wasn't reaching for anything, as it happened. He was merely sitting, as if a sudden bout of deep thought had overcome him. He actually didn't look terrifying, his large stature aside. She was faintly surprised to find herself still breathing whilst standing at his hearth, but perhaps her offer of just a few coins had been more appealing than she'd suspected.

"So," he said, lifting his head finally, "you want my aid, do you? In return for what? A handful of coins and a clean table?"

She stopped brushing crumbs off the table onto the floor and put both her hands behind her back. "I'm nervous."

"I intended you to be."

"I imagine you did."

"I don't like company," he said shortly.

"You'll like even less what comes crawling up your pathway once my brother creates another of what he fashioned in my mother's house."

The mage sat back and folded his arms over his chest. "Your brother?"

"Daniel of Doìre." She attempted a dismissive wave, but succeeded only in tipping over a mug she then had to rescue from tumbling off the table onto the floor. She set it back down on the table carefully, then took a deep breath. "He vows to destroy the world."

"The whelp of a village witch?" the mage said with a humorless laugh. "I don't think I'll lose sleep over the thought."

"You didn't see what he created to raze my mother's house and barn."

He snorted. "Surely any witch's get could have managed the like. And since you're one, why didn't you stop him?"

"I thought it might make a better impression on him to have someone swoop down and beat sense into his very thick head," she said honestly. "Someone with a terrifying reputation." She paused. "Someone like yourself, actually."

"I don't swoop."

She reached out and straightened a stack of books on his table that was nigh onto tumbling over. "Whyever not?"

"'Tisn't dignified."

"Then change yourself into a bloody dragon and singe him from tip to tail—"

She gasped and realized that her wrist was again on fire only after she saw why. The mage had leaned forward suddenly, caught her by the hand, and shoved her sleeve up to her elbow before she could protest. The pain winded her.

"What," he asked in a garbled tone, "is that?"

It took her a moment to catch her breath. "A spell," she gasped. "I touched—"

He released her so suddenly it was as if he too had been burned. He stood up, cursing viciously, then took her by the arm and pulled her across his floor only to push her out his front door.

"Seek aid elsewhere," he said curtly.

The door slammed shut behind her with a resounding bang.

Sarah gaped at the door for a moment or two in astonishment. Then she felt her eyes narrow.

"But I have nowhere else to turn," she shouted.

"Go away," came his voice quite audibly through the door. "You won't like what opens the door the next time you knock."

"I need your help!"

Only silence answered her.

Sarah stood there for several minutes, torn between wishing he would change his mind and open his door and hoping he wouldn't so she wouldn't catch an eyeful of something she wouldn't want to see. That was balanced nicely with her fury over the lazy, bad-mannered oaf's unwillingness to spend even half a day tracking down her brother and convincing him of the inadvisability of the course he currently contemplated.

Damn all mages to hell, where they could stay and rot.

She spun on her heel and strode away, leaving Castân to trot along after her. That stomping helped keep her warm for a bit until she reached the forest again and the chill began to bite. She looked back over her shoulder at the mage's house. Whereas it had a handful of moments ago looked merely rugged, now it took on other, more unsettling shapes. Well, one thing could be said for that ancient, crusty knave: he could weave a decent spell.

But he was obviously not going to weave one for her. She pulled Castân's blanket more closely around herself and reluctantly faced the rest of the hard truth: she was going to have to find her brother and stop him herself. As she had just seen, mages were unpredictable and, based on her experience, not particularly altruistic. Perhaps the man in the house behind her had the power to keep the entire world at bay and himself safe in his snug house, so therefore cared nothing for what her brother might manage. Perhaps he simply assumed he would never be troubled by things he imagined she should have been able to stop herself. She didn't hold out much hope that anyone else of a magical ilk would be any more inclined than he to see to the same thing.

Nay, she would see to Daniel alone, because she had no other choice. It wasn't the quest she wanted, and it wasn't one she went on willingly, but it was one of necessity. Unglamorous, unforgiving, unpleasant necessity.

She thought about the tales of Heroes she'd heard from the alemaster in the village, tales told to her during her youth when he'd been certain her mother wouldn't overhear them, tales of courageous men striding off into the deepening Gloom with their bright swords shining and songs of battle and victory on their lips. She'd heard a handful of tales about women as well—many of whom, oddly enough, had somehow thereafter found themselves queens of Neroche—who had challenged powerful forces and come away victorious. They had generally been skilled with either the sword or a spell, which had lent to them an undeniable advantage. There had been only a handful about ordinary souls who had undertaken tasks far beyond their skills or means. She supposed she would do well to avoid thinking on the terrible price those last souls had paid along the way or what that boded for her.

All she could do was stride into her own deepening Gloom and pray she had the strength to face what it contained.

Four

Ruith walked back to his fire to cast himself down into his chair there. He couldn't help but notice that spot on his table where that ridiculous wench had begun to clean with her apron. He supposed it could have been worse. She could have tried to clean him.

Of all the things he'd expected to have come to his door, she had been the last. Tales of the witchwoman Seleg's passing had reached him several fortnights ago, and whilst he'd suspected that any restraint her son might have shown earlier out of respect for his mother wouldn't last long, he'd hoped the fool would merely come to a bad end thanks to his own spells. Apparently that happy event hadn't come to pass yet, though Ruith was certain it couldn't be far off.

The daughter, Sarah he thought her name was, had always been something of a mystery. Rumor had it that she wove fine cloth out of wool and invisible tapestries out of spells. He'd never been one to give credence to the results of eavesdropping in taverns leagues from Doìre itself, but he could say that he had verified at least one thing for himself: she was astonishingly pretty. In a wholesome, weaverish sort of way, of course. And her hands had been green. For some reason, that had been rather reassuring.

Why those hands hadn't managed to prepare an extra spell or two a bit sooner to counter her brother's inevitable madness was a puzzle. Surely she should have given thought to the eventual unraveling of her brother's wits. It wasn't so difficult to seek out spells for use in such a case—

Unbidden, a memory came to him, a memory of sitting in front of a different fire with books sitting in piles around him. He could hear his mother's voice as clearly as if she spoke to him now.

Ruith, love, come away from the books and go to bed.

In a moment, Mother. I haven't yet found what I seek.

He couldn't say even now how much more time had passed before he'd looked up from yet another round of searching through heavy tomes full of spells—for there had been innumerable such searches—but he remembered on more than one occasion seeing his mother sitting across from him, simply watching him. His terribly beautiful, impossibly courageous, and determined mother, who had been watching him with love in her eyes.

Now that he was a man full grown and not a ten-year-old whelp, he suspected there had been sorrow in her eyes as well, for surely she had considered that the task lying before her was one in which she might perish. She also had to have known that there was little hope of his finding something to aid her, though he'd needed to feel as if he were aiding her somehow.

He pushed himself to his feet and began to pace before those memories caught him up. Unfortunately, all his pacing served was to run him bodily against the words he'd heard that silly wench bellow from outside his front door.

I have nowhere else to turn.

He scowled. He couldn't have cared less where she turned, even if it was only in circles until she came to her senses. He had much to do and none of it included going off to help her brother find wisdom. The fool in question had likely decided he was tired of the provincial nature of the county of Shettlestoune and had determined that stretching his wings was the wisest course of action. Who was he to deny a lad a decent adventure?

Besides, he was perfectly comfortable where he was. He had drawn his reputation around himself like a cloak and used it to hide quite happily for years.

Until today. That brassy wench had tromped through spells that should have given her pause, knocked on his door as if she'd had every right to, then crossed his threshold as if she hadn't minded all the other spells that someone besides him had seen woven across it, spells guaranteed to threaten and repulse.

He turned abruptly and walked across the chamber to fetch his bow from where it stood in the corner, already strung. He slung a quiver of arrows over his shoulder, then paused. He had a sword propped up in the corner as well, but he didn't think he could stomach getting that close to his supper before he slew it. The knives strapped to his back would have to suffice him where arrows did not.

He paused at the doorway, decided the witch's get had likely gone east, and turned west. Solitude was what he craved. Aye, that and something fresh to put into his stewpot.

He pulled his door to, then walked swiftly and quietly in the twilight, his bow loose in his hands. He wasn't unhappy with the bitter chill of the air for it cleared his mind in ways the warmth of his fire never could have. Having his silence disturbed had simply unsettled him more than he'd anticipated. His unease had nothing at all to do with that trail of magic he'd seen scorched into that quite lovely woman's arm.

He spent so much time attempting to ignore his unease that he didn't realize he was being followed until what was following him was almost upon him. It crossed his mind briefly that perhaps that man he'd seen in the hour before dawn had decided to make more of a nuisance of himself than he should have. If that were the case, Ruith wasn't above quickly disabusing him of that notion. He turned, drawing an arrow and fitting it to the string as he did so. But what stood twenty paces from him was not a man dressed in clothes better suited to a salon than a faintly traveled path through inhospitable woods.

It was a creature from nightmare.

The beast watched him with unblinking eyes that glinted in the twilight. Ruith was surprised enough by that that it took him a split second to realize that his greatest peril lay not in front of him, but behind him.

He spun to find another monster standing not an arm's length from him. He didn't think; he merely took the arrow he held and shoved it into the beast's eye.

It fell with a crash and a howl, thrashing about in a loud and unpleasant way. Ruith left him to it, then turned, fitted another arrow to the string, and let it fly into the troll that was now ten paces away, not twenty.

The monster continued to come, the arrow buried halfway into its chest.

Ruith managed two more arrows before he opened his mouth and found a spell of death there. It occurred to him instantly that whilst the words might have been there, the power to make them more than just interesting conversation most certainly was not. Any magic he might or might not have possessed, he had buried long ago. Releasing it without completely destroying the anonymity he'd carefully cultivated for a score of years was impossible. Death by ordinary means would have to do.

He pulled the knives from the sheaths on his back and flung

them together with all his strength into the creature's chest. It was borne backward, then it tripped over something in its path and fell with enough force to make the ground tremble.

Ruith looked about himself to make certain there were no more enemies to slay, then leaned over with his hands on his thighs and concentrated on breathing for a moment or two. It wasn't that he was opposed to taking another life to protect his own, though he didn't do it without great need. It was the look in that creature's eye, a look that said it had found what it had been seeking—

Which was, of course, impossible. For all anyone knew, he was a mage who had dwelt in the mountains for centuries, a mage of little consequence but fierce reputation. That someone—or some*thing*— should stumble upon him was nothing more than happenstance. He had been alone in the woods and therefore an easy mark for anyone wanting a bit of sport. Killing the first creature had likely enraged the second, which he could understand. Whatever he'd thought he'd seen in either of their eyes was just his sorry imagination running off with him.

He blamed that witch's get. She was obviously trouble.

He walked over to his first victim, wrenched his arrow free, and cleaned it in the snow that still lingered nearby in drifts. He paused, then squatted down next to the corpse and fingered what seemed to serve the fallen man for a tunic. He realized with a start that it was less a fabric than it was part of the beast itself. It was as if water had been formed into a shape, for it slid through his fingers, yet remained as it was, as if it were held together with some sort of spell.

A spell that gave off a very unpleasant odor when disturbed, truth be told.

He froze. It was an odor he hadn't smelled in years—

He rose abruptly, retrieved his other weapons, then strode away. Damn it, he should have brought a heavier cloak. He shot a baleful glance heavenward at stars that had begun to twinkle in the heavens. He wished the sun were still up where it might have provided him with a bit of warmth.

He suddenly stooped, snatched up a handful of pine needles, and shoved them against his face, ignoring the prickles. The scent trapped in his nostrils was one he wanted to rid himself of as quickly as possible. He threw the pine away after a moment or two. It didn't matter where he had smelled that smell before. What mattered was that he return home, lock his door, then try to regain the wits he'd obviously lost at some point along the way. Again, the blame could be pinned squarely on that bloody wench. If she hadn't arrived at his door with her very self setting his great room afire, he would now be enjoying a decent supper and an interesting book. She had driven him from his own home with her ridiculous requests, but no longer. He would return and be about his usual business of doing absolutely nothing that required any magic at all.

He walked unsteadily back the way he'd come only to realize his feet had taken him in a direction he hadn't intended to take. He stopped, swore, then swore again. He had no intention of walking all the way to Doìre to see if Sarah was merely imagining her brother's plans. He had even less interest in that terrible mark that ran up her arm, as if something evil had wrapped itself around her and burned her flesh. He had ale at home, a very fine pale ale that tasted a bit like apple when Master Franciscus had been feeling particularly generous with the contents of his root cellar. And he'd left bread to bake, bread he might find perfectly browned if he turned back now. That was a far more appealing thought than a three-hour walk to that inhospitable wreck the witchwoman Seleg had haunted for all those years.

Somehow his feet didn't seem to agree.

He dragged his blood-caked hand through his hair and cursed viciously. He did *not* want this. He looked west, where his house lay, his house full of things he'd made with his own two hands or bought from the very ordinary labor of those two hands. There was comfort there, and safety. It had been a refuge for him from the moment he'd managed to drag himself inside its front door.

He looked east with reluctance and no small bit of distaste. He had no use for an auburn-haired witch who apparently couldn't slap sense into her brother, who was surely not her equal in anything.

Nay, that was stating his reluctance poorly. There were simply no words to describe how thoroughly he wanted to avoid the path he could almost see shimmering in front of him. It looked a great deal like Fate and to say he wanted no more than a passing acquaintance with her was understating it badly. He knew if he took a single step toward the east, he would find himself enmeshed in things he had no stomach for.

He realized, with a start, that Fate was taking things into her own hands.

The silver path that ran under his feet turned quietly and relentlessly into something quite different even as he stood in its midst. It became first a stream, then a swiftly flowing river, glowing softly with a light of its own, full of spells that sparkled along the surface with a beauty that was difficult to look at.

It was Fadaire that slipped around his feet and tripped over itself with sweet laughter as it continued on its way. The water was more beautiful because of it, the air more full of things he couldn't quite see, the trees more inclined to whisper songs he couldn't quite hear any longer. It was so lovely, he didn't dare breathe lest he disturb its spell.

But suddenly, out of the corner of his eye, he caught sight of something running under the surface of the stream, something dark, putrid, noisome. It tried to mingle with the water running over its surface, but failed. Yet even so Ruith could smell an echo of what he'd encountered in the forest not a quarter hour ago. It was ruin, darkness, death—

A sound startled him.

He realized it was his own harsh breathing.

He reached out and put his hand on a tree to steady himself. He shook his head sharply and the vision disappeared. He was left as simply Ruith of nowhere in particular who had been perfectly content to be nothing but what he pretended to be.

Not a man who had begun to dream again on the night before desperation had sent a woman braving his reputation to come beg him for aid.

He took a deep breath. Perhaps he was making it all out to be more than it was. He could make a quick dash toward the witch-woman Seleg's house and see what sort of spells Sarah's brother had left behind. It didn't mean he had to weave any spell of his own, or actually do anything magical to sweep away the remains of what Daniel of Doìre had left behind. It didn't mean that he had to become involved. Surely.

He started walking, ignoring the fact that he felt like he was walking into a dream.

Or a future he'd always known would catch him up.

It took him just as long as he'd thought it would to reach the house. He approached silently, though he supposed the villagers standing there in a cluster with torches and whatever steel they'd had to hand were yammering too loudly to have noticed him. He listened to them speculate on whether or not the witchwoman's daughter lay under what was obviously the remains of her mother's house and barn, but he didn't care to tell them differently. He merely watched them until they tired of their discussion and trudged off back to the village to seek their beds. Very sensible lads, those.

He slung his bow across his chest, then walked out into the glade and looked by moonlight at the magic that lay in a heap there. He could sense the remains of it, but the spell was beginning to fade now that it had accomplished what it had been created to do. He watched for another half hour as it finally disintegrated, leaving only the faintest trace of having been there at all.

It was Olc. He didn't particularly care to think about why he

knew that. He was too busy being suddenly lost in his past, standing in a ruined, unpleasant keep, lingering just outside a chamber
full of spells that were equally unpleasant—

He rubbed his hands suddenly over his face, then turned and
walked away before he lost what few wits apparently remained him.
Daniel of Doìre's spell was poorly wrought, which meant anything
else he might attempt would be equally flawed. The lad could go
off and attempt a dozen terrible things and manage none of them.

Ruith continued on his way home, considering his duty done.
He wasn't responsible for what a stupid lad did with his time, or for
what spells that lad dabbled in that he shouldn't have, or even for
determining where a stupid, foolish, dabbling lad might have come
by spells that would have made any sensible mage ill just to look at
them. He had his own life to endure. He hardly needed to take on
the troubles of someone else's.

He made it home with a minimum of fuss. His bread was burned,
but he cut off the crust and settled for slices of the innards. Ten
minutes later, he was sitting in front of his own roaring fire with
a tall glass of apple-scented ale in one hand and a butter-slathered
piece of bread in his other. Of course he needed the fire because
it was still winter. His hands were shaking because he was hungry. He was cursing because it made him feel warm and happy to
toss a few expletives out into the midst of his chamber and watch
them hang there in the firelight. He anticipated nothing but a very
fine evening in which he could enjoy his warm bread and deli-
cious ale—

Whilst some silly wench with flyaway hair and an inability
to keep herself from dusting his table was out in the wild. In the
dark. Alone, save for her brother who had managed to use—albeit
poorly—spells he couldn't possibly have the bloodright to.

And not to forget possibly more of those creatures from hell
who would slay an unprotected woman before she could manage to
blurt out even a simple word of protest.

He wrenched his attention back to more interesting things: good ale, warm bread, and fire against his toes. Sarah would manage to do good and right wrongs without him. Just because she had knocked on his door and asked for aid didn't mean he had to offer it or even pretend to have heard her. Just because he had taken a brief, unremarkable foray out into a county he owed nothing to didn't mean he had to now hire himself out as rescuer of maidens faced with tangles they should have been able to unravel on their own.

Nay, he would leave that sort of thing to others. Perhaps those Neroche lads who didn't seem to mind it, or an intrepid fool from Meith who was more interested in having his name carved in stone along with other Heroes of legend than he was in not making a fuss. Ruith would be quite content with remaining out of sight, because he knew exactly what doom looked like and it didn't have a lovely visage and a scorch up her arm that he couldn't stop thinking about.

It didn't look like that at all.

He's going to go destroy the world.

And Daniel of Doìre's bloody sister was going to try to keep him from doing it.

Ruith looked at the bread in his hand, considered, then cursed vigorously.

He loathed traveling in the winter. He was certain it was going to snow. He was even more convinced that taking even a single step in a direction he didn't want to go would spell nothing but complete disaster for him. He had no desire to become involved with magic, or witches' get, or the righting of wrongs—

Or with rivers of elven magic that had been polluted by things ugly and deadly.

I have nowhere else to turn.

He looked at his weapons he'd propped up against a chair, looked at the books on the table that he had yet to read for the third time, looked at the fine supper that had been provided by eminently pedestrian, non-magical means.

And he thought about that woman who was out in the forest, alone.

He fought with himself for a good half hour until his bread was cold and his ale warm in his hand.

Then he cursed viciously, slammed his glass down on the table, and went to look for a warmer cloak.

Five

❧

Sarah knelt next to a pile of kindling and struck her knife against her flint. It would have helped if the moss had been dry, or if she had possessed anything of an otherworldly nature that might have been useful in convincing dry underbrush to light. Unfortunately, she was who she was and she was limited to what she had on hand, which wasn't much.

She set her knife down and blew on her fingers. Snow had begun to fall during the first night of her flight and continued on steadily ever since. At least she had boots, and she had taken her skirt and turned it into a makeshift cloak. She supposed that considering she'd spent most of the last two days running or walking as if the very demons of hell—or angry villagers, as might have been the case—were behind her, she should have at least been warm from that exertion. The truth was, all that running had done nothing but leave her exhausted and profoundly chilled.

She dropped her knife twice before she managed to take a decent hold of it. She started to curse, then stopped abruptly, less out of a desire to be ladylike and more from a desire to know if snow weighing down a branch in the distance had caused that cracking noise, or if it were something more sinister.

She wished desperately for light. Or a sword. Or the skill to wield the latter and create the former.

Castân was standing a handful of paces away from her, sleeping on his feet, seemingly unconcerned about what she thought she was hearing. Then again, he was a very confused beast, so perhaps he wasn't to be relied on. He had, over the course of their journey so far, grazed on too much dry grass, vomited it all up, dashed after a rabbit, then held it in his jaws and looked at her in consternation. She couldn't have agreed more. Magic was, as she had said more than once, a perplexing business—

A twig snapped behind her.

She froze, then reached down carefully for her knife. The blade was actually quite large and fierce-looking—chickens lived in fear of her, truly, along with several of the less gentlemanly lads down at the pub—but her hands were cold and clumsy and the blade seemed more unwieldy than it should have. But she was now convinced there was more in the woods than met the eye, so she would use her knife whether it came to her hand easily or not.

She staggered to her feet, then spun around to find a shadow standing ten paces from her. It was dark despite the snow that lay in drifts around her, and that did nothing to help her determine a strategy. She supposed when it came down to it, how she fought was less important than winning the battle, so she would just have to make do in the dark.

She ripped her skirt-turned-cloak off over her head so it didn't hamper her and brandished her knife. Her attacker tilted his hooded head, then reached up and drew two long hunting knives from sheaths strapped to his back. The steel glinted wickedly in the faint light, but Sarah didn't flinch. She had discovered from years of hard experience that the surest way to embolden an opponent was to show weakness. It was also advantageous, she had learned, to make certain her opponent thought her too much trouble to bother with.

She threw herself into the fray, such as it was, with her best curses, signaling to the man that he would be much happier to look for trouble elsewhere. Unfortunately, he merely stepped aside to avoid her thrusts, the lout. She followed them up with yet another barrage of parries, fully intending to drive her blade into his chest if possible, but he caught it between his knives, made an indulgent noise that was particularly annoying, then set her backward with a gentle push.

Sarah reassessed her situation with a cold detachment. The truth was, she was outmatched in strength and steel. Her opponent was sporting not only his knives, but a sword and bow. No matter how much bravado she possessed, vanquishing him fairly was out of the question. The best she might be able to do would be to disable him and run. Her mother would have done that and left him with a spell to remember her by, but Sarah decided she could perhaps forgo that additional pleasantry.

She feinted to her left, then held up her hand suddenly.

"Something in my eye," she said, blinking furiously and fishing about in her eye with the pinky of the hand that held her knife. "Nerochian rules of fair play, if you please, sir."

He hesitated, then nodded and rested his daggers against his shoulder.

She bent over as if she were truly suffering, made a few womanly noises until he stepped closer—no doubt to offer aid—then straightened abruptly and caught him full under the chin with the heel of her hand.

He gasped, staggered backward with a curse, then landed full upon his arse.

Sarah turned to flee, then she stopped still. It took her a moment to decide what seemed odd, but when she realized what it was, she felt her mouth fall open. She'd heard that voice before—and quite recently. She turned back around slowly to face her foe.

It was him. The profoundly unpleasant and terribly powerful mage up the mountain. She was so surprised to find him there that she did nothing but gape at him for several moments in silence. He had thrown her bodily out of his house and warned her never to come back, yet there he was?

She didn't suppose she should bother to ask him why he found himself on the ground in front of her instead of in his comfortable, if a bit dusty, house in the mountains. She revisited the idea of running, then decided there was little point in it, either. She couldn't outrun his magic and apparently she couldn't best him with her steel. All that remained her was a show of spine—or perhaps something he might not expect.

She held out her hand to him, to help him back to his feet.

He was still for a moment or two, then he returned his knives to the sheaths on his back as if he had done it thousands of times— which she was certain he had—and took her hand. Pulling him to his feet was more difficult than she'd suspected it might be, for he was rather solid for an old man, but she didn't waste any time thinking on that. She was too busy hoping he wouldn't do to her what she'd done to him.

"My apologies," she said quickly. "I thought you meant me harm."

"How do you know I don't?" he asked, reaching inside his hood no doubt to check the condition of his jaw. "Nerochian rules of fair play, my arse. Woman, that was profoundly unsporting."

"When outmanned, 'tis fair to use whatever advantage one has."

"I don't think that's part of their code."

"I might have heard that last part down at the pub," she admitted.

"I wouldn't be surprised," he said with a grunt. He shook his head and gave her a wide berth as he stepped past her.

Sarah frowned thoughtfully. He didn't seem angry, though he certainly had cause. She turned to watch him, suppressing the slew of other questions she had, beginning with why he found himself taking the same path she did, what his plans were, why he hadn't finished her off for the abuse to his chin, and finally, her sudden curiosity over whether or not he'd brought along anything tasty to eat.

The next time she set off on short notice on a perilous quest, she was going to be better kitted out.

He knelt down next to her wood, then looked up at her. "You couldn't just spell this into complying?"

"I'm trying to be discreet."

He didn't seem to find that unusual. He simply struck his knife against his flint until he had a decent spark. He carefully blew on the moss until it surrendered and began to burn. Sarah thought to ask him why it was *he* didn't spell the fire into a cheery blaze, but perhaps he preferred discretion as well.

He continued to feed his fire by degrees until it was warm enough that even she could actually hold her half-frozen hands against it and feel the heat. He did the same, sighing as he did so. His hood was still too far forward to see anything at all of his features, leading her to believe he was either horribly scarred, terribly wrinkled, or simply too ugly to be looked on without comments he perhaps didn't care to have voiced.

He rose with a grace that belied his centuries of magic making, then shrugged out of a pack and set it down. He was certainly dressed for travel. He wore not only very useful winter clothing but a bow, a quiver of arrows, and the hilt of a very long, unpleasant-looking sword. Either he planned to hunt or he took pleasure in terrifying his victims before he finished them with his magic. She didn't mind that, as long as she wasn't the one in his sights. With any luck, Daniel would find himself there and be repaid for all the frights he'd given her over the years.

The mage squatted back down, then reached inside his pack and drew out a loaf of bread. He tore it and handed half to her.

Sarah accepted it with all the enthusiasm of the starving woman she was. The outside was burned to a crisp, but she didn't care. It was without a doubt the best thing she had ever eaten.

She'd inhaled most of it before she thought to wonder if it had been poisoned or enspelled or subjected to some other dastardly bit of wizardly mischief. She paused, examined her stomach's reaction to the new addition, and decided that the bread had only been subjected to too much time in the oven.

He held out a bottle, which she took without thinking. She drank before she thought better of it, then realized what she was tasting. It was Master Franciscus's apple ale, something he rarely gave to anyone who didn't meet his approval. She didn't suppose the mage had intimidated his way into possession of it. The alemaster was a man possessing not only admirable calm but a quartet of well-used knives continually residing in his boots and his belt. Perhaps gold had been exchanged, along with a sizeable number of compliments.

She had one last drink on the off chance it might be her last, then handed the bottle back. Her companion set the bottle on her side of the fire, rummaged about in his pack, then handed her a bundle of cloth. She realized almost immediately that what she was holding in her hands was a heavy cloak. She looked at him in surprise.

"What's this?"

"What it looks like." He rose. "I'll go scout for a bit. You should sleep."

She maintained a neutral expression with effort. Sleep? With him watching over her? Was he daft? The rumors that swirled about the man were terrible and endless—and that was saying quite a bit considering the general character of Shettlestoune's inhabitants. She wouldn't have been surprised to listen to him weave any number of dastardly spells over her and laugh whilst he did so.

Then again, the man had endured her fist under his jaw and offered not even so much as a peep of a spell as retribution.

"I appreciate the suggestion," she managed, "but I don't need to."

He stood there for a moment or two, then shrugged, turned, and melted into the shadows of the trees.

She couldn't hear him moving, though that said nothing.

She took her knife out of her belt and drove it into the hard ground before her. No sense in not being prepared. The fire flickered softly against the wooden handle, which was cheering and unsettling at the same time. A complete stranger—and a very dangerous one, at that—had done something for her comfort without asking anything in return.

Astonishing.

She could scarce wrap her mind around it, so she pushed aside the gratitude she felt for a man who could have killed her with nothing more than a word and concentrated on the plans she had decided on during her first night of flight. Once she had rested for a bit, she would continue on over the hill to Bruaih, seek out the mage there, then bribe him to see to Daniel for her. Even if she had to stay a bit in town and work to earn enough to pay the mage his fee, she would do it without complaint. And once the mage was hired and Daniel seen to, her responsibility to the world would be discharged, and she could seek out her own very ordinary, unremarkable future.

She steadfastly refused to think about how far out of reach that future had become.

She rubbed her eyes suddenly. She yawned for good measure, then forced herself to stand up and shake off her weariness. She found her skirt and pulled it down over her head again, keeping her knife free of the waistband. She paced for a moment or two, stroked Castân soft ears and had a remarkably equine-sounding snort as her reward, then returned to the fire where she soon found herself sitting. She plumped the feed bag next to her not because she was going to use it as a pillow anytime soon but because she wanted to make sure it was still there, empty save for Lord Higgleton's coins. She perhaps should have sewn them into the hem of her apron. Her mother had done that with regularity, citing not only the security of having her gold close to her, but the added benefit of being able to take the apron off and use it as a weapon.

Her mother, Sarah could admit, had been a very resourceful woman, if not necessarily a nurturing one.

She looked briefly for the mage, but saw no sign of him. Perhaps he needed a bit of exercise to keep his creaking knees from giving way. She was still curious about why he'd followed her, but if there was one thing she had learned over the course of her five-and-twenty years of life, it was not to ask mages too many questions. Perhaps he was restless. Perhaps he always carried extra food and gear for potential guests at his fire. Perhaps she had gone too long without sleep and was now conjuring things up out of her imagination that couldn't possibly find home in reality.

She sat for as long as she could, then found that she could no longer keep her eyes open. If she didn't at least lean over and close her eyes briefly, she was going to either be ill or pitch forward senseless into the fire.

She laid her head down and closed her eyes.

Just for a moment.

She woke at some point during the night, or at least she thought she woke. She opened her eyes and saw the mage sitting cross-legged across the fire from her, holding his hands to the blaze. His stillness likely should have frightened her witless given that he was a mage and they were generally at their most dangerous when silently thinking deep, disturbing thoughts, but somehow the sight was surprisingly soothing.

"Why did you come?" she thought she might have said.

He was long in answering. "Duty."

"Couldn't agree more," she said with a sigh.

At least she thought she'd said as much. She wasn't as cold as she had been and that alarmed her until she realized she wasn't warm because she was freezing to death, she was warm because she was covered in his cloak.

She sighed again, then fell back into dreaming.

The sound of a loud slap woke her.

She opened her eyes and looked up to find a creature from the blackest pit of her worst dreams standing over her. She looked at his gnarled hands reaching down toward her and realized suddenly that she was not dreaming. The creature flinched. Sarah noticed that where there had been only a single arrow shaft protruding from his chest, now there were the well-worn wooden handles of two terrible hunting knives. The creature straightened, plucked thoughtfully at the knives for a moment or two, then threw back his head and howled.

His complaints were interrupted by three more loud thuds. The three arrows joining the knives seemed only to irritate the monstrous troll more, not deter him. Before she could make any more sense of that than the monster seemed to be trying to, she was hauled up to her feet and pulled through the remains of the fire. She found herself standing behind the mage as he cast aside his bow and drew his sword.

She absently beat at the now-smoking hem of her skirt, but that seemed far less pressing than wondering if the monstrous troll who was fussing with the weapons sticking out of his chest would die of his wounds or manage to stumble around the fire and be about his unfinished business. Or at least she wondered that until she watched the mage make quick work of dispatching him with his sword. Why he hadn't just felled the beast with a bit of magic, she couldn't have said and she didn't want to know. It was enough to watch the troll fall to the ground with a crash and not move again.

"Collect your gear," the mage said without so much as a change in his breathing. "And your useless hound."

Sarah admired his calm in the face of what seemed less a pleasant trip through ruffian-infested woods and now more of an involuntary stay in an unrelenting nightmare. She found she wasn't nearly so nonchalant about it. She hastily smothered the final embers glowing on the edges of her skirt and his cloak, retrieved her knife that hadn't served her one bloody bit, then snatched up her feed bag. She took a deep breath, then whistled very unsuccessfully for her hor—er, dog. Castân shuffled over, eyeing the fallen creature with suspicion and no small amount of alarm.

Sarah couldn't have agreed more. She watched the mage stride around the fire and go to retrieve his weapons. He was almost too efficient at the task, which made her wonder how he'd become so. Perhaps he found something unsporting about taking game by magical means. Perhaps he hunted things for pleasure alone.

Perhaps she needed to find a safe place to land where she could lock the door and fall apart in peace.

She needed a decent bit of sleep, that was all. She nodded to herself at that as she watched the mage stomp out the remains of the fire and pick up his pack. He snatched up his bow and pulled it over his head and across his chest, then turned toward her.

"We'll run."

Sarah nodded. She had spent the whole of her life running to escape a variety of things, so the thought didn't trouble her. She stumbled after the mage, leaving Castân to trot along behind her.

They ran for the rest of the night, walking only when she couldn't run any longer. She suspected the mage, despite his advanced years, could have run all night without pause and still continued on far into the next day. She didn't consider herself particularly weak, but she had to concede that after two days of flight and a terrifying awaking during the third night of her quest, she had finally reached her limit. Fortunately, at the very moment she opened her mouth to beg the man to stop, he slowed, then stopped and leaned over with his hands on his thighs.

She took the opportunity to fall to her knees in the snow and wheeze. She waited until the stars had stopped spinning in front of her eyes before she dug the heels of her hands into those eyes.

Hands were suddenly on her arms, dragging her to her feet. She hadn't managed to gasp from the pain of her injured arm being touched before she found herself being jerked behind her companion and heard the sound of a sword sliding from its sheath. She opened her eyes in time to see something stumbling from the woods they had just left.

"Stop, if you have any sense," the mage commanded.

The footsteps stopped immediately and a squeak was the only answer. Sarah peeked around his shoulder and found, to her surprise, that the beginnings of dawn revealed nothing more nefarious than Ned, looking very much worse for the wear. He looked at her in alarm, then drew himself up and brandished his own version of a hunting knife.

"Oy, you let her go," he said, taking a firmer grip on his blade. "Don't make me do something you'll regret."

The mage rested his sword point-down in the snow. "I wouldn't dare." He turned slightly. "Is he yours?"

Sarah nodded. "My mother's farm boy, Ned."

Ned leapt forward suddenly and pulled her over to stand next to him. He frowned, then put himself in front of her. Sarah would have smiled, but she was just too tired.

The mage resheathed his sword. Ned lowered his knife, which

was likely a good thing considering how badly his hand was shaking. Sarah couldn't blame him. The shadowy man standing five paces away was, she had to admit, terrifying. He didn't look to be on the verge of casting any spells, however, so she wondered if she might manage a question or two. But first things first. She turned to Ned.

"I sent you home."

"I went home, but me sire took me coins and tossed me into the barn to await the gypsies he'd sold me to."

She could hardly believe it. Ned was another mouth to feed, true, but he was a hard worker. When he managed to remember what he'd been told to do, that was. And assuming he could manage the task. She sighed deeply. In truth, he was just short of helpless, though it wasn't from a lack of intelligence or diligence. He was just a dreamy lad who would likely have been better suited to the life of an artist than a farmer.

It said something for his cleverness, though, that he had escaped his father's clutches. Farmer Crodh's barn was, rumor had it, an impenetrable fortress built for the express purpose of protecting his very rare and valuable milch cows from marauders who might want to liberate one or two of them and lead them astray. Nothing got free of that barn that Farmer Crodh hadn't let out himself.

"I'm impressed," Sarah said.

"There isn't a place built I can't escape," Ned boasted. He hesitated, then looked at her. "It might be my only skill."

Sarah didn't want to agree, so she said nothing.

"You didn't perchance bring anything to eat, did you?"

She shook her head. She wasn't about to ask the mage for anything else. Ned would have to wait until Bruaih where she could buy breakfast for him. She glanced at her unwitting defender, then glanced at what was behind him.

And she caught her breath.

The sun had begun to rise, and she had the most remarkable view of farmland that was . . . lush. There wasn't a clutch of sagebrush, or scrub oak, or stubby, spindly trees of other indeterminate make in sight.

She walked past her companions, feeling as if she'd opened her eyes for the first time. The mist that hung over the land in front of her, the beginnings of spring grasses, the rich earth of early ploughed fields . . . It was enough to render her mute and still.

"Duck!"

She realized the mage wasn't speaking to her only because when she turned around, he had his back to her. She watched as he pulled his knives free of their scabbard and flung them toward Ned.

Or over Ned, rather.

Her mouth fell open. It was one thing to see what she'd thought she'd seen the night before; it was another thing entirely to see a monster clearly in the growing light of dawn. The beast sported knife hafts in uncomfortable spots in his head, but still he fumbled for Ned, who was crouching in front of him, shrieking like a girl.

The mage drew his sword and heaved it. It found home in the troll's chest and quivered there as the beast fell backward and landed with a crash. The mage walked past Ned, gave him a rather smart slap on the back of the head that, blessedly, silenced him, then retrieved his weapons and cleaned them. He resheathed them all, then squatted down by the creature and studied it for a moment. Sarah didn't have the desire to get any closer to one of them than she had been already—twice.

"What an unpleasant-looking bugger," Ned breathed after he'd scurried over to hide behind her, "and I was talking about the beastie." He paused. "Though I *could* have been talking about the mage—"

"Ned!"

"But I've heard he's terrible scarred, Mistress Sarah. And that he avoids magic for fear that if he uses any, he'll undo the world."

Sarah wasn't one to give credence to tales told at the end of the evening down at the pub, but she couldn't deny that while ancient the man might be and powerful he might be, in the light of day he was nothing short of frightening. Hooded, cloaked, bristling with all sorts of pointy things he obviously knew how to use very well. Perhaps that was why he kept his face covered. If his visage was as fierce as his reputation, it might just be too much for those he happened upon.

Daniel, for instance.

She was tempted anew to ask him if he'd changed his mind about aiding her or he'd merely decided on a bit of a journey for pleasure, but he straightened and turned toward her before she could. The picture he presented, along with what Ned had just told her about his magic, was intimidating in the extreme. If she'd been a more timid soul, she might have taken a step backward.

But if she did that, she knew she could never make that step up. Not that it mattered, perhaps, to anyone but her. After all, it wasn't as if she had any intention of traveling much farther with the man facing her. Still, there was no sense in not at least presenting a picture of strength and confidence.

She stepped forward and folded her arms over her chest. It hid their shaking quite nicely, truth be told.

"I appreciate your aid in dispatching those . . . things," she began, "um . . . "

"Ruith," he supplied.

"Lord Ruith—"

"Nay," he said mildly. "Just Ruith."

"Very well, *Ruith*. I appreciate your aid last night and this morning. I'll be happy to repay you for the bread and return your cloak—"

He shook his head. "There is no need."

Sarah knew a good turn when she saw one and she wasn't about to spurn it. Perhaps that was his way of apologizing for throwing her out of his house. She nodded, accepting his gift, then cleared her throat.

"I must carry on—"

"Aye, because her mother's house fell down," Ned interrupted.

Sarah elbowed Ned firmly in the ribs, then turned back to the mage, er, Ruith. "I must carry on with my quest."

"Of course," he agreed. "I wouldn't think anything else."

She imagined he would—and had. "I'm going to Bruaih, for I need a mage to aid me in my particular bit of business."

"Many kings have likewise auditioned their mages," Ruith conceded, "so you are in good company." He pulled his bow across his chest, then looked briefly over his shoulder. "I think we should be away quickly," he said. "I'll come with you to Bruaih, then wait for you to decide your course."

She started to protest, then made the mistake of looking again at their very dead foe.

What if he wasn't the last one of those sorts of lads?

She reconsidered her plan to leave the mage behind. The truth was, he was handy with a blade, even though he should have been leaning on a cane and waggling his fingers to subdue his enemies. But since he seemingly wasn't, perhaps she would be a fool to refuse the companionship of his very sharp blades. Perhaps when the time came, she could simply put her foot down and remind him who was in charge. Perhaps she would hire instead the mage in Bruaih and have no need to remind him of anything at all.

"Very well, then," she said carefully. "I thank you for your aid."

He merely inclined his head. And waited.

An auspicious start, she supposed. She nodded briskly, then turned and wrapped Ruith of the mountain's cloak more closely around the skirt she had stuck her head through. She marched on ahead, as if she were truly about some noble quest, and left her companions to follow. And she hoped she was going in the right direction.

She tried not to think about the fact that since she no longer had all her gold, the wizard of Bruaih might not be at all amenable to going off on a little explore. Or that since Daniel had all her gold in his greedy hands, he might have gone anywhere in the great, wide world, and she might not find him before he destroyed everything he could see. Or that her help included a horse masquerading as a dog, a lad whose only skill was escape, and an ancient mage who apparently preferred steel to spells and fought with the agility of a man a tenth his age. All led, of course, by she herself, who had no idea how she would ever manage the task laid before her.

She was tempted to sit down and surrender.

But since she never surrendered, she would do what she'd always done in the past. She took a deep breath and began to string her loom with what warped threads she had to hand.

She could only trust that she would find the wool for the weft, and that the proper pattern would emerge in good time.

She put her head down and walked on.

Six

Someone was daft and Ruith was beginning to suspect it was him.

He walked next to a woman who had decided not a half hour ago that she would move about more easily if she attempted to pass herself off as a lad. The lad who had previously been attempting to pass himself off as a man was now wearing a skirt and a hood pulled forward in order to hide as much of his face as possible and avoid unnecessary brawling. He, however, was wearing the same disguise he'd worn for years, which meant that his gear alone would leave anyone with questions thinking that perhaps those questions were better left unasked.

Somehow, it didn't seem a very auspicious start to the present business.

He supposed some of his unease could be credited to weariness. The journey hadn't been difficult physically, though he would freely admit that Sarah had traveled at a pace that had left him spending most of his time running after her.

Nay, it was that he'd spent the past three days thinking on his past in an effort to find answers for things that perplexed him, such as why he'd lived in happy obscurity for a score of years only to find himself assaulted on the same day by creatures from hell and a witch's get from down the way.

Coincidence?

He suspected not.

He hadn't found any answers, his forays into memories he would rather have left unexamined aside. By the time he'd reached Sarah—and been felled by her—he'd almost convinced himself that the two brutes he'd slain had been aberrations.

Unfortunately, that hope had been dashed quite handily by the troll looming over Sarah the night before and the one lurking behind Ned earlier that morning. That added to the fact that he hadn't noticed Ned during any of his previous three days' travel had left him more unsettled than he wanted to admit. Perhaps the boy had simply taken a different road, or benefited from Ruith's weariness. Or perhaps he was simply adept at keeping himself undetected.

That seemed to be his only skill, though. That and blurting out whatever seemed to enter his wee head before any sort of guard he might have put on his tongue could convince him to do otherwise. At least he was fetching enough to pass for a gel, though slightly too tall.

Sarah, on the other hand, was far too lovely to be a lad and perfectly incapable of walking like anything but a wench. Ruith glanced at her, then closed his eyes briefly. No one would mistake her for anything but what she was because she carried herself like a gel. That and her hair—the color of cognac, he decided abruptly— kept escaping her braid, which she had managed somehow to wrap around her head and tuck under Ned's hat.

He rubbed his hand over his face and wished for something very strong to drink.

Her hair was making him daft. Well, she, actually, was making him daft. He had to get away from her as quickly as possible before her relentless determination to lead them into a fray she hadn't studied beforehand and her flyaway hair pushed him fully into madness.

He supposed it might be possible that he'd been a bit too long in the mountains.

He would have happily settled for that having been an excuse for being distracted by a woman he didn't know and was fairly sure would frustrate him endlessly if he did know her, but he couldn't. He had, over the years, frequented other places in other guises not entirely his own. The women he'd met were perhaps not from the lofty spheres his family would have chosen for him, but they hadn't been without their own distinctions. He was who he was, after all, and even though his own royal life had ended abruptly many years ago, he hadn't forgotten the protocols and traditions associated with that life.

In glittering salons and intimate dinners with very short guest lists he had moved without misstep. He'd played the mysterious nobleman at various palaces in various locales simply to ease his restlessness and escape his dreaming. Unfortunately, it had never accomplished what he'd hoped it would. His self-imposed vow of solitude had ruled him mercilessly and he had returned to his hot fire and rustic fare without undue protest.

But now duty had driven him from his refuge and he was surprised to find he actually regretted having to leave his mountain. He blamed that immediately on Daniel of Doìre's idiocy. The sooner he caught the lad and beat sense into him, the happier he would be.

He studiously avoided thinking on what had truly driven him

from his home, namely the more serious question of where Sarah of Doìre had come by that burn on her arm.

He had the feeling he wasn't going to like the answer to that at all.

He came to himself to find he was no longer walking in the pale winter sunshine down a street that was teeming with too many souls for his taste; he was leaning against the wall of an inn, staring at nothing. He looked around only to realize he was standing with a woman, er, with Ned, rather, and Sarah was nowhere to be seen.

"Where is she?" he demanded.

Ned was looking inside the inn with an expression of slack-jawed astonishment. That had been his expression since they'd first seen Bruaih in the distance, though, so perhaps it implied nothing untoward. Ned lifted a hand and pointed with a quivering finger inside the inn—a rather seedy inn, on the whole. Ruith would have bedded down there without hesitation—indeed he had once and found the accommodations to be every bit as disgusting as he'd imagined they might be—but he was not alone and his mother had taught him to be a gentleman.

Ruith found Sarah talking to the innkeeper, no doubt trying to negotiate the best price for a flea-ridden scrap of floor. He strode over immediately and took her by the arm.

"Sorry," he said briskly, flipping the innkeeper a piece of gold. "The lad is overtired and thought he recognized you."

The innkeeper fingered the coin calculatingly. "I don't know as he don't seem a bit familiar to me—"

Ruith put another piece of gold on the bar and held it there under his finger. "He's my nephew. I wouldn't want my sister hearing tales that I allowed him to cause any trouble. You, friend, wouldn't want to be the bearer of those tales."

The other man's glance rested for the briefest of moments on hilts of blades and the number of arrows Ruith carried on his back.

He lifted one eyebrow in acknowledgment, then pocketed the second coin after Ruith released it. He returned to shouting at his serving lads.

Ruith pulled Sarah across the tavern and out into the sunshine. He started up the street with her, assuming Ned would follow.

"Will you just let go," she said angrily, trying to pull her arm away from him.

"Nay."

"Damn you, you're hurting me."

He realized that he had hold of her right elbow. He released her immediately, for he knew the wound she bore there. He stopped himself just in time from rubbing the same spot on his own arm. He stepped to the other side of her and caught her by the sleeve.

"What?" she said impatiently, turning to look at him.

He nodded back the way they'd come. "That one robs his guests whilst they sleep. And he has a ready tongue for spreading all manner of gossip. I thought it best he not have any idea who you were or what your plans are."

"I would have discovered that eventually, I daresay," she muttered. She chewed on her words for a moment or two, then spat them out quickly. "I've never been here before."

"There was a first time for me as well and I left rather less well-heeled than when I'd come. And if you'd care for my opinion, I'll tell you that the next handful of inns are a bit safer than the first, though not much. Unless you're willing to sleep with a knife in your hand. Farther up the street is perhaps more what you're looking for."

She looked up the street warily. "I'll see what I can find that suits my purse."

He nodded, though he had no intention of allowing her to pay for him. He supposed there was little point in saying as much. It was, as she'd reminded him more than once that morning, her quest. He was more than happy to leave it in her hands, for doing so seemed to keep her from asking questions he wasn't sure he wanted to answer, such as why he'd thrown her out of his house only to chase after her hours later. In the end, he supposed he would simply give her the answer he could most easily give himself, that he was merely there to help her look for her brother. With any luck at all, that would be the extent of it anyway.

He watched her lay siege to the street they were on, searching for a decent place to stay, all the while surreptitiously counting her coins. He was accustomed to prissy women who had all their needs catered to immediately by an army of servants, not lassies who wore sturdy and quite sensible boots and seemed terribly determined to do things without aid. Sarah reminded him a bit of his mother, which he wasn't at all sure was a good thing, though she was a scrappier, fiercer, more intensely determined version of his mother—and his mother had been very intense.

He watched Sarah walk away from the fifth place she couldn't afford before he could bear it no longer. He stopped her before she continued on doggedly up the street.

"Let us make a new bargain," he suggested.

"I didn't realize we had an old bargain," she said grimly.

"I believe we did. You were going to allow me to trail along after you whilst you looked over several mages to see who might suit you best. And since you are about the heavier labor, I think you should allow me to see to the inns. That will leave you free to look for just the right lad to suit your purposes."

"I cannot—"

"You could consider it my contribution to the cause."

She looked suddenly quite impossibly tired. "My pride demands that I say nay."

"But your good sense suggests that you put your pride to bed and then follow it there."

She sighed. "I'll repay you."

"Of course," he said, because he had the feeling she would fight

him right there in the street if he said her nay. He'd been counting her coins right along with her and guessed just how many she
didn't have. Why she hadn't been better prepared, he didn't know.
Perhaps her plans had somehow gone awry.

"I need a place for Castân," she said quietly.

He nodded at the stables behind her. "I think they'll take him
there, given that he seems to prefer hay."

Sarah glanced at that drooling mess, who had indeed found a
stray pile of last year's final cutting and was contentedly crunching
on it. She considered for a moment or two in silence, then looked
at Ruith.

"He's not a dog."

"I was beginning to suspect that."

She looked up at him searchingly. "I don't suppose you would
change him back to what he was. For a certain price, of course."

"Not here in the street," he said, because it was easier than giving her reasons that would only lead her to ask other questions and
dig again into her very light purse. He flipped Ned a coin. "Feed
yourself and the dog inside, lad. Stay out of sight until we come
back to fetch you."

Ned nodded and clicked at what had no doubt been a decent
chestnut gelding at some point in the past. They disappeared into
the stable without fanfare. Ruith nodded up the way.

"The Silver Swan is a safe place," he said. "We'll stay there."

"I'll agree to it only because I'm not in the habit of arguing with
my elders," she muttered. "This time."

He could only imagine the conversations they would have when
she realized he was not exactly who he'd been pretending to be. He
put that thought aside for use as a distraction later and walked to
the inn with her.

He found the innkeeper and negotiated for a quiet room in
the back on the upper floor where there was a modicum of safety.
He followed the man to it, saw that a fire had already been lit in

the hearth, then lifted the curtain slightly and looked out the window. There was a garden below, covered partly by a small roof jutting out from the floor beneath him. Useful enough if a hasty leave-taking was required. He handed the man the full price for a single night and a pair of meals, then escorted him out the door.

He shut it, then took off the majority of his weapons and propped them up in a corner. Knives down his boots would be enough for the morning. He looked at Sarah.

"You'll be safe enough here, I daresay," he said, walking over to the door.

"Where are you going?"

"Out for a walk," he said. He put his hand on the latch, then paused. "Lock the door after the maid comes, and please sleep. I'll take the key and return when I've had a look around."

She stood by the fire, wrapped in his spare cloak, her face grey with weariness. "I don't understand why you won't just cast a spell, or waggle your fingers, or some other such rot to find him. This seems like a great deal of fuss for something that could be solved so simply with magic—though I can't believe I'm suggesting it." She shook her head slowly. "I must be losing my wits."

"You aren't," he said simply. "As for the other, there are times when 'tis best to go about your business without leaving a trail of magic behind for others to follow." He opened the door. "I'll return."

She only watched him, silently.

He left the chamber, shut the door behind him, then found another doorway to linger in and wait. He supposed his life would have been much easier if he'd allowed himself even a simple spell of un-noticing, but since he couldn't, he'd become very adept at blending into crowds and standing in shadows.

He remained very still as a maid with a pair of serving lads arrived with enough food to feed half a dozen souls. They were let in, then all three left without incident. Ruith waited until he heard the lock turn before he took himself downstairs and through the great room. He left the inn, then turned to his left and walked quickly along the street, mingling with townspeople hurrying about their own business.

Bruaih wasn't a large place, but it was enormous when compared to Doìre. Ruith had been there many times over the years and found it to be nothing more than what it purported to be: a bustling hamlet of not a single honorable soul. Only in Shettlestoune, or so the villagers said with pride, never mind that Bruaih wasn't technically part of Shettlestoune county. Close enough for a sloppy spell, or so the saying went. Geography aside, the town lived up to its self-proclaimed reputation. Ruith expected to be lied to, cheated, and robbed if at all possible every time he set foot in the place. There was, he had to admit, a certain clarity of purpose that came with that manner of doing business.

He suspected Daniel of Doìre wouldn't fare very well trying to cheat cheaters, which might turn out to be very useful indeed.

He spent the morning walking through the market with his hand on his purse, nosing about the odd shop selling potions and sundry that the mage up the way wouldn't have lowered himself to produce, and sitting in a darkened corner in the seediest pub in town where he could eavesdrop in peace. All of it produced nothing more interesting than reports of Master Oban being even more stingy and high-handed than usual, which he'd already suspected, and a raging headache, which he'd acquired from listening to off-key musicians attempting to play whilst still laboring under the influence of things imbibed the night before.

He walked back to the Silver Swan by a fairly circuitous route simply from habit, then went upstairs and hoped for the pleasure of even a cold luncheon. He was weary, his head pained him, and he imagined that the search for Daniel's trail could be taken up again later in the afternoon without undue trauma having been inflicted upon the world. For the moment, sleep was what he needed, sleep that followed something decent to eat.

He knocked on the door instead of simply walking inside the chamber because his mother had somehow managed to instill a few manners in him, then let himself in when there was no answer.

Sarah was asleep on the floor in front of the hearth. He was somehow unsurprised to find her there instead of on the very comfortable-looking bed. No doubt she had left that for him since he had paid for the chamber. He was tempted to use it, but that might have left him sleeping more deeply than he wanted to.

He started to remove his cloak, then hesitated. He supposed he couldn't spend the next few days with Sarah—assuming that was how long it took to find her brother—never showing his face. He didn't consider himself particularly vain, but there was no denying that his particular ancestry was difficult to hide.

Then again, given how enormous Sarah's eyes had been as they'd walked into Bruaih, perhaps she had less experience with the world outside Doìre than she cared to admit. She might look at him and find him not only nothing out of the ordinary but actually quite repulsive.

At present, he wouldn't have been at all surprised.

He tossed his cloak over the foot of the bed, yawned hugely, then went to sit in a chair in front of the fire. He ate without tasting any of it, then helped himself to a mug of ale that couldn't compare on its best day to Master Franciscus's poorest attempt. It was almost cold, however, and useful in washing down his meal, so he didn't complain. Then he set his mug aside and paused. He had fully intended to close his eyes and have a bit of rest himself, but instead he leaned his head against the back of his chair and simply watched Sarah of Doìre as she slept.

She was, as he had noted before, remarkably pretty, even with the dark smudges under her eyes and her fingers still slightly green from whatever she had likely been dyeing before her mother's house collapsed under the weight of Daniel's poorly wrought spell. He wondered what her life had been like, all those years with a brother dabbling in things he shouldn't have been and a mother whose reputation for crotchetiness rivaled even his own. Perhaps she had found solace in weaving her own spells into whatever cloth she had made.

Why she hadn't used some of that magic she'd inherited from her reputedly quite powerful mother to stop her reckless brother was something he honestly couldn't fathom. Had the fool convinced her that she was not his match? Had she been intimidated enough to believe it? He couldn't imagine it, but he'd learned the hard way that the world was full of quite a few things he never would have imagined in his youth.

He rose, fetched his cloak, then spread it over her carefully. She shifted, sighed, then fell back into slumber. If she dreamed, she didn't show it.

He envied her.

He didn't envy himself, however, when he woke to a tremendous crash. He leapt up, then clutched his head in his hands as the chamber spun violently around him. He didn't have headaches often, but they were terrible when they came and they were usually brought on by dreams of magic.

Or screeching players with no sense of pitch.

He froze at the feel of steel against his throat.

"Sit down, you villain."

He sat back down without hesitation, then managed to pry his eyes open far enough to find it was Sarah standing at the other end of his sword, far enough away that he couldn't reach her without impaling himself on something he'd sharpened quite thoroughly himself not a fortnight earlier. The crash had, he suspected, been a tray full of pewter bowls dropped on the floor to purposely wake him.

"Don't move," she said in a low, deadly voice, "or I'll kill you."

He was happy to be as still as she wanted him to be. He peered at her blearily. "Do you know how to use that? Perhaps you should put it away before you hurt yourself—"

He shut his mouth abruptly at the look on her face.

"I don't particularly feel like putting the blade away," she said in that same very dangerous tone of voice, "and, aye, I can use this quite well, thank you very much."

He suspected that might very well be true. She hadn't been without skill in the forest, even caught as she had been, unawares and exhausted. The tables were well and truly turned now and he imagined she wouldn't be interested in any talk of Nerochian rules of engagement.

"Now that we understand each other, you'll want to give me answers to my questions, beginning with what you've done with my mage."

He took a careful breath. "I am he—"

She moved more quickly than he'd anticipated. Before he could so much as utter a peep in protest, he found himself sitting with one of his knives driven into the chair a hairsbreadth from his ear and the other an uncomfortable finger's width from his throat. His sword was quivering where it had been thrust into the floor, well out of reach of any of his limbs.

"I see no blood spilt," she said, sounding greatly displeased, "nor spells wrought, but he is gone and you are here."

He gingerly reached up to still the blade still twitching next to his ear. He didn't attempt to move the other bit of steel so close to his skin he could smell it. In his current condition, he likely couldn't have brushed it aside before she'd slit his throat.

"Are you paying for the damage to the wood," he asked lightly, "or am I?"

She wasn't amused. "It seems a pity to waste such a face as yours, but I will if I must. Now, give me the truth whilst I've the patience to hear it. Who are you and what have you done with my mage?"

He would have, he decided, given her whatever she wanted if she would just stay where she was long enough for him to uncross his eyes and look at her properly. But since it was all he could do simply to squint at her, he supposed he would have to content himself with her outrage over someone having absconded with, well, his own poor self.

Her mage, indeed.

" 'Tis a bit complicated," he began, mustering up the most trustworthy look he could.

"The truth is rarely complicated," she said shortly, "unless you have something to hide, which I suspect you do." She looked at him coolly. "You sound like Ruith, but you cannot be him. For one thing, you're supposed to be centuries old, which you most certainly are not."

And he was saved from answering by the sudden pounding on the door. The next thing he knew, his other knife was residing in the arm of the chair, between the fingers of his left hand.

"I'm *not* paying for *that*," he said faintly.

She shot him a displeased look. "Don't move. I'm not finished with you, and I have my own blade."

He imagined she did. He closed his eyes gratefully, then winced as she stepped on his foot, hard, before she walked over to the door. She managed to convince the souls clustered on the other side of the door that she had had a nightmare and knocked mugs and things to the floor in her fright.

He understood that.

He listened to her ask for a brief list of herbs, then heard the door shut quietly. He supposed he should have watched her to make certain she wasn't going to kill him for vexing her, but all he could do was lean his head back against the chair and concentrate on breathing carefully. He heard his knives come free of the wood near his ear and hand, and his sword from the floor. The table was then pulled to one side. He knew he should have offered aid, but he found he couldn't. It was all he could do to keep his eyes closed and allow himself the pleasure of sounds of company.

It was slightly unnerving how much he enjoyed it.

He had just decided he should be about hardening his heart when he felt a touch on his knee. He opened his eyes and found Sarah sitting on a stool at his feet.

"Drink."

He realized only then that he had dozed off, for he didn't remember having heard her brew anything. He accepted the cup she handed him, then sniffed. "What is it?"

"Something that will reveal your true wizened, wrinkled, impossibly ancient and unpleasant self," she said curtly. "Drink it and be thinking on a very believable tale that will explain why it is you aren't the old gent I was led to believe you were."

He sipped gingerly. The moment the infusion slid down his throat, he felt the edge come off his pain. The tea wasn't enspelled, but somehow it didn't need to be. He felt the crease on his brow lessen just as easily. He let out a deep, rather unsteady breath.

"Thank you."

"You're welcome."

"How did you know my head pained me?"

"You were squinting. Let me have your hand."

He surrendered it because she gave him no choice. She pinched an excruciatingly painful spot between his thumb and pointer finger, which left him gasping until he realized after a rather brief period of agony that his hand had ceased to pain him and so had his head.

He finished his tea, because he thought he would be wise to, then looked at her in astonishment.

"You *are* a witch."

"A lowly brewer of teas, rather," she said, releasing his hand and sitting back, "but you are most certainly not what you're purported to be. Who are you?"

"I told you who I was."

Her eyes narrowed. "I can give you that headache back, you know, if you persist."

He almost smiled. "You cannot."

"The hilt of your sword might have a different opinion."

He did smile then. He didn't imagine that even with having taken care of a farm for her mother—for he assumed Daniel hadn't been of any help at all—and her perfectly adequate skill with a knife, she would manage to do any damage with his blade. And he couldn't believe she had the heart to slaughter anything that wasn't required for supper, her fierce words aside.

And she still had hair the color of cognac lit by fire.

"I know what you're thinking."

He met her eyes. "I imagine not."

"Stop stalling," she said sternly. "How old are you?"

"How old are *you*?"

"A score and five and I'm not the one answering the questions."

"Aren't you?"

She glared at him. "I want answers. Stop your bloody smirking and give them to me."

He sobered himself as best he could, then reached out and took her right hand in both of his. He ignored, also as best he could, the fact that an inordinate and unlikely amount of pleasure went through him at such a simple thing. He didn't have to push her sleeve up her arm to see the damage because the spell that had burned a trail in her skin had left an echo of its mark on the white of the fabric.

"Tell me again where you came by this?" he asked quietly.

"Likely the same place you acquired yours."

He froze and met her eyes. "What did you say?" He tried to ask it carefully, but he feared it had come out rather harshly.

She reached out to touch his right wrist. "'Tis a mirror of mine."

She looked at his skin with a detachment he couldn't possibly match.

He leapt up out of his chair so suddenly, he tipped it over and almost knocked Sarah off her stool. He caught her, steadied her, then released her as if she'd burned him.

Which she had, actually.

"Let's go walk," he said, even though he would have preferred to run.

She looked up at him as if he'd suddenly sprouted horns.

He couldn't offer any explanation or excuse for his behavior. He sorted his gear into piles, put his cloak on, and strapped his knives to his back. The rest could be left behind without incident. His sword was too distinctive to be easily resold and his bow and arrows were etched with the symbols of his making. There was, at least in Bruaih, some honor still left amongst thieves.

He saw out of the corner of his eye that Sarah was putting her hair back under Ned's cap, then covering her attempts at looking like a lad with his cloak. A hopeless case, but there was no point in telling her that. She went to stand by the door as he secured the window a final time, then crossed the chamber.

"It was a spell," she said quietly. "That which burned me. I touched something on my brother's table, just a simple—"

"It's all right," he said hoarsely. "I don't want to know any more."

And he didn't. He didn't want to know any more, because he feared he already knew too much. The only question that remained was how she, a simple village witch's get, could see something that had happened to him in his dreams. The question of why the burn on her arm mirrored his was one he wasn't going to answer, even if his life depended on it.

He opened the door and walked with her out into the passage-way, leaving the conversation behind in the chamber where he didn't need to look at it any longer.

Seven

❧

Sarah walked along with Ruith of wherever he'd come from and looked unhappily at her surroundings. She didn't care for crowds, especially rough ones full of thugs for which not even the admittedly intimidating man next to her was deterrent enough for the more opportunistic souls. She had, in the time it had taken her to walk from the inn down one street and up another, fended off three attempted poachings of her feed bag and a very enthusiastic youth looking for a kiss.

He'd gone away sporting a bloody lip.

Ruith hadn't lifted a finger to help her with that lad, though he had unbent far enough to give a particularly evil-looking man who'd gotten too close to her a hearty shove. After that, he'd merely walked between her and the press of humanity with his hood pulled up over his head far enough to shield his face and his hands tucked into his sleeves. She wasn't sure if what she'd said about his arm had sent him scampering back into a terribly unyielding silence or if it had been merely the temporary loss of his blades that had distressed him enough to render him so implacably unapproachable.

She had no regrets for her actions. She'd woken back at the inn, warm and comfortable, only to sit up and find that she was locked in her chamber with a complete stranger. She considered the possibility that he'd killed her mage and found the exertion to be such that a wee nap had been necessary, but that had lasted only until her head had cleared and she'd decided that if he had killed Ruith, he likely would have killed her as well—and she was still breathing.

Until she'd gotten a full view of her companion's face and lost her breath abruptly.

She had decided, after a moment spent recovering from *that*, that the impossibly handsome man snoozing in the chair before her had to be Ruith, but if that were the case, then he had misled her deliberately about his identity. She'd been perfectly content to repay him a bit for that before she'd become distracted by the headache she could see wrapped around his head in an ever-tightening swath of pain. Once his brow had unfurrowed far enough that she thought he might be equal to answering a few questions, she'd apparently made the mistake of commenting on the burn she'd noticed on his arm. The wound hadn't been visible in the same way hers was. It seemed as if the magic that had left its mark had been purer somehow . . . as if it had been something come from a dream.

She had no idea why mentioning it had set him off so. Mages were, as she'd learned over the years, unpredictable and generally foul-tempered. That should perhaps have been enough to tell her all she needed to know about him. Obviously, he was more powerful than she'd feared. How else could he have lived in that house for centuries, yet had none of that living show on his face—

She felt her mouth fall open briefly before she managed to shut it. He couldn't be one of those damned elves she'd heard tales about once too often, could he? They were, from what she understood, full of magic, majesty, and themselves. She had decided when she'd been ten-and-three and quite empty of anything she considered desirable, that if there were ever creatures to loathe, it was elves.

In this, her mother actually agreed, which Sarah knew should have given her pause, but it hadn't. She had spent copious amounts of time scorning the elves she'd heard about in Master Franciscus's tales and feeling perfectly content to do so.

She glanced sideways at Ruith, then shook her head. Nay, he couldn't be. For one thing, he wasn't dressed in fine silks and adorned with all manner of precious gems. And he was altogether too familiar with pedestrian means of protecting himself. Elves limited themselves, she was quite certain, to spells. And they were cleaner.

But if he were just a man, and he was indeed the mage on the hill, how was it, then, that he looked so young? Had he killed the old mage and taken his house and his reputation, or had he simply found the place empty and decided it was well suited to his purposes?

The questions burned in her mouth until she thought she would go mad from keeping them to herself. But at the very moment when she thought she just might blurt them out and the potential for being overheard by miscreants be damned, Ruith slowed, stopped, then turned to her. She could see only shadows of his face, but now she—unfortunately—knew what those shadows hid. "I didn't kill the old mage."

She shifted uncomfortably. "I never suggested that you had."

He shrugged lightly. "I imagined you might be wondering. I would have been wondering the same thing, in your place."

"Thank you," she managed. She was wondering half a dozen other things, but since he didn't seem inclined to elaborate on more personal matters, she forbore. Again, obviously not an elf, else he would have been willing to talk about himself endlessly.

She cast about for something to discuss that might be less touchy. She put her hands into her apron pockets only to realize she was still masquerading as a lad and had no pockets. She leaned back against a wall and affected a casual pose she most certainly didn't feel.

"Did you find any sign of Daniel this morning on your walk?" she asked.

He put his hand on a heavy doorway that lay between them and relaxed just the slightest bit. "I heard nothing but the usual gossip of shopkeepers and market men. If he's here, he's well concealed."

She waited, but he said nothing more. She certainly didn't want to give him any more rein with her affairs than he likely already thought he had, but in truth, she had little idea where to start looking for her brother short of walking up to the town wizard and making inquiries there. She considered, then looked up at him.

"I'm not opposed to suggestions," she said slowly, "about where to start with all this."

"Even the noblest of Heroes has the odd, helpful squire," he conceded.

She frowned. "Are you laughing at me?"

"I wouldn't dare," he said, sounding very much in earnest. "And if you'd like the odd, helpful suggestion, I think we should first visit Master Oban. If your brother's intentions are as he said, he would most likely want to eliminate the competition—or at least attempt to."

"Any suggestions on where this Master Oban might be found?"

Ruith took his hand off the door. "The entrance to his house is never found in the same place, which leads to merriment and hilarity for those who seek him."

She smiled in spite of herself. "You don't care for that sort of thing."

He rubbed his hand over his face suddenly and shook his head sharply. "Nay, I've little patience for the silliness of some mages.

But, as that is how Oban manages his affairs, we're left with no choice but to subject ourselves to his antics."

"Where do we start?"

"He could be hiding anywhere."

Sarah looked down the street behind Ruith, then at the door he'd been leaning on. It was a heavy wooden door, rough-hewn and sturdy, but quite unremarkable.

And then she blinked.

She blinked again, but the vision didn't disappear. She reached out and trailed her finger along the doorframe.

"There's something on the door behind you."

Ruith looked, then shook his head. "I don't see anything."

"'Tis covered with runes."

"Is it indeed?" he asked, sounding faintly surprised. "Where?"

She ran her fingers over the doorframe, but that didn't bring the characters into better focus. She supposed she should have been surprised she could see them at all if Ruith couldn't. What she did know was that they were of a most magical sort and she didn't care to look at things covered with magic—for more reasons than just her aversion to mages and their ilk. She took a deep breath and pushed aside the usual thoughts that accompanied that one, ignored the fact that she had no sight, nor special gifts, nor ability save what allowed her to tell chartreuse from apple green, and had a better look. The sooner she described them, the sooner she and Ruith would be about her business.

"They're written in Croxteth," she ventured.

"That's interesting," Ruith said, sounding intrigued. "Can you make out what they say?"

Sarah had the same sensation she'd had as she'd stepped away from the forest earlier that morning, as if a layer of wool had been pulled from her eyes. She supposed there were more layers still, but even so she had a definite clearing of her sight.

Odd.

Perhaps it was nothing more than the leagues she had put between herself and Doìre. To be sure, her heart had lightened with every step.

She pulled herself back to the task at hand and studied what she could almost see.

"I think most of them have to do with power and magnificence and the superior quality of the cloth used in Master Oban's robes."

Ruith made a noise that might have passed for a bit of a laugh in someone else. "How fortunate we are that your mother did not neglect your education in the tongues of magic, else we might still have questions on that score." He leaned against the door again. "What other secrets are you hiding?"

She felt a thrill of fear rush through her before she could begin to stop it. Too many years of hiding who she was had obviously taken a toll. But since there wasn't any possible way Ruith could know even the first thing about her, she had to believe his question was an innocent one.

"Oh, just the usual things a witch's daughter can do that no mage would lower himself to," she said lightly. "I'll tell you one of my secrets for every one of yours you reveal."

"I suppose that will leave us discussing the weather."

She imagined so. She studied the runes trailing up and down the doorframe and winding around the latch like a vine. "I can actually get along in quite a few tongues," she conceded, "though not as many as I would like. What of you?"

"The same," he said easily. "I had to do something during all those centuries of hiding in the hills, didn't I?"

"If you're a score and ten," she said with a snort, "I would be surprised."

He tilted his head slightly. "Do you think so?"

"You don't really want to discuss this right now, do you?"

"Nay, I do not," he agreed. "I think we should rather be about this business and see what it yields."

Sarah supposed she might have hit closer to the mark than he was comfortable with, though he didn't retreat back into the silence he'd wrapped around himself earlier. Perhaps she would wear him down eventually and discover all his secrets—

Which would leave her open to his discovering an equal amount of hers. Fortunately, she had no plans to be traveling with him long enough for any of that. She had plans of her own that didn't include a man wearing more weapons than necessary and sporting a face that was distracting in the extreme. She had her duty to the Nine Kingdoms to fulfill, then she was going to be about her own future. Ruith would no doubt wish to return to his house on the hill where he could retreat back behind his terrible reputation and have his own measure of peace, though how he could find it in Shettlestoune, she couldn't imagine. She wouldn't have set foot in the place again if her life had hung in the balance.

Ruith knocked on that door that was covered in endless praises to Master Oban and his marvelous magic. A small square slid open and a long nose appeared protruding from it.

"What do you want?"

"An audience with His Magnificence," Ruith said politely. "We bear gifts."

Two eyes looked down that nose skeptically. "What sorts of gifts?"

"Small, round ones."

"Let me see."

Ruith produced two gold coins, then handed them into fingers that had replaced the face in the opening. The fingers fondled the coins for a moment or two, then retreated back into darkness. The door over the little window slid shut.

Sarah waited for a moment or two, then looked at Ruith. "Perhaps the wizard is not receiving visitors."

"Could be."

"Do you think Daniel threatened the mage?"

"So Oban won't open to us?" he asked in surprise. "Of course not."

"He can be intimidating."

Ruith snorted. "Your brother is nothing more than a very small annoyance in a world too large for his power. I have the feeling he will try to intimidate a mage or two, find himself slapped for his trouble, then slink off in shame and set himself up as a village wizard in some obscure locale to the south where neither you nor I will need travel to find him."

She wanted to believe him. She would have given all the gold in her purse plus whatever she might have earned over the rest of her life to have believed him. But she couldn't.

She had seen what Daniel could do.

Ruith pushed away from the wall. "We'll work harder at chatting up this lad here and see if I'm not right about the other."

He knocked again, deposited another three coins into the gate-keeper's questing fingers, and was informed that was enough for a single entrant. Ruith stuck his foot in the door when it opened, then pushed it open far enough for Sarah to go in first. He followed, shutting the door securely behind him. The gatekeeper eyed him warily, then scuttled back into what apparently served as his sitting room.

Ruith started along the passageway. Sarah followed him, loosening the knife in the back of her belt as she did so. She was prepared to find any number of souls loitering about with her death on their minds, but to her surprise she saw no one save a kitchen lad who took one look at Ruith, squeaked, and fled.

They saw no one else until they reached a door on the upper floor that was covered with the same sorts of runes that adorned the front door below. Sarah looked at Ruith.

"I think he's here."

Ruith tried the door handle, but it was locked fast. He picked the lock with tools he produced from some pocket or other, then he very carefully turned the knob. Sarah leaned up on her toes and looked over his shoulder.

The chamber was exactly as she imagined it would be, full of very fine furniture, an enormous, elegant hearth, and cases upon cases of expensive things to dust. There was a man sitting in front of the fire with his back to the door. The wizard, obviously, judging by the height of his pointed hat and the robes that flowed over the sides of the chair and cascaded down to the floor. He was, quite thankfully, alone.

Ruith motioned for her to stay behind, which she chose to do without hesitation. She stood in the shadows and watched him pad silently over to the man. He stopped to the mage's left, well within his line of sight, and made a low bow.

"Master Oban?"

The wizard threw himself to his feet, but the motion seemingly overbalanced him. Before Ruith could reach out and take hold of him, he'd gone sprawling on the floor. Sarah hurried over and pulled his very heavy chair back a bit whilst Ruith righted the side table that had taken a tumble along with its master.

The mage looked up at them, then began to scream.

Silently.

Ruith took hold of the man and pulled him to his feet. The mage fought him, but he wasn't any match for Ruith in size and strength. Ruith set him with surprising gentleness back into his chair, then pushed his own hood back from his face and looked at the wizard gravely.

"What befell you, Master Oban?"

Sarah was ready to ask the same thing, but then she had a decent look at the mage's face. He wasn't so much disfigured as he was slightly . . . empty. As if something that had been there before had been removed—and not very well. He mouthed spells, but nothing happened. He picked up a very ornate wand, golden and sparkling, and waved it frantically at Ruith. Sarah watched a poorly woven and exceedingly slow-moving spell waft its way through the air like eiderdown. Ruith stepped aside, leaving the spell whispering harmlessly past him.

The mage looked at them both for a moment in silence, then he put his face in his hands and began to sob. It was done in profound silence, which made it all the more terrible. Sarah perched on the edge of the man's chair and put her hand on his back. He reached up and fumbled for her hand until she gave it to him. He held on tightly and continued to grieve.

Sarah looked up at Ruith. "What do you think happened to him?"

His expression was very grim. "I'm not sure." He pulled up a stool and sat down in front of the old mage. "Can you tell us what befell you?"

It took another few minutes before Master Oban finally dragged one of his velvet sleeves across his face, then nodded. He seemed to recapture something of himself, because he suddenly waved his wand around furiously, sending more spells scattering around him. Sarah watched them bounce harmlessly off things and disintegrate. He then leapt up and began an involved pantomime where he played two characters: himself, by all accounts; and apparently another evil, sneaky mage. A fight ensued and, despite Oban's masterful strategies and impressive defenses, his voice was taken from him.

Sarah caught sight of Ruith's face during the last bit of Oban's tale and was surprised by his expression. He said nothing, but he watched Oban as if he'd seen something almost too horrible to face. She almost reached out to him, but stopped herself just in time. He visibly shook aside whatever had troubled him, then assumed an expression of sympathy.

Curious.

She turned her thoughts to what the runes below had proclaimed about Oban's utter magnificence. She wondered about her brother and how Ruith had been certain he didn't have enough power to do anything but be an annoyance. But what if he had found a way to take things from others?

Their voices, perhaps?

Or their power?

The thought was so horrifying, she instinctively turned away from it . . . and then she looked at it again. How many times had her mother wished aloud that she could add to her own power and lamented the fact that she knew no spell for such a thing? How often had Daniel simply listened to her rattle on without adding to the conversation? Sarah had always assumed he was simply allowing their mother to go on so she would think kindly of him when he wanted something from her. Now Sarah began to suspect he might have been thinking about something else entirely.

Her only question now was how in the world he ever would have found such a spell.

"Master Oban," she said slowly, "did someone steal more than your voice?" She paused. "Perhaps your power, too?"

The mage stopped in mid-retelling of his tale, then turned to her and nodded vigorously, but that shouldn't have caused the sound of breaking glass. Sarah realized then that the glass Ruith had been holding had slipped through his fingers and shattered against the marble floor. She rose from where she'd been sitting on the edge of the chair to help him, only to find Master Oban in her way. He held up his thumb and forefinger pinched together and looked at her pointedly.

"But only a bit," she guessed.

He looked down his nose at her and jerked his head once in a brisk nod. Of course. It likely wouldn't do for anyone to believe he was less than he had been.

She cleared her throat. "Was it a man, a dark-eyed man with blond hair?"

Master Oban's eyes widened suddenly, and he nodded.

"I fear that was my brother," she admitted. "We're trying to find him and stop him from doing any more damage—"

The mage pulled his cloak more closely around him and tapped her aside with his wand before he marched unsteadily toward the door. He looked back over his shoulder at them, then pointed pointedly at the passageway.

Sarah looked at Ruith. "I think he wants to come with us. Do you need to rest—"

"Nay," he said hoarsely. He rose, crunching glass under his boot. "I am well."

He didn't look well, but she wasn't going to argue. She followed him from the chamber not out of any desire to defer to him, but rather because she thought she might better catch him that way if he keeled over.

Master Oban, however, seemed perfectly happy to be off hunting Daniel, if the alacrity with which he descended to his kitchens was any indication. He found a rucksack and began to load it with dainties that likely wouldn't survive the trip out of town. She watched him for a moment or two, then looked up at Ruith, who looked better than he had before. Then again, he'd poached a substantial piece of cake and was putting it where it was intended to go.

Man first, mage second, apparently.

Master Oban paused in his packing and wandered out of the chamber.

"I believe we've made another acquisition," Sarah said with a sigh.

"He'll slow us down," Ruith said grimly. He poured two glasses of wine, handed one to her, then sipped at his own. He paused, then drained the entire glass in one slow pull. He drew his sleeve across his mouth and shook his head. "Give me a reason, any reason at all, why we shouldn't leave him behind."

"Because he might know something useful?"

He cursed, set his glass down, then began to pace restlessly. Master Oban came trotting back into the kitchen from points unknown with several bottles that he shoved into his sack without regard to the cakes and delicate pastries he'd already packed first. Sarah watched him hurry off to rummage through his silver, then looked again at Ruith, who had stopped pacing and was merely standing there, watching grimly.

"What befell him, do you think?" she asked before she thought better of it.

He looked at her, opened his mouth, then shut it again and shook his head. "What I'm thinking doesn't bear repeating. 'Tis so fanciful that even I think I'm mad to entertain it." He scratched his right wrist, then flinched. "I forget about this."

"I wish I could."

He studied her for a moment, then sighed. "I'm sorry for it. As for the other, I think we can safely assume that your brother was about his business, then left town before he was caught. Unless you think he might still be loitering somewhere here."

"He might be at a bookseller," she said without hesitation. "He was always looking for more spells, and 'twas certain he couldn't find them in Doìre—"

She jumped at the sound of a pounding on a doorway at the front of the house. Oban popped up from where he'd been rustling around in a chest of linens, stuffed a handful of things into his pack that was already overflowing with spoils, and hauled it up onto his shoulders. He waved for them to follow and sprang for the back door.

She followed, with Ruith hard on her heels. They slipped through the garden and out into a street she hadn't seen before. Sarah wasn't sure who had been trying to get into the wizard's house, but she knew she didn't want to meet them if Master Oban didn't.

She supposed it might have been easier to blend in if she hadn't been hurrying off with a tall, profoundly dangerous-looking man and an ancient wizard dressed in purple velvet robes and a tall, pointy purple hat, and waving a wand that scattered spells around him like seeds.

'Twas little wonder Ruith was cursing rather more loudly than necessary.

He finally stopped them on a corner. "I have to have my gear," he said in a low voice, "and we have to get out of the village before we're not able to."

"I'll fetch Ned—"

He shook his head. "Too dangerous. Just take Oban and wend your way east until you reach the road. Many companies stage their wagons there. I'll follow with the lad and your hound." He paused. "If the choice is between you and the mage, leave him."

She nodded, though she wasn't sure she could do it. She watched Ruith walk off swiftly into the light of the setting sun, then turned to Master Oban.

"Listen to me," she said sharply. "If you want to live, hide your gear, keep your head down, and follow me."

His mouth fell open, but he took off his hat and put that and his wand under his cloak just the same.

Sarah towed him along behind her, ducking into the first shop she saw when she heard shouts in the distance. It happened to be a bookstore, which she thought to be fortuitous for a potential sighting of Daniel—until she realized she'd lost Oban. She found him fondling what were obviously books of spells, but she didn't have time to look and neither did he, no matter how vigorously he flapped his arms in protest when she pulled him away.

It took a good half an hour to duck in and out of front and back doors, but she finally found herself on the outskirts of town with the sun going down behind her and a road full of dust in front of her. She looked over the wagons critically, wondering which one might be willing to take on an unusual quartet of travelers without asking too many questions.

She selected a likely suspect, then walked over. The four horses already hitched were large and sturdy and the wagon seemed to be well stocked. Her coin might buy them at least a few meals from the wagon master if she were very polite.

She left Master Oban thinking on her command that he not move, then approached the man and waited until he'd turned from his business to greet her. To her profound surprise, the man turned out to be none other than Master Franciscus.

"What are you doing here?" she asked in astonishment.

He shook her hand with a smile. "Deliveries in the north, my girl. What are *you* doing here?"

"Don't ask." She pulled her purse from her feed sack and held it out. "I need you to hide us."

"Us?"

"That mage there, Ned, me . . . and the mage from up the hill."

Master Franciscus ignored her coins and instead put his hand on her head the same way he'd been doing for as long as she could remember.

"I sense quite a tale here, but I'll wait until we're a more comfortable distance from Bruaih to pry it from you. I assume your other companions will find us?"

"I certainly hope so." She paused. "Do you have oats, perchance? Or carrots?"

"Carrots?"

"I brought Castân. He won't need many. Ned will eat what he doesn't, I imagine."

"And the lad from up the hill? What will he require?"

She looked at him sharply. "What did you call him?"

Franciscus lifted an eyebrow and smiled. "I've shared the occasional cup of ale with him, Sarah, and I've two good eyes. I assume you do too."

"I—"

"I'd better go see to your other mage before he becomes a little too cozy with any of my kegs," he said, turning away. "We'll set off momentarily. Don't lose yourself."

She wasn't sure she hadn't already begun to. She paced restlessly until Franciscus was ready, then followed along after his wagon as he drove off into the twilight. She had the oddest feeling, as if she were walking in another world that wasn't hers. She drew her hand over her eyes and shook her head for good measure, but that didn't help her any. Her surroundings seemed sharper somehow, no matter what she did. In time, she gave up trying to ignore those surroundings and settled for concentrating only on the ground in front of her feet.

Ruith and Ned caught up to them before long, with Castân trotting along dutifully behind them. Sarah walked along behind them all far enough into the night that she was very grateful indeed when Franciscus called a halt and they made camp.

Ned wolfed down a supper suitable for a lad of ten-and-six, rolled up in a blanket, then closed his eyes and began to snore happily. Castân deigned to lie down, but he made a particularly horse-like noise as he did so. Ruith reached over and fed him a wizened, nasty-looking carrot. Castân crunched it happily, then rested his head on his paws and looked at Ruith worshipfully.

Sarah sat on the other side of the fire from them and watched as Ruith pulled out a stone and began to sharpen one of his knives. He looked much better than he had before, so much better that she wondered if she'd imagined his actions in Oban's private chambers.

Only she could still see the trail of spell on the back of his hand, glinting silver in the moonlight.

She looked up from her contemplation of his hands working his steel to find him watching her. She attempted a smile, but failed.

"I'm worried," she admitted. She glanced at Oban, because she couldn't help herself, then looked back at Ruith. "Can Daniel be found without magic?"

"We're only a pair of days behind him and I can't imagine he suspects he's being hunted," Ruith said easily. "He'll become careless, and then we'll have him."

She wished she had that sort of faith in her brother's stupidity, but she knew him better than that.

Ruith set his knife aside. "You should sleep. The road will be long tomorrow."

She shook her head. "You first. I have too much on my mind now. Besides, Master Oban will keep me company."

He hesitated. "I'm not entirely convinced we won't see more of those trolls. They move silently."

"I'll listen carefully."

He hesitated, then nodded. "Very well, a pair of hours. No more."

She nodded, then watched him stretch out near the fire. Castân rose, lumbered over, then lay down at Ruith's back, snorting a time or two contentedly before he stretched his front feet out and rested his head on them. Sarah would have smiled, but the sight of her horse who was now a dog because of things she couldn't control was too unsettling to allow her to. She rose and began to pace the perimeter of the camp silently. And she hoped Ruith was right about Daniel, that his conceit would be his undoing.

She didn't want to think about what other lives he would ruin if not.

Eight

❈

Ruith dreamt.

He found himself in a forest he didn't recognize, though that was perhaps nothing noteworthy. There were many places in the world where he hadn't walked. This, however, was a forest full of things that didn't normally find themselves growing together with limb and leaf.

The forest was full of sheaves of paper.

He walked under boughs laden with single pages, past trees wrapped entirely in parchment. He made the mistake only once of reaching for one of those sheaves. The spell apparently written thereon leapt up and wrapped itself around his wrist, crawling up to his elbow before he could jerk his arm away. He cursed viciously and ripped himself away from the tendrils that subsequently waved in the wind as if they had been bits of a spiderweb disturbed, or some sort of monstrous, multilimbed creature determined to wrap itself around him and consume him.

He didn't care for either image, actually.

He continued on for a bit longer until he thought the spells might have gone back to sleep, then he leaned over and looked at what was written on the parchment. He drew back in revulsion, for he recognized not only the hand but the words.

Those were his father's spells.

He walked away, fighting his gorge and his ire. He'd watched secretly as his father had penned many of those spells, collecting them all like vile, twisted seeds into a single place where he might plant them at will and watch them spring up into something evil. He, along with his brothers, had memorized all of those spells as the opportunities presented themselves, though they had made solemn vows never to use any of them.

He suspected that he might have broken that promise without another thought if he'd had his father in front of him.

He continued on, though he felt himself slowing as he realized that he was no longer in a forest he'd never seen before; he was in a place he recognized.

He looked at the path that continued to wind through those parchment-covered trees. He didn't want to follow that path, for he knew very well where it led, and he had no desire to visit that locale ever again. His feet, unfortunately, seemed to have a much different idea, for they carried him where he most certainly didn't want to go. He steeled himself for what he knew lay in the middle of the glade he could now see opening up in the midst of that forest.

Only instead of what he expected to find, there was something entirely different.

And all the more horrifying because of it . . .

Ruith woke with a start, realizing only as he almost fell over that he was on his feet. Sarah had him by one arm and Ned by the other. They wore identical expressions of astonishment.

"'Tis nothing," he said, his voice sounding rough to his own ears. "Too much rich food from supper last night."

Ned released him with a shrug and walked off, apparently following his nose to something more interesting. Sarah didn't let go of his arm, which was likely all that kept him upright.

"You were shouting in a language I didn't recognize," she said quietly.

"My misspent youth," he managed. "Or, as I said before, too much time alone in the mountains."

She frowned thoughtfully, looked at him once more rather more searchingly than he was comfortable with, then released his arm slowly.

"If you say so," she said doubtfully.

He attempted a smile. He supposed it had been rather less of a smile and more of a grimace, but 'twas the best he could manage at present. He watched as Sarah walked away to rouse the fire that someone—Ned, no doubt—had let burn out during the last watch. He bent his head and rubbed his hands over his face, though that was of little use dispelling the horror that hung about him like smoke.

He looked around him in an effort to put himself where he was instead of continuing to be lost in a dream he hadn't asked for. Ned had been sent off to look for more dry wood. Master Franciscus was preparing what would no doubt be a rather cold breakfast if things didn't change soon. Sarah was kneeling next to the fire, trying to coax it back to life. Master Oban waved his wand over the fire, but all that business produced was something that grew into a head-sized bubble and floated off. He leapt to his feet, mouthing a silent curse, and ran off to chase what he'd created.

It had been, Ruith could admit without any hesitation at all, a very long pair of days.

He lost his balance slightly as Sarah's horse-turned-dog leaned up against him, then sat in a friendly fashion on Ruith's foot and put his head within easy scratching distance. Ruith obliged him gladly. Anything to forget things he didn't care to dream about and ends to dreams he had no desire to sleep long enough to discover.

He watched Sarah as she fought with her own flint and whatever dry moss Ned had been able to find. And as he watched her, he wondered about her. The witchwoman Seleg had not been without substantial power, or so reliable rumor had said. After all, she'd spawned the illustrious Daniel of Doìre. Sarah should have inherited her share of power as well, yet there she was trying to light a fire in as unexceptional a fashion as he might have himself. She had no reason to shun her magic, yet she did so just the same.

She sat back on her heels, blew her hair out of her eyes, and looked up at him. "It's hopeless, I think. Too wet."

"Then why don't we gather everyone up and take the road," he said, wanting nothing more than to walk until he'd left his nightmare behind. "We'll eat as we walk. I think we might manage to catch one of the straggling companies today if we make haste. They might have tidings of untoward happenings in the area."

She rose and nodded. "How much longer to Firth, do you think?"

"Another handful of days. We'll buy more supplies there."

"I'll go collect Ned and Oban."

He nodded and watched her go before he stomped out the soggy remains of her attempts at a fire, then went to look for Franciscus. The alemaster was hitching up his ponies to the wagon and had obviously already secured his load. Ruith discussed with the man their plans for the day, then collected his gear and strapped it to himself. He spent another few minutes hiding the details of their camp. Others would know someone had come by, but they wouldn't have any idea about the number of the company. He wasn't sure why he bothered. Their trouble lay ahead of them, not following along behind.

He walked off a ways and stood looking over still-sleeping farmland. He could see the faintest outlines of mountains in the

distance. Those were the Mealls, the mountains that began as foot-
hills, then grew into a protective ring about Lake Cladach before
marching north to form the western boundary of Ainneamh. He
hadn't seen them in a score of years. He could hardly believe he
might actually set eyes on them again in the near future.

His dream came back to him suddenly, and he wondered about
it, though not for long. He had enough to think on with Sarah's
quest.

Unless there were mages who had grown into vast amounts of
power whilst he'd been ignoring the world on his mountain, there
was no one with the ability to take another's power save the usual
suspects and he wasn't quite ready to think on any of them.

Even if by some miracle Daniel had found the sort of spell to
take things that weren't his, he would never have the ability to use
it. The lad couldn't weave a decent spell of Olc to destroy a house
and barn with any flair. He wasn't going to manage something as
delicate as ridding a mage of his voice. Oban still had his power.
His loss of voice could be explained easily. Ruith was sure he would
get to that explanation when he was at his leisure.

He looked back to find most of the company collected by the
wagon. Sarah was standing apart, bent over something she held
in her hands. He knew without looking any more closely what she
was doing. He'd caught her more than once poking about in that
wee purse of hers, counting her coins with a look of intense dismay
on her face.

Worry about her situation had kept him quite nicely from thinking about his own, but he knew that couldn't last for long. There
were things swirling around him, things from nightmares, things
he was managing to ignore only out of sheer will. It couldn't last
forever.

His recent dream was proof enough of that.

He set himself to shepherding the company in the right direction, then found himself walking next to Sarah, which wasn't

anything unusual. Ned and Oban had taken a liking to each other
from the start. The mage gestured wildly in an attempt to make up
for the loss of his powers of speech and Ned did nothing but watch
him in slack-jawed fascination. A perfect combination, to be sure.
Castân trailed along after the pair, clomping steadily and drooling
prodigiously. Master Franciscus seemed happy enough to manage
his horses and wagon. Ruith couldn't blame him. It seemed rather
the safest place to be.

He looked to his left to find Sarah studying him from out of the
corner of her eye. She'd been looking at him in much the same way
ever since they'd left Bruaih.

It made him nervous.

"What do you think befell him?" she asked suddenly, with a
slight nod at Master Oban. "What of Daniel's make, I mean."

Ruith didn't want to discuss it. He felt as if he were walking
along that path through woods he never wanted to see again in
what he was fairly certain would be an excessively long lifetime.

"I don't know," he hedged.

"A mage cannot steal another's soul, can he?"

Ruith shrugged. That was all he could manage, given that he was
doing everything in his power to continue to breathe normally.

Steal another mage's soul, indeed. Words could not begin to
describe the dread that had sprung up around his heart. It wasn't
possible, of course, but what if Daniel had come by a spell fashioned by a lesser mage, perhaps a spell of Taking? Perhaps he
might have, even with his inferior skills, used it well enough to
take something from another mage.

Such as his voice.

"You don't think Daniel was using a spell he found on that page,
do you?"

Ruith felt the world grind to a halt. He stumbled to an ungainly
halt right along with it, then looked at Sarah slowly.

"What page?"

"The one that attacked me in my mother's house."

He swayed. He didn't mean to, but he couldn't help himself. "What?" he managed.

She stopped next to him. "I went in his bedchamber to look for a bottle of potion for a customer who had come seeking aid for her daughter. I'd thought I'd simply used that tincture without thinking, but the bottle had been of a particular make, with a tear running down its side." She looked up at him. "I always thought that particular bottle looked a bit like a well that had somehow become too full and left its contents slipping down its sides."

Ruith felt a bit like a horse had just kicked him in the gut. It was all he could do not to lean over and suck in air that he couldn't seem to find whilst standing up straight. He found that all he could do was stare at Sarah, mute, and wish with fervor that she would stop speaking.

"I suspected that Daniel had taken that particular bottle because I saw a thread of his spell in my mother's workroom in a suspicious place," she went on, still watching him closely, "so I went into his bedchamber to look for it. It was there that I saw the page lying on his table. I would have thought nothing of it, even considering that it was torn in half and scorched along its edges as if it had been rescued from a fire, but what happened when I reached out to touch it makes me think it was more than a simple sheaf." She paused. "Odd, isn't it?"

Ruith couldn't answer. It was all he could do to remain where he was. He knew with a certainty that made him almost ill that he wasn't going to want to hear the rest of her tale.

"I reached down to pick up the page," she continued slowly, "and a spell written there leapt up and wrapped itself around my arm."

Ruith closed his eyes briefly. It wasn't possible that she'd had happen to her whilst awake what had happened to him in his dream. The similarities were interesting, but surely not significant.

But if his father's spell had attacked him in a particular way, and a different spell had assailed her in precisely the same way, could it not be possible that the author of the spells might be the same?

"I wonder if Daniel used a spell from that page," she mused. "He seemed particularly fascinated with it. Nay, that isn't the right word." She paused, then met his eyes. "Obsessed. He was obsessed with it, so much that he was unable to look away from it once he'd cast his eyes on it."

"And you think he used the spell from that page on Master Oban?" he asked thickly.

She studied him for a moment or two in silence. "I never said that."

She didn't have to. Ruith didn't want to look at what events pointed to, but he realized he was fast approaching the point where he knew he wouldn't have any choice. There was only one spell in his father's collection whose purpose was to take power from another mage. It was almost unthinkable, but what if that spell had found itself in the hands of a fool who had tried to use it—unsuccessfully, fortunately—on a mage he could see walking now thirty paces in front of him?

His father's spell of Diminishing?

He shook his head, because the thought was too terrible to contemplate. His father never would have let that be found. It had been his most precious possession, a thing of evil he had created at the height of his powers, a loosing of forces that should rather have been left buried and secret.

A bit like that morning at the well, truth be told.

"Ruith, you don't look well."

"Sympathy," Ruith said hoarsely.

She put her hand on his arm. "Do *you* think Daniel is using a spell he found on that page?"

"I don't know," he ground out.

Because he didn't know, he decided abruptly. The truth was,

Daniel could have found anything akin to it, something a much lesser mage had invented, something that wasn't equal to what an equally foolish mage with little power would have attempted to use with only marginal success.

"Why would Daniel want his voice and not his magic?"

"Bloody hell, woman, I don't know!"

Sarah didn't look at all surprised by his outburst, which made him regret it even more than he already did. She merely took her hand off his arm, lifted an eyebrow, and walked on without further comment. Ruith caught up to her when he could move again, but she said nothing. She merely clasped her hands behind her back and walked, studying the mage in front of them as if she could wring answers to her questions from the air that separated them.

Ruith found himself suddenly back in his dream, walking along a path he couldn't bear, breathing air that was full of putrid spells, reaching out to steady himself but finding his skin scorched each time he encountered other pages—

"I think that's the village, don't you?"

He'd never been more grateful for anything in his life than he was at the sight of a distraction not a league away. He caught Sarah by the sleeve, but carefully. He was walking on her right and 'twas her right arm that bore the wounds of . . . his father's spell.

He had to simply breathe for a moment or two until he thought he wouldn't sick up onto her very sensible boots what he'd managed to eat as he walked.

"Can I fetch you wine?" she asked, looking up at him searchingly. "Truly, you look unwell."

He shook his head carefully. "Forgive me," he said without hesitation. "I was not growling at you."

"I should have realized—"

"Nay, Sarah," he said quietly, "it wasn't your doing." He paused for a very long moment. "I don't care for magic."

That was an understatement, but there was perhaps no sense in elaborating at present.

"Neither do I."

He took another in a very long series of deep breaths. "It wasn't you," he said, again.

"One of your secrets?" she asked lightly.

He nodded.

"I won't ask, but I will buy you breakfast if there's a decent inn available. We'll leave Daniel to his madness for the morning."

He knew he could do neither—allow her to feed him or forget about her brother—but he agreed just the same and forced himself to carry on with renewed vigor. Perhaps they might manage a decent meal, which he would pay for, another blanket or two, and other things to take his mind off things he couldn't face, such as dreams, scribblings of mages, wounds that couldn't possibly be inflicted by swords . . .

It took only half an hour to reach the village. Ruith had planned to make a quick and very discreet visit to a seller of sundries for supplies, but he realized immediately that he wouldn't manage it. Master Oban was recognized for what he was before they'd set foot past the most outlying house, and that seemingly called for pleasantries and formalities that Ruith was certain might carry on for the rest of the day.

He first leaned against a rock wall separating two fields, then he sat upon it, then he had to force himself not to stretch out and nap.

And given that he knew where that would lead, he resisted the urge without hesitation.

In time, the mayor stopped lavishing praise upon Master Oban and turned to the other members of their company. Ruith kept his seat on the rock wall in an effort to avoid either questions or praise. He was more than happy to watch it be bestowed on Sarah, whom the tall, thin politician seemed to think the next worthiest candidate for his attentions. Ruith listened to the flatteries with half an ear and kept his head down. He didn't like the aftereffects of dreaming. His head hurt, his spirit was wearied, and he wanted nothing more than to sit with his feet up and do his best to work through several glasses of Master Franciscus's latest offering. He glanced at the wagon in the distance, then sighed with genuine regret. Too far and too many souls to thread his way through to reach the prize.

"What happened?"

Ruith looked up at the sound of Sarah's voice. He realized instantly that she wasn't talking to him; she was conversing with the mayor. Her tone wasn't so much panicked as it was full of unsurprised resignation, as if she'd anticipated the tidings, however unpleasant.

"Our mage," the mayor said with a shiver. "He was fine yesterday when I saw him for the sowing of the ceremonial beet crop, but not this morning for the turnips, which is why I thought it wise to make a visit and see if aught ailed him." He paused. "I think it best to show you what befell him rather than attempt to tell you."

Ruith met Sarah's gaze and saw his own unease mirrored there. It was one thing to hope that Daniel was a fool and Oban had been an accidental success; 'twas another thing indeed to be faced with the possibility that perhaps Daniel had been more successful than they'd feared.

He hopped off the wall, then followed the company as they were shepherded to the local mage's house, but he remained without as the others were ushered bodily inside. It wasn't that crowds troubled him overmuch; he simply preferred to proceed only after he had investigated the lay of the land, unlike Sarah of Doìre, who plunged ahead with enthusiasm, deciding upon a course and doing what needed to be done without hesitation. He envied her the ability to do so without thinking her choices to death.

Voices were raised in alarm and dismay. Spells came floating back out the door, spells that were of Oban's make; of that he was certain. He ducked under a pair of them, then took a deep breath and steeled himself for the worst as he eased into the house.

He wasn't prepared for what he saw.

He put his hand on the doorframe for support, because he had to. He schooled his features so they wouldn't show what he didn't want others to see.

Because he knew the man lying on his cot, a former shell of himself.

He forced himself to breathe evenly. He couldn't say that he had known very many people in his past, but he knew the man lying there. Seirceil of Coibhneas, he was sure of it. Not a very famous mage as mages went, nor a very powerful one, but a profoundly decent and kindhearted one. The sort of man, Ruith had heard, that one would be overjoyed to meet on a rainy night after a long journey. Ruith had no doubt that Seirceil had opened his door to Daniel freely, invited him inside, fed him, made certain he had clothes and food enough for the rest of his journey, and then . . .

Well, 'twas obvious he had been repaid with harm.

A particular sort of harm that made Ruith quite ill. If Seirceil could be called more than barely alive, Ruith would have been surprised. Actually, it was worse than that. He was most certainly quite well in body, but his soul had been ravaged. Ruith rubbed his hand over his face. It was all he could do to stand where he was and not turn, walk out the door, and begin to run.

Away from what was before him.

Away from his past.

Away from the path he could now see had always been laid out beneath his feet, a path he didn't want to walk, a path he was equally convinced couldn't be walked by anyone else.

"Why don't Sarah heal him?" Ned blurted out. "She's a wit—"

Ruith watched Sarah clap a hand over Ned's mouth before he finished. He was happy to see Ned contained as often as possible simply as a matter of principle, but he wondered that she wanted her skills to be hidden. Perhaps he shouldn't have, given his own propensity for the like, but he did just the same.

He felt a light touch on his arm and looked to find Sarah standing next to him. Her face was full of exactly what he was feeling.

"Was it Daniel?"

He took a deep breath. "Aye, I imagine so."

She looked up at him searchingly. "Can you not do something for this mage?"

He had to look away because he simply couldn't bear having her look at him that way any longer. Unfortunately, that left him looking at Seirceil of Coibhneas, lying there ruined because he'd not recognized evil as it stood on his doorstep. And whatever else might be said about Daniel of Doìre, it had to be conceded that he was improving in his craft. Master Oban had suffered a glancing blow; Seirceil had taken a full, frontal assault. If he woke again, Ruith would have been surprised. If he woke to himself, 'twould be a miracle.

Ruith felt for Sarah's hand, squeezed it briefly, then turned and walked out of the house. He had to, or he was going to make some unwholesome noise that would frighten more than just him.

I cannot use a spell was what he would have said to her if he'd been able to.

And he couldn't. He had vowed, as he'd crawled into that empty house in a county that every last bloody one of his relations would have refused to even dignify with a mention at supper, that he would never again use a spell. It was the only way he could guarantee that what had slain his entire family—

He began to run, but soon found himself standing still in the middle of a sunrise that couldn't possibly penetrate the darkness that surrounded him. He wanted to, but he couldn't deny the truth of what he was seeing.

Mages were being drained of their power. The spells for such a thing were few and the few keepers of those spells brutally determined to keep them private. Ruith could bring only three of them to mind: Lothar of Wychweald, Droch of Saothair, and the most famous practitioner of them all, Gair of Ceangail.

His father, as fate would have it.

He leaned over with his hands on his knees and wished for nothing more than ignorance. Ignorance, no magic, no memories . . .

And no woman with flaming hair who had come to him for aid and found him completely unequal to the task.

He continued to breathe in and out because it kept his gorge down where it belonged. He could no longer block out the vile, unseen forest that hemmed him in on all sides, the forest that he was quite certain was a symbol of all the evil his father had perpetrated over the course of his thousand years of life. He could no longer ignore the fact that it was one of his father's spells that had first wrapped itself around his wrist—

Or that the same sort of spell had wrought the mark on Sarah's wrist as well.

And if that was the case, and she had earned the wound by touching a page of spells on her brother's table, he could no longer deny that somehow beyond reason and beyond any plot devised by King Darius of Gairn's most clever and evil bard, Daniel of Doìre had come by a page from his father's private book of spells.

The questions now were how had he come by that page and was the spell of Diminishing written there? Worse still, if that page had been set free on the world, had others? And where were they?

He looked behind him, but Sarah was no longer standing by him. She was walking back to Seirceil's house, no doubt to do for the poor man what she could.

He took a deep breath, then turned and walked away.

And then he began to run.

Nine

Sarah walked back into the house and wondered what in the hell she was going to do now.

She hovered on the edge of the little group clustered around the mage's bed. Ned continued to look at her as if he couldn't fathom why she didn't just spew out a spell and relieve the man's suffering. Master Oban was looking at her with equal expectation, his wand apparently at the ready to add to whatever she might combine. Only Master Franciscus wasn't watching her as if he expected her to do something mighty.

She wondered, absently, why Ruith didn't volunteer to do it for her.

"Mistress?"

She realized the mayor was talking to her, then nodded and walked over to stand next to him. She looked at the man lying there in the bed before her and frowned. He looked perfectly sound in body, but there was something missing, something she couldn't quite see.

She turned to the mayor. "I think herbs will serve him best at first, so let me see what your fields will provide. I'll return soon."

He looked terribly indebted, which made her feel very guilty indeed. She hurried out of the house and was very grateful for the chance to catch her breath. She walked away because she needed to at least look as if she were doing something, never mind that she suspected nothing she would be able to do could possibly aid that poor man inside.

She walked along a handful of rock fences but saw nothing particularly useful. There were more things than she would have found in hours of looking in Doìre, but nothing that spoke to her as a means of healing the mage's distress. She walked until she realized she wasn't alone.

Ruith was standing there on the edge of a field, breathing heavily as if he'd just run a great distance. He stood in the early-morning sunlight, staring into the north as if he saw horrible events unfolding right in front of his eyes. Sarah almost turned and walked away, but there was something about him that worried her. He was rigid, as if he stood on the edge of some terrible precipice and only luck was keeping him from throwing himself off.

She walked over to him quietly and touched his elbow. Too late, she realized it was his right elbow, the one that bore the marks apparently only she could see. He flinched, hard, then startled out of his dream. He turned and looked at her.

"I'm sorry," he said hoarsely.

She didn't need more words to know what he was talking about. He had already refused to help the man inside, and he was refusing again. She could see that rejection didn't come without cost, though. There was obviously something dreadful going on inside him, something that wouldn't—

Her thoughts screeched to a halt much like Castân on a good day in his youth.

Not wouldn't. *Couldn't.*

She realized with a startling flash that she now knew what the truth was. It wasn't that he didn't *want* to use any magic, or that he was purposely making her daft by leading her on merry chases through nests of thieves and thugs to look for her brother when all it would have taken was some sort of finding spell. Nay, it wasn't that. The truth of it should have been plain from the start, but she hadn't been looking hard enough to see it.

Ruith couldn't aid her, because Ruith had no magic.

It was the only answer that made sense. How he had managed to live all those years up on the side of that mountain without it was a mystery, though she supposed it would have been easy to keep up that appearance of fierceness. Certainly his physical presence would have been enough to do it. Perhaps he had relied on spells left behind by the former mage. Any other sorts of terror could have been cultivated with words alone.

She took a deep breath and felt a great deal of tension ease out of her. She couldn't even be angry with him. He had built his life around what others took to be true. Telling them they were mistaken, admitting that he might not possess what they assumed he did, would not only be a blow to his pride; it might spell the end of his life.

She understood that perfectly, actually.

She decided abruptly that the only thing she could do at the moment was continue on as they had been and pretend nothing had changed. It was one of the things she did best, that ignoring of what might upset the balance of everyone's life but hers.

Somehow, though, when it came to preserving the equilibrium of the man standing in front of her, she didn't mind it.

"I'm going to look for herbs in the village," she said. "I'll take everyone with me so they can fetch supplies." *And so you can have a few minutes to yourself.* "Would it be inconvenient for you to go stand guard over that poor mage?"

He shook his head silently, his eyes full of terrible things.

She hesitated, then cast caution to the wind. "Can I help you, Ruith?" she asked very quietly.

He looked at her, startled, as if the thought of someone else offering to ease his pain was one he'd never entertained.

"Nay," he said roughly. "I am well."

He continued to say that, but she didn't believe him. She wasn't going to press him on it, though. Even mages who apparently weren't mages but only men still had pride enough to want to save.

"I'll be off, then," she said. She wasn't altogether sure she should leave him alone, but she was not his keeper, nor his mother, nor his . . . well, his anything else. He could surely get himself back across the fields to the mage's house without her aid.

She turned and walked away. She would have to do one more sleight of hand and prepare herbs that passed for something more potent. Whether or not they would help that poor destroyed man lying in that bed was yet to be seen.

She entertained the idea of leaving her companions where they were, but she changed her mind when she saw them straggling out of the mage's home. They would surely find Ruith with enough time and for some reason, she just couldn't bear the thought of them seeing him in his present condition.

She collected them all, including the villagers, and shepherded them all into the center of town. It took only moments to reach it and even less time for Master Franciscus to suggest that a visit to the local pub to taste the wares, even at such an early hour, was an appropriate use of their time. Sarah shot him a grateful look, then waited until they'd all trooped off to be about their business.

She took a deep breath, then looked around. The village was only slightly larger than Doìre, though considerably more attractive. The apothecary was located near the village green, and marked by an important-looking sign hanging over a sturdy door. Sarah went inside and stopped still to breathe.

The smells were almost as overwhelming to her as her first sight of the fields near Bruaih. She opened her eyes to look about her and could scarce believe the abundance there. Shelves upon shelves stocked with jars, bottles, and sachets full of wholesome-smelling things. Sarah put her hand on the doorframe for a moment to steady herself. Perhaps there was something strange about the shop, for she could have sworn she saw little shadows fixed to all the tinctures and potions and bags of herbs, shadows that bespoke their virtue and healing powers. She rubbed her eyes, then looked again, but echoes of the herbs were still there, faint but sure.

She pushed away from the door and floated along an aisle, seeing things she'd never seen before and hoping no one would notice how she periodically had to hold on to shelves and counters to keep herself from drifting away. By the time she made it to the far end of the shop, she wasn't sure if she were dreaming or awake.

"Hello, dearie," said a well-worn, comforting voice.

Sarah blinked, feeling as if she had just woken, to see a wizened old woman standing behind a counter, filling sachets full of good things.

"Ah, good morning," Sarah managed. "I've come for a few herbs."

The woman looked at her from surprisingly clear blue eyes. "For Lord Seirceil?"

Sarah blinked. "Is he a lord, then?"

"The youngest son of an obscure nobleman from Meith," the woman said placidly. "Too kind for his own good, or so it would seem."

"Do you know what befell him?" Sarah asked carefully.

The woman continued to scoop and fill. "Things are stirring in the world, my gel, things that had slept for many years. There are rumors of creatures from the north hunting a particular magic." She looked up. "And a particular bloodline."

"Is that what attacked Lord Seirceil?" Sarah asked, feeling her mouth go dry.

The old woman shook her head. "The evil that attacked him is not the same, though I suspect in the end, we'll find it connected." She smiled. "But all things are connected in the end, aren't they, dearie?"

Sarah felt suddenly quite ill. This was the reason she loathed magic. She didn't want to be pulled into a web of things she couldn't see—or hadn't been able to see before, actually—things that were beyond her abilities to control, or best, or even wrap what was left of her poor wits around. She wanted to find Daniel, stick a knife between his ribs, and be done with him. Then she wanted to find a peaceful place, a *safe* place, a place free of all magic save the use of the word her customers might make to describe her handwork.

She wasn't sure she could go back into Seirceil's house and see what her brother had left of him.

"You don't think just a mage harmed your wizard?" Sarah heard the words coming out of her mouth and wished she could have stopped them, but 'twas too late. "A blond man, carrying his arrogance about his shoulders like a fine cloak?"

The woman frowned thoughtfully, tapping her scoop against the end of her wrinkled chin. "Saw one of those sorts earlier this morning, but there was a cloud surrounding him, so I can't say as he's the one you're looking for. You might have a look, though, lovey. You can see, can't you?"

Sarah had absolutely no response for that.

The old woman pushed a large sack across the well-worn wood. "Take those, my gel. Do with them what you think best."

Sarah fumbled for her coins, but the woman shook her head. Sarah would have argued, but in truth she was feeling very ill, and she wasn't altogether sure she wouldn't need to find somewhere to sit down sooner rather than later. She nodded her thanks, because that was all she could manage, then staggered out of the shop, clutching a heavy bag of what she assumed were herbs.

She was so busy concentrating on keeping her feet that she didn't realize she'd almost knocked someone else off his until he stumbled about in a flurry of velvet and lace.

"Oh, my apologies," Sarah said quickly, reaching out a hand to steady him.

The man straightened, then turned slowly and smoothed his hand down the front of his blue velvet coat. "Not to worry, my dear. My fault for not seeing you, of course." He inclined his head. "I hope you suffered no lasting damage from our encounter."

Sarah looked at the man standing three paces from her and forced herself not to recoil at the darkness she saw clinging to him. She shook her head, sure she was imagining things. He was nothing more than a very handsome man of indeterminate age, dressed in a dark blue coat that accentuated his very fair hair and skin. He reminded her a bit of Daniel in his coloring, though certainly not in his dress. He was obviously a gentleman of quality and fortune, if his clothing was any indication.

"Nay," she said, dragging herself back to herself. "I am unhurt."

"I wish I could say the same," the man said with a long-suffering sigh. "I find myself, however, lost in a foreign land with no friends or family. Or means of travel, if you can fathom that."

Sarah didn't dare suggest that he use his feet. His boots were too shiny for anyone who might have been familiar with a more pedestrian means of getting from place to place than a carriage with a team of perfectly matched horses.

The man tilted his head and looked at her. "You wouldn't know of any companies leaving this primitive outpost. Would you?"

"I am not the master of my company," she said, stalling, "and I'm not sure if he has the patience for being the minder for any additions."

The man lifted an eyebrow, then inclined his head as he took a step back. "Of course. I understand. A good journey to you, then."

Sarah nodded, then watched him turn and walk away. She could honestly say he appeared to be nothing more than a man, so perhaps she had sent him off without reason.

She contemplated going after him, then shook her head. She had trouble enough behind her without adding to it. She had a quick look for the rest of her group, but saw none of them. Obviously, the pub had been as interesting as Franciscus had hoped it would be.

She held the herbs close to her chest and breathed in their healing scent. Perhaps she could fashion a tea from them and have it serve Lord Seirceil in some manner. Unfortunately, she had the feeling that no amount of tea was going to give Ruith any ease—

She stumbled, then came to an ungainly halt as she remembered her realization from earlier.

Ruith had no magic.

And if he had no magic, how could he help her find Daniel? And if he couldn't, how would she possibly manage it on her own? Or if Daniel continued on his present course, would there be any mages ahead of her left to try to enlist in her quest?

She toyed again briefly with the idea of simply sitting down and giving up. That wasn't something she'd ever allowed herself in the past, but she was tempted to at present. The task before her had again become too large, too full of things she had no desire to face, too far beyond any of her capabilities, only now she didn't even have a crotchety, supposedly ancient mage to aid her. She was left with a mage damaged by her brother, an alemaster and a lad, and a man who was obviously something far different from what he wanted others to believe he was.

And herself.

She wished she had the power to weave a tapestry large enough to stretch over half the Nine Kingdoms, with threads that would tempt Daniel so greatly that he would follow them in an ever-tightening circle until they led him into a clutch of wizards with no interest in anything but keeping the world free of foolish lads tinkering with things beyond their ken.

But she didn't have that power, so she would make do with what she could do and hope that answers would come from where she hadn't looked for them.

Ten

Ruith stared off into the full light of the morning sun. The light should have been a relief—daylight always was—but it did nothing to cure either the chill in his heart or the darkness in his mind.

You can never outrun your demons, son.

His father had told him that once, a year before his death. Ruith had found it ironic at the time considering how he'd felt about the demon who was his father, but he had to admit now that Gair had spoken the truth. He could likely run every day for the rest of his life and he would never outrun either his past or the path that was laid out in front of him that he knew he had to take.

No matter through which forest it led.

That first step along that path, however, was more difficult than he'd suspected it might be. He stopped, then realized he wasn't going to be able to take another step. He could only stand there, trembling like a horse faced with an impossible task and torn between the fear of it and the gentle but relentless command of its beloved master that it walk on.

. . . Inconvenient for you to go stand guard over that poor mage?

Inconvenient. Ruith smiled bitterly over the word. Inconvenient to do what required so little effort? He shook his head, got hold of himself, and forced himself to continue on as he should have. He ignored the way his legs shook, didn't think about how he had to wipe his palms on his thighs more than once, didn't allow himself the luxury of contemplating anything that might lie before him.

He was, however, enormously grateful when he reached Seirceil's house to find that Sarah had done as she'd promised and taken everyone with her to the village. He managed to get himself inside, hopefully without anyone having marked his weakness. He drew his sword to aid him in fulfilling the task of protecting Seirceil he'd been given, but had to lean it against the wall because his hands were shaking too badly to hold it.

He paced from the door to the hearth and back a score of times, two score, three, until he lost track and feared he might begin to wear a trench there soon. He was torn between his past, the present, and the continual vision of a woman who made allowances for him he didn't deserve and was too damned grateful for the pitiful things he managed to do for her.

He stopped again at the bedside and looked down at Seirceil of Coibhneas, lying there half mad, and knew that it could have been worse. Even with his dimmed vision, he could see that the mage's power had only been grazed, not taken. Daniel of Doìre would never manage anything more with only half a spell. Seirceil's mind had been cleaved in twain, but magic could heal that. A simple spell, half a dozen words at best. A spell he'd used scores of times without thinking in his youth to mend broken bird wings, lameness in his mounts, scrapes on his sister's knees—

He took a deep breath. It wasn't as if using that spell meant he then had to change himself into an eagle and fly to the schools of wizardry at Beinn òrain where he would announce that he had returned from the dead and was ready to work all manner of mighty magic to delight and astonish. It was a simple spell. A spell that would do good instead of evil.

It wouldn't change his life.

He could then rebury his magic as easily as he had twenty years ago and not feel even the slightest twinge of regret. In fact, the entire process of releasing his magic, repeating dutifully the words of a spell of healing, then shoving that magic back down inside himself where it belonged might take less than a score of heart-beats if he hurried. And there wouldn't even be any finger-waggling involved.

And no one to see what he'd done.

He wished he had an hourglass so he might time himself at the task to consign it to the realms of merely interesting scientific experiments, but since he didn't, he would simply be about it in as businesslike a manner as possible. He took a deep breath, then turned to examine the spell he'd used to hide his magic.

There were, as he and a childhood friend had discovered whilst about their happy work of appropriating the spell in question, three ways to undo the burying. He could uncap the well containing his magic—an unsettling mental picture if ever there was one—slowly and with great deliberation, which would require time but leave no one the wiser. The second way was more to the point—and proportionally more jarring to the mage—but still just as secret. Ruith imagined more than one dwarvish soldier had used that to release a bit of extra strength when faced with the business end of someone else's sword. The roughness of the spell surely wouldn't have been noticed in battle.

The last way took a single word only, but even the book had suggested such a thing never be used except in the most dire of need, for it would send ripples of magic outward for thousands of leagues and anyone with any sensitivity at all to the like would know who had wrought the spell.

Ruith settled for the second, repeated the words silently without hesitation, then steeled himself for the return of something he was certain he hadn't missed.

And for a moment, he panicked, for he felt nothing at all.

And then the well geysered up, far into the reaches of his soul before his magic cascaded down over him with the power of a thousand pounding waves. He fell to his knees because that magic gave him no choice.

He couldn't see. He could hardly breathe. He groped for Seirceil's hand, held it hard, then spoke the spell aloud. He didn't wait for it to take effect before he gathered up his power and shoved it ruthlessly back where it had come from and capped it all before he thought better of it.

It hurt to do that, truth be told, more than he'd thought it might.

Seirceil opened his eyes and looked at him before Ruith could leap to his feet and bolt. Astonishment filled his face. "I know you."

"You don't," Ruith managed.

"That was Camanaë," Seirceil whispered in awe. "I know those healing words."

"Forget them, forget me, if you have any mercy in you."

Seirceil smiled, a small smile that was so full of goodness, Ruith had to look away. He didn't deserve it. He released the man's hand, stumbled to his feet, and felt for the hearth. He stood with his back to the door, fully intending to flee the very moment the stars completely obscuring his vision dissipated.

Unfortunately, he heard the door open behind him before he could manage anything but to keep himself on his feet.

"Ruith?"

'Twas Sarah. He kept his back to her and concentrated on breathing.

"What befell you?" she asked urgently. "Did someone come?"

He realized she was standing in front of him, looking up at him. He didn't have time to say anything before she'd found a chair and pushed him down into it.

"Are you ill?"

"Nay," he rasped. "Sympathetic. Again."

"Daft, rather," she said shortly. "I had intended to brew this for him, but I think at least some of it had better be for you. Sit there and don't move."

Heaven help him, he didn't think he could. He closed his eyes and listened to her about her work, listened to the others who came in time, listened to talk that should have made sense to him, but didn't. When Sarah pressed a cup into his hand, he drank without question.

It was marvelous and full of virtue he could taste as it seeped into his flesh. He managed to open his eyes in time to watch her give more of what she'd brewed to Seirceil.

How things happened after that, he couldn't have said. Events took an alarming turn without his being equal to stopping them. He watched helplessly as Seirceil sat up and began to vie with Sarah in attempting to make everyone comfortable. If Sarah wondered why Seirceil had suddenly regained his faculties, she didn't say anything. Perhaps she credited it to herbs, which Ruith had to admit had certainly restored him quite thoroughly.

Seirceil was very forthcoming on his last memory, which was of Daniel of Doìre thanking him for supper and informing him that for dessert he would have Seirceil's power.

Ruith wasn't at all surprised.

He was surprised, however, to find himself an hour later walking from the village of Firth with a motley crew that he wasn't entirely sure wouldn't be the death of them all.

Sarah he would have kept quite gladly. The rest of them, perhaps not. Ned was babbling all sorts of things he likely shouldn't have to

Seirceil, who had decided he could surely be of use to them in some fashion. He was presently tying himself in knots trying to listen to Ned and flatter Oban at the same time. Seirceil had brought along yet another hound, a yipping one that fluttered about Castân, pestering him until Castân, in true horselike fashion, kicked out with one of his hind feet and sent the annoying thing flying.

Ruith approved.

Sarah dropped back to walk next to him. She said nothing, but Ruith could almost hear the wheels turning. He didn't volunteer anything. Seirceil had looked at him closely a number of times already, obviously because he simply couldn't help himself, so Ruith had taken to wearing his hood over his face again. The less comment made, the happier he would be. With Sarah, though, he didn't hold out much hope she wouldn't tell him exactly what she thought. He only hoped he could bear it when she did.

"I have a plan."

Ruith tripped in spite of himself. "Another one?"

She looked up at him seriously. "A more necessary one, perhaps."

He could scarce wait to hear it.

"This is difficult to discuss," she said, sounding as if it were very difficult indeed, "but I think we cannot go on any longer pretending."

He found it difficult to breathe all of a sudden.

She looked up at him unflinchingly, then reached up and pushed his hood back where she could apparently see enough of his face to satisfy her.

"I'm not sure what it is you're hiding," she said very quietly, "or why you're hiding it, but it's obvious to me you have reasons for both. I also think I've asked you for magic when you're unable to give it. I'm sorry. I've put you in a terrible position."

He had to stop, because he was simply too winded to go on. "What?"

She put her hand on his arm, gently and briefly. "I would like to ask you not to be a mage, but to be my guardsman. An *elite* guardsman, of course."

He blinked. He had to blink again. It was all he could do not to stick his fingers in his ears.

"A hired sword?" he managed, narrowly avoiding choking on the words.

She nodded quickly. "Aye. You're very skilled, too skilled for my purse, surely, but I promise you I'll pay you what you deserve in time—if you can be patient for that payment. I am short what I intended to have at this point." She smiled, though it was a very strained smile. "Skill with a blade is hard-won, I know, and the fact that it is what you possess instead of magic is something to feel only pride in."

He could hardly believe his ears. The daft wench was trying to spare him embarrassment. He could only gape at her, speechless.

She smiled gently. "I realized it this morning. There is nothing to be ashamed of. Not everyone in the world has magic. In truth, I think the world might be better off if no one did."

He had to agree with that, but he decided he would have to agree later, when he could wrap his mind around what she was saying.

She thought he had no magic.

And she was trying to spare him any discomfort over that fact.

"We'll go on more easily without cluttering up our lives with spells," she continued. "In time, I'm sure we'll find a way to stop Daniel, then undo what he's done so far. Perhaps we'll eventually collect enough injured mages to make up a single whole mage, then the lot of them can do what needs to be done. But until then I'm quite sure I need a guardsman to watch over me." She looked up at him. "Is it a bargain?"

Ruith looked down to find that she'd held out her hand, as if to seal that bargain.

He wasn't sure if he should haul her into his arms, or use that hand to spin her away from him and nudge her in an entirely different direction before his descent into madness was final.

He did neither. He simply turned and walked away. He had to, whilst he still had some control over himself.

He walked five paces, then stopped. He took several deep breaths, then shook his head. Madness? He was fully in it and the blame for that could be laid at the feet of that astonishing woman standing behind him. He rubbed his hands over his face, then turned and walked back to where she was standing. She had dropped her hand to her side, though, and she looked as ready to bolt as he generally felt himself.

He stopped a pace away from her, then held out his hand. He waited until she reluctantly put hers into his; then he bent over it with a courtly, formal bow even his mother's mother could have found no fault with.

"I would be," he said, straightening, "honored to serve you thus, my lady."

She pulled her hand away and smiled uncomfortably. "You're daft."

"I'm afraid so."

She laughed a little and it was like sunlight streaming down into the very depths of an impenetrable forest. Pure, pale, and so very welcome.

"They're leaving us behind," she said. "Well, save for that damned dog of Seirceil's. Tell me again why we had to bring him?"

"So he can torment your horse."

She smiled. "I imagine so." She looked up at him briefly. "I'm tempted to ask you if you ever had magic, but perhaps that is too personal a question."

"Once, perhaps," he said quickly, before he thought better of it. The words were easier than he'd thought they might be. "Not now."

Only that wasn't exactly true. He realized with a start that he hadn't managed to stuff all his magic back down into that well. There was a tiny bit running around inside him, inciting all sorts of anarchy. He started to chase it, then he stopped himself. He would later, when he had the peace to do it properly. For now, he had more than enough to occupy his time.

Master Oban called for Sarah and she shot him a smile before she ran to catch up to the others. Ruith watched her go work her magic on someone besides him.

She had tried to save his pride. She was currently trying to save two very damaged mages as well. She collected souls as she likely collected skeins of yarn, waiting until the perfect pattern presented itself so she could weave them all into something beautiful.

He was starting to think she was going to use him in that pattern as well.

He grasped for his fast-departing shreds of common sense. He didn't need to be woven. He wanted to find Daniel, use his magic a final time to stop the whoreson, then put it all behind him and go home. He wanted his roaring fire, Master Franciscus's pale ale, and his very pedestrian, unmagical life.

Instead, he was out in the wild with a maker of beer, two grievously wounded mages, a farm boy who should have still been tied to his mother's apron strings, and a woman who carried an evil-looking hunting knife tucked in the back of her belt and was far too perceptive for his comfort.

If her brother was out to destroy the world, Sarah of Doìre was out to save it.

If the woman had been a man, she would have given the Heroes marching pompously into the Gloom a reason to scamper back home with their tails between their legs. Or she might have cut their money from their belts, thanked them, then run off in the other direction to use that gold for her own, more useful purposes.

He shook his head for the hundredth time since he'd met her

and wondered how he was going to survive her, much less the task she had set before them.

Hired sword.

His father would have been appalled. His mother would have likely smiled, then told Sarah she had put him in his place quite nicely. His brothers, well, his brothers would have laughed themselves sick over it. His wee sister likely would have looked at Sarah and found her quite to her liking. Then again, Mhorghain had been but six when she'd been slain, so perhaps he was imagining her in ways she wouldn't have become. She now would have been a score and six, not much older than Sarah herself—

He turned away from those thoughts before they pained him. He took a deep breath, then let it out slowly. He would be exactly what Sarah had asked him to be, because it was safer that way. And he would take those little bits of magic he hadn't managed to corral and return them to their place the first chance he had.

And then he would think on a way to find that bloody Daniel of Doìre so he could render the fool senseless and rifle through his gear to see just what sort of spells he might be carrying in his pack. He didn't imagine he would be surprised by what he found, which was all the more reason to find Sarah's brother sooner rather than later before he realized his sister was following him and decided turning his vile spells on her would be good sport.

Ruith put his head down and concentrated on the ground in front of him.

Aye, the sooner he managed it, the better.

Eleven

Sarah stood by a window in a very lovely inn and looked down at her hands by the last of the sun's setting rays. They were no longer green, which was perhaps the only improvement she could see over the past few days. The journey from Firth to their current city of Iomadh hadn't been difficult physically, but it had seemed longer than it should have. She supposed that had much to do with the thoughts she couldn't manage to escape.

She feared she might be losing her mind.

She wasn't one to give in to any sort of dramatics, but she was seriously beginning to question her ability to carry on. It wasn't worry that she might not manage to find Daniel, or that even if she did find him, she might not be able to subdue him. She fully intended to try to bribe the wizard of Iomadh somehow to see to her quest for her, as she'd resigned herself to the fact that she couldn't do it herself. She was well aware of her limitations when it came to things magical.

Nay, it wasn't that.

It was that she was seeing things.

She had wondered, at first, if the entire county of Shettlestoune was under a curse that left the inhabitants slightly blinded to all but what was passing directly beneath their noses. That would have explained nicely the clearing of her sight now that she was somewhere else, but Master Franciscus didn't look as if he were being delighted by the same, and she couldn't bring herself to ask him if he thought her mad lest he agree wholeheartedly that she was. Ignorance was a comfortable nest to linger in, in the right sort of circumstances.

She had asked Ruith, in an offhanded sort of way, if he thought things were a bit more interesting to the eye of late, but he had only frowned and shaken his head.

So, it seemed it was just she who was being subjected to views of things that weren't there. After a while, she'd begun to suspect that either her vision was deteriorating or her mind was. Or both. That, added to the burn on her arm that grew worse with every day that passed, had left her almost more concerned about her own self than Daniel and his mischief.

"Ready?"

She looked at Ruith, who had come to stand just inside the doorway of the chamber they'd taken for the day to use as a potential refuge should things go south with their plans. Ready? Aye, she was ready to finish her quest quickly, whilst there was still something left of her to do so.

She smoothed her hand over her velvet cloak and adjusted her matching skirts. She didn't dare touch the blouse that was simply bristling with rows and rows of finely wrought lace. It felt more like armor than fine clothes, and she wasn't altogether sure it wouldn't leave marks on her hands. She felt absurdly overdressed, but Ruith had been adamant that at least one of them needed to be of a certain stature to gain entrance to the wizard's palace, and since he had been hired to protect her, it was fitting that she look the part of nobility.

At least she had on her leggings and boots underneath her skirts. She might have been pretending to be a fine lady, but if necessary, she wanted to be able to dash for the nearest exit.

Ruith, however, looked like nothing more than what he was: a secretive man, cloaked, hooded, sporting more sharp things than any man with sense should have. He'd left his bow behind with their companions without the city walls, but she half suspected that had been an oversight.

She didn't bother peering into his hood to see his expression as she passed him. He had been grim from the moment they'd left Firth. He had avoided Master Seirceil completely and distanced himself equally from Ned and Master Oban. She might have been tempted to think he was shunning her as well, but he'd kept her within arm's reach for the whole of the journey. As if he'd been trying to protect her—which, she supposed, was what she'd hired him to do. But conversation had been minimal, at best.

"Any tidings about this wizard here?" she asked as she followed him from the chamber and along the passageway.

He shook his head. "None but the usual noisings that he's too important for simple magic and that the odds of seeing any but his underlings are not good."

She waited to question that until they were standing outside the inn, hovering on the edge of a swiftly flowing river of townspeople, more townspeople than she'd ever seen in one place together. It was distracting, but when she started to see flickers of things she wasn't sure were really there, she pulled herself back to herself and looked up at Ruith.

"And you think we'll manage to convince his guards to open the door?"

He reached out and settled her hat more firmly on her head. "I think they'll be falling over themselves to let you in, dressed as you are in your finery."

"You're trying to humor me so I don't stick you for forcing me into this bit of frippery," she said with a scowl. She couldn't be entirely sure, but that had almost sounded as if that could have been mistaken for a compliment. "I will repay you for it, believe me. And my revenge will be unpleasant."

"If you were all that tormented me, Sarah of Doìre," he said with a sigh, "my life would be quite lovely indeed." He took a step backward. "Let's see what our good lord Connail has been doing with himself for the past few days."

"Or if he's had a visit?"

"I didn't want to say that, but aye, that's something to see as well." He pulled his hood forward and inclined his head. "After you, my lady."

She felt altogether ridiculous marching up the street in clothing she couldn't have afforded if she'd saved for a year and trying to keep her head under a hat with that damned feather that continually fell over her eye. She hazarded the occasional glance at those who passed her. No one seemed to think anything of her save a few lads dressed in equally ridiculous outfits who sent interested glances her way. She supposed she might manage the ruse after all.

Connail of Iomadh was apparently every bit as impressive as he thought himself to be if his house was a good reflection of the mage. Sarah had to fight not to stand there and gape at the ornate gilt door that opened not onto a simple house but onto what could only be termed a palace. She had never seen anything so fine. Not even her imagination had produced anything close to it.

She looked at Ruith. "Here?" she squeaked.

"Allow me to make sure your path is free of undesirables, Your Ladyship," he said, stepping in front of her.

Sarah listened to him confidently and with a distinct trace of hauteur in his voice talk their way into the palace and all the way up the stairs to Lord Connail's receiving chamber.

She could hear the shouting before they reached it. Ruith paused, then shrugged and knocked. She knew what he was thinking. Perhaps Connail was inside with Daniel, which would save them time and trouble in continuing to chase after him.

The door was wrenched open and a mage stood there, his robes askew, his hair looking as if he'd had a fright that had left it standing straight up. He took one look at Ruith, squealed in fear, then shut the door—onto Ruith's foot.

That didn't seem to bother Ruith overmuch, for he only grunted, then pushed the door open and walked into absolute chaos. Sarah would have suggested that perhaps a measured retreat might be in order, but she didn't have the chance. Ruith ushered her over to a corner, bid her stay there, then walked as easily into the middle of what looked to be a pitched battle as if he really were the madman she had always thought he might be behind that handsome face. She stood in the shadows and attempted to identify the players and shout out a warning if someone tried to sneak up behind Ruith and stab him. The mages were the easiest, only because they were the most richly dressed. There were five of them clustered in a group near the fire, braying loudly at a set of guardsmen who had trooped in, apparently looking for trouble. She didn't know all that much about city guardsmen—Doìre certainly didn't have any—but surely these lads wouldn't kill first and ask questions later. Perhaps things would go well after all.

That hope was summarily dashed when another man strode out into the chamber swathed in a black robe and wearing a golden hat that was at least half again as tall as he was.

She paused. Perhaps *strode* was the wrong word. She had thought the cane he leaned upon was actually his wizard's staff, but he leaned too heavily upon it for it to be merely something for magic making.

He started shouting at the guards and poking at them with his staff. That worked fairly well until he lost his balance and went down, leaving one of the guardsmen reaching for him.

His magelings didn't care for that, apparently.

Sarah watched, openmouthed, as all-out war ensued. She looked for Ruith to shout a warning but saw that he had already stepped back away from the fray. He was talking calmly to what were apparently two of the more disinterested palace guards.

She began to look around the chamber for possible exits. Unfortunately there was only one in plain view and that lay behind Ruith and his companions. She was trapped for the moment, but Ruith was still breathing so perhaps the time to panic hadn't come yet. And what blades wouldn't solve, wit might, so she looked around her to see what that might reveal.

She had been deposited into a darkened spot between a wall and a large case. She saw nothing out of the ordinary until she eased out of her hiding spot and realized she was within arm's reach of what had to be the most valuable of Lord Connail's treasures.

The entire cabinet was covered with strands of something she supposed were spells of protection. She recognized none of them, then she froze. She was accustomed to seeing, or imagining she was seeing, bits of Daniel's spells that he'd inadvertently left behind, but those had been nothing more than strands of black, fraying threads. Identifying their use—save for anything untoward—had always been beyond her.

But now, things had changed.

She didn't touch the spell, but she leaned over to have a closer look at it. There were several languages of magic, and her mother had insisted she attain fluency in them all. Putting power behind the words had been, of course, another matter entirely, but she could certainly repeat a spell with as much skill as the next mage. The spell before her had been fashioned from Wexham, the favored magic of the rulers of Neroche. She could see that because, she realized with a start, she could see the words of the spell not so much scattered over the strands of the spell, nor wrapped around those strands, but woven into them.

As if the spell had been a tapestry and Wexham had been its warp threads.

She would have lingered over that astonishing realization, but the shouting behind her made it impossible to concentrate. She looked over her shoulder to find the undermages fighting with spells and the guards brandishing swords to convince them to stop. Ruith was now leaning back against a wall with one foot propped up underneath him, looking as if he were simply waiting his turn in a crowded pub. Apparently, they weren't in danger yet.

She turned back to the spell and noticed the tiny barbs on each strand, barbs put there to inflict enormous damage on anyone foolish enough to try to sweep the spell away. She wasn't foolish, so she immediately gave up any idea she might have had to rid the case of magic and have a closer look at what was inside.

She was certainly no expert in the matter of trinkets, given that her mother had preferred stockpiling gold rather than things to dust, but it appeared to her that everything that resided safely behind very finely wrought glass was there because of its power, not its beauty. She immediately dismissed vials, jewelry, and obviously quite well-used wands in favor of the center spot. There, under glass, was a case lined in what looked to be blue velvet of the finest quality.

But whatever had lain there before was there no longer.

Sarah leaned over carefully and examined the case's lock. It wasn't broken, but that said nothing. Perhaps it didn't require a key; it required a spell. A pity she possessed nothing equal to opening it. She wondered what had been so precious that it had required such care and security.

She looked around and found a torch sitting in a sconce to her left. She fetched it and held it close enough to see but not so close that the spell was disturbed. She was no king's riddler, but she thought she might be able to divine the impression of what looked to have been a book.

Or a page of a book, rather.

The thought of a single page of magic being held so dear gave her the chills, so she turned away and looked for something else to think about. She replaced the torch and walked slowly back to her original spot. She leaned against the wall and watched as the chaos in the chamber deteriorated into something of a pitched battle. She pulled her knife out of her belt because it seemed prudent, though she wasn't sure she would accomplish anything past having someone trip and fall upon it.

She began to feel a faint bit of alarm when Ruith drew his sword. He didn't call for her, though, or even look at her, so she took that to mean she was safe enough where she was. He worked his way over to stand with his back to her, which made her feel even more comfortable.

Bodies soon went scattering. Pointy hats followed, or were thrown into the fire with robes, or plunked down hard onto heads and followed with rather unfriendly fists to covered faces.

Mages. What an unruly lot.

A lad of some stripe or another came flying suddenly across the chamber and landed full on the case to her right. Glass shattered immediately. He screamed as he fought his way out of not only glass but spells, then staggered across the room and fell, of course, into the fire. That seemed to trouble him less than what he'd just endured. He pulled himself to his feet and spent equal time beating out flames and trying to wipe spells off himself.

Sarah saw that the lad had done her a favor. The glass on the center case was shattered and the spells completely ruined. She eased past Ruith and quickly liberated the blue velvet on the point of her knife. She didn't take the time to see what sort of magic it might have been covered with. She merely folded the cloth and stuck it down the side of her boot. It was sharp, somehow, and painful, but that only increased her determination to have a look at it later, when she might see if there was more there than just the outline of a page.

A doorway she hadn't noticed across the chamber opened suddenly and red-coated guardsmen poured in. Those weren't city guards or wizards' guards. These were lads from an entirely new employer.

"Time to go," Ruith said, taking her by the hand and almost jerking her off her feet as he leapt for the door they'd used to come in through.

He might have gained it if it hadn't been for who she assumed was Lord Connail flinging himself at the door and using his body to block it. He looked at Ruith, who had lost the anonymity of his hood over his face at some point in the recent scuffle, and his mouth fell open.

She understood. As steely eyed and unromantic as she considered herself to be, she had to admit that looking at Ruith left her slightly affected. Perhaps in the same way a bad cold might— namely feverish—but affected just the same.

Ruith tried to push the mage aside, but Connail wouldn't budge. Sarah stepped up beside Ruith to use a few of her fine-lady manners to tell the lout to move, but she was distracted by the sight of Connail's right hand. The fingers were jutting out at odd angles, as if they'd been broken.

"What befell you?" she asked loudly, over the din.

"Trouble," Connail managed, still gaping at Ruith.

Sarah understood why he couldn't seem to concentrate. Ruith was profoundly handsome. Then again, Connail wasn't too far behind him in beauty. Or he would have been if it hadn't been for a long, thin scar that ran from his forehead, over an eye, and down his cheek. Sarah studied him for a moment or two, then decided the scar didn't matter. He was handsome, but there was something in his aspect that was very hard, as if years of trauma had found their way into his visage.

"Where are you going?" he asked Ruith.

Ruith hesitated, then sighed. "We're looking for a particular lad, Daniel of Doìre. This is his sister—"

Ruith didn't finish, and the reason he didn't finish was he was too busy keeping a suddenly cursing Connail from throwing himself at her. Sarah ducked behind Ruith not because she couldn't reach her knife, but because her skirts were hampering her ability to truly engage in a decent fight. Best to let someone in trousers see to it.

She watched Connail land to her left. He tried to push himself up, but he made the mistake of putting weight on his broken fingers. He cried out in pain, then lay there on the ground, cursing furiously.

"I'm trying to stop him," Sarah said pointedly, "not aid him."

Connail took an unsteady breath, then nodded. "Very well, then. I'll come along to help you."

"You won't," Ruith said immediately.

Connail looked up with bloodshot eyes. "I have answers you want and tales to tell, tales you won't have if you leave me behind."

Ruith sighed, looked briefly over his shoulder at the fight still in progress, then reached down and hauled Connail to his feet. Sarah ushered the mage out the door with perhaps more enthusiasm than she should have, for he stumbled and went down heavily again. Ruith pulled the door to behind them just as something slammed into it. A blade, by the look of the point of it coming through the wood. Ruith pulled Connail back up to his feet again and looked at him seriously.

"Keep up, or we'll leave you behind."

Connail nodded, took a firmer grip on his cane, and limped quickly down the passageway after Ruith.

Sarah lost her hat somewhere during that very dodgy trip out of the palace, tripped on her skirts once too often, and then didn't argue when Ruith took one of his hunting knives and slit the cloth from waist to hem. She was left with her leggings, the shirt that probably would have repelled everything but a sword, and the jacket that flapped along behind her almost as frantically as Connail did.

At one point on the street, Ruith urged them into a deep, darkened doorway, then stood in front of her and Connail both. His sword gleamed dully in the lamplight from the street. Connail was absolutely silent, though she had been listening to him wheeze for the past ten minutes and suspected she knew what it was costing him to be still.

They stood there long enough to listen to several groups of different sizes chasing or being chased. She supposed they were fortunate indeed that either they had remained unseen or those who had seen Ruith had decided he was most definitely not worth the risk of engaging.

Ruith finally resheathed his sword and stepped out of the doorway. He looked up and down the street, then turned to them.

"Let's go. Don't fall behind, my lord."

Sarah walked quickly next to him down the street, until he put his arm around her shoulders and pulled her close. He did that, she realized with a start, because they were being followed—and not just by Lord Connail. She started to look over his shoulder, but he tightened his arm quickly.

"Don't look back."

She took an unsteady breath. "Think we'll die?"

"Of course not," he said, sounding surprised. "I wouldn't be much of a guardsman if I couldn't get you safely in and out of a nest of second-rate mages, would I?"

Connail muttered a succinct and pointed curse, but left it at that.

Sarah managed a smile. "What now?"

"We'll fetch our gear," he said, "then bolt out of the city, leaving our clumsy companion to follow after us as best he can. The guards won't bother with us after we're on the road, for we'll outrun them."

"I think you have too much faith in my abilities to run long distances," she said.

He shook his head, then opened the door to their inn. "It took me two days to catch you after you left Doìre. That says something."

"It says that you walked."

He smiled briefly, then looked over his shoulder at Connail. "Find a shadow to hide in. We'll return in a bit." He didn't wait for an answer, but merely ushered Sarah inside. "I didn't walk," he said. "Well, not all the time."

She paused. "You can be very . . ." She stopped because she realized there wasn't a good way to say what she was thinking without either offending him or offering sentiments that she shouldn't have. He was her guardsman—a hired one, at that—and she needed to treat him as such.

It was difficult when he smiled.

"You can be very kind," she said finally.

"See what you think after I finish with Connail," he said with another faint smile. "Let's fetch our things, then make haste."

That haste, however, didn't seem to preclude a quick meal or a bit of time lingering over a very decent mug of ale. Sarah enjoyed it, tried to pay for it, and had a snort as her reward. She supposed there was no point in arguing further, so she merely sat back and looked at her companion.

He was leaning back against the wall, fingering a spoon absently. He was sitting far enough in shadow that he apparently felt his hood unnecessary, though she supposed it would have been better for her peace of mind if he had covered his face. He was, she could admit freely, easily the most handsome man she had ever seen. Handsome, chivalrous, and slightly rough around the edges. A far cry from her brother, who screamed like a gel when he saw a spider and tended to use vile spells to make up for his lack of manliness.

She realized Ruith was watching her and smiled reflexively. "What?"

"What were you thinking about?"

"What a woman my brother is."

He lifted his eyebrows briefly. "He seems to have done a man's work here."

"Did he?"

"He terrorized the lads at the palace and assaulted Lord Connail, but I don't know that he made off with what he came for." He pursed his lips. "I don't suppose we can leave the mage behind."

"We could, but I don't think things would go well for him."

Ruith sighed deeply and rose. "Then let's fetch him and escape the city whilst we can."

She nodded, then left the inn with him. They collected Connail, who was muttering curses, then walked quickly along the street until the street turned into a smaller road through a less populated bit of village, then a well-worn track that soon left houses and huts behind. She took a deep breath only to realize Ruith was doing the same.

"I've never seen a town so large," she said with an uncomfortable smile.

"I've never liked a town so large," he said, pushing his hood back off his face and dragging his sleeve across his brow. "I won't be unhappy to leave it behind." He looked over his shoulder at the mage twenty paces behind them. "I don't suppose it would be polite to run."

"It wouldn't be," Connail called pointedly.

Sarah looked at Ruith. "Nothing wrong with his ears, apparently. Or your manners."

"To my eternal shame."

Sarah smiled until she found herself suddenly taken by the arm, her left one fortunately, and tugged forward.

"Now that we're finally at our leisure, my dear," Connail said smoothly, "why don't you tell me again who you are and how it is you found yourself related to that piece of filth I encountered the day before yesterday?"

"I am Sarah," she said. "He was Daniel, and if you don't stop holding on to my arm so tightly, I'll take my knife and remove your fingers from your hand to spare you any chance of them being broken in the future."

She could have sworn Ruith snorted. It might have been a chuckle. She wasn't sure, though she was quite certain he didn't seem inclined to leave her alone with Connail. His presence immediately to her right was proof enough of that, she supposed.

Connail removed his good hand without hesitation. "No need to rile yourself, my dear. I'll leave you be." He looked over her head at Ruith. "And you, my wee rustic, what were you doing in Iomadh?"

Ruith lifted a shoulder in a half shrug. "Looking for answers to questions."

"What questions?"

"You've already answered them," Ruith said, "and for that we thank you. And now that I think on it a bit longer, I suspect that you might manage to make it back to town before the watch locks the gates for the night, if you hurry."

"Oh, nay," Connail said, shaking his head slowly. "That sneaking wretch stole something from me and I want it back. Once I have it, I'll go and you can do with him what you want." He considered Ruith for a moment or two. "Aren't you curious what I lost?"

"Not particularly," Ruith said wearily, "though I suppose you'll feel compelled to tell us just the same."

"I lost a book," Connail said, his eyes glittering in the faint light of the waning moon. "Or, rather, a single page of a book. I wonder why anyone would want that?" Sarah didn't look at Ruith. She didn't dare. She could feel him stiffen for a mere heartbeat, so quickly that she might have thought she'd imagined it if she hadn't traveled with him long enough to sense it. "I wouldn't presume to guess," Ruith said, very quietly.

Connail smiled. "Wouldn't you?"

"I am a lowly swordsman," Ruith said in measured tones. "Such things are far beyond my ken."

"We must all be satisfied with our limitations, I suppose," Connail said.

"Indeed, we must," Ruith agreed.

Connail looked at Ruith for another long moment, then tripped and caught himself heavily on his leg before he fell. He said nothing thereafter, but simply concentrated on keeping up with them.

Sarah remained next to Ruith, walking silently until they reached where the others had camped to wait for them. She wondered about Connail and why he seemed determined to vex Ruith. She would have warned him that he was harassing the wrong man, but she supposed he would discover that soon enough on his own.

The others in their company made a fuss of Connail, which seemed to please him greatly. She accepted a cup of ale from Master Franciscus, then watched Ruith do the same. He seemed uninterested in the goings-on, but she could see he was watching Connail closely enough.

"He's what I expected him to be," she remarked idly.

"Hmmm."

She considered a bit more, then leaned back against the wagon. "He seemed surprised to see you."

"He mistook me for someone else."

Sarah added that mystery to her list of things she would press him on when he wasn't paying attention—if that day ever came. He was too canny for his own good. It must have come from so many years pretending to be what he was not.

"Where to now?" she asked.

He sighed. "Your brother has been going from city to city, which has made following him easy, only because there is but one road out of Shettlestoune. Gilean lies yet ahead, but after that we must either turn left toward Angesand and Neroche, or right, toward the mountains. Caernevon is there, to the north, and it is a major city, but I'm not sure it would be a place your brother would go."

"Why not?"

"The mage there comes from a long line of wizards wearing six rings of mastery on their hands. Even his guardsmen there are full of serious magic. Daniel would find it difficult indeed to gain entrance into the wizard's hall and if he managed that, he wouldn't get any farther." He shook his head. "These lads your brother has visited so far are children in power by comparison."

"Even Connail?"

He looked at the man holding court near the fire, then drained his cup and set it inside Franciscus's wagon. "Aye, even him." He nodded toward the fire. "You sleep. I need to pace."

"Perhaps I should set his fingers."

"Or you could wait until tomorrow when I might actually have the presence of mind to enjoy the noise."

She smiled briefly. "Why did we bring him?"

"I have no idea," he said grimly. "I'll go have a walk and see if I can't divine the answer to that. It may take me all night." He put his hands on her shoulders and turned her toward the fire. "Go sleep. You need it."

She wanted to tell him he was the one who looked as if he should sleep, but he had already released her and melted into the shadows. She drank again of Master Franciscus's finest, then walked back over to the fire. She had meant to tell Ruith about the velvet swatch in her boot, but she supposed another day of secrets wouldn't matter. He looked as though he had enough on his mind already.

She walked over to the company, ignored Connail's piercing look, and stretched out in front of the fire. She stared at it, watching the shape of the flame and the echoes of the wood's memories weaving in and out of it as it burned, then closed her eyes because she was simply too tired to look any more at things that were more than they should have been.

Sleep, however, did not come easily.

Twelve

Ruith stood in the shadows with his arms folded over his chest and came to two conclusions.

First, Connail of Iomadh was going to die very soon on the end of a very sharp blade if he didn't learn on which side of the fire to place his sorry arse.

And second, Sarah of Doìre had no magic.

The first he put away to chew on at a more opportune moment. The second was far more intriguing, so he turned to examine it more closely.

He wondered why he hadn't seen it before. He supposed he could have blamed weariness. He hadn't slept well—or much, actually—in almost a fortnight. It had spared him foul dreams, but little else. In truth, that was too convenient an excuse for not having realized earlier what one of her secrets might be. He hadn't seen what was in plain sight because he had either been staring at

Sarah like a slack-jawed sixteen-year-old—and given that he had a perfect view of one of those on a daily basis in Ned, he knew of what he spoke—or doing his damndest to ignore her, her bloody flyaway hair, her pale eyes that took in more than what she should have been able to see, and her hands that continued to weave every damn thing but spells.

He paused. He was beginning to think he swore too much. His mother wouldn't have approved.

But she would have approved of Sarah.

Sarah, who had never once in his presence made any magic at all. Sarah, who was now starting the fire by hand whilst making a production of weaving a spell over it with such a convincing manner that Seirceil had closed his eyes as if to better listen to her lovely voice and Oban was voicing his approval with silently woven spells that set flowers and butterflies dancing about her head.

Connail was likely too busy flattering her to notice anything, Franciscus was working on preparing a pot to put over the fire, and Ned was tending the animals. That left only him to stand there and wonder if she would notice if he set fire to her wood with a bit of his own magic.

Before he could think that through fully, much less act upon the idea, her spark caught; then she concentrated on blowing it into a flame that she then fed surreptitiously whilst turning the full force of her very pale green eyes on Connail, who seemed every bit as affected by her as might have been expected.

Ruith leaned back against Franciscus's wagon, suppressing the urge to beg the man for a hefty tankard of ale in which to drown his thoughts, and allowed himself a brief moment of repose and speculation.

How was it that Sarah had lived her entire life as a witchwoman's daughter without having inherited any of her mother's magic? Had her mother known?

Did Daniel know?

He imagined that it had been an unspoken secret. The question was, why? What reason would her mother, a woman notorious for her foul temper, have had for not berating her daughter for her lack of magic? Unless she had, but Sarah had certainly never given any indication of that. Not that she would have said anything about it, he supposed, even if he'd asked. After all, why would she? It wasn't as if he'd been forthcoming with any of his secrets.

But he wondered about hers, just the same.

And speaking of secrets, Ruith couldn't stop himself from looking at Connail of Iomadh, who had his fair share of them. He was currently making a great production of warming his hands at the fire. He had been, for the past half hour since they'd made camp, entertaining himself by regaling anyone who would listen with tales of mighty magic wrought and arrogant mages humiliated. By him, of course. Ruith pursed his lips. Connail was just like his father, whom Ruith knew not only by reputation but by an unpleasant encounter or two.

Peirigleach of Ainneamh and some tavern wench had produced Connail three hundred years ago, or so the tale went. Ruith wasn't at all surprised that Connail had styled himself a great lord in a relatively small city far enough from his home so that he wasn't bothered by nosy relations, but large enough where he could be genuflected to whenever he passed. It would have suited his ego perfectly and perhaps been the start of repayment for the slights he no doubt endured from his father's family whenever chance encounters occurred. Connail had made no mention of having found Ruith's face familiar, though he'd certainly looked closely enough in Iomadh. That could have been for any number of reasons, though—

"Shall I spin a tale for you all?" Connail asked brightly. "Something so horrifying as to defy belief?"

Oban and Seirceil seemed amenable enough. Sarah was too

busy feeding her fire and looking as if she would have rather been anywhere but where she was to offer comment. Ruith caught her eye and gave her a faint smile. She lifted an eyebrow, then started to crawl to her feet.

"Oh, nay," Connail said, catching her by the arm quickly. "You'll want to stay for this."

Sarah looked torn, likely between a desire to be polite and an equally strong one to pull the knife from her belt and use it on the fool sitting next to her. Ruith almost smiled, for he could plainly see the thoughts flit across her face. She sat back down, apparently with great reluctance, and nodded warily.

Connail obviously needed no encouragement to begin. "I had lived many years in Iomadh," he said, settling in comfortably and sending Ned off to refill his mug of ale, "enjoying the luxuries I had provided for myself, taking on the occasional apprentice and teaching him just enough for him to be useful. But not too much, lest he prove . . . troublesome. But you understand that, don't you, Master Oban?"

Strands of werelight sparkled and swirled around the camp, coming to join themselves to the fire. Ruith shook his head slowly. Oban agreed, apparently.

"Of course, there is a danger in setting oneself up as a powerful mage in a large city," Connail continued, "for one then draws attentions to himself that he might rather avoid. I, however, had wasted little time worrying about it, for I knew I was equal to the task of protecting myself. Besides, I had a small garrison of mages at my disposal, should I have fallen ill, or been weak from making too spectacular a piece of magic. Unfortunately, the beginning of my tale comes not in my comfortable abode, but as I was out traveling about the countryside where I found myself in a rustic tavern in Gilean—which happened to be the only place within miles where one might have a decent cup of ale. Nothing to compare to yours of course, Master Franciscus."

Ruith watched Franciscus lifted his mug slightly in acknowledgment of the compliment, though he said no word.

"I don't admit weakness often," Connail said, "but I will concede that on that particular night, whilst I was well into my cups, I might have made mention of my magic. And being in Gilean, I thought it might be instructive for the inhabitants if I offered my thoughts on a certain wizardess who happened to live in the area. She had, you see, caused me to lose a position at a certain prince's palace because she said my magic was too dark and unpleasant."

Ruith wasn't unused to exercising an austere sort of control over himself. It had served him well in the past. It served him well at present, for it took every smidgen of it to keep himself from displaying any reaction to those words. The only wizardess he knew living near Gilean was Eulasaid of Camanaë.

His grandmother, as it happened.

"So you disparaged a wizardess," Franciscus said, moving to set his stew to boil over the fire. "Not very chivalrous, are you?"

Connail smiled, but it was not a warm smile. "I have learned to hold my tongue since then, thanks to a lesson on the subject from a most unlikely source."

"Oy, but by who?" Ned asked, his eyes very wide.

"I'll get there in good time, young one," Connail said. "For now, I'll say only that I dragged myself back home and gave no more thought to the evening than I might have an unremarkable meal. It was over and forgotten before I lay my pounding head on my luxurious silken pillow. It never occurred to me that on another night such as the first, a dark and stormy night where the wind howled and the rain lashed the windows, that I might find myself regretting my words."

"Did you, indeed?" Sarah asked, not looking up as she continued to feed her fire.

"I did, indeed," Connail said smoothly. "Thank you for asking. And to answer the unasked question of what possibly could have befallen a powerful mage such as I, let me tell you. There I was, sitting in front of my fire a scant month after my outing, enjoying a fine, rare wine imported from Penrhyn and listening to the wind howling outside, when who should have simply appeared in front of me but a man. He was unannounced, unescorted, and obviously uninvited, but before I could open my mouth to chastise him for his poor manners, he bound me so I couldn't speak."

There was complete silence save for the crackle and hiss of the fire. Ruith was rather more grateful than he should have been for a very solid wagon to lean against.

"Of course, I wasn't unwilling to use the sword hanging over my mantel," Connail continued, "but I found that in addition to rendering me mute, the whoreson had rendered me immobile as well. I could only watch in stunned silence as the man pulled his hood back and revealed himself to be the youngest son of that particular wizardess I had spoken of in the tavern. I knew the man not only by sight but by reputation, and there is no shame in admitting that I knew at that moment I had made a terrible mistake. I was fully prepared to apologize—profusely, if necessary."

"And was he willing to have that," Ned asked, his eyes absolutely enormous in his face, "or did he demand a duel with swords at dawn?"

"Swords, my lad, were not the man's first choice," Connail said with a faint smile. "He was more inclined to choose a weapon that would inflict a more lasting, painful wound. As for the other, who knows? I'm not sure an apology was what he was after."

"What, then?" Ned asked, edging closer to Sarah, presumably to use her as a shield if things went south.

"He wanted my magic."

Ruith felt his mouth go dry.

Connail shrugged. "He took it, of course. Every last, perfect drop of it, then stretched like a cat and made himself at home in one of my chairs. He finished my bottle of wine, and watched me weep until he apparently tired of the sport. That took longer than you might suspect." Connail smiled at Sarah. "Care to know his name, my dear?"

Sarah shook her head just the slightest bit.

"I'll tell it to you just the same, for the knowing of it might serve you at some point." He paused dramatically. "It was Gair of Ceangail."

Master Oban's wand quivered with his fear, causing several squeaking things to appear and flap off frantically. Even Seirceil looked a bit unsettled. Ned only gaped at Connail.

"Oy, who is that?"

Connail shot him a look of distaste, then turned back to Sarah. "Surely, you've heard of him."

"Nay," she said faintly, "but I don't know very many mages."

Ruith found himself the unhappy recipient of a quick look from Connail, a look full of hate and several other unpleasant things. He wasn't at all surprised, for he imagined Connail suspected quite a few things he hadn't considered before. Ruith had always thought he resembled lads from his mother's side of the family, but perhaps he looked more like his father than he'd feared. And apparently Connail thought so too.

The only mystery remaining was why Connail didn't blurt out the truth right then and there.

Connail turned to Sarah. "Perhaps your rather secluded upbringing has left you without the tales you'll need to know to move in a larger world. Let me tell you of Gair of Ceangail and what befell him."

Sarah looked as if she would have rather been sticking needles into her eyes than listen to Connail of Iomadh bludgeon her with tales about mages, but she was apparently on her best behavior, for she didn't just up and leave.

Ruith wished she had.

"I should say first that the particular evening I spoke of was over a century ago. After that time, Gair wed an elven princess, sired six strapping sons and a beautiful daughter on her, then continued on his journey to madness, a journey I believe he began in my house. You see, my dear Sarah, the spells he was using, or rather that particular spell, take not only a mage's power, but some of his own . . . peculiarities. When Gair seized my power, he took along with it a bit of my own madness and arrogance." He nodded at Sarah. "I am willing to admit my failings freely. I consider it a virtue."

Ruith imagined he did, and he wished heartily that Connail had cultivated the virtue of keeping his bloody mouth shut.

"By the time I had recovered enough to pay heed to the events in the world—and that took several decades—I realized that perhaps my revenge on Gair would be meted out by Gair himself."

"How so?" Sarah asked uneasily.

"He had acquired enough power that he thought himself able to do anything, including opening a well of evil. I understand he boasted he would open it, then shut it quickly, simply to display his marvelous strength. That he intended to open that well, then take all the evil to himself is, I believe, closer to the truth. But we don't know that, given that we have no one to ask who might have known Gair's mind."

Ruith forced himself to merely watch Connail as if he'd been one of Ehrne of Ainneamh's bards, spinning a tale of evil to send chills down the spines of children listening.

It took more effort than he wanted to admit.

Connail lifted an eyebrow at him, then returned to doing his best to entertain Sarah.

"Of course, the well was too much for him. What he'd loosed sprang up, then poured down and slew everyone in his family, including him."

"How terrible," Sarah murmured.

"I think it a mercy. Can you without horror think on how

vulnerable the world would have been had Gair survived? And can you imagine the danger that would have been augmented had any of the sons lived, they who were full partakers of their father's magic?" Connail shivered. "Terrifying."

Sarah shivered as well. "Fortunate, then, that they didn't."

"They would have had the power to destroy the world, surely," Connail said thoughtfully. "I know I wouldn't trust one, were he alive. Perhaps the lad might look safe enough, but Gair looked sane enough in the beginning, or so I understand. His madness was unpredictable, or so 'tis rumored, and all the more dangerous for it."

Sarah rubbed her hands together and tucked them under her arms. "Is there more?"

"There always is, isn't there, my sweet?" Connail said pleasantly. He had a sip of his ale, then shrugged. "Before that business at the well, I understand Gair thought so much of his magic that he gathered all of his spells into a single tome, a book that never left his person. In time, as he grew to realize that no one around him was as clever as he, he took to hiding the book in his library. He amused himself by enspelling all the books there so that the titles shifted continually, effectively hiding that very desirable bit of writing. I've also heard that after Gair died, the library at his keep caught fire. Several of the books were saved, but I understand a terrible battle ensued over their possession. Things were torn, manuscripts were divided, men were maimed and killed."

"What happened to the book?" Sarah asked. "That book of spells?"

Ruith could scarce hear her words. He wondered, in a way that left him feeling slightly queasy, if she were thinking the same sorts of thoughts he was.

"The book of spells," Connail said, "was scattered on the wind like so many seeds, destined to fall into fertile soil, germinate, and grow up into quite lovely gardens of particularly vile spells. The location of these gardens remains a mystery to most, I imagine.

Some don't realize what they have; others don't dare show it, lest they find themselves—how shall I put it?—ah, yes . . . dead. The wise ones, the brave ones, display their page of history with pride."

Ruith imagined they did. He glanced at Sarah to find her studying Connail silently.

"Why do I have the feeling you know this personally?" she asked.

"Because you are as astute as you are lovely," Connail said smoothly. "Once I heard of Gair's demise, I decided that I would see how much of his book I could find. I planned to collect it all, then destroy it so that his magic might have an end. There could have been no greater hell for him than that."

"And did you find any of it, Lord Connail?"

Ruith found Master Franciscus standing at the edge of the firelight, his arms folded over his chest, his stirring spoon held in one hand as if he brandished a knife.

Connail looked at him, an eyebrow raised slightly. "Aye, I did, Master Franciscus. It took me ten years, but I finally found a single page of the book. I might have found more, but I am, as you see, no longer suited to arduous journeys."

"And what sort of spell did the page contain?" Franciscus asked.

"Nothing for you to use in your alemaking, my good man," Connail said with an indulgent chuckle. "The spell was one of Reconstruction. For those with less experience than I in these matters, a spell of Reconstruction is one in which a thing can be remade into something else but only for a certain amount of time. An annoyance for the subject so reconstructed, but not life changing." He rubbed his hands together suddenly. "Of course, once I had the page, even just that page, I found I couldn't destroy it. It was . . . mesmerizing."

"Was it, indeed?" Sarah asked reluctantly.

"It was," Connail said, looking at her with a light in his eye that wasn't entirely pleasant. "Mesmerizing and perfect in every way. Evil though Gair might have been, it is undeniable that he was a master at his craft." He shook his head. "I obviously didn't have the magic to work the spell, but I could look at it every day and imagine I did. And I could imagine that Gair was too dead to do the like." He shrugged. "A cold comfort, true, but a comfort nonetheless."

"Where did you find the page?" Seirceil asked.

"In the bottom of a peddler's cart."

Ruith was somehow unsurprised. He couldn't say that he didn't share Connail's joy over the fact that someone besides Gair of Ceangail had even a small a piece of his bloody life's work, except for the fact that now Gair's damned spells weren't walled up inside his own black soul. They were out in the world, where they could have been found and used by anyone with enough magic to attempt them.

That said nothing about what would be left of a mage not equal to the strength of the spell.

Perhaps Daniel of Doìre would use the spells in his possession once too often and go mad as a result, though Ruith didn't hold out much hope for that happening before Daniel wreaked undeniable havoc—

"But the page is gone now," Sarah said, interrupting his thoughts.

"Aye," Connail agreed. "Your brother took it, after he tried to take my magic." He held up his right hand. "I laughed at him when he failed, and he broke one of my fingers. I mocked him further and he broke another." He paused. "I think one day I must learn to curb my tongue. I just never know what sorts of details are going to come spilling out at an inopportune moment."

Ruith imagined so. He supposed Connail could decide this was an inopportune moment and tell everyone there that he, Ruithneadh of Ceangail, was Gair's youngest son. Sarah would look at him in horror, or with distrust, or not at all.

He wasn't sure which of the three would have been worst.

"What was the spell Daniel was trying to use?" Sarah asked.

Connail looked at her with an emotionless stare. "Gair's spell of Diminishing. The one used on me a century ago. Your brother only has enough of the page to be irritating, not dangerous, though he's certainly strapping enough to do a bit of physical harm. My only comfort is that your charming brother doesn't realize that what fraction of the spell he has will eventually begin to turn on him." He shivered. "It has a mind of its own, that spell."

Sarah climbed ungracefully to her feet. She pulled her cloak around herself, then took a step backward, almost going sprawling over Castân. She caught herself before Ruith could leap forward, then looked down at Connail.

"Thank you for the tale," she said. "It was most interesting."

Connail held up his hand and looked at the fingers Sarah had set that morning. "Consider it repayment for this fine work. Perhaps when you're better rested, you would care to try a spell of healing on them."

"Master Seirceil is better at that sort of thing than I am," Sarah said quickly. "I'll go look for wood."

Ruith realized she was coming for him only as he found himself being taken by the arm and pulled along, out of the firelight. He went, partly because it was Sarah doing the pulling, but mostly because he too had had enough of tales about things he didn't care to discuss.

"I didn't like any of that," she said in a low voice, once they were out of reach of the firelight. "I don't think I'll sleep well tonight."

The moon was but a sliver, not nearly enough light for him to see her face properly, though he had no trouble feeling her fingers digging into his arm.

"At least Gair of Ceangail is dead," Ruith said, understanding completely her feelings. "You've nothing to fear from him."

She looked up at him. "But I think we all have something to fear from his spells. Especially if they fall into the wrong hands."

Ruith rubbed his hand over his mouth, then sighed. "Only if those hands understand what they have. How much does your brother know of history? Of mages and that sort of rot?"

"Daniel knows very little, I imagine," she said with a shrug. "He went to school, though they weren't happy to have him, as you might guess. Whether or not he paid attention at his lessons, I don't know. He was too busy thinking on ways to torture small animals, I daresay."

He pursed his lips. "I'm sorry you had to live with him for so long."

She smiled, one of the more genuinely happy smiles he'd seen her wear. "You know, as difficult as it's been to travel and as often as I've had to swallow my pride to accept aid—your aid, mostly—I have enjoyed being free of him." Her smile faded. "I don't think it will last, though. It can't last, if I'm to accomplish what I must."

He nodded, because he had no choice. He would have spared her the journey as well, but he couldn't. Seirceil hadn't seen but a hooded and cloaked Daniel, Oban couldn't shout if he recognized him, and Ruith had the feeling Connail would have retained the knowledge out of spite. Nay, Sarah would have to come if only to identify her brother.

Though he couldn't help but feel there was more to her presence near him there than just that.

He pulled her cloak—his cloak, rather—up to her ears and tugged it closer around her. He put his hands on her shoulders and looked down at her.

"You should sleep—"

"After that?" she interrupted. "I told you I couldn't. Since you don't seem to sleep either, we'll not sleep together." She pulled away, then offered him her elbow.

He looked at her in surprise, then smiled. "Are you escorting me now, my lady?"

"It's just Sarah, though I can see how you might be confused given the blouse I'm still wearing."

"You seem to like the ruffles."

"I most certainly do not, but I can't divine how to get them off. I'm not entirely sure that seamstress didn't sew me into the bloody thing."

He smiled, because he suspected she had it aright, offered to have a look at her prison in the morning, then took her arm and walked with her in a large circle about camp. It occurred to him suddenly that he hadn't seen anything of the creatures from nightmare since the forest. He couldn't imagine that he'd been so fortunate as to leave them behind entirely, but perhaps the trolls were uneasy around such a large group. That was all the more reason to stay with the wagon.

He supposed he wouldn't be able to manage that forever. He had the feeling that Connail had unbridled his tongue more than he'd let on to earn those four broken fingers and the one twisted thumb. Perhaps he'd taunted Daniel with his knowledge of the author of those pages, if only to politely point out that Daniel wasn't and would never manage to work one of Gair of Ceangail's spells.

Ruith didn't suppose that would stop him from trying.

He considered that invisible path before him and attempted to reconcile it with Sarah's quest. It was perhaps better that he now knew for a certainty what Daniel had in his possession and what he was seeking. If his goal was to visit every mage in the south and take their power, that made his path easier to follow.

But what if Daniel's intention was different? What if he actually, in some wee part of his deluded mind, thought that wasting time with minor mages and half-written spells was beneath him and he would be better served to look for the source of those spells?

Ruith stopped himself before he considered that even a moment longer. He had a plan and that was to stop Daniel before he traveled much farther and convince him that the path he'd put his foot to led only to death.

Ruith knew that very well.

He looked at Sarah. "Weary?"

"Not if it means going back to camp and listening to that pompous arse babble any longer."

He managed a smile, then started on another circle with her. And he ignored the fact that each circle led him back to where he'd started, back to the realization he could hardly bring himself to face.

His father's spells were out in the world and mages were finding them.

And he was the only person alive who knew those pieces of magic well enough to recognize them.

Thirteen

Sarah walked along behind the company, looked at her hands, and wondered why they were equal to some tasks, yet completely incapable of the simplest of others. They had carded wool, spun it into thread for weaving and yarn for knitting, and sported a rainbow of colors from her dyeing.

But they had never once been used in even the most pedestrian piece of magic.

She supposed she might have continued on quite happily not caring that her hands could only do things any village gel would have learned at her very unmagical mother's knees if it hadn't been that she was continually surrounded by an apparently never-ending supply of mages. Wounded ones, unmagical ones, ones who couldn't seem to stop themselves from decorating everything in camp with things that sparkled and fluttered and bloomed. She found herself

wishing that, just once, she might use her hands for the same sort
of thing. She'd been fighting that thought for the past four days,
since Connail had told that horrible tale about Gair of Ceangail
and his evil. If *she* had possessed any sort of power, she would have
used that power only for good.

Unlike her brother.

She took a deep breath, then concentrated on the road in front
of her. She was bringing up the rear because she feared that if
she had to listen to Connail tell another of his magnificent tales of
might, magic, and lads who had come to him wishing they could
possess even a fraction of his charm and wit, she would do him
an equally mighty insult. Likely to his mouth where he might be
required to spend several days wondering how it was her fist could
leave such impressive bruises.

She turned away from that appealing thought and allowed
herself the pleasure of watching the countryside they walked
through. They had left the last of the vast farmlands behind earlier
in the day and begun a slight but steady climb into terrain that
was more lush and green than she'd imagined anything could be,
even in winter. Even though the snow seemed to be giving way to
bouts of rain and the damp air made even the rain seem unpleasantly cold, she hadn't cared. She could see evergreen trees in the
distance.

It was as if she walked in a dream.

She wasn't sure anyone else was enjoying it as much as she was,
especially Ruith. He was pleasant enough when they were walking together alone, but that was a rare occurrence of late. The last
time she'd had two words with him had been three mornings ago
when he'd cut her ruffled monstrosity from her to leave her standing there quite happily in her everyday tunic. She wished she could
have cut Connail away from Ruith as easily.

Unfortunately, wherever Ruith was, Connail seemed to want
to be. She watched them walking thirty paces in front of her and

knew that Connail was picking at Ruith again, as if he simply couldn't stop himself from needling the man every chance he had. Why, she just couldn't fathom.

Ruith's only reprieve seemed to be going off every day for hours at a time to hunt. She didn't begrudge him the time alone, partly because she understood the need and partly because he always returned with something useful for the stewpot. She had happily turned the tending of that stewpot over to Master Franciscus, who was a much better cook than she.

Indeed, the entire company seemed to have fallen into roles suited to their particular talents and desires. Master Franciscus drove his wagon and saw to their meals, Ned tended the horses, and Seirceil watched over Master Oban, who hadn't regained his voice but seemingly didn't miss it much. He had become very adept at expressing all manner of things with spells.

Seirceil insisted his magic was intact, but he used it only with great reluctance and seemingly not very successfully. He'd attempted a fire one night but it had gone awry and only Master Franciscus rolling him in the dirt had put out the blaze that had sprung up all over him instead of the wood. Magic the man might have still had, but something had happened to him to alter it. It was as if the weft threads of his piece had been cut, leaving the rest of the weaving to unravel frantically and without any discernable pattern.

And if Daniel was responsible for that, she couldn't bear to think what other things he might manage before they could stop him. She had begun to wonder if that sort of thing would become their means of determining where Daniel had been, that trail of mages who were only partly damaged. Connail didn't seem anything but pleased by it. He was convinced Daniel would eventually realize that all he could weave were flawed spells, he would see reason, and then he would stop even attempting any magic.

Sarah knew better. He wouldn't stop until he had destroyed the world, even if it was only one mage at a time.

She spent most of the day watching the ground at her feet, having grown increasingly unable to look up and enjoy her surroundings, unable to taste the brew Franciscus pressed on her every few hours. The farther she walked, the less sure she was that she was going in the right direction, or doing the right thing. She felt as if a storm were brewing, and she would go mad if it didn't break soon.

"Ho, there! Lord Seirceil, see if he lives."

Sarah looked up to watch Franciscus struggle to control his normally very obedient horses. He convinced them to halt, set his brake, then jumped down off his seat and hurried to the side of the road where Seirceil was leaning over a body lying there in the weeds.

Sarah approached, then found herself running into a hand. She frowned up at Ruith, who was stopping her without looking. *I don't need protection* was half out of her mouth before she managed to shut it around the whole of her thought. If he wanted to trot out his rusty manners, she wasn't going to argue.

Perhaps he would want to use them again and take her for a walk that evening. She still hadn't had the privacy to show him the velvet cloth she'd filched from Connail's chamber. She would be happy to be rid of the thing, for it had begun to leave welts on her leg. She wasn't sure it wouldn't do the same to Ruith, but even so perhaps he would be willing to carry it for a bit.

She managed to look around his shoulder and the clutch of arrows in her way. A man lay on the ground, groaning. He was finely dressed and might have been handsome if it hadn't been for the bruises on his face—

She blinked in surprise. It was the same man she'd seen in Firth as she'd been fetching herbs for Lord Seirceil. Obviously, he'd continued to travel and apparently he'd done so on his own. She was slightly surprised to find him in his current condition given that she hadn't seen anything of ruffians or thieves along the way. Perhaps Ruith had been more deterrent for their own company than she'd thought.

Odd, though, that in all their walking, they hadn't seen the man before.

Within moments, he was sitting up, accepting drink, and trying to make sense of what had happened to him. He seemed to be less distressed about the condition of his face than he was by the fact that the lace had been ripped off his sleeves and his collar.

"He's a fop," she said under her breath.

Ruith shot her an amused glance, then turned back to listen to a tale so fanciful, she was sure he would snort in derision and walk away.

He didn't. He merely put up his sword and studied the man as he spoke. Seirceil was offering what aid he could along with Franciscus and Ned. Oban was expressing his concern with roses that wept crystal tears. Sarah admired them as they marched on their long stems in a funeral procession to the man, then past him. Perhaps Oban was better off away from Bruaih. Surely no one there could possibly have appreciated his talents.

Sarah made polite conversation with the man and expressed what she hoped was an adequate amount of sympathy when it was called for. But she found herself, to her profound surprise, sharing the opinion that was written quite plainly on Connail's face.

The traveler wasn't quite what he seemed.

His name was Urchaid, or so he claimed, and he demurred when asked where his home might be found. *Too famous*, he'd admitted modestly. Unfortunately, his native land was the only thing he was modest about. Within a quarter hour, he had pontificated on everything from magic to the proper method of field dressing a rip in one's trousers. Sarah began to look on Connail with a friendlier eye. Urchaid might have been, admittedly, the most handsome man she'd seen save Ruith, and his deep, melodious voice should have been enough to soothe even the most fractious of ill-mannered mage's spawn. There was, however, something about him, something that bespoke his absolute love of himself and all that made up his fascinating life that grated on her.

Perhaps he was an elf. She wouldn't have been surprised.

Camp was pitched right where they'd stopped, without delay. Sarah looked at the others. Save Connail, who was carrying on some sort of conversation with himself under his breath that couldn't have been pleasant, no one else seemed to think anything of their new addition. Perhaps her unease had less to do with Urchaid and more to do with the fact that her calf felt as if she'd shoved a handful of nettles down her boot or perhaps it had to do with the fact that if she didn't escape Connail's irritating self, she would kill him with Master Franciscus's heaviest stew ladle.

She eschewed supper and hastened away from the fire at sunset, before anyone else could volunteer for the first watch.

She paced well outside the perimeter of their camp, listening intently for things that might be out of the ordinary, holding her knife loose in her hand on the off chance she found something untoward. She walked until she found herself standing at the place where Urchaid had lain, moaning delicately and placing his hand against his fevered brow. Oban's roses were still there, lying side by side in a row, as if they'd been laid out deliberately.

Only now they were black.

And they were weeping bloodred tears.

Sarah reached down to touch one only to have them all disintegrate. All that was left was a pile of ashes that vanished once she breathed out.

She straightened and felt something slither down her spine. Perhaps Oban's spells were going awry just as Seirceil's were, or perhaps there was something about the ground where she stood that rendered things what they shouldn't have been.

It surely wasn't anything more sinister.

She took a step backward. That was it, surely. She shivered and rubbed her arms briskly, then stepped backward again until she was standing in the middle of the road. She looked up into a sky full of stars, but they were cold and unfriendly looking. The moon was nothing but the thinnest sliver, a deep yellow that was more like an eye watching her than a heavenly body looking down on her benevolently.

She took a deep breath, then let it out slowly. She wondered why some things were nothing more than what they seemed, and others were layered with traces of things she didn't expect.

She shivered briefly under Ruith's cloak, then started to walk again. The longer she walked, the calmer she felt. Taking the measure of a man by the reaction of Oban's spells to him was unreliable, nothing more. Besides, she might have been seeing things that weren't there. It had been at least a fortnight since she'd slept well at night, and perhaps almost that long since she'd eaten anything that tasted as it should have. It was weariness that colored her vision. There was nothing amiss with members of her company. Even the woods surrounding her were reassuringly quiet—

She froze. That wasn't exactly true.

"I know what you're hiding, my false rustic."

Sarah let out her breath very carefully. That was Connail, his voice a harsh whisper in the dark. She couldn't imagine he was talking to anyone but Ruith, for he was unfailingly polite, if not a bit condescending, to everyone else. She couldn't fathom what Ruith had done to deserve it. After all, he'd consented to spiriting the mage out of a dangerous city, fed him, allowed him to travel along with them. What more did the man expect?

"And I imagine I know *why* you're hiding what you're hiding," Connail added.

"Do you?" Ruith said mildly.

"Of course I do," Connail snarled. "I've been guarding my tongue, but I could stop. Then we'll see how the rest of your company views you, especially the little wench."

Sarah stepped forward to listen a bit more, but she apparently disturbed a warren of rabbits, for two of them went racing off. By the time Sarah's heart had calmed down enough for her to hear, the conversation had moved on.

"And *that*," Connail was saying, "is the reason for my silence."

Sarah cursed silently. She wasn't one to eavesdrop, but she suspected that these were details she might want to know. What could Connail possibly be holding over Ruith's head? His lack of magic? She moved closer until she could see both of them. She was tempted to walk out into the clearing and speak the truth aloud, to save Connail the trouble, but she supposed Ruith didn't need her to fight his battles for him. The coldness in his voice was proof enough of that.

"Say what you like about me," Ruith said, his words clipped. "At this juncture of my life, nothing can harm me."

Connail laughed, but it was a very unpleasant sort of laugh. "You say that now, but you haven't thought it through. Nay, my friend, I'll keep your secret. But in return, I want what you know. And you know *precisely* what I'm talking about."

"Never," Ruith said flatly.

Connail glared at him for several very long moments, then he took a step backward.

The weak fool.

"You'll regret that," Connail said angrily. He glared at Ruith one more time, then turned and stalked unsteadily off.

Ruith bowed his head and dragged his hand through his hair.

Sarah watched him for several minutes in silence, until he finally sighed and departed for points unknown. She waited for a handful of minutes until his footsteps receded, then rubbed her arms briskly. She was suddenly quite chilled, though she couldn't account for it. Obviously Connail knew Ruith far better than he'd let on. And Ruith knew it.

She turned and started toward the fire, then leapt back with a squeak.

Urchaid stood there, silent and unmoving.

"'Tis dangerous to be out here alone," he said softly.

She opened her mouth to give vent to a bit of bluster, but found it was unnecessary.

"She isn't alone."

Sarah had never been so happy to see the glint of a sword hilt in her life. Ruith stepped around Urchaid and came to stand next to her.

"Too much walking might be dangerous for you, my lord," Ruith said, inclining his head. "Shall we help you back to camp?"

Urchaid took a step backward. "How thoughtful your concern is, my friend. I seem to have forgotten your name . . ."

"It's forgettable," Ruith said. "Head straight through those trees. You'll see the fire shortly."

Sarah was perfectly content to allow Ruith to pull her away. She didn't dare look behind her as she walked with him into the shadows. He said nothing and she had no desire to break the silence. They walked directly away from the camp and into the midst of a farmer's freshly ploughed field. Ruith stopped, finally, then simply stared off into the distance. She wanted to ask him what it was Connail held over him, but decided that whatever it was, it was none of her affair. If Ruith wanted to tell her, then he would. If not, she was likely better off.

But now that they had a bit of privacy, she turned to what she'd been putting off.

"I took something from Connail's house," she said.

He looked at her. "Did you, indeed? What?"

She hesitated, then reached down and pulled the piece of velvet from her boot. "Something from his case of precious things. I haven't looked at it, lest someone notice it, but I can tell there is magic involved." She took a deep breath. "I know you don't have any magic, but you seem to know quite a bit about it, so—"

"My parents had a bit of magic," he admitted slowly. "I am schooled in the theory of it, if not necessarily the practice."

She was surprised by that, but perhaps the fact that his parents hadn't passed on their abilities to him was embarrassing to him. She held out the square of cloth. "Do you know the page Connail was talking about? The page from Gair of Ceangail's book?"

"I've heard tell of it, aye."

"This is the cloth that page was resting on. I'm not sure how much you'll see in the dark, but I think the words were burned into its surface."

He accepted the swatch, then flinched and dropped it immediately. Sarah looked at him in surprise.

"Did it burn you too?"

He blew out his breath. "Aye, but no matter." He reached down and picked the cloth up again. He looked up at the sliver of moon, then peered at the cloth intently. "I fear we'll need to leave it for the morning."

"You keep it," she said with a shiver. "I have welts from it on my leg already." She looked at the cloth, but she didn't dare touch it again. "Do you truly think Daniel is trying to collect other pages of Gair of Ceangail's book?"

Ruith took a deep breath. "I'm beginning to."

"What will we do?"

He folded up the cloth and shoved it down the side of his boot. It must not have pained him as much as it had her, for he didn't flinch. "We'll continue along after him." He looked up at the sky again, then turned to her. "I think he might be the one who attacked Lord Urchaid."

"Do you think so?" she asked in surprise. "Then we're not far behind him."

"I think we still have a fair amount of travel before us," he said slowly, "for I suspect Urchaid was lying there longer than he claims. Perhaps to admit otherwise would be too great a blow to his pride."

"Is he an elf?" she asked.

"I don't think so," he said, frowning. "Why do you ask?"

"Because he can't seem to stop talking about himself," she said with a snort. "And he's very handsome, in a cold, unpleasant sort of way."

Ruith's mouth twitched. "Does he have any other flaws I should have noted?"

"I have a list, but I also think I have a hole in my boot. My toes are damp."

He smiled and put his arm briefly around her shoulders. "Let us make one more circle, then go back. We'll leave Urchaid's heritage unexamined. I don't think I've the stomach for it tonight."

She agreed without hesitation. In fact, she was happy to leave several things behind her as they walked back to camp, namely the burden of carrying that quite obviously enspelled scrap of cloth. Now, if only she could have avoided another pair of things at the fire, she would have been content.

They walked back into camp a quarter hour later to find the company gathered around the fire, enjoying something of Franciscus's make that smelled fit for a king's table. Sarah sat down next to Franciscus and watched Ruith sit across the fire from her. Urchaid reached out to hand her a cup of something, but upset Franciscus's stew onto the flames in the process.

"Oh, I imagine that's my fault," he said, looking faintly surprised. He frowned, then looked at her. "I don't suppose, my dear, that you have the energy to see to this for us?"

Sarah fumbled for her flint, but Urchaid shook his head.

"Magic, my dear Sarah, is what's needful." He smiled. "I understand your mother was quite powerful. Surely this isn't beneath you."

Sarah would have silenced him if she could have, the obnoxious fool. Unfortunately, all she could do was what she always did in like situations. She demurred. "I prefer to be discreet," she said.

"Better warm than discreet," he countered. "Don't you agree?"

She would have perhaps said something she might have regretted, for she didn't care at all for the mocking expression on his face, as if he knew something he shouldn't. Fortunately, Seirceil interrupted her before she could speak.

"Go on, Sarah," he said gravely. "I'll join you. What sort of spell shall we use?"

"I don't know," she stammered, feeling completely flustered. Every eye was on her, most with expectation she couldn't meet even on her best day.

"Let's try Croxteth," Seirceil suggested. "I'm sure we both can manage the simplest spell of fire-making."

Sarah nodded, though she felt a little ill as she did so. If his magic had not returned to him in some useful fashion, the jig would, as Master Franciscus was wont to say, be up. She took a deep breath, then repeated the words with Seirceil, because she couldn't do anything else. She was actually quite surprised when the fire sprang to life. It certainly hadn't been her magic that had done the work. She looked quickly at Seirceil, but he was only watching her with a gentle smile on his face, as if he understood completely.

"Well-done," he said quietly.

"Thank you," she managed, vowing then to weave him something spectacular at her earliest opportunity. "I couldn't have done it without you."

He waved aside her thanks, then turned to Oban, who was about his usual work of filling the flames full of things that glistened and glowed, strands of colors not found in the usual bit of business consuming wood. She didn't dare look at anyone else, but she could feel Urchaid's eyes on her. Speculating on what he knew—or thought he knew—was bound to leave her not sleeping well. She turned instead to look at the fire Seirceil had made and Oban had embellished. Then she realized that wasn't all that was there.

Someone had added something else. It was so profoundly beautiful, that last bit of magic, that she could hardly look at it, yet she couldn't look away. It twisted and tangled with the flame, wrapping around the fire and the wood a whispered song that only she could hear. It was as if it had been something out of a dream.

"Where is Lord Connail?" Ned asked suddenly.

Sarah blinked, pulled away from what she'd been watching, feeling suddenly quite bereft. She looked at Urchaid, who lifted a shoulder in a half shrug.

"He had something stuck in his throat," Urchaid said dismissively. "He wandered off to see to it before Sarah and her swordsman came back."

Sarah pursed her lips. What he likely had stuck in his throat were the things he'd intended to say about Ruith. It was odd, though, that he should have left the safety of the company. He complained endlessly about the necessity of traveling with them, but he was never out of earshot of Franciscus's wagon.

"I'll go look for him," Urchaid said, rising to his feet easily. "Perhaps I'll even take the first watch, so you all can rest. No need to thank me."

Sarah watched him go, saw that Ruith was watching him as well, then turned back to the fire. The magic that had been there before was there no longer. She would have grieved for its loss, but somehow, she saw an echo of it in Ruith's face as she glanced at him. His eyes were full of the loss she felt.

Perhaps he too wished that something so beautiful could come from his hands.

She shook her head slightly and closed her eyes. When she opened them again, Ruith was looking at the blade he was sharpening. It was just as well, for she had other things besides magical flames to think on. The morrow would bring what it did, a closer look at the cloth, more lovely vistas she'd never before imagined, perhaps even a few questions for Urchaid that might reveal something besides that flawless exterior he took great pains to maintain.

But for the night, she couldn't help but look at the fire, remind herself of the beauty she'd seen wrapped in the flames, and think on the many things she hadn't expected to see when she'd walked away from Doìre with the ruins of her mother's house behind her.

She supposed those memories might carry her through what she suspected she would face sooner rather than later.

Fourteen

D anger came in many guises.

Ruith leaned against Master Franciscus's wagon and contemplated the truth of that. He'd suspected, as he'd closed up his house on the mountain, that putting his foot to the path he'd sensed lying before him would spell trouble. He'd thought he might have to come to grips with his beliefs about magic and its useful-ness. He'd feared he might encounter a reminder or two of his past. He'd actually expected that at some point, he might find that his soul had been shattered.

He had just never expected that to happen thanks to a woman who had spent her time the evening before looking for magic in his face.

He hadn't intended to add anything to the fire Seirceil had started for her. Sending a flicker of a flame to dance along the wood had been an afterthought of sorts, nothing grand or useful. But it had been beautiful and she had obviously seen it.

That in itself was unusual.

"And where do you think they've gone off to?" Seirceil asked, his face full of worry.

Franciscus shrugged, though he looked no less worried. "I've scoured the surrounding countryside for hours, but seen nothing of either of them."

Ruith rubbed his hands first over his face, then together, though he wasn't sure what sort of aid he expected from either action. He and Franciscus had been sitting at the fire the night before, discussing the virtues of the widow Fiore's garden and just what sort of cider Franciscus could brew with a bushel of her green apples and a modest cutting of her lavender. Realization that neither Urchaid nor Connail was back had hit them both at the same moment.

Ruith had risen to go look, but Franciscus had waved him back down, saying he could easily sleep during the day and leave his draft horses to follow the road without incident or direction from him. Ruith had agreed reluctantly, but he hadn't slept. He had put his weapons within easy reach and wondered about the missing men. There was no reason for either of them to have disappeared, unless Urchaid had irritated Connail a bit too much and Connail had stabbed him, then limped off.

But there had been no trace of either of them.

"Perhaps we should just continue on without them, then," Seirceil said quietly. "I don't like to speak badly of anyone—"

Franciscus smiled and put his hand briefly on Seirceil's shoulder. "In this case, my lord, I think you could safely express a desire not to travel farther with either of them and still be considered kinder than they deserve. And aye, I agree. We'll be off and leave them to follow—or not."

Seirceil's expression didn't relax any, but he nodded just the same. He smiled briefly at Ruith, then went to gather up the various and sundry who were vexing Sarah over breakfast.

"You light the fire," Ned cajoled.

"We've already eaten," she hedged.

"But that were cold," Ned complained. "Just a brief bit of warmth, then you can put it right out again."

Ruith watched Sarah dither. It was so contrary to how she usually conducted herself that he felt certain it was an adequate reflection of the conflict going on inside her. He shook his head. If trailing after her brother, who was apparently doing his damndest to gather up pages from a book of spells, wasn't enough to unsettle her, being part of the current madness certainly was.

"'Tis too trivial a thing for her," Seirceil said, putting his hand on Ned's head. "Something better suited to a child. I'll see to it, since that is about the extent of my skill at present."

Ruith winced, but Seirceil's words were completely without rancor. It wasn't exactly true, for Seirceil did possess magic. It was unreliable, though, even for such a simple thing as fire.

He could remember vividly the first time he'd called to fire in his mind and wrapped it around a single twig without so much as the slightest lifting of his smallest finger. He knew he should have been chiding himself for all the things he'd set on fire as a toddler before his mother had convinced him to exercise a modicum of self-control, or damning himself for now adding a simple bit of Fadaire to what Seirceil was doing, but all he could do was watch a headstrong, beautiful, ferociously determined woman look at the fire as if she saw things he could not.

She looked up at him with tears in her eyes.

Damn it anyway.

He reached for that very thick protective crust he'd built around his heart and found to his dismay that it wasn't nearly as substantial as it should have been. He suspected he knew on whom to lay the blame for that. He tried to scowl, but that didn't work either.

He grasped for shreds of common sense in a last-ditch effort to save his sanity.

Sarah wasn't the right sort of girl for him. He needed, were he to actually manage to find anyone to wed, a girl with courtly manners, the ability to tell which fork to use first at dinner, and an innate grace and unfailing command of the niceties of lofty conversation and flatteries. A gel with a big dagger, a quick tongue, and eyes that saw far too clearly were not what he wanted—er, needed.

But he couldn't look away as she sat there and looked into a fire that he hadn't created entirely himself, but had certainly added things to to make it burn in an especially beautiful way.

Because he liked her.

Very much.

He drew his hand over his eyes. He had to run before he did something stupid. Perhaps he would slip off that night and run all the way to Gilean. It was still some fifteen leagues from where they were. Even if they managed five leagues that day, the rest would take him all night, even if he ran hard. By the time he reached the place, he would have surely invented a reason he'd needed to come with such haste.

He turned into Franciscus before he realized the man was standing there watching him.

"I didn't see you."

"Apparently."

He pursed his lips. "I was just watching over the company."

"Never said you weren't, lad."

Ruith shot him a look but Franciscus only smiled pleasantly— and unrepentantly.

"I'm going to run ahead to Gilean tonight," Ruith muttered, "because I think the journey will do me good."

"Clear your head?" Franciscus asked politely.

"Allow me to escape meddling old men."

"I am not old. I'm seasoned. And I'm not meddling, I'm observing."

"You're going daft," Ruith said. He started to turn away, then hesitated. "You'll watch after Sarah whilst I'm away?"

"With both eyes and a dagger in each hand."

Ruith paused. "I don't trust Urchaid."

"We could hope he's dead."

"If someone was murdered last night, I imagine it wasn't him," Ruith said grimly, "but I've been wrong many times before. Please keep Sarah close."

"I will, but tell me what you're about. Something to do with our present business?"

Ruith considered, then leaned against the wagon again and looked at the alemaster. "I think there will come a time when I must go on ahead," he said slowly. "And I'm certain you'll need to be about your own affairs sooner rather than later." He chewed on his words for a bit. "I fear Daniel is determined to have a few more of those spells he's laid hands on. I'll actually be a bit surprised if he continues on with his harassing of local mages. I fear he has a different plan."

"Care to share it?"

Ruith wasn't sure where to begin. He had looked at the velvet cloth of Connail's Sarah had made off with and it was indeed a perfect imprint of his father's spell of Reconstruction. It wasn't necessarily a dangerous spell, though he supposed under the right circumstances, he who found himself reconstructed might find himself unable to protect himself against further assaults. Fortunately, Ruith highly doubted Daniel would use it with any success on anything that moved.

But if he managed it to any degree, he might redouble his efforts to find more of those sorts of spells.

Ruith looked at Franciscus and forced himself to maintain a blasé expression. "What do you know of Gair of Ceangail?"

"Other than the tales Connail has seemed determined to bludgeon us with?" Franciscus asked. He shrugged. "Just rumors. There are many nasty little mages weaving dark spells, but few of note, wouldn't you agree?"

Ruith nodded and refrained from comment.

"Lothar, Gair, Droch of Saothair, and Wehr of Wrekin, of course, come immediately to mind, though Gair, at least, was rumored to have manners and a decent bit of charm. I can't speak with any authority about the others."

A decent bit of charm. Ruith pursed his lips. Aye, his father had been charming—to others. And to his family, when it suited him. Unfortunately, the mercurial changes in temper had been swift and all the more terrifying because of their unpredictability.

"Ruith?"

Ruith unclenched his fists, realizing only then that he needed to. He managed a smile. "I was just thinking that if Daniel knew what he had in his possession, he might be willing to see if he could have a bit more of it."

He couldn't bring himself to talk about his father's spell of Diminishing. He had watched his father completely strip other mages of their power at least a score of times. He didn't like to remember the particulars, so he didn't. Even the fact that Daniel possessed but half of that spell was enough to turn his blood cold. If Daniel found the other half, even if he didn't possess the power to wield the entire thing fully, he could do terrible damage.

Ruith didn't want to think about what would happen to the world if someone with a substantial amount of power got hold of both halves of that spell. Daniel might think he could undo the world, but he was hopelessly lost in delusions of grandeur. But the spell of Diminishing in the hands of Lothar of Wychweald, or Droch of Saothair?

Devastating.

"And you suspect you know where Daniel might be going?" Franciscus asked.

Ruith dragged himself back to the conversation at hand. "I think Ceangail's as good a place as any to start a search. But I can't walk all the way there and I can't take a large company with me. Especially one that includes that damned Oban, continually waving his wand and covering us with rainbows and whatever else he sends scampering around us at all hours."

"Unicorns."

"I was trying to forget that."

Franciscus laughed briefly and reached up to put his hand on Ruith's shoulder. "I am too. You go tonight and I'll keep things together here. If worse comes to worst, Oban will create us an army of mythical beasts to charge our enemies and blind them with their twinkling."

"I knew there was a reason we needed him," Ruith said dryly. He took a deep breath, then nodded. "I thank you, my friend." He paused, then looked at Franciscus seriously. "There are things that hunted us in the woods of Shettlestoune. Things that weren't precisely human, I don't think. I think 'twas me they were seeking, but I can't guarantee that. But felling them is no easy task."

"Then why don't you leave me your weapons and I'll teach Ned to use them."

"When I'm dead and no sooner," Ruith said without hesitation. "The lad would ruin my arrows, put chinks in my sword, and lose my knives. You'll just have to watch during the nights. But I'll leave you most of my gear. I won't need it on my present errand."

"You'll be back, then."

Ruith nodded, though he was less sure of that than perhaps he should have been. He needed to find Daniel of Doìre and stop him, which might entail going into places where he wouldn't have taken his worst enemy. Taking Sarah along to those places was out of the question.

But if he didn't take her, he might not recognize Daniel in a crowd, which would leave him losing the chance to stop the man.

Worse still, he might possibly be leaving her in the sights of monsters and mages she couldn't simply discourage with her hunting knife.

"I'll be back," he said. "In a day or two."

Franciscus looked at him and considered for a moment or two. "Shall I continue on to Slighe, then?"

"Were you headed that way?" Ruith asked in surprise. "I assumed you would turn west for Angesand or make for Penrhyn." He frowned. "Actually I hadn't given much thought to your journey's end past being grateful for your company now."

"And my ale."

"And your cooking," Ruith added with a smile. He thought for a moment, then nodded. "If you're going through the mountains, then aye, you could make for Slighe, though I have many miles to travel before I would find myself there."

"You and Sarah, you mean."

"Of course," Ruith said without hesitation.

Franciscus looked at him closely, then pursed his lips and walked away. Ruith watched him go, then turned to go help Seirceil break camp.

It took him longer to reach Gilean than he'd intended only because he spent too much time thinking, which left him walking instead of running. He supposed, as he walked through a relatively crowded market, that that thinking was what had allowed someone to follow him without his having noticed.

Truly, he was in desperate need of sleep.

He yawned, stopped to purchase a rather wizened apple from an equally wizened-looking farmer, then leaned in close over the fruit.

"Might I use your alley?" he asked politely.

"For that lad behind you?" the man asked with a toothless grin. "Have your little brother following where he shouldn't, eh?"

"Absolutely," Ruith agreed. He had a nod for his trouble, then wandered away, doubling back behind carts and humanity until he had a clear path to the very tiny alleyway behind that seller of last year's fruit.

He waited until the boy, Ned he assumed, had come walking by, then jerked him off his feet and into the dark.

He froze at the feel of steel against his throat. It was only then, after he realized that his assailant was gasping because he had hold of her—aye, that was *her*—right wrist, that he swore and released her.

Her blade didn't move.

"I didn't think you could kill with your left hand," he said carefully.

"I can, if I need two old hens for the stewpot and my right hand is holding one of them." She pulled her knife away and resheathed it. She cursed. "I must find a mage to heal this arm."

He had to stop himself from making werelight, then had to bite his tongue to keep from cursing a bit more. He pulled her sleeve gently up her arm and relinquished the idea of not swearing. The grooves were yet deeper than they had been the day before and the blackness still spreading. He supposed there would come a time when there was naught but rot.

He was going to have to do something about it.

It wasn't that he hadn't wanted to, as long as that something had nothing to do with magic. Unfortunately, there was no denying that what ate at her flesh had nothing to do with a normal wound and everything to do with some vile spell.

Of his father's, as it happened.

"Can a mage heal himself?" she asked, looking up at him in the faint light of the morning sun.

He lifted an eyebrow briefly. "Many have tried, or so I've heard. Unsuccessfully, I might add."

"Do they merely fail at the task or is there something more interesting that happens?"

"I couldn't say." He gently pulled her sleeve down over her arm again. "I think the binding principle is that healing can only be given away."

"Lest a mage hole up in a cave by himself and forgo any contact with others?" she asked, looking up at him unflinchingly.

He shifted uncomfortably. "I'm just your guardsman," he said. "What would I know of any of it, in truth?"

She pursed her lips. "Some guardsman. Where were you last night?"

"Running."

"Not all night." She frowned up at him. "I'm paying you to guard my back and here you are, having scampered off without a word."

She reminded him sharply of his six-year-old sister who'd been slain. He had a very vivid memory of Mhorghain putting her hands on her hips and glaring up at their eldest brother, who'd stood three feet taller than she, when he'd tried to tell her what to do once too often. Ruith had to lean back against a very handy wall until he could catch his breath. He attempted a smile, but that only seemed to irritate Sarah more.

"Do you *want* me to leave you here, bleeding to death in this alley? And stop your bloody smirking. You're not as immune to me as you think you are."

If she only had any idea . . . Nay, he wasn't immune at all.

"Don't do it again," she added. "Leave me, that is."

He bowed his head and rubbed the back of his neck for a moment or two, then looked at her from under his eyebrows. "Very well," he said, finally. "I won't."

"I should point out that you didn't leave me before; you deserted me. 'Tis a more serious offense."

He pursed his lips to keep from smiling, which he supposed would have resulted in his being altogether more familiar with her blade than he wanted to be. It was all he could do not to pull her into his arms and hold her there until his delight bubbled over into laughter she most certainly wouldn't have appreciated.

Dangerous paths, indeed.

She nodded toward the market. "Let's be off. I'll buy you breakfast before you laugh yourself into a faint."

He pushed away from the wall, then put his arm around her shoulders. "I'll pay. If I have to watch you count your coins again, I'll kill your brother for the vexation when we meet. By the way, how many did he steal?"

"Four hundred and ninety-three."

"I hope they gave him a backache from having to carry them," Ruith said with a snort. "We'll eat, then go look at horses."

She looked up at him in surprise. "For the company?"

"For you and me."

"I can't afford a horse."

"Then I suppose I'll have to leave you behind."

He could hear the wheels grinding miserably inside her head. "I could earn—"

He squeezed her shoulders, then released her and took her hand. It was her right hand, so he held it very loosely. Better for her skin, necessary for his sanity. "I wasn't serious, Sarah. 'Tis part of our bargain. You look for your brother, I see to inns and transportation."

She was very quiet as she allowed him to weave a path through the market. He bought food, two very lovely, slim daggers that were engraved with runes he was certain were neither elvish nor of dwarf make, but rather something from some noble house or other.

They had been fashioned to fit a woman's hand and tuck down the sides of slim riding boots or perhaps down an over-ruffled blouse such as the one folded resentfully and left behind happily under Master Franciscus's wagon seat. The sight of them made him smile, so he handed them to Sarah without comment and promised himself a better look at them when he had a chance.

He didn't realize she hadn't said anything at all until he was walking with her along a fairly wide road that led west, out of town toward where the horse breeders plied their trade. He looked at her to find her looking straight ahead with tears standing in her eyes. He stopped and stared at her in astonishment.

"What is it?"

She looked so devastated, *he* almost wept. Hard on the heels of that came the intense desire to turn and flee. He was not good with women who wept, the sum total of his experience with wailing females being limited to his younger sister's very rare bouts of it. He hadn't been her primary comforter—nor her primary tormentor, it should be noted—but he'd been passing fond of her and he'd never shunned her company. He'd seen her weep only when she'd truly injured herself, or when she'd been afraid. He'd never blamed her for either. She'd certainly had cause enough for the latter.

But a grown woman who wouldn't even look at him as she stood there with her eyes closed and tears running down her cheeks?

Now, *that* was terrifying.

But he was nothing if not resourceful, so he turned her to him and drew her with rather less grace than he might have liked into his arms. She was not a willing weeper. Indeed, he wouldn't have known she wept if he hadn't felt his tunic growing damp and heard the occasional hiccup.

He murmured soothingly, punctuating that with the occasional curse lest she think he'd gone completely daft, and tried to decide what would achieve better results, patting her back or stroking her hair. He was afraid he had patted a bit too hard and encountered a few too many tangles and pulled rather too vigorously, but what did she expect? He was, as he would have readily admitted to any passerby who looked capable of rescuing him from his current predicament, not good at that sort of thing.

Sarah finally pulled away, laughing uneasily as she dragged her sleeve across her eyes. "Thank you."

"Is it over?"

"I think so."

"Then you're welcome," he said with feeling.

She looked up at him, her eyes very red, then she smiled and took his arm. "Let's press on."

He walked with her, feeling quite pathetically grateful she hadn't completely fallen apart on him. But hard on the heels of that came the idea that he should ask her what was amiss.

"Sarah—"

"It was the daggers," she said shortly, tugging on him and walking faster. "A very lovely gift."

He knew that he should have dug a little harder to find out why such a gift would bother her so much, but he suspected he might not need to. For all he knew, she had never had anyone do anything nice for her.

"Where now?" she demanded.

"We'll find horses, then decide," he said, happy to discuss something a little less tender. "I left most of my gear with Franciscus, so we'll need to go back and fetch it. Then we'll be off to find your brother. I think we'll manage more easily if we ride."

"And what are we going to do once we find him?" she asked in a suddenly weary tone.

"You'll hold him whilst I cut his entrails from him and hang him from the nearest tree with them."

Her eyes widened briefly. "Savage."

"Efficient."

"I was talking about you, not your methods."

He smiled in spite of himself. "I think I should be offended."

"Flattered, rather," she said. She looked at the knives she carried in one hand. "Thank you for these. Truly."

"You're welcome. Truly."

She shook her head. "I'll never manage to repay you, not for the horse, not for these." She took a deep breath suddenly. "Which stable shall we visit?"

"At the end of the road. Hardest to get to, but worth the effort."

"Have you been here before?" she asked in surprise.

"Aye," he said, but he didn't elaborate. He didn't dare. He'd come with his father's father when he'd been barely eight summers, just they two for a look to see if there might be decent horseflesh to be had. It had been a particularly marvelous journey, full of adventure and pretending to be a mere traveler along with his grandfather, who was famous for going about in homespun. He had never once dreamt that pantomime might become his life in truth.

He pulled himself away from that memory and looked at her seriously. "Can you choose horseflesh?"

"And ride too, if you can believe it. You can thank Master Franciscus for it, though. Those lessons gave me a reason to be out from under my mother's . . . scrutiny."

"Stirring up insurrections in some farmer's field, were you?"

"Something like that."

Avoiding her mother's rages was more likely, or so he suspected. He reached out and pulled her into his arms again before he thought better of it. He held her close and closed his eyes when he felt her arms steal around his waist.

"Come on, you wee feisty wench," he said roughly. "I'll buy you a horse."

"I don't need sympathy."

"I'm not offering you sympathy," he said, though he most certainly was. "I'm buying you a horse. We'll see who is the better rider, and then the loser can spend the rest of the day polishing the victor's tack."

She pulled away and looked up at him. "Have you ever ridden a horse, Ruith?"

"I had one as a boy." He'd had more than one, actually, waiting for him in a handful of locations. He didn't bother to mention that whilst he was very fond of riding, he had been rather more fond of throwing himself off whatever steep inclines had been available and turning himself into something very fast with wings before he hit the ground. He pulled himself back to himself, then nodded toward the street. "Let's see what's available, then you'll remind me what to do. I haven't ridden in years."

Two hours later, they were leaning their elbows on a horse fence and watching a selection of very fine stallions be worked in an arena.

"These are exceptional," Sarah said very quietly.

Ruith nodded in agreement. "They are. I imagine they have Angesand blood in their veins."

She looked at him with a frown. "But I thought the lords of Angesand never allowed their horses out of their care, and if they did, they required absolute guarantees that the beasts wouldn't be bred."

"All true, to my knowledge," Ruith said, "save for one relatively obscure incident several centuries ago in which Alan of Gilean spirited away a particularly lovely Angesand mare from the king of Neroche's summer palace at Chagailt. He bred her several times and produced himself a very fine living. Briefly."

She leaned against the fence. "What happened to him?"

"Treun of Angesand hunted him down, pulled out his entrails, and hanged him with them in his own barn." He lifted an eyebrow. "Savage, isn't it?"

She laughed a little at him. "You're not very original, are you?"

"I'm just entertaining you for the sport of it."

"Then 'tis very well-done. I'll be even more impressed if you can talk that man over there out of a pair of horses and have any gold left over."

"What, these lame nags here?" Ruith said dismissively. "Look you at those strange and ungainly growths on their hooves."

She leaned close. "I think they're wings."

"I'll look for other flaws, then."

"Best of luck with that." She looked at him sideways. "How is it you know so many things?"

"I have an extensive library at home," he said, "with tomes full of gossip and speculation."

She said no more, but she did smile more easily and she did indeed have a way with horses. He paid a fair price for two very fine nags with what he wasn't entirely sure weren't wings on their hooves. He gave Sarah a leg up, then swung up into his own saddle with as much grace as he could muster—which wasn't much, given the day he'd had so far—and turned with her back toward town.

The road was fairly empty, but he supposed that didn't matter. He had no intention of sampling his horse's canter at the moment anyway, given the fair likelihood of his falling off upon his arse. So he remained at a walk, listened to the wind in the branches of trees thinking about breaking forth into buds, and contemplated the great pleasure of riding next to a woman who seemed content to enjoy the same.

He nodded at souls that they passed, not paying them much heed past avoiding trampling on them.

And then he froze. He hardly dared look behind him but he was fairly sure he recognized the two men he had just passed. Sarah looked at him, then back over her shoulder. She frowned.

"Ruith, those lads are coming back toward us."

"Fly," he said without hesitation.

She did, and so did he. He didn't look back, and he heard no shouts or calls to stop and explain why he was where he was when he was supposed to be dead. He drew his hood over his face, but the wind had other ideas.

He supposed the lads he'd passed would think they had perhaps been overtired, or overfed, or over-aled and imagined what they'd seen. Surely they wouldn't rush back to Lake Cladach and tell their employers whom they thought they'd seen.

Surely.

He hazarded a glance behind him but saw nothing. His secrets were still safe and he wouldn't soon find himself hunted down so he could explain things he wasn't ready to.

At least not yet.

"You're losing!" Sarah called over her shoulder.

Aye, more than just the race. His sanity, his peace, his heart . . .

The list was very long, indeed.

Fifteen

❧

Sarah set a pot of water to boil and glanced at her right wrist. Ruith had bought a salve from an herbalist during their walk through the market earlier that morning and whether it had been enspelled by someone else or simply worked because of who had put it on her arm, it had eased her pain greatly. The marks were still there, but not so black. She had the feeling it would take a mighty magic indeed to cure her. That would have to come later. First, she had to come to terms with the fact that she was now the very fortunate, if not slightly mortified, owner of a very fast horse. That horse would be, in the morning, wearing the tack that his purchaser was now sitting in front of the fire cleaning.

She had won the race.

They had caught back up with their reduced company earlier that afternoon to find that there was still no sign of Urchaid or Connail and no one had any idea what had befallen either of them. Connail had seemed angry enough to have taken a blade to Urchaid, but Urchaid had also possessed a certain coldness that had bothered her. That there had been no sign of a struggle, nor any remains left behind, was troubling. She couldn't credit either man with magical mischief, but what did she know?

She knew, actually, that she was ready to be done with magic altogether.

Ruith had discussed plans with Franciscus after their return, then informed the mages and Ned that if they wanted to live, they would do well to stay close to the alemaster, who had more hidden in the false floor of his wagon than his finest reserve of cognac. Sarah had heard the things Ruith had left out, such as the danger involved in shadowing Daniel more closely and the dodginess of the places he might be visiting.

She had no doubt that Ruith intended to leave her behind again, his fine promises aside.

She cursed him under her breath as she fetched a pot to use for the tea she intended to make. He would find that she was a very light sleeper indeed and a better rider. He wasn't going to be going anywhere alone.

She looked up, froze, then dropped the cast-iron kettle into the fire.

A stranger had walked suddenly and without pause into the midst of their camp. She fumbled for her knife, realizing only as she couldn't seem to grasp it that she also had two slim, lethal-looking daggers down the sides of her boots thanks to Ruith's generosity. She didn't bother to reach down for those given that Master Franciscus seemed determined to make up for her lack of weapons with his axe in one hand and a barrel hook in the other. Ruith had an arrow fitted to a string.

The arrow dipped, then fell from his hand. He gaped at the stranger as if he'd seen a ghost.

Oban rose immediately to his feet and upended the remains of his supper into the fire on top of her pot, and that bloody dog of Oban's yipped until Ned reached over and brought it onto his lap where he could muzzle it. Seirceil didn't seem as astonished as he perhaps should have been, but that one was prone to keeping his humors quite settled. She glanced at Ruith, who looked no less stunned than before, then turned to study the stranger.

He was dressed very simply in traveler's garb: an unremark-able cloak, worn boots, a hat that had seen better days and sported feathers, which she realized, on closer inspection, were actually fishing lures. Perhaps that explained his lack of weaponry, though she supposed that might have been a gutting knife tucked into his boot.

Before she could find her voice to ask him who he was and why he'd turned Ruith as pale a shade of white as he himself seemed to be, he had stepped forward and thrown his arms around her hired sword.

He wept.

It took Ruith a moment or two, but there were soon tears run-ning down his cheeks as well. Sarah looked away out of respect.

In time, Master Franciscus walked over to the man and inclined his head slightly. "Welcome to our fire," he said. "We've just fin-ished supper, but we can prepare more, if you like. Perhaps you have traveled far and are hungry?"

"Thank you," the stranger said simply. "Something to drink would be most welcome."

"And who is 'e, do you think?" Ned asked in a whisper that wasn't quite a whisper. "He looks a bit rough around the edges, I'd say."

Ruith stepped back and dragged his sleeve across his eyes. "This is my grandfather." He paused. "It has been many a year since last we met."

"Oy, his grandpappy?" Ned said, scooting behind Seirceil. "He don't look a day over a score."

Ruith's grandfather, who indeed didn't look much older than
Ruith, only smiled. "Clean living, my lad, and a distaste for sweets.
You might think about it."

Ned frowned. "I don't know—"

Franciscus shot Ned a look. "Stay out of my sugar barrel, Ned,
and keep your teeth." He turned to Ruith's grandfather. "I'll prepare a light meal for you, which will give you a moment or two of
privacy with your grandson."

"Thank you."

Sarah watched Ruith walk off with his grandfather into the
shadows, but not before he'd sent her a look over his shoulder.

He was undone.

It was very much later, after all the others save Franciscus had
gone to sleep, that she sat and worked on a sock with the knitting needles Franciscus had thoughtfully tucked away under the
bench of his wagon along with several skeins of wool she had spun
for him. He was diligently working on a pair of mittens. For at
least an hour there had been nothing but the comforting sounds of
the fire cracking and popping at their feet and the barely percep-
tible tick of their needles as they worked.

"I didn't know Ruith had family alive," Sarah remarked at one
point.

"I didn't either. I wonder if he knew."

She didn't look up from her work. "He has secrets, I think."

"Aye."

She looked at him briefly. "I think he appreciates that you
haven't told them."

Franciscus held his mitten away and looked it over critically.
"I'm in the business of secrets, my gel. Not that I know any of
yours."

"I don't have any."

"Save how it is you spin such lovely yarn," he said, fingering the mitten and sighing with pleasure. "A more eloquent man might call it magic."

Sarah would have responded, but Ruith and his grandfather walked back into the light of the fire. It was obvious they had both shed their share of tears, though the grandfather was now smiling. Ruith still looked a bit winded. The grandfather shook hands with Franciscus and accepted a cup of ale, which he tasted, then praised effusively. She scrambled to her feet when he turned to her, and held out her hand to shake his in her most manly fashion. Grandfather he might have been, but there was no sense in his not knowing that she was a woman with her own mind and her own quest.

"Grandfather, this is Sarah of Doìre," Ruith said quietly. "It is her errand I'm on."

Sarah found her hand held on to whilst the older man—if a fortnight in age could have been called older—made a low, formal bow over it.

"'Tis a pleasure, lady," he said, straightening. "I am Sgath of a very tiny little fishing spot just over those hills, really not worth mentioning. I apologize for having stolen your guardsman for the past pair of hours, but I see that you have needles there that are surely protection enough."

Sarah put her sock behind her back and shifted uncomfortably. "Sorry—"

"Oh, not at all," Sgath said with a smile. "And I don't know about you all, but I would very much appreciate just a scrap of ground to sit on for a bit and rest my old bones."

Sarah sat, eyeing him critically. He didn't look a day over two score, truly, but perhaps he was full of a magic that had preserved him. Ruith had said his parents had had a bit, so perhaps one of them had inherited their bit from that man named Sgath.

The name seemed familiar somehow, but she couldn't place it. It wasn't as if she was well versed in the souls who peopled the rest of the Nine Kingdoms, even if Sgath had been someone of note. Perhaps he seemed familiar because he looked like Ruith. Not so much that she would have immediately identified them as kin, but there was definitely a resemblance there.

She watched Ruith watch his grandfather as if he still couldn't quite believe his eyes, or as if he'd just discovered a lovely bit of something that he was afraid might disappear if he looked away. She didn't want to envy him, but she couldn't help it. Sgath seemed delighted just by Ruith's existence. It seemed ridiculous to be as old as she was and find herself wanting so badly that same thing in her own life—

She put away her knitting abruptly and leaned over to Franciscus. "I'm going to go see to the horses. Shall I see to yours as well?"

"You can if you wish, my gel," Franciscus said with a smile. "Though you spoil them overmuch."

"You're feeding my horse carrots," she pointed out.

"He brings me rabbits, thankfully being too confused to know what to do with them himself, which leaves them for my stew. 'Tis a fair trade."

She nodded, rose, and walked away. By the time she reached the horses, she had forcibly shaken off her melancholy. That wasn't her natural state, so it sat very ill on her shoulders. She was very happy for Ruith that he should encounter, after what had to have been a very long time, a relative he obviously loved so much. And she didn't envy him his family, for life was difficult enough without it. If he had been so fortunate as to have run across a relative he cared for, then she could be nothing but pleased for him. She turned around to look for a brush and ran bodily into the man for whom she had so diligently wished only good things. She took a step backward, a deep breath, and ahold of her womanly emotions. She looked up at him and attempted a smile.

"What a happy coincidence for you."

He rested his hand on her horse's neck and fussed absently with his mane. "I didn't expect this." He was silent for quite a while. "It has been many years."

"He is obviously overjoyed to see you."

"And I him," Ruith murmured.

She elbowed him out of her way. "Go back to him. I can see to these beasts. I'll even tend your grandsire's horse over there. I can see he's rather finer that these spectacular specimens here."

"A trueblood," Ruith admitted.

"Your grandfather must be very wealthy."

"Just choosey," Ruith said. "About his horses and his fishing gear."

She brushed for a minute or two in silence, then stopped. She couldn't look at him. "If you need to go now, I'll pay you and you can be on your way."

He didn't say anything.

She didn't dare look at him at first, but when he remained silent, she supposed she might as well. The moon was beginning to wax again, but it was of little use. She could see little but what the stars would reveal, which might be more than she could bear. She had no other choice, though, so she looked at him.

He was merely resting his arm on Osag's neck, watching her with a very grave expression on his face.

"And what would you give me as my payment, Sarah of Doìre?" he asked quietly.

She didn't flinch, but it took most all of her self-control not to. She had next to nothing, but since that was all she had, that was all *he* would have unless he wanted to tell her where he was going so she could have gold sent to him later. She moved past him, then went to fetch her gear from its secret location under the wagon seat. She pulled out her feed sack, rummaged around in it unnecessarily because there was only one thing inside, then drew forth her very small collection of coins. She closed her eyes briefly, then turned and walked over to where Ruith was standing. She pulled the knives from her boots, then held them and her bag of coins out to him.

"There. That is all I have."

He took the three things without comment. He tucked the knives under his arm, then opened the bag and spilled the contents out into one of his hands. He contemplated the meager pile of coins for a moment, then poured the coins back into the sack and drew the strings closed. He stood there for several minutes without moving until Sarah could bear the silence no longer.

"I know it isn't enough—"

"It isn't."

She knew she had no right to be angry, but she found she was just the same. "And this comes as a surprise to you? You knew I had no gold—"

"I don't want your gold," he interrupted.

"Then what do you want, you bloody, arrogant, unfeeling—"

He reached out and pulled her into his arms. She protested, loudly, mostly because the hilts of her daggers were pressing painfully into the soft spot just inside her shoulders. Ruith pulled back, took the daggers and tucked them into the back of his belt, then paused.

"Are you going to shout now if I attempt that again?"

"Nay," she said shortly. "I'll just pull my knives from your belt and stab you. Why don't you simply be about your demands whilst I still have a modicum of pride left to bear them?"

He clasped his hands behind his back, though he didn't step away from her. The bloody lout, he might as well have been clutching her to him.

In that divine embrace she wished she hadn't protested.

"I want you," he said gravely, "to come with me on a journey."

"We already have a quest, which you're obviously ready to abandon."

He shook his head slowly. "I'm not and a few hours of conversation with my grandfather at his summer house—"

"He has a *summer* house?" she asked in astonishment.

"'Tis very small," Ruith said with a smile. "It gives him a place to take his grandsons to keep them out from underfoot." He paused and chewed on his words for a moment or two. "Unless you'd rather not."

He sounded unaccountably hesitant.

She frowned fiercely, because it helped her keep control over that little bit of something beautiful that threatened to sprout up in her heart. "Do you *want* me to come with you?"

"I believe I asked you to."

She had to clear her throat roughly, for it was either that or weep and she had already wept once in front of the man. She would not do it again.

"I'll come," she said, dredging up a stern look. "How else will I keep you from scampering off if I don't keep you within blade's reach?"

He reached out and tucked a lock of hair behind her ear, then he frowned and tried again. "It doesn't stay."

She blew out of her eyes a bit of the fringe that seemed determined to frame her face no matter what she did to it. "I don't plan it that way."

He put her coins back into her hand, gathered up her curry comb and brush, then put his arm around her shoulders. "I'll rebraid it for you in front of the fire. Leave the horses. I'll come tend them later."

She knew she should have protested, but she found she simply couldn't. She watched him toss the brushes into the wagon before he walked with her back to the fire.

A handful of moments later, she was trying to keep her eyes open whilst Ruith brushed her hair with something Oban had conjured up for him. Whatever else that mage's faults, he certainly knew how to see to life's luxuries with aplomb. He was busily working on ribbons for the end of her braid, creating strand after strand only to spell them into oblivion when they apparently didn't suit.

"I can find a bit of rope," Ruith said loudly.

Master Oban opened his mouth and looked at him in horror. He then scrunched up his face and frowned fiercely as he turned away from silk and concentrated on velvet.

Sarah closed her eyes and smiled to herself, for more ridiculous reasons than she wanted to admit. She was warm, for a change, she was safe, a truly novel feeling, and she was, for the first time she could remember, leaving the untangling of her mane to someone else.

"You must have had sisters," she said with a sigh.

"One," he agreed quietly. "Once."

She turned around to look at him so quickly, she almost pulled the hair he was braiding not only out of his hand, but out of her head. She winced. "I'm sorry. I didn't think."

He shook his head with a faint smile, then put his hand atop her head and turned her back around. "You needn't tread carefully around me."

"Nor you, me."

He began to brush again. "I think I disagree. You have too many knives on your person for me to dare." He paused. "You'll have to show your knives to my grandfather when we've a bit of privacy. He might be able to translate the runes that I cannot."

She looked at his grandfather, who was deep in discussion with Franciscus, then shook her head. "He looks old enough to be your brother, nothing more."

"He never takes dessert."

She smiled. "Liar."

"I'm not," he said promptly. "As he said himself, he's quite careful about his diet. I think his youth is due to all the time he spends out of doors, but I could be wrong."

She suspected there was more to Sgath's youthful face than an avoidance of sweets, but what did she know? Her mother had been ancient for as long as Sarah could remember.

She closed her eyes again and listened to Ruith discuss with a silent Oban the appropriate color of ribbon for a woman on an important quest, listened with half an ear to Sgath and Franciscus discuss the location of their favorite taverns, and did her best not to fall asleep.

In such peace and safety, it was difficult.

She could have sworn Ruith had just put his hands on her shoulders and told her he was finished before she heard shouts and felt herself be yanked up to her feet and set aside very gently.

Actually Ruith shoved her behind him so hard she went sprawling, but she supposed she was grateful for it when she sat up and saw what was making an absolute wreck of their camp.

"Ruith!"

She watched Ruith catch his sword that Franciscus had managed to snatch from the wagon. He drew, turned, and almost found himself skewered by a monster that stepped through the fire as if it didn't feel it at all. The others scrambled out of the way. The dogs screamed in terror. Or perhaps that was Ned. She honestly couldn't tell and it seemed a little strange that she was obsessed with determining the truth of it.

Better that than watch the battle going on in front of her.

Sgath had somehow laid hands on Ruith's bow and quiver of arrows and he was using them well against what had become a trio of trolls. Franciscus proved to be a more than adequate warrior as he took on the third of the attackers—or at least it seemed so until Sarah realized that the alemaster's axe was no match for a troll with seeming inexhaustible strength and inhuman speed. She found herself with one of the knives Ruith had given her in her hand. When it came to hunting supper, she was better with a trap, adequate with a bow and arrows of her own that were at least a third smaller than what Ruith used, and rather handy with a knife.

But those were rabbits or the odd overfed quail. These were far beyond her experience. In the end, she supposed there was nothing to lose but Franciscus's life, so she flipped the knife to hold it by the tip, then flung it with all her strength into the third beast's eye.

It screamed as if a hot poker had been thrust into its skull.

Ruith turned to look, then tripped and went down. Sarah gasped, but she could offer no aid, nor, seemingly, could anyone else. She tossed her other knife to Ruith, who caught it, shook the sheath off it, then thrust it upward into the chest of the beast who had tripped and fallen over onto him.

The shrieks were deafening.

She ran over and started to pull the monster off him. She had help. Seirceil was frail, but surprisingly strong. Other hands soon joined in and within moments, Ruith was freed. He sat up slowly, wincing. Sarah looked down at him in horror. The front of his tunic was drenched in blood.

"Ruith—"

He shook his head sharply. "Not mine, don't worry." He accepted his grandfather's hand up. "I think perhaps we should carry on."

"I think we should carry on separately," Franciscus said, resting his axe against his shoulder. He handed Sarah back her knives, cleaned and bearing no mark of their recent activity. "I'm not sure how to say this politely, Ruith my lad, but those creatures weren't interested in anyone but you."

Sarah looked at Franciscus in surprise. "What are you saying, then?"

He looked at her. "They were coming for our wee swordmaster there. Didn't you notice?"

"I'm embarrassed to say I was too busy trying to keep myself alive to notice anything but how best to do that."

Sgath laughed and began to clean used arrows on the greening grass. "I fear my answer is the same as Mistress Sarah's." He looked up at Franciscus. "But I think you have it aright. They weren't interested in me."

"I'm not certain I wasn't just the easiest target," Ruith said, panting. "Perhaps we should try an experiment. I'll take a different route and we'll regroup in a handful of days and see who has survived."

Sarah wasn't sure what was louder, Seirceil's hound's yipping or Ned's squeaking. She couldn't say that she wouldn't be happy to be free of both.

Franciscus only laughed and went to collect his charges. Sarah stood there, clutching the knives Ruith had given her and feeling them very warm in her hands. She looked down in surprise and saw firelight glittering along the edges of the blades she hadn't managed to yet resheath.

Firelight that wasn't being reflected from the pile of smoldering coals ten paces from her.

"We need to go now."

Sarah tore her attention away from what she held in her hands in time to see the look Ruith gave his grandfather. Sgath tried to lift Ruith's tunic, but Ruith shook his head sharply.

"Leave it. Let's go."

"Don't be a fool, Ruith—"

Ruith started to argue again, then sighed. He pulled up the edge of his tunic himself, then cursed. The blood he wore was most definitely more of his than he no doubt wanted to admit to.

"Did one of them stick a knife through you?" Sgath asked in astonishment.

"Just a wee nick," Ruith said dismissively. "I've gone soft."

"Aye, in the head," Sgath said. "We need—"

"To find someone with magic, aye, I agree," Ruith said. "As I have none, we'll have to search—"

Oban elbowed Ned aside. He pushed the sleeves of his courtly robe up to his elbows, took a firm grip on his wand, and waved it over Ruith, scattering what Sarah could have sworn were fat black-and-yellow bumblebees.

But the blood was gone and the wound closed. Ruith didn't look much better, but he also was no longer sporting a hole in his side. He smiled at Oban, complimented him on the added delights they'd enjoyed with that bit of healing, then went to collect his weapons.

Sarah watched him carefully. He moved more easily, but she just couldn't believe that was all there was to it. She thought about that whilst she commended Castân to Ned's care, bid farewell to the mages, then turned to Franciscus for a final word.

"That didn't heal him," she said bluntly.

Franciscus looked at her, clear-eyed. "Then I suppose you'll have to see to it."

"You know I cannot," she said in a very low voice.

"Sarah, my sweet gel, I know nothing of the sort," he said, though he was a terrible liar and exactly what he knew showed quite plainly on his face. "You'll find what you need along the way, perhaps," he offered. "Put him to bed and tend him. I know where your lad is making for. We'll wait for you there."

She nodded, because she could do nothing else. She collected her gear, such as it was, and walked over to find Sgath saddling Ruith's horse for him. She ducked under Ruith's arm and pulled it over her shoulders.

"Lean on me," she commanded.

"I'm we—"

"Lean on me, you fool," she whispered harshly. "Now, do you need me to ride with you to keep you in the saddle, or can you manage that?"

"A beautiful woman with her arms around me for as long as I look feeble," he gasped. "I think I'll drag the entire affair out endlessly."

"Shut up."

"Does that mean you're reneging?" he managed.

Sarah looked at Sgath, who didn't appear nearly as lighthearted as his grandson. He helped Ruith up into his saddle, then looked at her.

"Can you hold him?"

She nodded without hesitation. "How far?"

"How fleet are your horses?"

"How much speed can your grandson bear?"

Sgath smiled briefly, then gave her a leg up. "Follow me. We'll be there by dawn if we make haste."

She nodded, wrapped her arms around Ruith's waist, and pulled him back against her. He wouldn't lean, though.

"I might fall off and ruin my visage," he panted.

"You have an overinflated opinion of the fairness of your face."

"All the more reason to stay awake longer so you might point that out a time or two more."

She would have attempted something else to take his mind off the wound that had started to ooze again—she could feel it—but she couldn't. She was more worried than she wanted to admit—and not just about Ruith's side. He had it aright.

Those monsters weren't coming for her, they were coming for him.

She wondered what an unmagical swordsman who'd lived for two decades in the mountains of a county that all sensible men avoided could possibly have done to attract such creatures.

And there she had thought finding Daniel was going to be the most dangerous part of the journey. She realized now just how wrong she'd been.

Sixteen

Ruith had had better journeys to Lake Cladach.

He supposed the only thing to be grateful for was that he honestly didn't remember much of the current one. Sarah had shaken him awake several times, which meant he'd slept away most of the night, and she had held him close, which he wished he had paid more attention to, and she had managed to keep him on his horse after they'd stopped long enough for his grandfather to dismount and catch him before he fell off and truly did do damage to his face.

"Herbs, sir?" Sarah asked, following hard on Sgath's heels.

"You'll find a variety of things down by the lake, my dear," Sgath said, grunting a bit as he set Ruith on his feet. "Don't lose yourself, though. Sunrise is near, but the woods are still very thick."

Ruith looked blearily at Sarah. "Take him at his word and be careful, though I'm more worried about you becoming enamored of the surroundings and forgetting to return."

She put her hand on his back. "You talk a great deal for someone in such pain."

"I'm not in such pain," he said, and that was true. He was past pain. He was in absolute agony. Whatever had been on that creature's knife had done more than a usual bit of damage. Either that, or Oban's spell had been less useful than he'd dared hope it would be.

He watched Sarah walk off, then leaned heavily on his grandfather as they made their way to the house. It would have been very strange indeed to consider that he was walking where he hadn't in a score of years and never thought to again, but he was far too busy thinking on whether or not he would manage to survive the day. He jumped when a fire leapt to life in the hearth, then looked at his grandfather.

"Perhaps you shouldn't. She thinks I have no magic."

"I gathered that," Sgath said dryly, "but I didn't imagine that included me."

Ruith pursed his lips. "I did tell her that my parents had magic, so I suppose she might assume you have a bit, but that doesn't fit in with your persona as a simple fisherman, does it?"

"I could be a modest mage," Sgath said with a bit of a shrug. "One of those lads too humble to make a fuss." He frowned. "I'm not sure I understand why your Sarah hasn't healed you."

Ruith caught his breath as he stepped wrong, then had to concentrate on simply walking for a bit. He paused at the doorway to one of the bedchambers and looked at his grandfather.

"She cannot. She's the witchwoman Seleg's daughter, but she apparently has no magic."

Sgath looked at him in surprise. "Why not? Seleg is—"

"Was—"

"Very well, she *was* very powerful. Her daughter should have inherited some of that."

"You would think so, wouldn't you?" Ruith said, clutching the doorframe to keep himself upright. "Could we discuss this later? I think I might be ill soon."

"You don't look good," Sgath agreed, "which begs the question about where *your* magic is and why you didn't have it to use to protect yourself." He frowned. "I sense only an echo of it."

"Didn't I tell you about it last night?" Ruith asked sourly.

"I thought I was having a nightmare. Now, come over here and lie down, lad, before you fall there."

He shook his head. "I'll ruin the bedding. Just let me sit and bleed on that chair over there." He was appalled by how hard he was leaning on Sgath, but there was nothing to be done about it. He sank down onto a hard wooden chair and leaned back with a ginger sigh. "I didn't expect this."

"I have the feeling, son, that you could say that about many things," Sgath said. He sat down on the bed and smiled faintly. "So, first things first. What am I to do with this hole in your side?"

Ruith winced. "Admit to a little power, if you must."

"I don't see that you have a choice," Sgath said, "or you won't last until morning. I would like one answer, however, just to set my mind at rest. What did you do with your heritage?"

Ruith met his eyes steadily. "I took it all, every last drop of the magic I possessed, shoved it into a well inside myself, and shut it all in with a spell of concealment I stole from Uachdaran of Léige."

Sgath closed his eyes briefly. "I suppose I understand why."

"Just so you know, I had help with the appropriation of that bit of magic."

"Let me guess," Sgath said, pursing his lips. "Miach of Neroche convinced you it was something you both needed to round out your ever-growing collection of things you shouldn't have memorized."

Ruith managed a smile. "I convinced him, for a change. I imagine I shouldn't admit how often that was the case, lest my lily-white reputation find itself sullied." He looked up at the sound of a footstep. "Here is Sarah."

"I'll see to it."

Ruith closed his eyes and surrendered gratefully to events he wasn't responsible for controlling. He listened to his grandfather and Sarah discuss herbs and healing and the fact that she had never in her life imagined such a beautiful place as what she could see from Sgath's front porch. Ruith suspected he might have slept for a bit because he woke to the feel of cold air on his side, followed by cold fingers on his skin.

"See?" she said quietly. "There is something there. Some thread of something . . . wrong."

"I can't see anything."

Ruith opened his eyes to find them both kneeling in front of him, peering intently at his side. Sarah looked at Sgath.

"That black thread of something there," she said, touching Ruith's skin near the wound. "'Tis barbed and covered with drops of something I don't know how to name." She looked at Sgath. "Poison, perhaps?"

Sgath shook his head. "I have no idea, my dear, for I can't see it at all. But my sight isn't as clear as yours."

Sarah studied Ruith's flesh for a moment, then drew forth one of her knives.

"Are you going to finish the job?" Ruith asked, feeling faintly alarmed.

She met his eyes. Her face was full of what another might have called determination, and that no doubt in spite of the fact that her other hand resting on his knee was trembling. Determination, apprehension, and no small bit of plain fear.

"I'm thinking on how that creature screamed when it encountered my knife in his eye," she ventured. "I wonder what this knife would do to that thread if I were to try to pull it from your flesh?"

"Leave me shrieking in pain?"

"We'll try just the same," she said, looking closely at his side. She reached out and touched what looked to be nothing.

Ruith felt a white-hot strand of pain flare, then disappear. Sarah cut off her sleeve and stanched a new flow of blood.

"Interesting," Sgath said, sounding more interested than he should have been. "And what, Sarah my dear, is that horrible business on your arm?"

"Nothing," she said dismissively. "It was much worse before Ruith made me a poultice. I need to find a mage to tend it properly, I think."

"Hmmm," Sgath said, "well, perhaps you'll find one in your travels—and rather sooner than later, if you want my suggestion. I might have something in a cabinet that might serve you until that happy day. Now, shall I be about healing this lad so he can have a nap? I'll take you for a walk and show you all the best spots for catching lake trout, if you're interested."

"Only if I can try my hand at it using one of the lures you have poked into your hat."

Sgath reached up and felt his head, then laughed. "I left in such haste, I'd forgotten what I was wearing. Of course, my girl. You'll have your choice. But let's see to my grandson here. What sort of thing shall we use?"

"I only know things of my mother's," Sarah admitted, "though they have never worked for me. Have you nothing of your own to use?"

"Perhaps."

"Then you do it," Sarah said without hesitation. "I'll keep him from running away."

Sgath laughed softly. "As you will, my dear."

Ruith closed his eyes and sighed deeply. He was quite happy to listen to his grandfather use a modest though quite efficacious spell of Camanaë. His grandfather had no bloodright to it, being of Ainneamh himself, but he certainly had the power to use whatever suited him.

Ruith felt the wound heal as if it had never been there. He opened his eyes and looked blearily at the pair kneeling in front of him.

"Better," he managed.

"Sleep," Sgath suggested.

"I just might."

"We'll leave you to it," Sgath said, rising and offering a hand to Sarah.

Ruith felt Sarah's hand briefly on his head, smiled reflexively, then waited until he heard the chamber door close before he stripped off his clothes and crawled happily into bed, feeling as lighthearted and secure as a ten-year-old. He closed his eyes and listened without compunction to the conversation going on briefly on the other side of the door.

"He never sleeps," Sarah said. "I think he has nightmares."

"Then we'll watch over him today and see if he can't manage a decent bit of napping. He'll be safe enough in the house, I daresay, whilst we go see what the lake will surrender."

"Aye, please," Sarah said, sounding as if nothing could have delighted her more. "You're fortunate to call such beauty yours."

"I am merely its steward for a few years," Sgath said modestly, "but aye, I am fortunate."

A few years. Aye, Ruith thought to himself, twelve centuries full of them at last count, and that didn't add to the tally the years he'd lived in the land of Ainneamh where flowers never ceased to bloom.

He heard the front door shut. Sarah would be perfectly safe with his grandfather to protect her and he himself would be the happy beneficiary of the spells that guarded his grandfather's land, even a little house that lay a league around the top of the lake from Sgath's true home.

He sighed deeply, then turned over and fell into the first peaceful sleep he'd had in years.

He woke to the smell of supper. He could tell from the light in the window that the sun would be setting soon, which meant he had slept most of the day away. He had to admit he'd needed it. Perhaps he could convince Sarah to take her turn and actually have a full night's rest.

He had a wash, donned clean clothing that had doubtless been conjured for him by his grandfather, then walked out and followed the glorious scent of something he hadn't cooked himself.

He almost tripped over the equally glorious Sarah of Doìre, freshly washed and dressed as well, sitting in front of the fire and drying her hair by its heat. He'd never in his life seen hair like hers. A riot of curls that straightened into fatter, less numerous but no less lovely curls after a day or two in a braid. He was tempted to offer to braid her hair for her, but that would have meant taming it and he wasn't sure he wanted to see that happen quite yet.

He sat down on a stool behind her, within easy reach on the off chance she needed her hair brushed for her. She looked over her shoulder at him.

"You look better."

"I feel better, thank you," he said with a smile. He rested his elbows on his knees. "How was the fishing?"

"Your grandfather's lure made all the difference," she said. "And you'll be pleased to know he did the cooking."

"I never said you couldn't cook."

She pursed her lips at him, then turned to Sgath. "I won't tell you what he *has* said about my turns at the cooking fire. We'll just say he prefers what Master Franciscus combines in the pot."

"Appalling," Sgath said, with mock horror. "I worry about his manners."

"I wouldn't admit it to him, but his manners are quite lovely. After all, he did buy me a horse and a pair of daggers."

"Rather he should have bought you flowers, or something made from silk."

"Oh, he did buy me a silk blouse," Sarah said without hesitation. "But I made him cut it from me before I took a knife to it myself. Too many ruffles."

Ruith met his grandfather's startled eyes, then smiled as Sgath burst into hearty laughter.

"Then perhaps daggers are more appropriate." He put his hands on his knees and rose. "Let's go eat, children; then Sarah should have a rest, given that she provided us with supper."

An hour later, Ruith was lingering at a well-worn table with his grandfather and his . . . er, *friend*, and he found himself marveling at the complete improbability of being where he was. He was sitting with a grandfather he'd never thought to see again and it was as if no time at all had passed. He was nursing wine he was certain his grandfather *hadn't* distilled in the shed behind the house, and he was looking at a woman who made the room sparkle with her smiles, her laughter, and her obvious enjoyment of one of Ruith's favorite people.

Which she was also fast becoming.

He felt pressure on his toes and focused on her. "What?" he asked with a smile.

"I think you need to sleep again," she said. "You're daydreaming."

He shook his head slowly. "Just enjoying."

She set her glass away from her and hid a yawn behind her hand. "I fear if I enjoy any more, I'll fall asleep with my face in my plate and wake not remembering why I'm wearing what I couldn't finish eating."

Sgath pushed his chair back immediately and rose. Ruith rose without being asked, because his mother had taught him decent manners in spite of himself.

"I'll show you to another bedchamber," Sgath began.

"Nay," Sarah said quickly. She took a deep breath and put on a smile. "I appreciate the offer, my—" She looked at Sgath and laughed a little. "I keep wanting to call you *my lord*, but I can't fathom why."

"My wife says exactly the same thing," Sgath said without hesitation. "But you needn't, Sarah dear. You might call me anything you liked and I wouldn't take offense. Now, about your sleeping—"

"The fire will be more than enough," she said. "I would actually prefer it, if you don't mind. Doors make me feel trapped. There's no reason for it, of course." She shrugged. "I just prefer the fire nearby."

Ruith decided it was best not to even look at his grandfather, first because he couldn't bear to think of Sarah living with that hellishly unpleasant witch in Doìre, and second, in the language of Camanaë, his father's first language, Ruithneadh meant *fire*.

Not that Sarah would have known that.

He was tempted to poach the rest of that bottle of wine, shut himself behind a sturdy door, and drink himself into oblivion. But before he could truly examine the merits of that plan, he found himself standing with Sarah in front of a pallet and blankets his grandfather was currently making up for her. Sgath had centuries of practice, having done the same countless times for other guests. Even the high ones of Camanaë and Ainneamh hadn't been above a night or two in Sgath's Folly, as they called it.

"This has been very nice," Sarah said quietly. She looked up at him. "Thank you for bringing me."

"Thank you for making it so I was able to eat supper," he said with a faint smile.

"I don't think I did very much," she said. She paused. "Your grandfather's power is . . . immense."

"He has been a good steward of it," Ruith said, wanting nothing more than to avoid discussing that, or how she knew, or what else she knew. He put his hand on the small of her back. "Shall I stay with you—"

She smiled a quick smile. "I think you can guard me just as easily from outside, if that fire your grandfather built in his pit is where you're headed."

"Do you mind?"

"Don't be daft." She pointed to the door. "He made do quite politely with me, but I know he's anxious to have you to himself a bit more."

"Call me if you need me."

"I will." She smiled. "Get on with ye, lad, and ease your grand-daddy's heart."

He did, though he did look over his shoulder once as he paused at the doorway. Sarah was standing in front of the fire, holding her hands out to its blaze, looking almost at peace. It was the first time he'd seen her so and he looked perhaps a bit longer than he should have. She glanced at him, smiled, then waved him off before she turned back to the fire.

He stumbled out of the house, down the steps, and along the path that led the short distance to the roaring fire his grandfather had indeed built in his pit. He found his grandfather sitting on a two-foot-high slice of a tree that was one of many surrounding that fire that he'd no doubt started by hand. Sgath was, as it happened, that sort of man.

Sarah would have approved.

Ruith took another step forward, but had to stop. He could see as if it were happening afresh a scene in front of him. His mother sitting with her parents-in-law, laughing as she held her daughter on her lap. Some of his brothers had been sitting at their grandfa-ther's feet, listening to him spin some impossible tale of glory and ogres, whilst others had been enjoying the remains of their meal.

He could see himself holding a book up to the fire, squinting to read it by the flickering light. It had been a book of spells. He was fairly certain he'd eventually taken the book inside and read it by that fire that Sarah was currently warming her hands against.

He had been, he had to admit, obsessed.

"Ruith?"

He blinked and the scene was gone. He was a little winded, but since that seemed to have become his normal condition of late, he thought nothing of it. He walked over to sit on the stump next to his grandfather, accepted a cup of mulled wine, and sipped. He sighed in pleasure.

"Lovely."

"Been drinking stream water, son?"

Ruith laughed a little uneasily. "You don't want to know what I've been drinking, Grandfather."

Sgath reached out and put his hand on Ruith's shoulder briefly, then held his own cup between his hands. "You told me very briefly last night of your adventures these past twenty years. I suppose I can draw my own conclusions as to why you didn't drag yourself here where you would have been safe and comfortable. Or should I inquire as to the specifics?"

"Don't," Ruith said, more sharply than he intended. He attempted a smile. "I'm sorry. I meant—"

Sgath shook his head, just as sharply. "I shouldn't have asked. But one day, Ruithneadh, you and I will descend into my very fine cellar across the way, indulge quite thoroughly in too much of what we find there; then you will tell me what your heart cannot bear to now. But here, I want you to tell me what it is you're about and what that has to do with a certain fiery lass resting so peacefully inside the house."

Ruith smiled. "She is fierce, I'll admit."

"She would have to be. I'm surprised she survived her mother's temper without having it embitter her. I'm even more surprised anyone braved that woman's temper long enough to spawn any children with her. How did your lady remain so sweet?"

"I would imagine 'tis a combination of having spent as little time with her mother as possible and a resolve to be nothing like her."

"Determined, is she?"

"Frighteningly so." He considered the fire for a bit, then sighed. "Her brother is the reason she left home and I followed her. She asked for my aid, thinking I was a centuries-old, vile-tempered curmudgeon—"

"Who I'm sure you patterned after Sìle of Tòrr Dòrainn."

Ruith laughed in spite of himself. "I fear I had no opportunity to display any of my maternal grandfather's most autocratic ways to the locals, though he no doubt would have considered it a vast compliment to his admittedly quite superior self."

"He would have," Sgath agreed. "So, that lovely woman sought you out, then what? You fell for her instantly?"

"I haven't fallen anywhere."

"Ruithneadh, you are a terrible liar."

"And you're a terrible romantic."

"I want grandchildren. And I like the look of her."

"A witchwoman's daughter?" Ruith asked quietly. "A witchwoman's daughter who doesn't have a shred of magic to her name?"

"Perhaps you underestimate her. She lit the candles for supper."

"*I* lit the candles for supper," Ruith said dryly, "whilst she was admiring your fishing gear."

"I hadn't noticed," Sgath said promptly. "I was distracted by the thought of more grandchildren. And how is it you did what she could not? I thought you said you buried all your magic with that dastardly spell you and the youngling from Neroche pilfered."

Ruith shrugged. "I briefly freed it to heal Seirceil of Coibhneas.

I don't think I managed to stuff it all back where it belonged." He shot Sgath a sideways look. "Little bits of Fadaire escaped. They've been causing me trouble ever since."

"I would say they *would*, being what they are, but that would disparage your sweet mother, which I could never think to do." He set his cup aside, then leaned back with his hands wrapped around his knee. "What did you and Miach want that spell for, anyway?"

"To hide dessert from our elder brothers," Ruith said solemnly.

Sgath laughed. "That doesn't surprise me, especially considering Adhémar's fondness for sweet cakes."

"If he doesn't weigh twenty stone by now, I'll be surprised," Ruith said sourly. "How is the illustrious king of Neroche? As obnoxious as ever?"

Sgath smiled deeply. "I've avoided any royal visits from him, though I did manage to drag myself to his coronation, out of respect for his parents. I'm certain he's slowly driving Miach mad, or so Miach says when he can endure Tor Neroche no longer and comes to visit. He arrives on wing, as you might imagine, shakes off in my courtyard whatever shape he's taken, then happily lingers at my table as long as I'll let him before I send him off to bed." He shook his head. "You would like him still, I imagine. The mantle of archmage has sobered him, but not soured him. I assume you heard of his calling."

"I assumed it would fall to him should something happen to Queen Desdhemar," Ruith agreed. "Riding accident, or something less pleasant?"

Sgath looked at him, openmouthed. "She died rescuing Miach from Lothar's dungeon. Good heavens, Ruith, where *have* you been?"

Ruith realized his own mouth was hanging open. "What in the hell was he doing *there*?"

"Being an arrogant young man, I imagine. He won't talk about it, but I understand from others that he was riding the border without a guard and found himself overcome. Desdhemar and Anghmar both perished rescuing him." He shook his head and sighed. "He keeps Lothar on the far side of his northern border, though I can't help but feel things will come to a head between the two of them someday. 'Tis a pity, really. I think Miach would like nothing better than to retreat to some piece of land near Chagailt and grow turnips. He's spent his share of time eyeing my vast stretches of fertile farmland, if you're curious."

"No lady for him yet?"

"I think Adhémar's tried several times. You know Miach, though. He can be slightly . . . How shall we say it?"

"Intense," Ruith said without hesitation. "Driven. Colored by an annoying tendency to do good at any cost. All character flaws, I'm sure. He should watch his back. He'll find himself falling for some wench someday who'll send him in circles."

"I can scarce wait to see who she'll be," Sgath said with another deep smile. "I imagine he would offer the same happy wish to you, did he know you were alive. But we digress from details I want and you don't want to give. Your lady came to you for aid and you did what?"

Ruith knew he should have corrected his grandfather. Sarah was not and likely would never want to be his lady, even if he wanted her to be such—which he was fairly certain he didn't. He fully intended to do for her what he'd offered to, then retreat to his house and hide.

Only now, he might have to make the occasional visit to Lake Cladach. And if Sgath and Eulasaid knew, then word would eventually leak out and his other grandparents would know and then he would most definitely need to visit there.

And he would have to visit Sarah as well, and make certain she was safe, and happy, and had enough sheep to provide the wool she needed for her art.

"Ruith?"

He looked at his grandfather. "What?"

Sgath smiled. "You know, I offered her a bit of land down the way. There's that little clearing that I've been keeping to myself for the past few centuries. Just right for a little house, on the right part of the lake for the sun to warm a garden, close enough that a quick walk would bring her to the big house."

The big house. Taigh-mòr, it was called, and it rivaled any elven palace he'd ever traipsed through.

Ruith looked at his grandfather. "Are you trying to kill me?"

"I want more grandchildren."

"Don't you have enough?"

"I want some from you."

Ruith rolled his eyes, because it was either that or heartily agree with his grandfather that providing those joys for him was a perfectly reasonable thing to do.

Sgath waved him on. "I'm vexing you overmuch. Go on with your tale. Sarah sought you out, but you didn't tell me why."

"She feared her brother was off to do evil," he said, turning his thoughts in less pleasant directions. "She was particularly concerned about a torn page from a book she had seen briefly on her brother's table. We found another page she's sure was in the same hand." He had to take a deep breath. "It was a page from my father's book of spells."

Sgath's eyes widened briefly, then he rubbed his hands over his face. "Hell."

"Well, I'm afraid that's what we'll be living in if I don't find it."

Sgath stared into the fire for several minutes in silence, then looked at him with a sigh. "What spell was it, do you suppose, that the lad had found?"

"The spell of Diminishing."

Sgath's verbal reaction was quite a bit more vile that time.

Ruith shrugged. "I suppose we're fortunate that someone

laboring under a severe overestimation of his power found it—and that he only has half of it. And I'll answer what you haven't stopped swearing long enough to ask. Sarah's brother, Daniel, has gone from mage to mage, trying out what he has. He's managed to take one man's voice—but that only because the mage wasn't expecting it. The second man lost a bit of his . . ." He shook his head. "I'm not sure how to describe it. 'Twas Seirceil of Coibhneas who was attacked. He didn't lose his power; he lost his ability—temporarily—to make it do his will. He's recovered now, mostly, though still unsettled by the experience. But anything else? Nay, Daniel hasn't managed anything else."

"Is he making up the end of the spell, or has he looked for another spell of Taking? Perhaps Lothar of Wychweald's?" Sgath added with a fair bit of distaste.

"I have no idea." Ruith paused. "Do you think that my father would have purposely scattered his book, or . . ."

"I would choose 'or,'" Sgath said without hesitation. "I heard a rumor that the library at Ceangail was burned. 'Tis possible that someone found his private book of spells and took it, then perhaps lost it, or fought over it, or hid it intending to come back and fetch it later. Have you any idea where Daniel came by what he has?"

Ruith shook his head. "I understand the spell of Diminishing was found in a peddler's cart. Daniel stole my father's spell of Reconstruction in Connail of Iomadh's hall. That one was, I fear, mostly intact, though I suspect Daniel doesn't have the power to use it properly. Not as my sire would have used it."

"Your father's imagination knew no bounds, unfortunately," Sgath agreed. He looked at Ruith seriously. "What of those beasts I saw last night? They seemed particularly interested in you."

"So it seems." He paused for a moment or two before he could go on. "They are fashioned from some sort of substance that seems . . . well, liquid, for lack of a better word."

Sgath frowned. "Indeed? How many have you seen to know this?"

"I killed my first pair in the mountains, a month ago perhaps. I examined one's tunic and found it solid, yet not. More unsettling still, it gave off an odor I recognized." He paused, then met his grandfather's gaze. "It was the same stench of evil that came from the well."

Sgath closed his eyes briefly, then looked at Ruith. "Ah, my boy, I'm so sorry."

"So am I," Ruith agreed, striving for a lighter tone, "for I daresay it means I should make a visit there to see what's afoot. Fortunately, I have the diligent Daniel of Doìre paving the way for me, first no doubt to the well, then to Ceangail itself."

"But you won't take Sarah to either place," Sgath said, sounding faintly horrified.

"I don't think she'll stay behind," Ruith said slowly, "though I certainly don't want her to come with me." He paused. "In truth, I'm not sure where she would be the safest. As canny as he is, I'm not sure I would trust Franciscus to guard her."

"Oh, I don't know about that," Sgath said, with a faint smile. "You might be surprised at that one's resourcefulness. But I understand your thinking. There is no better guardsman for a lass than a man who loves her."

Ruith shot his grandfather a look he blithely ignored. Perhaps it was better not to pursue it. Sgath would only bludgeon him the more with demands for offspring.

Sgath sighed suddenly. "'Tis a pity my son chose such a path. I grieve for the harm he did to so many others besides himself."

"Was he ever thus?" Ruith asked, before he thought better of it. It was a question he hadn't been able to ask in his youth. He'd been far too busy hating the man and looking for every way possible to help him destroy himself.

"That, my boy, is something I ask myself even now," Sgath said with a weary smile. "Your grandmother and I had seven children, as you know, and Gair was the youngest. One doesn't particularly want to look at one's offspring and see darkness, but I will concede that there was even from an early age a lack of empathy. His elder brothers were quick to offer aid when called for, his sisters compassion, but Gair would simply stand to the side and watch, as if the trouble didn't touch him."

"How did he ever convince my mother to wed him?" Ruith asked in disbelief.

"He could be very charming, as you well know. He was certainly on his best behavior with her, apparently long enough to sire seven children. I wasn't unwilling to believe that fair Sarait had wrought a miracle and inspired a change in his nature." He paused and stared into the fire. "It wasn't you, or Mhorghain, or even Gille or Eglach who drove him to madness, if that's what you've wondered."

"Then who? Keir?"

"Nay, it was none of you, yet perhaps all of you together. I think it angered him more with each child that he might have spawned something to rival his power or his place in the world."

"Do you feel that way about your own children?"

Sgath looked at him in surprise, then he laughed. "Of course not, you wee fool." He laughed again, then shook his head. "My only complaint with my children is that after all these centuries, you would think they could have provided me with more grand-children to bring here and teach to fish."

"Do you even have an accurate count of your grandchildren any longer?"

"Forty-nine," Sgath said with a smug look, "and that doesn't include their very fine mates, or their children, or their children's children. And even though I keep building on, they keep repro-ducing. 'Tis an endless task for me, but a welcome one. I will say, however, that there are several little ones who insist on sleeping with your grandmother and me when they visit."

"How terrible for you."

"I'll send them to sleep with you after you finish your quest and you can suffer their toes digging into your back all through the night."

Ruith was torn between pain at the thought of being the only of his family alive to visit, and a surprising feeling of happiness that he might actually have a place to go where he would be welcomed for who he was. He looked at Sgath. "I'll come."

"Alone?"

Ruith dragged his hand through his hair. "Stop matchmaking."

"I like her."

Ruith sighed. "So do I."

"Finish your quest, then woo her."

"I'm not sure she'll want me once she learns who I am."

"You are not your father," Sgath said seriously, "but that's a conversation for another day as well. Go see to your quest, find that fool of a brother your lady has, and stop him, but keep in mind that you have a place to come to when you're finished."

Ruith nodded, because he couldn't speak.

"And if there turns out to be more to this quest than stopping Daniel of Doìre, remember that there are still those in the world who would aid you without question."

"You?" Ruith asked quietly.

Sgath's eyes glistened suddenly, but he snorted quickly—no doubt in an effort to distract from it. "Me? Of course not. I'll be building on more chambers for your children. I was thinking you might try some of your mother's kin, actually. I'm certain Sìle is always up for a decent adventure."

Ruith smiled in spite of himself. "If he can drag himself away from his supper, that is."

"I want it noted that you said that, not I, though that is the reason I never go on quests. It disrupts the digestion." He put his hands on his knees and rose. "Go to bed, son. I'll walk about the place and see to our tranquility."

Ruith looked up at his grandfather. "Don't you have spells for that sort of thing?"

His grandfather only laughed and ruffled Ruith's hair on the way by just as he'd done dozens of times in the past. Ruith scowled at his back.

"Is there an age at which you stop doing that to your grand-children?"

"Four hundred ninety-nine," came the answer over Sgath's shoulder.

Ruith smiled to himself, then rose and stretched. He took his mug back into the cabin, set it in the sink, then went to look for a blanket. He found one easily, then stretched out in front of the fire with his head near Sarah's. He leaned up on one elbow and looked at her, asleep with her hands curled under her chin and an expression of complete peace on her face.

He looked for quite a while, truth be told.

She stirred after a bit. "You smell like fire and night," she murmured.

"And you're so beautiful it hurts me to look at you."

Her eyes opened and he realized she hadn't been quite as asleep as he'd thought.

"Strange," she said very gravely. "I think that about you too."

He closed his eyes briefly, then laid his head down, brushing her hair out of the way first. If there was a finger's width between the tops of their heads, he would have been surprised.

He knew he should have thought about his plans, or considered his father's madness, or invented some other plan that might have been useful in saving the world.

Instead, he reached up and laid his hand on the floor and hoped he wasn't making a terrible mistake. In truth, he was taking a terrible risk, but there was no turning back now. Not from the path that led into darkness, not from the path that might possibly lead to the ruin of his heart.

She put her hand in his.

He closed his eyes and slept.

Dreamlessly.

Seventeen

Sarah sat atop her horse and looked back down the path. The trees were too thick to give her a perfect view of the lake, but there was enough there to please her. Snow was still on the ground in the higher elevations, but along the shore she could see the rich soil giving way eventually to a particularly lovely beach. She knew she shouldn't have been surprised. The entire place seemed charmed somehow, as if there were someone watching over it who loved it very much.

"Ready?"

She looked at Ruith and shook her head. "Another moment or two, if you don't mind—" She winced. "I'm sorry. I wasn't thinking about you. You must be anxious to put it behind you now the decision to carry on has been made."

Not that he'd seemed particularly anxious that morning. She'd woken to find him sitting on the floor at her head, talking to his grandfather, who sat next to the fire. They had been engaging in a friendly discussion about who was a more reliable producer of drinkable wine, the brewers of Penrhyn or the elves of Ainneamh. They didn't seem to come to any conclusion, but during the discussion, she had her hair brushed and braided by a man who had seemed perfectly content to linger over the task.

His mien did change after he and Sgath had had a quiet word apart down by the lake. She had left them to it, mostly because she had felt uncomfortable intruding on their time as much as she had. That, and she hadn't wanted discussion of the world outside Lake Cladach to color her memories of it—

"Sarah, there was never any doubt about what I intended to do," Ruith said quietly.

She pulled herself back to the present and looked at him, his dark hair shining in the sun, his too-beautiful face wearing a very serious expression, and found it was all she could do not to fall off her horse, bid him do the same, and fling herself into his arms.

The past day had been very hard on her heart.

"Look your fill, my lady," he said gravely. "I don't blame you."

She found that quite suddenly she couldn't see as much as she would have liked. Perhaps she was weary. Perhaps it was just that she had felt, for the first time in her life, at peace and safe. Leaving it behind had been more difficult than she'd suspected it might be.

"I never imagined such a place could exist," she said, shrugging helplessly. "The flowers . . . well, they *glow*. And the trees whisper when you walk under them. The water laughed as your grandsire and I waded out into it. And over it all is laid some sort of magic that seems to wrap itself over and around the entire place to keep—." She shut her mouth suddenly. "I suppose you knew that already."

He shook his head slowly, his eyes wide. "I don't think I would have heard any of that, or seen it, even if I had been paying attention."

"What were you doing the last time you were there?"

"Flinging knives into targets I'd strapped to trees."

She smiled in spite of herself. "I imagine you wouldn't have wanted to hear what they said during that."

"I imagine not," he agreed. "I was a lad of ten summers. I was more concerned about keeping up with my brothers than anything else."

"How many did you have?"

"Five elder," he said with a shrug. "All gone now, save me."

"I'm so sorry," she said, feeling altogether sorry she'd asked. "I shouldn't have said anything."

"I should have told you sooner. I won't give you the rest of the tale now, but I will someday. For now, tell me what else you saw," he said abruptly, "and I'll see if it matches my memories."

She was very happy to describe all sorts of things for him, flora, fauna, and animal life that seemed to be so much more aware than she'd imagined they could be. She was torn between looking at him and looking back at the land behind her.

She was surprised to realize she wasn't sure what she wanted more.

Her dream lay behind her. Sgath had promised to introduce her to whoever owned that little cove he'd showed her, the one that lay to the south where the sun was just right for growing all sorts of things. She could easily imagine a little house there, with sheep grazing on the hill behind it and a garden to the side. She would have been close enough to Gilean to sell her weaving, but far enough away that no one would have troubled her.

Odd, but it sounded far more lonely than it should have.

"What did you think of Sgath?"

She looked away from the lake and turned to Ruith. She smiled. "He was . . . " She had to think about the word for moment or two. "He was whole."

Ruith looked at her with a puzzled frown. "How do you mean?"

"I mean he was who he is, though I think he possesses a great deal more magic than he lets on." She shrugged. "I'm not good at seeing much, though I am better than I was before."

"What do you see in me?"

She pursed her lips. "I think you're fishing for a compliment."

He blew his hair out of his eyes. "And I would deserve what I had in return, believe me." He shook his head. "I even slept quite well last night, but here I am asking ridiculous questions."

"It isn't," she protested. She had seen many things, but most of them had to do with the perfection of his face. She supposed those weren't what he was asking. She studied him for a moment or two in silence, then smiled faintly. "You are the sun behind a cloud."

He blinked. "What?"

"A very large, intimidating cloud, if that makes you feel any better."

His eyes widened. "What do you mean?"

She shrugged. "You, whatever you are and whoever you are, are hidden behind something rather intimidating." She shrugged again, because it sounded completely daft. "I slept quite well too, but perhaps it wasn't enough."

Actually, she'd slept less well than she would have liked to claim. The pallet was marvelously soft and comfortable, the fire seemingly always at the perfect temperature, and the protection that enveloped the house a tangible thing. Even holding Ruith's hand in front of her face hadn't been a burden.

On the contrary.

She was fairly sure she'd slept a goodly amount, but not particularly a goodly quality. She couldn't even credit it to sleeping so close, albeit chastely, to a man, something she'd never done before. It began and ended with the fact that Ruith disturbed her. She thought about him when she should have been thinking about her quest, or her funds, or what would happen after her quest was finished.

Actually, after having spent the night with his hand wrapped around hers, she supposed she was finished before the quest had a chance to do the same to her.

She met his eyes. He looked no less startled than he had before, but added to that was something else. She shifted uncomfortably.

"What is it?"

He shook his head slowly. "You are a remarkable woman, Sarah of Doìre," he said. He smiled faintly. "Have you looked enough, or shall we stay a bit longer? I'm talking about the lake, of course. You, fortunately, have me to look at anytime."

She felt her mouth fall open. "Why, you vain peacock."

He laughed and it was like sun streaming out from behind that very dark cloud that obscured much of who he was. "I'm teasing you."

"I don't think you are," she said archly. "And aye, I was thinking on the lake." She looked over her shoulder one more time, then she had to turn away before the tears that had sprung suddenly to her eyes overwhelmed her. It had nothing to do with the beauty she was leaving, or the uncertainty before her, or the man who seemed to be wrapped up in both.

Especially not him.

She felt her hand be taken, gently of course. It was the hand Daniel's page had ruined. Nay, that wasn't right. It had been Gair of Ceangail's page to assault her, for what reason she couldn't fathom. She looked down at her hand in Ruith's, then up at him.

"I should have asked your grandfather to look at this before we left this morning," she said, "though it is better than it was, somehow. Perhaps there is healing in the woods."

"I daresay there is. And I'll admit I'm loath to leave these woods, as well. There is something here that is very . . . safe."

"That's the other thing the trees do," she said before she thought better of it. "They watch. But the trees down there don't." She nodded down toward the path they had yet to ride. "At least the ones at the feet of the mountain don't."

"Sarah, what else do you see?" he asked with an uncomfortable laugh.

She shrugged helplessly. "I don't know. Magic, mostly." She swallowed less comfortably than she would have liked. "I never saw anything in Doìre. I don't know what's happening to me." She paused. "I thought there for a bit that I was losing my mind."

"I don't think so." He looked up at the sky for a moment or two, then at her. "There was—*is*, rather—something less than wholesome about Shettlestoune as a whole and Doìre in particular. Something that deadens sight and causes spells to go awry."

"Do you think so?" she asked in surprise.

"I wouldn't know, but I've heard as much," he said. "But I don't think the same holds true here until we reach those unhelpful trees you spoke of. I suppose then I'll have to be the one to keep us safe." He took a deep breath. "Shall we go?"

She nodded, though it was a reluctant nod. She had one last look at the lake behind her, saw a flash of sunlight on a ripple, then turned away. She wanted to believe she would see it again, find herself in a place halfway as lovely, but she wasn't sure she would manage it.

But she would hope for it just the same.

It took a day of hard riding to catch up to the company, and half a se'nnight later as she walked along behind them, she wished it had taken much longer. Whatever peace she had found on Lake Cladach had been replaced with nagging worries that seemed to affect Ruith just as greatly. They saw no sign of Daniel, but that was no guarantee that he wasn't stirring up trouble somewhere.

It came to the point where Ruith's mutterings under his breath began to vex not only her but the rest of them as well. He finally shot her a meaningful look, then announced that he was going to ride ahead and see how the road looked. Even Oban, who seemed less eager than she to be without him, had shooed him on freely.

That had been earlier that morning. Now she studied her knife as she walked, trying to decipher the runes etched into the blade and wrapped around the hilt. She had little success, though she couldn't deny that they gave her a certain measure of security if only because they had already proven themselves in battle. She would have felt better if Ruith had been walking next to her with his own selection of sharp things, but since he wasn't, she would just take what comfort her blades gave her and make do.

At least she hadn't seen anything more of the trolls—yet. She hadn't wanted to ask Sgath about them for it seemed an invasion of the purity of his home, but now she had no choice but to face the possibility of seeing them again. She also wondered, when she could bear to, what mischief Daniel was combining. Ruith was convinced he would hunt for more of the pages of that book, but where those were to be found, neither of them knew. She suspected Ruith had an idea, though, for he often spoke with Master Franciscus about forks in the roads they came to periodically. Ever he chose the right-hand one, the one that kept close to the feet of the mountains and led north.

She woke with a start, realizing that she had dozed off as she walked. And in that moment of sudden waking, three things became terribly clear.

Dusk had fallen.

Second, she had fallen far behind the company and neither she nor the rest of them had noticed.

And lastly, she was standing in front of her brother.

His spell slammed into her before she could blurt out the slightest protest. She had no idea what sort of spell it was, but it rendered her blind. She supposed she should have been grateful for that. At least she could only see but a shadow of her brother standing in front of her. She couldn't imagine she wanted to see his face.

"What are you doing following me?" he spat.

"I wouldn't waste my time with—" She gasped as the ground came up to meet her, hard. Darkness fell around her, a darkness so thick she couldn't breathe.

He cursed her. She knew he was pacing back and forth next to her, snarling, as if he could find no other way to express his anger.

"If you had any magic," he spat, "I would take it."

"I know," she managed.

He stopped suddenly. "You do? Well, of course you do if you've been following me. And I've only begun my work."

"I believe that."

The darkness receded just the slightest bit. She breathed very carefully. She might have had no magic, but she was very skilled in the art of keeping the focus off herself and onto someone else. She wouldn't lie, but she would deflect until she could deflect no more.

Daniel hadn't moved. "Why are you following me?"

"I wanted to stop you," she said, "but I couldn't find a mage to do so."

"And what of this company of fools?"

"They're traveling with Master Franciscus on his journey north." That was the truth. Franciscus was heading north and the others were traveling with him. Whatever else they were doing was none of Daniel's business.

"And what of the tall one? The one with all the weapons?"

"My guardsman," she said, before she thought better of it.

Daniel laughed heartily. "Is that what he is? You'll need him, though I imagine he won't be able to save you from what I'll unleash."

"Please don't tell me—"

"I will," Daniel said, beginning to pace again, "because I *want* you to know what I'm going to do, so you can watch it unfold."

Sarah remained silent. If she could encourage the fool to go on, so much the better.

"You won't know anything of these names, being the uneducated country wench that you are, but there are in the world only three black mages of note, and I intend to surpass them all."

"Do you?" Sarah asked, then winced as the darkness increased suddenly. It was as if she were being crushed under a wagonload of rocks. "I mean, of course you do," she gasped. "Of course."

The darkness eased slightly.

"There is a place of power," Daniel said contemptuously, "one hidden from all but the most skilled. I was there before, in the winter, but I didn't have the right spell to take what I needed. I won't make that mistake again."

Sarah imagined he wouldn't.

"Breathe comfortably for a few more days, sister," he said, leaning over her. "Breathe and dream. Once I have what I want, you won't be able to do either very pleasantly. Here, let me give you a taste of it now."

Sarah fell headfirst into darkness and knew no more.

S he dreamt.
   She walked along a road, much as she'd been doing for what seemed

like weeks on end. The company was ahead of her, marching along into darkness only she could see. She tried to call to them, but her voice came out as nothing but a croak.

She tried to run, but the faster she went, the slower her progress until she could no longer see her companions. She wrapped her arms around herself and looked for a shelter of some sort. The wind had come up and brought with it a frigid rain. She wasn't accustomed to rain, as a rule. In Shettlestoune, it rained only once a month, a singular, unpleasant downpour that washed away things that would have likely been useful.

This was different. It was a light rain, barely more than a mist, but it was relentless. It occurred to her, as her hair began to hang in damp locks against her neck, that a fire would have been most welcome.

She looked to her left and saw a fire in the distance. It burned with an eerie blue light that wasn't particularly welcoming, but she thought she might not be in a position to be choosey. She left the road and trudged over to it through a marshy, unpleasant-smelling field. She hugged herself more tightly and bowed her head against the rain until she stood in front of the fire and could see it for what it was.

It was a single sheaf of parchment that burned but was not consumed.

She stared at it stupidly for a moment or two, then reached down to pick it up. It leapt up and wrapped itself around her forearm in precisely the same way Daniel's page had, only this time she didn't manage to rip her flesh free of its hold. It tightened itself around her until she was weeping from the pain. She finally remembered the knives in her boots and managed to pull one of them free. It slit through the spell without any trouble. The spell fell back into the fire, hissing and crackling.

Sarah stumbled away, cradling her arm to herself. Every time one of her tears would land on her skin, the tear would flare up into a flicker of flame that she would have to blow out.

Her company was nowhere to be seen. The only thing visible were fires, small fires she suspected might be like the page she'd left behind.

She walked endlessly, catching glimpses of flames every now and again. In time, she grew so tired that she fell to her knees. She knelt in the mud for hours before she managed to raise her head and look again. A fire, brighter and warmer than the others, was there in front of her, shining like a beacon.

It was Ruith.

She called to him, but his back was turned and he couldn't hear her. She shouted until her voice was hoarse. She crawled, but somehow his light grew fainter and fainter.

She took a final deep breath and shouted his name.

He didn't turn.

And then the world began to shudder violently . . .

Sarah woke to find someone shaking her. She looked up and found Ruith there, kneeling over her, shaking her and calling her name. He was breathing heavily.

"What?" she asked, blinking.

"I heard you calling me," he said, panting.

"She didn't say aught," Ned said, leaning over Ruith's shoulder.

Sarah saw the look Ruith sent Ned's way, which had him scampering off abruptly, then searched his face for some of what she'd seen.

"I couldn't catch you," she said. "I tried."

He smiled reassuringly. "It was a nightmare, Sarah. You fell behind, fainted, and dreamt. Perhaps the rain overcame you."

She nodded, because she didn't want to tell him the truth with an audience there. Ruith pulled her up to her feet, sent the rest of the company off with reassuring words, then put his arm around her shoulders and walked with her in the opposite direction.

"I heard you screaming, even if no one else did," he said in a low voice. "What befell you?"

"My brother."

Ruith stopped still and gaped. "Impossible."

She shook her head. "He cast some species of vile spell upon me and I fell. That was when I began to dream."

"Do you feel him nearby any longer?"

"How would I know?" she asked crossly. She rubbed her eyes suddenly. "Forgive me. Nay, I do not feel him nearby, but I've no gift for that sort of thing." She paused. "I don't suppose you can feel him."

He shook his head slowly.

"Do you think we should look for someone who can?"

He sighed and dragged his free hand through his hair. "I've considered it, but I have my reasons for not wanting to." He looked off into the setting sun for a moment or two, then turned her around and started back toward the wagon. "I'll tell you of them when the others are asleep."

She nodded and continued on with him. He didn't take his arm away and she didn't ask him to. She was actually quite happy for the protection.

Two hours later, she was sitting on the back of Franciscus's wagon, watching Ruith repair the fletching of one of his arrows. She wondered about him, where he'd learned to do that, why he had found himself leagues away in that horribly intimidating house when he could have just as easily been living with his grandfather on that glorious lake behind her. It couldn't have been that they didn't want him. Sgath hadn't seemed angry with Ruith. On the contrary, he had seemed overjoyed to see him, as if he'd thought he'd lost him and been thrilled to have him back.

Very strange.

"Are you going to tell me now why we don't find a mage who can take us to Daniel immediately?" she asked.

He looked at her briefly, rose from where he'd been sitting, and put his arrows into their quiver and the quiver into the wagon. The sword and the knives he generally wore strapped to his back joined the blade there. He walked over and leaned against the side of the wagon where he could speak softly and be heard.

"Because I think he knows things that might be useful if he's left to investigate them."

"What sorts of things?" she asked in astonishment.

He shrugged. "Where to find more pages of that book, perhaps."

"Gair of Ceangail's book?" she managed, her mouth suddenly quite dry.

"Aye," he said very quietly. "Gair of Ceangail's book."

"What a horrible man," she said without hesitation. "Horrible and evil. Why did he ever write that accursed book?"

Ruith shrugged. "I don't know that anyone will ever know the true reasons, though I suspect Connail had that aright, at least. It was to flatter his enormous ego, to show the world that no one else could work magic in quite the way he could."

"But surely he had to suspect those spells might fall into someone else's hands."

"Aye, but who would have the power to use those spells successfully? Gair was a thousand years old before he wed Sarait of Tòrr Dòrainn, fathered his children, then slew them all, the poor wretches. His power was immense, his arrogance boundless. There are others alive who might match him in both, but I imagine they're wrapped up in their own egos and have no time for traipsing about the countryside, looking for spells they perhaps wouldn't be able to manage."

She studied him for a moment in silence. "You do care about this, don't you?"

He looked at her in surprise. "Did you think I didn't?"

She managed half a smile. "Ruith, I never know what to think about you. You're a mystery."

"Not worth solving," he said with a weary smile. "But, aye, I do care. Because of Lake Cladach and scores of other places just as lovely, or unlovely, or full of souls who don't deserve to have their lives destroyed by a lad with nothing to check his madness."

"Aren't there other black mages out there attempting what Daniel plans?" she asked.

"Your brother is not a black mage. He aspires to nothing more than dirty grey."

She blinked, then laughed in spite of herself. "I think the worst thing you could possibly do to him is mock him. He's very sensitive to that sort of thing."

"Most evil mages are," he said.

Sarah wanted to ask him how he could possibly know that, but he seemed disinclined to elaborate, so she didn't press him. Besides, he was more talkative than she'd ever heard him be before, and she wasn't about to interrupt him now.

"And aye, there are mages enough with the power to undo the world," he said, clasping his hands together and studying them. "There are those who have both the power *and* the spells to do so, but at least for now there are things that give them pause. The tantalizing thought of more power, or another mage who threatens them if they act, or sheer laziness."

"Are mages lazy?" she asked.

He shot her a look. "I wouldn't know, but I imagine there are a few who are. And as for our dingy little pretender, 'tis better to have him collecting things he can't possibly do justice to than have another with the power to truly use them finding them without us knowing it."

She smiled faintly. "You sound as though you're off to save the world."

"For you," he said quietly. "For you, and my grandfather, and the widow Fiore who grows lavender that Franciscus covets."

"I think he covets more than her lavender."

"Aye, I imagine he does," Ruith said, and he smiled as well. "So we'll save the world for her, and him, and us. We'll allow your brother to continue on and we'll follow. And we'll hope to hell we can stop him before he does something stupid." He reached out and ran his hand down her braid that hung down her back. "You should sleep, Sarah."

She shook her head. "I'm afraid to."

He straightened and walked around the end of the wagon to take her hand. "I'll help you."

"Are you going to clunk me over the head with your sword?" she asked as he reached into the wagon for his knives, then led her over to one of the large, heavy wheels. He sat and pulled her down to sit between his legs, then set his knives down. "Nothing so nefarious. I'll just hold you. My mother did it for me often enough in my youth."

She looked at him. "How maternal of you."

He pursed his lips and pulled her back to lean against his chest. "You are a mouthy wench."

And you are impossible, she wanted to say. Impossibly handsome, impossibly chivalrous in a rough, very formal sort of way, impossibly mysterious.

And rather comfortable, as far as pillows went. She put her head on his shoulder and closed her eyes. She was certain she wouldn't sleep, but there was something unwholesomely comforting about sitting with a man who had two very deadly knives resting on either side of him.

"Sleep in peace, Sarah," he said very quietly. "I'll keep you safe."

"And if I dream?"

"I'll wake you if I feel you start."

She nodded, then felt the tension seep out of her. She sighed as she felt his arms come around her. She was quite certain she had never in her life been held thus by anyone, much less a man who wasn't her brother—not that she would have ventured that close to Daniel if she'd had a blade to her throat—but she found she became accustomed to it far more quickly than she'd suspected she might. Peace sank into her soul and she sighed in relief.

"Ruith?" she managed, because she knew she had to ask him one last thing before she slept.

"Aye?"

"I want to know where we are tomorrow."

"Why?"

"I want to see if it matches my dream."

"Again, why?"

"Because I dreamt of books that were on fire. I think I can find them again if I have a map."

He sat up so quickly, she almost earned a kink in her neck for her trouble.

"What?"

She rubbed her neck and looked at him crossly. "There's nothing more to it than that and there's no use in describing anything tonight because you can't draw a map in the dark."

"You vile wench, you can't leave me with that and no more," he said faintly. "Besides, the moon is almost full. I could draw quite a few things you could see."

"It was likely only a dream."

"Or a vision," he countered. He looked at her, then sighed. "You're right. There's nothing to be done about it tonight. But I'll draw you a map in the morning, then we'll see whether you were dreaming or not."

"And if I wasn't?"

He rubbed his hand against her back. "If you weren't dreaming, then we'll have a few pages to collect, I suppose."

She nodded, then met his gaze. "Do you want me to tell you what else Daniel said tonight, or shall I wait until the morning?"

He closed his eyes briefly. "Am I going to be happy about it?"

"Are you happy about any of this?"

He put his arms around her and gathered her close again. "I refuse to answer that lest it reveal me to be overly sentimental and dispel any lingering fear you have of me."

"I don't fear you."

He sighed lightly. "When was it you stopped?"

"The night you caught up with me in the forest. I bruised you terribly—"

"You didn't."

"Liar, you still have a mark on your chin. I knocked you flat, yet you did nothing but build me a fire and save my life. I think I knew then that you were a softhearted sap."

He laughed, apparently in spite of himself. "You have an appalling lack of respect for my reputation, but I'll let that pass. Tell me what that fool said before we must needs discuss these more uncomfortable subjects any longer."

She shrugged. "He said he knew of a place of power, a hidden place where he would obtain more power. And after that, I think he intends to look for more pages to add to his collection."

Ruith was very still. In fact, he was so still that she finally tilted her head back to look at his face.

"Ruith?"

He shook his head, started to speak, then shook his head again. "I don't worry about him finding spells. If Connail couldn't, your brother won't manage it. As for the other, that place he seeks, let me think on it whilst I watch over you." He tightened his arms around her briefly. "May you have a peaceful, dreamless sleep."

"I'm sorry that my brother has caused you this trouble."

"I fear, love, that your brother is the least of our worries," Ruith said quietly.

She wished she could believe that so easily, though she supposed that was preferable to the alternative. If he thought Daniel was only a small, insignificant problem, then what other horrors did he think they would face? She closed her eyes and hoped for sleep.

She didn't suppose she would manage it.

Eighteen

❧

The day was full of sunshine.

Ruith stood on the bank of a river and watched the boat bobbing gently there. The river was one that flowed from Tòrr Dòrainn and the boat was one of his grandfather's. He knew that because the wood whispered its pleasure at being called on to carry the daughter of the king and her children, and the river whispered sweet Fadairian spells as it lapped against the dock. Ruith started toward the end of the pier, but found he suddenly couldn't move.

A spell bound him in his place.

He frowned, then felt a chill slide down his spine as he watched his father step onto that boat, drawing all the light to himself. Ruith's siblings huddled suddenly together. His eldest brother, Keir, drew their mother behind him, as if to protect her. The boat ceased to whisper and the river fell silent. There was nothing in the air but an anxious stillness.

His father cast off and the boat floated away down the river. Ruith watched it go, trapped on the dock by things he could not best. He would have called out a warning, but he was mute.

And then he was suddenly no longer trapped, but he still could not speak. He found himself flying above his family in the shape of a mighty eagle, crying out to them in his harsh voice, trying to warn them with words they couldn't understand.

And then he realized where the river led.

He shook his head, for it made no sense. The rivers of Tòrr Dòrainn might have flowed north until they reached lower elevations, but then they wended their way around the mountains and south where they gathered with other rivers that turned into mighty waterways that were eventually diverted into lands owned by farmers grateful for even the echo of magic that aided their crops.

The river he flew above flowed north, up into the mountains, through rugged terrain, until it flowed into a forest. A particular forest that he'd seen before, walked in before, run from before. He knew what lay ahead for his family in that forest, but he could do nothing to stop their progress. Their course was fixed and there was no turning back.

No matter how loudly he cried out . . .

He woke and found himself standing, holding on to someone so tightly he was half surprised he hadn't hurt them.

Only he realized he had.

He released Sarah immediately, then took her hand and looked at her arm. He didn't dare push her sleeve up lest it do more damage to her skin than the spell had already done. He drew a knife from his boot and slit her sleeve up to her elbow.

His fingerprints had joined the black trails there.

"I'm sorry," he said hoarsely.

She shook her head. "I didn't feel it, truly."

He didn't believe it, for there were tears streaming down her cheeks, but there was no point in arguing with her. He cut off her sleeve so it wouldn't touch her skin, then tucked the material down his boot with his knife. Perhaps there was something there, something buried in the cloth that would eventually tell him what was buried in her flesh.

His grandfather hadn't been able to tell. Sgath had tried to heal her whilst she slept, but said there was something in the wound he could not cure. He suggested that once Ruith had the spell that had assaulted Sarah in the first place, he might find the answer. Ruith hadn't mentioned his own wound, and he knew his grandfather hadn't noticed it or else he would have said something about it.

Odd that Sarah could see things Sgath could not.

Ruith wasn't sure if Sarah's scorched flesh had to do with his father's spells, or his book, or things he couldn't yet see. All he knew was he was going to have to do something about it very soon or she wouldn't recover.

He put his hand lightly on her shoulder. "Daniel first, then we'll turn the Nine Kingdoms upside down to find a healer who can remedy that."

She shook her head. "Too much trouble."

"Then we'll just turn one of the Nine upside down, but we *will* find a way to see you whole." He rubbed his hand over his face. "Was I talking in my sleep?"

She looked up at him, clear-eyed. "You weren't, but I was sitting in your arms, watching over you after a fashion, and I saw your dreams."

He dropped his arm to his side and felt his mouth slide open. *"What?"*

"Not that I understood your dreams, of course," she said. "I simply saw a forest, and a river running into it. That's when you started to scream, but apparently I was the only one to hear it."

I thought you didn't have any magic was almost out of his mouth before he could stop it, but fortunately his self-control hadn't left him entirely.

"You see too much," he managed.

"I know." She paused. "It seems to be growing worse with every league we travel." She looked up at him. "I'm back to thinking I'm going mad."

"If you are, I'm traveling along that long, sloping road with you," he said with a sigh. He touched her arm lightly. "I'll help Master Franciscus with the horses, then perhaps you and I will ride on ahead."

"After you draw me a map."

He nodded, for he hadn't forgotten. He would have preferred to dwell on the happy pleasure of having Sarah of Doìre in his arms, but all he could think about was what she'd told him.

She knew where pages of spells were.

And her damned brother was going to go to the well and see what he could have from its innards.

Ruith cursed silently and thoroughly as he walked away to tend to horses. Daniel apparently knew what he wanted, even if he wasn't precisely sure how to have it. And if he knew where the well was and what it could provide him, there was no reason to believe he wouldn't go to Ceangail's keep itself and see what could be had there.

Unfortunately, Ruith knew exactly what Daniel would find there. Darkness. Unrelenting darkness and souls wallowing quite happily in it. His mother had suffered her time there only because she'd known her husband might become suspicious of her if she refused to accompany him to his adopted home.

Perhaps Daniel intended to find the rest of Gair's book there, then bind it all back together, and attempt to work magic from it. Ruith wasn't so much worried about what Daniel might do, but he was very concerned what someone more powerful might do if they have that collection of immensely powerful spells in one place.

Once the company was ready to go, he sent them off and

remained behind with Sarah. He squatted down and sketched out a map in the dirt for her. They were traveling along the north-west corner of the forest that sheltered Ainneamh within its magi-cal boughs. Ruith wished he could claim that he couldn't feel that magic, but the truth was, he could. It was only the faintest echo of song teasing the back of his mind, but aye, he could feel it.

It was beautiful.

He supposed he could leave the company to its fate, take Sarah, and beg asylum there. After all Sgath was the son of Ghèillear of Ainneamh. Though King Ghèillear had long since passed from the world, his name was revered and a kinship with him would have been honored. Ruith could have found a corner of the kingdom, built Sarah a house with a weaving chamber for her, a library for him, and an enormous hearth for them both where they could sit in the evenings and speak of the simple things of the day. They would have been free from darkness and the road ahead that led places he knew he wasn't going to want to go.

"Ruith?"

He looked at her, kneeling in the dirt next to him, and had the overwhelming urge to lean over and kiss her. Or ask her to wed him. Or perhaps both, or one right after the other.

She frowned. "Are you unwell?"

He had no idea how to answer that. He could only shake his head and look down, trying to remember where he'd been before his mind had wandered off into paths he dared not tread. He couldn't take her into Ehrne of Ainneamh's kingdom for two rea-sons: Daniel of Doìre and monsters that were looking for him alone. He couldn't bring the latter with him and he couldn't ignore the former.

"Ruith?"

He dragged himself back to the map before him. "This road here," he said, clearing his throat roughly, "winds past the elven kingdom of Ainneamh—"

"Does it?" Sarah asked in surprise.

"We won't go for a visit if you'd rather not."

"I might say something I shouldn't," she admitted. "About their terrible beauty or enormous arrogance."

He smiled. "You would perhaps be justified—at least in the latter. The truth is, not many manage to cross the borders of Ainneamh and even fewer escape to tell what they've seen. Though we could attempt a quick peek, if you wanted."

"At this point, Ruith, I would be happy to see anything that wasn't on fire."

He reached out and smoothed his hand over her hair before he thought better of it. He had to do it a time or two more until he had the urge to put his arms around her and never let her go completely under control. He attempted a smile.

"I'm sorry."

She shook her head. "This is my quest. I knew when I set out that it would be difficult."

He imagined that was true, but he also imagined that she had, as he had, grossly underestimated just how difficult it would turn out to be.

He looked down at the map in the dirt and fiddled with the lines for a bit, drawing the road north and west that led first to Coinnich before it wended its way south of Chagailt and caught up with the main road that led from Angesand north to the crossroads. From there, it was a long and difficult journey to Tor Neroche, the palace of King Adhémar, or an easier road could be taken east to the country of Penrhyn where the wine was tart and the princesses acidic.

Not that he knew that personally. He had traveled as a child, of course, but not after—

"You didn't sleep well."

He focused on her with an effort. "Forgive me," he said with a sigh. "I'm not particularly tired. Just lost in thought." He forced himself to concentrate on the map before him. "We'll travel north

a bit longer, then turn east, skirting the northern border of Ainneamh. The road will become more difficult there as it winds up
into the mountains. If we turn north again, we'll eventually reach
Slighe, the crossroads that is, surprisingly, the last village of any
size before the plains of Ailean. I suppose if you cared to, you could
travel past the Sgùrrach mountains and turn north. Léige is there,
the dwarvish kingdom, as well as other places that I'm not particularly familiar with."

She looked down at his map. "And that place of power that Daniel spoke of? Do you have any idea where that might be found?"

He traced the road with the tip of his knife. He watched as
that blade wound its way northward from Ainneamh, through the
mountains, to the keep of Ceangail. It was a fairly simple journey
west to a forest near the grim, unrelenting mountains that had protected his father's keep. So, aye, he had a rather good idea where
Daniel's destination might be found.

Would that he didn't.

"There is a forest here," he said, having to force himself to trace
and not stab the innocent ground in front of him. "In that forest
there is rumored to be a well of power." He looked at her to find her
watching him without any sign of distaste or terror.

He couldn't guarantee she wouldn't feel both if he allowed her
anywhere near the place.

Which, now that the reality was staring him in the face, he
would do only if he were too dead to stop her.

"We'll scout out a few less dangerous locales first," he said, fingering the hilt of his knife. "Just to see if they've seen him." Just to
see where he might safely leave her behind.

She studied the map, then pointed to a crook in the road. "There
is a barn here. We should see what's there."

He had to force himself to breathe evenly. "Can *you* see your
brother?"

She shook her head slowly. "Just the pages, and perhaps not

even those. I could just be dreaming. I can't see the ones he has, but I'm not sure why not."

He had no answer for that. He couldn't imagine Daniel was clever enough to bother using a spell of concealment.

"I'm not sure there are words to describe how much I don't want to do any of this."

He rose and pulled her to her feet. "I imagine every Hero of note said the same thing at one time or another. I don't blame you for it."

And he didn't. There were, as it happened, no words to describe how much he didn't want her to come any farther along the road that lay before them. His only comfort was that her road would end soon. He would go to the well, stop Daniel, then go back and fetch Sarah. They could collect the pages in relative safety, destroy them, then move on with their lives.

She nodded, then watched him silently as he erased the map with the toe of his boot. She didn't move, though, when he reached for the reins of their horses. He paused and looked at her in surprise.

"What is it?"

She hesitated. "Now that I can see the pages, do we need Daniel?"

Ruith considered the reins in his hand for a moment or two, then handed her hers. "I think that he still has a part to play in this all," he said slowly.

"I suppose you have it aright."

He couldn't blame her for questioning the plan, or for worrying. He had spent his share of time wondering if he was making a terrible mistake.

But the alternative was to unearth what he'd buried a score of years ago. It was one thing to briefly use magic for the purpose of healing Seirceil; it was another thing entirely to use it to seek out and destroy another human being. He had been faced at every turn with what his father had once been and then become, and he couldn't set a single foot to that path.

Nay, he would find Daniel and stop him by normal means. If

he couldn't track and subdue a simple village witch's brat without the aid of his magic, then the past score of years had been ill spent indeed.

Nay, he would do it without magic and succeed.

He had no other choice.

It was nightfall before they reached the barn Sarah had indicated. They sent the company on to make camp, then stopped on the pretext of needing a bit of horse liniment. Ruith chatted with the farmer as Sarah looked at things no one else could see. The expression on her face was difficult to watch. He would have given anything to have spared her the fear that was plain in her eyes, but he could do nothing for her save hold her when her task was through. If he knew nothing else, he knew that there were some things that one could only do alone.

She walked into the barn behind the farmer, then paused in front of a tack trunk pushed up against the wall. She looked at the farmer and smiled. It was more of a grimace, which the farmer seemed to notice right off.

"Are ye ill, miss?" he asked, a worried frown on his brow.

"Nay," she croaked. "I'm finding myself . . . ah . . . *called*, if you will, by a collection of, er, spells—"

The farmer's face brightened immediately. "Ah, a witch's get, are you?"

"Um—"

"My best draft horse fell lame yesterday," the farmer said promptly. "Rock in his hoof and now he won't put weight on it. Don't suppose you'd want to fix that, would you?"

Ruith was impressed by her ability to master the panic he could see flash in her eyes.

"My powers are unpredictable so far from home," she said quickly, "so I wouldn't dare promise anything. In case it went awry, of course. But if I could just have a wee look inside your trunk just the same?"

The farmer frowned. "Then I don't know, missy."

Ruith held up two pieces of gold behind Sarah's back, which the farmer immediately saw.

"Look away," the man said, taking and pocketing the gold with alacrity. "The trunk isn't mine, actually. My brother bought it from another lad clearing out and moving south. Makes a handy seat for a bit of ale in the afternoons, but I've never looked through the gear inside. Mind if I watch?"

"Of course not," Ruith said, though he imagined Sarah did. He watched her hands shake as she opened the lid. He caught that lid before it fell back down on her fingers, then made a great production of moving things about to give her time to catch her breath.

"Where?" he murmured.

"On the left," she managed. "In that rolled leather cover."

He pulled aside layers of rags and cracked leather halters and reins to reveal just what she'd said would be there. He took out the rolled-up sheaves, then untied the leather strands that held them together. And there in his hand he held the unthinkable.

A scorched but imminently legible copy of his father's spell of Shapechanging.

"Roll it up," Sarah said harshly. "Before it burns my eyes to cinders."

He did so, startled. He turned to the farmer and made him a low bow. "Many thanks, good sir. This is precious to my lady here. I'm sorry we can't do anything for your horse."

"Horses," the farmer corrected. "I've a mare just foaled who isn't doing well. Even if your lady could just try, I'd be much obliged."

Sarah looked as if she would have been much obliged to have shaken the farmer's hand and bolted, but she seemingly suppressed the impulse. Ruith considered, but not overlong. He took a deep breath, then silently uncapped his magic. He was more prepared than he had been the last time, but still he stumbled as it rushed back through him. He caught himself heavily against a stall, then felt Sarah's arm go round his waist immediately.

"Are you unwell?"

He shook his head. "Nay, just hungry. I don't think I want to stay for pleasantries."

"I certainly don't," she muttered under her breath. "I don't think I can heal his animals."

"They don't look like they need it," Ruith said. "We'll give them a pat and be on our way."

"You *did* pay him, I suppose."

He would have agreed with her on that, but he was too busy trying not to be crushed by what he'd managed so easily at the age of ten. Obviously, he'd become soft in his dotage.

He had also obviously lost any finesse he'd once possessed. He healed those two horses on his way out of the barn, thoroughly and hastily. He supposed the beasts were grateful, but not overly. The mare snorted at him in disgust and the draft horse tried to bite him.

Nothing more than he deserved, no doubt.

He gathered up every last drop of what he had and shoved it back down into the center of himself before he could think about it, or spare the effort to realize how quickly he'd become accustomed to even that small, unruly bit of his birthright leaping and tripping through his veins.

"You look terrible."

Ruith put his arm around her shoulders because he had to. "I feel terrible."

He listened to her thank the farmer again for the look in his trunk and apologize for healing spells seemingly unexecuted. Ruith could only concentrate on putting one foot in front of the other until they reached their own horses. He managed to get himself into his saddle without causing his mount undue discomfort, then held down his hand for Sarah. She looked up at him in surprise.

"What?"

"Ride with me," he said hoarsely. "I need aid."

She put her foot on his, then swung up behind him and put her arms around his waist. "I think you need less aid than you do coddling. Or is it all just a nefarious plot to grope me whilst I'm otherwise engaged in the all-consuming task of keeping you from falling off your horse?"

"Grope you," he gasped. "You, lady, have an overly healthy opinion of your charms."

She laughed a little, then took his reins from him, clicked to her horse, and steered his horse in the right direction.

"I'm taking your mind off the fact that you look as if you're nigh onto sicking up your lunch onto that poor farmer's back porch."

He couldn't speak, for he wasn't entirely sure he wouldn't still delight her with that spectacle. He concentrated on breathing until they had left the farmer's house far behind. The road was well lit thanks to the moon, but even with that light he couldn't see the company ahead. He supposed that was a boon, lest they see him before he had recovered enough to avoid questions about what had befallen him. He held himself upright with his right hand on his thigh and allowed himself the pleasure of holding Sarah's hand wrapped around his waist. When he thought he could manage it, he sat upright without aid and reached back to put his arm around her.

"Woman, if the happy day comes when I'm at my leisure to give you a proper mauling," he managed, "rest assured it won't be because I need to be distracted from puking."

"You great barbarian."

He smiled because he could hear the smile in her voice. He patted her briefly, then went back to holding himself upright simply because he suspected he might indeed fall off his horse if he didn't. He was more grateful than he would ever have admitted that Sarah was strong enough to keep him in the saddle. He wouldn't have thought burying his magic would have taken such a toll on him, so perhaps that work on the horses had been more demanding than he'd suspected.

He didn't particularly care to think about what that augured if he had to do any serious magic in the near future.

Time passed and so did his weakness. By the time they reached their company, camped well off to the side of the road, he almost felt himself.

Or he would have if he'd had nothing more pressing to think about than supper and what to read by the fire afterward. Unfortunately, supper didn't sound appetizing, and he knew exactly what he would be reading because it was burning a hole in his leg where he'd shoved it down his boot.

He swung his leg over his horse's withers, then jumped down and felt rather fortunate that he managed to stay on his feet. Then he turned and held on to the saddle for a moment until his legs were steady beneath him. He put his hand on Sarah's knee and looked up at her.

"Thank you."

She covered his hand with her own. "My pleasure."

He hesitated, then smiled. "You don't have an overinflated opinion of your charms, you know. I really was trying to keep from puking into that poor man's rhododendrons."

"I imagined you were."

"You're very lovely."

"And you're daft," she said, rolling her eyes. "Move over so I can get off your horse and tend it and mine. You should find a seat by the fire."

He might have been not quite himself, but he was still as much of a gentleman as he could manage. He tended his own horse, saw Sarah fed, admired her whilst she ate and he did not, then insisted she roll up in a blanket by the fire and sleep. Once she was safely dreaming, he took himself off to sit on the back of Master Franciscus's wagon and have a much-needed cup of ale.

"Find what you were looking for?"

Ruith looked at Franciscus over the rim of his cup. "And more, I fear."

"I can only imagine." Franciscus patted the haft of his dagger meaningfully. "You be careful with her, you young rogue. I feel a certain proprietariness where she's concerned."

Ruith smiled faintly, then watched Franciscus draw one of a handful of daggers he seemed inordinately fond of and begin to slide a sharpening stone down its already quite wicked-looking length. He watched, waited for the ale to work its magic, then waited a bit more until he could manage the question he likely shouldn't have asked.

"Was it terrible?"

Franciscus looked up. "Her life?"

Ruith nodded.

Franciscus considered his knife for quite some time before he answered. "Seleg was an unpredictable and unforgiving woman. Sarah craves, I believe, peace and beauty above all. There's a reason for it, I daresay."

"That must be why she weaves."

"That, and she's likely just fond of pretty colors."

Ruith pursed his lips. "She obviously spent too much time with you in your alehouse. You influenced her in an unwholesome way."

Franciscus smiled. "She is lovely, isn't she? Lovely and tenacious and unafraid."

"Throwing herself headlong into things and wondering how she'll master them after the fact," Ruith said with a deep sigh. "Aye, she is." He looked at Franciscus. "I'm going on a little errand."

"Where to?"

"North."

"There's a lot of that to choose from," Franciscus said easily. "Care to be more specific?"

"I think I know where Daniel's going and I'm going to follow him. Alone."

"Sarah won't like it."

"She can swear at me when I return."

"She will," Franciscus said tranquilly. "What will you have us do? Shall we continue on to Slighe?"

"If you would," Ruith said. He set his cup aside and looked at one of the very few friends he'd had over the past twenty years. "Tell her something cheerful, will you? Some tale of beauty to counter all that bilge Connail spewed at her."

"He seems inordinately fond of Prince Gair, doesn't he?"

Prince Gair. Ruith hadn't thought of his father as that, well, perhaps ever. He was technically a prince of Ainneamh through Sgath, though fortunately so far from that throne that the title had been meaningless.

"Or seemed, rather," Franciscus said. He considered his dagger a bit longer. "I wonder what happened to him."

"I imagine Urchaid killed him."

Franciscus looked up at him. "Why?"

"He talked too much."

"Why would Urchaid care what Connail said?"

"That is a riddle I can't begin to answer," Ruith said wearily. "I'm not even sure I would want the answer if I knew where to look for it."

"You have enough to think on," Franciscus said seriously. "Leave the riddles to me. And aye, I will tell Sarah something pleasant. Perhaps favorable tales of the princes of Neroche. There are several of them, I believe, and all quite eligible. I'm sure she would enjoy those thoroughly."

Ruith pursed his lips and stood up. "And here I was fooled by how amiable you look on the outside."

"'Tis a façade, my boy," Franciscus said, stretching his hands over his head and yawning, "to hide my black heart. Go sleep, and I'll keep watch. If you're going to go, though, you should go before she wakes."

"I agree."

"Whatever she takes out of my hide, I'll take out of yours, so don't thank me yet."

Ruith smiled, then went to lie down near the fire. He was exhausted enough that sleep should have come easily.

Instead, all he could do was see in his mind's eye the barn, the lamplight, the look on Sarah's face as she'd forced herself to look for things only she could see. He wasn't sure where she'd come by that seeing, but he knew he didn't envy her. And he didn't envy himself what he knew he would be seeing in a pair of days.

In the end, all he knew was that he was going to keep her from having to see the same thing if it meant strapping her to the fullest keg of ale in Franciscus's wagon.

Nineteen

Sarah stood in the faint light of dawn and wondered if the man facing her was going to draw his sword soon and use it on her, or if he would simply fasten her to her horse and let it drag her behind itself off to points unknown.

Ruith looked capable of either.

She'd known the night before that he was planning another bout of desertion. He should have spent more time practicing his looks of innocence in the mirror, for he was particularly incapable of taking the broadside of a pointed question and not sailing away quite low in the water, as it were.

She frowned thoughtfully. It was entirely possible that Franciscus had told her too many tales of the sailors of Aigeann and their fantastical ships. For someone who had grown to womanhood in the driest, most unmagical place possible, she had an appallingly large store of nautical tales running about in her head.

The force of Ruith's glare pulled her back to herself. She returned his look coolly and listed silently his offenses, to stiffen her spine, beginning and ending with the fact that he'd snuck away before dawn and ridden like a demon. She'd anticipated the like and had followed him within minutes. That following had been made all the easier by the page of Gair of Ceangail's book he still had stuffed down his boot. It was like a beacon, faint but undeniable, calling to her from leagues away. She was fortunate she'd been able to see it shimmering in the predawn countryside. It also helped that her horse was as fast as Ruith's but she was lighter. That, over the course of several leagues, was what had made the difference.

She looked at the man now standing in front of her, bristling with not only full-blown, manly indignation but an impressive clutch of weapons as well, and decided that perhaps they had talked enough about their future plans. Actually, there hadn't been much talking. There had been shouting, a few threats, and quite a bit of cursing.

And that had been just her side of it.

Ruith was, she was surprised to find, coldly furious. She couldn't fathom why. It was, after all, *her* quest. If she couldn't be involved, what was the point in it?

Well, apart from the obvious goal of keeping her brother from plunging the Nine Kingdoms into utter entire ruin.

She folded her arms over her chest and looked at him. "I'm baffled," she said, feeling quite thoroughly that and nothing else. "This is *my* quest—"

"Not this part of it," he said curtly.

She wanted to tell him he was being completely unreasonable, but she didn't think that would get her very far. She took a purposely deep breath and spoke very slowly. "Well, since this part has to do with looking for Daniel, doesn't that apply to me as well?"

He glared at her. "I'm finished with this conversation."

"So am I. Let's ride."

He ground his teeth. She knew that because she heard him do it. He looked at her for a moment in silence, swore quite vilely, then turned and walked away. He forgot his horse, which she supposed would irritate him further. He finally stopped, dragged his hands through his hair, then turned and strode back to stop just a handsbreadth from her.

"Please go back," he said simply.

She hadn't seen that coming. He looked sincerely worried, though she couldn't imagine why. She reached out and put her hand on his arms crossed over his chest. He was not relaxed, for his forearms were like granite under the sleeve of his tunic.

"And if I can see things you cannot?" she asked, quite reasonably to her mind.

He pursed his lips, but said nothing.

She didn't back away. If there was anything she had learned in all her years with horses and mages, it was to never show weakness no matter the threat. She didn't bother to even attempt a smile, though. It was all she could do to stare up into his remarkably lovely eyes—bluish green, she decided—and not go a little weak in the knees. But that wouldn't serve her at present, so she forbore.

"I have been of little help so far," she said honestly, "and caused you a great deal of trouble. If in this small thing I can be of use, how can you deny me the chance to repay you for your efforts on my behalf?"

"I think I'd prefer years of you cooking me dessert," he muttered. "Or not cooking it, which is likely safer."

She almost smiled. "Aye, you have that aright." The thought of repaying him thus was indeed appealing until she realized abruptly the truth of it. She would likely find herself cooking for him as he fell in love with someone else, wed her, gave her children—

"Sarah."

She was surprised at how much that bothered her. She frowned up at him, then realized she couldn't see him very well for the tears that had sprung suddenly and without warning to her eyes. She cursed, but that did nothing to rescue her from her folly.

She never wept, and she certainly wasn't weeping now. She was overcome by enthusiasm for the task ahead and that had overcome her weak, womanly form. Either that, or she had looked at Ruith's spectacular face once too often and was losing every shred of good sense she'd ever had. She supposed she was grateful to find herself suddenly gathered into strong, secure arms and held against a sturdy chest. Safety wasn't at all overrated and she had enjoyed far too little of it over the course of her life. Just a moment or two more of it wasn't going to turn her soft, surely.

"I am walking into darkness," he said quietly, so quietly he was almost inaudible. "I don't want you to be there with me."

She put her arms around him and held on, because she had to keep herself from turning and bolting the other way. She had no desire at all to walk into darkness with or without him, but she'd known from the start that she was setting her foot to a path she wouldn't enjoy.

"I can see those pages," she said. "Even in the daylight. If what you're hunting has to do with them—and I know it does so don't bother protesting—then why *wouldn't* you want me along?"

He swore succinctly. "Didn't we just have this conversation?"

"I didn't like the ending of it."

He snorted out a laugh, sounding thoroughly exasperated. "Damn it, Sarah, I will not yield."

"Neither will I."

"You will when I strap you to your horse and tell it where to take you."

She lifted her head and met his gaze. "You won't manage that."

He lifted an eyebrow. "You underestimate me."

"And you me."

He pursed his lips and pulled her close again. "Very well, it might not be easily done, but I *could* send you back to the company if I chose to."

"Continue to think that, if you like."

He sighed deeply and simply held her in silence until his silence became hers. She didn't want it to. She might have been mouthy, as Ruith would have said, but she was no fool. She had perfect recall of how she'd felt in that barn, or when Daniel had stood in front of her, or while she'd watched her mother's house fall and caught a whiff of the magic involved. If Ruith intended to be involved with anything remotely resembling what her brother had become entangled in, he was going to be facing those things.

And so would she if she went with him.

"I'm afraid," she said, then she realized what she'd said.

That seemed to make some sort of decision for him. He loosened his hold on her so he could look her in the face.

"That is the first sensible thing you've said all morning."

"I'm lying to instill a sense of confidence in you," she blustered. "You know, all those manly feelings of protection and chivalry and . . . well, things of that nature."

She'd intended to sound sure of her self, but her voice quavered as she said the words.

Damn it anyway.

He took her face in his hands and kissed her. On the forehead, but that was a start, she supposed. He looked as if he might have liked to kiss her a bit closer to her mouth—such as on it, truth be told. Perhaps she had laid out his future for him prematurely.

Or perhaps she was mad to even be thinking on any of it when she was fairly certain she was about to walk into hell.

He closed his eyes very briefly, then took a step backward. But he kept his hands on her shoulders.

"I don't like this, *but*," he added, no doubt to cut off her protests, "in truth, I like even less the thought of you being in the company of useless mages and a lad whose first instinct is to hide behind your skirts. I fear not even Franciscus could protect you as I would wish it."

"Then I suppose you'll have to do it."

His expression didn't lighten. "There may come a time, lady, when I cannot. What will you do then?"

"Survive. I have before."

"Doìre is a child's playground compared to where we're going."

She tilted her head slightly. "How would you know?"

He looked momentarily startled. "I, ah, read quite a bit."

And one of the books he should have read was how to maintain a lie over the course of several days. She wasn't sure why he felt the need to be less than forthcoming with her, but he certainly did. She studied him closely.

"What else do you know?"

"Vast amounts of lore, speculation, and outright gossip," he said, dragging his hand through his hair wearily. "I'll entertain you with it whilst we ride. But there may come a point where I insist you remain behind with the horses. And that you will do, or we go not a step farther in this quest."

"If you promise you'll make me a bow and some of your arrows."

He blinked. "Why?"

"I'm a decent archer," she said without any excess of pride. "Or I was before Daniel used my gear for kindling. It has been many years, but I think I could remember how they're used. I assume you made your own."

"I did."

She walked away from him and swung up onto her horse. "Let's go, then, that you might be about that sooner rather than later."

He hadn't moved. He looked up at her. "I don't like this."

"I never said you had to."

He pursed his lips. "How will anyone believe I can control any of the events surrounding a stupid, arrogant wizardling when I can't manage to control his headstrong, impossible sister?"

"I promise to look properly cowed if we meet anyone you want to impress."

He rolled his eyes, swore at her a bit more, then went to retrieve his own horse.

Sarah looked at the mountains in the distance. They were rugged and beautiful and covered with evergreen trees. But there was something else there as well.

Something dark.

She drew her hand over her eyes, took her reins, and followed Ruith when he set off.

And she didn't look at the mountains again.

They traveled for most of the morning in silence. Ruith seemed to have much on his mind and she supposed the less he thought about her presence, the better off she would be. But when they stopped to water the horses, she had to at least attempt some bit of innocuous conversation.

"Why do black mages decide on that path?" she asked. She listened to the words come out of her mouth and thought that perhaps she should have kept her mouth shut.

Ruith looked at her in surprise, then hesitated before he sighed. "Who's to say? I suspect ego is involved. One doesn't gain much notoriety for going about secretly doing good, does one? But inspire terror, or make war for your own ends, or destroy something beautiful, and there you have a tale fit for telling in pubs across the world."

"But what if you have only a little power?" she asked. "Daniel doesn't seem to be particularly good at his spells, so I can't imagine he'll become famous."

"As I said, he'll never achieve more than a dingy white as his final color," Ruith said. "But I suppose a lad can dream. As for the others . . . " He shook his head. "Others have possessed power enough to achieve their ends without undue effort."

"All for the sake of ego?"

"Or revenge." He boosted her onto her mount's back, then swung gracefully up onto his own horse. "Several of the more persistent and unpleasant black mages of this world were tossed out of the schools of wizardry for dabbling in things they shouldn't have, or denied some coveted spot in a royal house they had no claim to. Others simply chose darkness when they could have as easily chosen light. Some were born to privilege and great power, but chose to scorn it and rebel against it."

She watched the countryside for a few minutes in silence. It had been relatively lush that morning, but now it was much less so. As if some sort of flood had washed over it and left it barren except for the weeds that had grown up to take the grass's place.

"Was Gair of Ceangail the worst of them all?" she asked. "Connail seems to think so, though he perhaps wasn't an unbiased raconteur of tales."

"I can't say," Ruith said carefully. "Lothar of Wychweald has killed scores of his own progeny. Wehr of Wrekin left his family alive, but he turned all of them save a handful to darkness. Droch of Saothair is not a pleasant soul. I understand he has a brother who wouldn't dare find himself within arm's reach, but perhaps he is kinder to his children. But Gair?" He took a deep breath. "His evil is particularly egregious considering who he was and how noble his birthright."

"I don't know much about him," she admitted, "save what Connail told me, which was more than enough. His poor parents, though. Did they live to see him turn to evil?"

Ruith nodded. "They live still. His mother is Eulasaid of Camanaë, a powerful wizardess in her own right, his father S—ah, an elven prince of Ainneamh." He shook his head as if he strove to free it from some sort of dream. "Their children have been perfectly content to live their lives, love their offspring, and contribute to the world as they could. All save Gair, their youngest."

"At least his evil died with him," she said, with a shiver. "All save the spells, I suppose."

"Aye, save those."

"Are they sound spells?" she asked. "Those spells of Gair's?"

He was quiet for several minutes. "They are," he said finally, "without exception exceptionally elegant. Simple, direct, and devastatingly powerful."

"A pity he chose darkness."

"It is."

"Am I talking too much?"

He shot her a look, then relented and smiled a bit. "You're trying to distract me, aren't you?"

She lifted one shoulder in a half shrug. "Both of us, perhaps, though I'm not choosing a very distracting subject. Are there *no* tales of good mages? You have to have at least one tucked away in your store of gossip and hearsay."

He smiled. "Let me think for a moment or two about an appropriate subject, then I will."

Two days later, he was apparently still thinking. Sarah had found as time went on that he was not so much unwilling to speak as he was incapable of speech. She understood completely. The journey had been endless, broken up only by stops to eat, water the horses, and sleep when they hadn't been able to go on.

Nights had been the worst. She had insisted on watching her share of times, sitting next to Ruith with his knives stabbed into the ground next to her, fingering his arrows and distracting herself by marveling at their perfection.

But that hadn't driven the shadows away.

Now she was simply too frightened to speak. She hadn't asked Ruith much about their destination beyond wondering where they were headed. He had mentioned a forest. She wouldn't have imagined in her worst nightmares the sort of forest she now knew he had been talking about.

The trees were evergreens, looking old and stately even from a great distance. It should have been a pleasing place.

But somehow it wasn't.

She realized why once she drew close enough to the trees to see them clearly. She looked quickly at Ruith but there was absolutely no expression on his face. Not surprise, nor horror, nor curiosity. He was pale and very quiet. She realized then that he hadn't said anything that morning. She thought they might have discussed what she'd managed to stuff into her saddlebags to use for breakfast, but she couldn't remember if that had been that day or the day before. In fact, the entire journey had begun to feel like a very long, relentless descent into nightmare.

She looked for somewhere to leave the horses, but there was nothing but the forest surrounded by that barren, noxious-looking plain. To her right were the beginnings of those rugged mountains that swept up into the sky at a certain point, but there was no shelter there either. Either they would have to convince the horses to remain under those accursed boughs or they would have to turn the beasts loose and hope they returned. She stole another look at Ruith, but he was so deep inside himself that she seriously doubted he would even hear her, much less understand her.

She grew more uneasy with every hoofbeat until she could bear it no longer.

"Ruith?"

It took calling his name three times before he blinked, but he did, then turned to her.

"Aye?"

"I don't think the horses will go into the trees."

He looked at the forest, then nodded. "Agreed."

"Do we tie them up, or turn them loose?"

He looked at her, then at the trees, then fell silent, as if conversing with her was just more than he could manage. He continued to watch the forest loom in front of them until he simply stopped his horse and sat there, fifty paces from the edge of it.

She understood why. It was an even more horrifying place up close than it had been from far away. Spells hung from the trees, spells that were torn and ragged. It was if the entire place had been draped in some unpleasant fabric that had subsequently suffered a tremendous storm that had clawed it to shreds.

She looked at Ruith, but he didn't acknowledge it. He simply stared at the trees in front of him for so long that Sarah began to worry about him. Well, more than she'd been worrying already.

"Ruith?"

He turned to her, but he wasn't seeing her.

"The horses?" she prompted.

"We'll tie them," he rasped.

"And if something comes?" she said. "What then? They'll drive themselves mad trying to get away."

He drew his hand over his eyes and shook his head. "You're right, of course." He dismounted ungracefully, then began to methodically remove his weapons from the saddle and strap them to himself. "We'll send them away and call them back when we're finished. If worse comes to worst, we'll continue on without them."

She nodded and slid down off her horse. She didn't have any gear to speak of that she wasn't already wearing, so she shortened her stirrups to keep the irons off Teich's sides, then tied up the reins so he wouldn't tangle himself if he had to make a quick dash to somewhere safe. She supposed Ruith would think her daft if she gave her horse instructions on how to survive the next several hours, so she merely shared a short mental picture of escape with her mount, then turned and waited for Ruith to join her.

She didn't want to walk into the forest, but there was no other alternative. She drew closer to Ruith.

"What is it that lies in this forest?"

He took a deep breath. "You'll see."

She suddenly didn't want to see, but if he could go forward, then so could she.

It was a singularly unpleasant journey. She was apparently the only one who could see the spells hanging down from the sky above like tangled, putrid vines. She pushed them aside with her hand at first, but just the touch of them on her skin made her recoil with revulsion. She drew one of the knives from her boots to do the duty for her, but it wasn't long enough. She finally tried one of Ruith's arrows poached from the quiver on his back. It seemed to make less of an impression on the spells than her steel, but it was of some help at least.

She was so busy concentrating on keeping things from falling down on her head and across her face that she didn't look at Ruith until he stumbled and caught himself heavily on one leg. She realized only then that he was pale as death.

"Ruith!"

He leaned over with his hands on his thighs and sucked in great lungfuls of air. He straightened in time, but looked no better.

"We'll press on."

She drew his arm over her shoulders. "Lean on me."

"Nay—"

"Lean on me, you stubborn fool," she said sharply.

"You have no care at all for my dignity," he managed.

"I'll heap all manner of compliments on you when we're free of this place to make up for it. Where to now?"

"Ever inward," he said, then he leaned on her the slightest bit. "Thank you."

She shook her head and continued on with him. The trees grew closer together, the spells thicker, the gloom more impenetrable.

And the farther they walked, the worse Ruith looked until she thought he might not manage to walk any farther.

Several times, she caught him just before he walked into spells strung across the path like spiderwebs. Those seemed to bother him more than just the general feeling of fear that seemed to be as woven into the air as the trees were planted in the ground.

"We cannot go on," she said, at one point.

"We must."

She started up again with him, but he grew whiter with every footstep until she was convinced that even if he survived the journey into the forest, he wouldn't live long enough to escape it. She started to say as much.

Then she realized they had reached their destination.

The trees had thinned, then disappeared to reveal a glade in front of her. She realized the glade wasn't empty, so she quickly pulled Ruith off the path with her. When she was fairly certain they couldn't be seen, she stopped. Ruith sank to his knees, breathing shallowly. She leaned over and put her hands on his shoulders.

"What can I do for you?" she asked softly.

"Nothing," he rasped.

"You can't stay here," she said, feeling very worried indeed.

"I must. Is your brother by the well?"

"I'll go look, but first let me make you comfortable."

He didn't argue when she pulled his bow over his head and removed the quiver of arrows from off his shoulder. She knelt, unbuckled his sword, then removed that as well so he could sit back on his heels. He reached up and groped for her hand, squeezed it, then dropped his hand back to his thigh. She put her hand briefly on his head, then quietly walked away until she could see what lay in the middle of the forest.

The glade there was large, much larger than she'd suspected it might be, and in its precise center was a well. It was perhaps three feet tall, made of unremarkable rock, with a stone cap closed atop it. She studied it for another moment or two, then frowned as she realized what seemed so strange. Caps on wells weren't unusual, she supposed, though she'd seen them only on wells that were dry and owned by farmers who didn't want children and grandchildren falling down them.

But why would a dry well find itself in the midst of a forest full of spells?

Daniel was standing by the well. Sarah watched him busily trying different spells to get it to do something. Open, shut, disintegrate: who knew? She leaned against a tree when the view became slightly tedious. It was difficult not to snort at his increasingly grandiose movements. He finally grew so frustrated at his lack of progress, he put his hands on his hips and began to shout at the rocks. When he drew a sword she hadn't known he had and started to hack at the stone, she supposed she might safely leave him to his madness for a bit and see how Ruith fared.

She walked back to find him kneeling in the same place, breathing in and out very carefully. She squatted down in front of him.

"Why does this place make you so ill?" she asked.

"I don't know."

"You're lying." She could see that on his face without any special gift of sight. "Have you ever been here before?"

He only bowed his head and rubbed his hands over his face. "Ask me later, I beg you."

She was unsettled enough by his tone to agree. "Daniel is there."

Ruith only nodded, as if he'd expected nothing less.

"What is that well full of?"

He looked up, his face ashen. "Power."

She would have fallen over, but Ruith's hand shot out and kept her balanced. She closed her eyes briefly, then looked at him.

"He wants to have it."

Ruith nodded.

"Is it evil?"

"It was, once. What it is now, I can't say." He took a deep, unsteady breath. "What is your brother doing?"

"Trying to open it, I think. First he tried a few spells. Now he's just hacking at the stone with his sword."

Ruith's expression lightened just the slightest bit. "He isn't."

"He is. Shall I go see what else he's combining?"

"I'll come—"

She put her hand on his shoulder and forced him to remain where he was. "There's no need. I'll go have a look, then return."

He began to struggle to his feet. "You shouldn't—"

"And neither should you." She pushed him toward a tree and propped him up against it. "Stay there. I'll go have another look, then tell you what I found—"

"Nay," he said sharply, "I must come." He took another breath, deeper this time. "If you would hand me my sword and bow, that would help."

She supposed there was no point in arguing with him about it. She fetched his sword, but slung his arrows over her shoulder and kept his bow herself. She put her arm around his waist and walked slowly with him until they were within sight of the glade. Ruith's breathing was a painful-sounding rasp in the stillness. He put one hand out on a tree and leaned heavily on it, but he kept his other arm around her shoulders.

"What should I do?" she murmured.

"Stay here whilst I see to him," Ruith said without hesitation. "But I must catch my breath for a bit longer before I do."

"Are you ever going to tell me what ails you?"

He squeezed her shoulders slightly. "Aye. When you cut it from me with a dull knife."

She didn't release him. "He's now trying to set the stone on fire. What do you think?"

"I think he underestimates the peculiar properties of this forest," Ruith said grimly. "If he's not careful, he'll set himself on fire."

Daniel chose that moment to do just that. He flapped his arms frantically and attempted to beat out the sparks that had leapt up and attached themselves to his tunic.

Before she could stop him, certainly before she thought better of trying to stop him, Ruith had walked unsteadily out into the glade. Daniel turned around in time to have Ruith catch him under the chin with his fist and send him sprawling. Sarah would have complimented Ruith on his technique, but she didn't have the time.

She was too busy trying to find her breath to shout that they were not alone.

Twenty

❧

Ruith heard the twang of his great bow and turned about in surprise.

Sarah stood there, killing things from nightmares as they lumbered into the glade. The bow was too big for her, but she was managing it with admirable skill. He shook his head briefly and wondered if there would come a time when he wouldn't be surprised by something she was able to do. He left her to it and turned back to his most pressing problem.

Just as a precaution and because he was beginning to stir, Ruith pulled Daniel of Doìre to his feet by the front of his tunic, elbowed him firmly in the face, then let him slump down to the ground, groaning. One less useless thing to worry about. He stumbled across the glade, unsheathed his sword, and put himself between Sarah and a trio of trolls. The arrows wouldn't last forever and it was taking Sarah at least four to bring down each of the creatures coming toward her. Once those were exhausted, she would have nothing standing between her and death but him and his sword.

And he knew instantly that that wouldn't be enough.

Not even the fact that the trolls were coming for him would be enough to save her if he didn't call upon more aid than his sword and bow could provide. He put himself at her back, feeling her elbow bumping into his arm each time she loosed an arrow, and made a decision.

He took a deep breath, then released all his magic.

It should have sent him to his knees, but he kept himself upright through sheer willpower alone and began to kill things with a spell of death that came all too easily to his tongue. He had never used that spell—a spell his father had perfected, as it happened—though he had often imagined how it might be to try it out on his father, the arrogant bastard—

"I have no more arrows!"

Ruith put his left hand behind him and yanked her against his back. He turned in a circle and fought with sword and spell, keeping evil at bay with the first and killing with a spell of Olc that was augmented far beyond what it should have been by an anger he hadn't realized he had burning in him like a raging fire.

A quarter hour later, he dropped to his knees, stars swimming in front of his eyes. He had never in his life been so exhausted, not even twenty years ago after he'd managed to drag himself up to the door of his house, crawl inside, then collapse in front of the fire.

"Ruith, you're burning up," Sarah said, her hand on his back. "Are you ill?"

"Nay," he gasped. "Are they all dead?"

"They are," she said, sounding completely unsettled. "I'm not sure what killed them, though. There are more here than we could have seen to."

He couldn't answer. He had to simply breathe until he thought he could see straight. He supposed it was going to take more time than he had to manage that. He squinted at the glade, full as it was of the bodies of his enemies, and saw it as he'd seen it a score of years earlier, with his mother lying there—

"Daniel isn't here."

He wrenched himself away from that memory. He supposed Sarah had it aright, but he honestly couldn't tell for certain. He continued to simply suck in air for another precious moment or two, then reached for her hand.

"Can you fetch my arrows?" he rasped. "I'm sorry to ask it—"

"Don't be daft," she said briskly, walking away from him. "I'll hurry."

He supposed she was wise to. He had no sense of time passing, but he imagined Sarah had worked very quickly. She returned with two score arrows in her hand.

"I didn't clean them," she said apologetically.

"We'll do it later," he said. He used his sword as a means of getting himself to his feet, then incinerated the bodies almost without thought. Sarah gasped, but he said nothing. He merely buried his magic again, carelessly and incompletely, but it would have to do. He resheathed his sword and wished he had the strength to strap it to his back.

Sarah did it for him, pulled his bow over her head, then drew his arm around her shoulders.

"We have to hurry."

He knew she was right. He only hoped they would manage to hurry quickly enough.

He ran with her, a stumbling, ungainly run that he was sure wouldn't end any other way but with him flat on his face in some location where he wouldn't want to be. He continued to run, though, because he knew that if he didn't get out of the forest, if he didn't get them *both* out of the forest, they wouldn't simply die.

Nay, their fate would be far worse.

Because whoever was sending those trolls had obviously had enough forethought to have them seek out those with particular characteristics. Magic, perhaps, or something else desirable in their blood. Ruith couldn't have said and he wasn't sure he wanted to know the truth of it.

He just knew he couldn't stop running.

He woke to the smell of hay in his nose and the crunch of it under what felt like his own cloak. That he had no idea where he was or how he'd gotten there was profoundly alarming. He let his eyes adjust to the gloom and realized that it was perhaps closer to day than he'd first suspected. He was still for a moment or two, then he carefully turned his head and looked at the soul breathing very softly beside him.

There were dark circles under her eyes, as if she hadn't slept in far too long. A pity it did nothing to diminish her beauty. He turned carefully so he might have an unobstructed view of her face.

He wondered how it was that a woman of her mettle and courage—and loveliness—had ever found herself as the daughter of Seleg of Doìre, a woman of uncommon ugliness inside and out. He wondered how it was she'd survived all those years with her brother picking at her, no doubt belittling her for her lack of magic, likely never appreciating her for all the things she could do.

He speculated for a while longer about how the hell she'd managed to get him from his last memory, which had been ducking under one of the final, putrid spells of illusion and disorder that had hung from the boughs of those accursed trees, to his current place, watching her dream. How he'd come from there to where they were was perhaps one of the more miraculous things that had happened to him . . .

Well, since he'd first seen Sarah on his doorstep.

He reached out and carefully brushed a few stray hairs from her forehead. She smiled faintly and he thought he just might weep.

If he hadn't been such a hard-hearted bastard, that was.

He had to clear his throat roughly just the same. "You aren't asleep," he said, his voice sounding hoarse to his own ears.

She opened her eyes and looked at him with another faint smile. "It wasn't for a lack of trying, believe me. Unfortunately, you think too loudly."

He continued to tuck strands of hair behind her ear, one by one, until he simply couldn't lift his arm any longer. He covered her hands curled under her chin with his and sighed deeply.

"Thank you."

"For what?"

"I'm alive, and I no longer feel like death. I suspect you might be responsible for both."

"Might be."

He smiled, partly because of her modesty and partly because he actually didn't feel as destroyed as he should have. Killing magic was, he had heard, quite exhausting. He had used magic in his youth constantly for a thousand things he hadn't thought twice about, but he had never made a piece of magic as large or as deadly as the one he had in the glade.

Then again, he was no longer a lad of ten summers. He had fury to spare. He supposed it should have worried him a bit, that anger, but he decided he would think on that later, when he'd forced himself to come to terms with the ruthless actions he'd taken. After all, he hadn't destroyed those creatures for pleasure, he'd done it to save Sarah's life and his own skin. It wasn't as if he'd walked casually up to a nearby mage, taken tea with him, then stripped him of every particle of his magic just for the sport of it—

He felt Sarah's fingers intertwine with his.

"Don't," she said, looking at him seriously. "Whatever you're thinking on, don't. Not today."

"Have you been eavesdropping on my dreams?" he asked, trying to achieve a light tone. He failed miserably. If she had any inkling of the darkness of his dreams, or of how he'd failed where he should have succeeded—

"Ruith."

He dragged himself back to her with an effort. "Aye?"

"Leave it. Whatever it is, leave it."

He stared at her in silence for a moment, then cleared his throat again. "What did I dream?"

"You didn't, for the most part," she said. "When you did, it was all darkness." She squeezed his fingers. "You didn't cry out, if that eases you any. But you seemed to sleep better if I slept next to you, so I did. I will admit," she added lightly, "that I am rather bruised because of it."

He felt his mouth fall open. "Did I hurt you?"

"You held me rather tightly now and again," she said dismissively, "but I expected nothing less from a man with an unhealthy respect for the fairness of his own face."

He couldn't smile. "Forgive me," he said without hesitation. "I didn't know—"

"Of course you didn't," she said. "I shouldn't have said anything about it." She kissed the back of his hand as casually as if she'd been doing it for years, then untangled her hands from his. She sat up and brushed the hay out of her hair, then shivered. "'Tis cold here. I thought we were finished with winter."

"Not in the mountains," he said, suppressing the urge to pull her back down next to him and wonder how it was he'd been so weary that he hadn't known he'd had her in his arms. He pushed himself gingerly into a sitting position and looked about himself. The stall wasn't overly large, but it was enough for the two of them and his entire collection of wood and steel, most of which lay on the other side of Sarah within easy reach. He looked at her gravely. "You brave gel."

She shrugged, though it wasn't perhaps as convincing as she might have wanted it to be. "I fear I gave the farmer a goodly bit of your gold for the stabling of our horses and yet more for his secrecy. I thought it worth the trouble to pay richly for both."

"I would have done the same thing," he said. He rubbed his hands over his face, shook his head to clear it, then looked at her. "How did you manage to get us both here?"

"I'm stronger than I look," she said with a smile. "And we were fortunate that our horses came when I whistled. You weren't altogether coherent at the time, but you managed to get yourself up on your horse when I shouted that you had to and you stayed there without my having to tie you on. I was prepared to ride with you, but you wrapped your arms around Osag's neck and didn't let go until we reached this farm. We're three days east and a bit north of that . . . that place."

She related the events as if they'd been nothing, but he wasn't fool enough to believe she hadn't paid a substantial price for what she'd done. He looked at his hands for a moment or two, then slid her a sideways look.

"And how do I begin to repay you for this? Shall I rebraid your hair for you or let you sleep?"

"Both," she said with a smile, "but the last first. I will admit I'm tired. You're damned heavy."

He laughed a little in spite of himself. "I daresay I am." He rolled off his cloak and patted the spot he'd just relinquished. He waited until she had argued with him for a bit, then given up and taken his place. He covered her with her own cloak, then smoothed the hair back from her face. "I'll go chop wood or find something to trade for another meal or two and a bit more secrecy."

She looked up at him seriously. "The farmer has magic."

"Does he?" Ruith asked in surprise. "How do you know?"

"He hid us."

"From prying eyes wanting a look at the lovely daughter of the witchwoman Seleg?" he asked with a smile.

"From my brother."

Ruith felt a little winded. He trailed his fingers through the hair at her temple a time or two, but his hand trembled as he did so, so he stopped. "Indeed."

"He's on his way to the keep at Ceangail," she said, looking at him seriously. "I only know because I heard him ask the farmer for directions. I'm assuming he didn't find what he needed at that well."

Ruith shook his head. "I imagine we would likely know of it otherwise."

She put her hand over her mouth and yawned suddenly. "I'm sorry. I'm not sure I can stay awake much longer."

"How long has it been from the well?" he asked.

"Six days. Three to get here, then three secluded here in luxury."

"I owe you a fortnight at a palace," he said, with feeling.

She smiled and turned toward him, her eyes already closed. "Where you can see to the garrison and I can join the weaver's guild. At least there we might have a decent place to sleep, though, so I accept. Though this is a very . . . comfortable . . ."

He didn't imagine she would finish that thought anytime soon. He waited until she was well and truly asleep, then he collected the knives that went down his boots. There was no sense in terrifying the farmer with anything else, though if the man had magic, perhaps he was less disposed to being intimidated than others of his ilk.

Ruith didn't think he wanted to know what sort of magic the man possessed.

Six hours later, he had chopped a month's worth of wood and rid himself of his lingering malaise. He happily accepted a basket with things that gave off steam and smelled quite edible, then walked back to the stall, ducked under the spell of un-noticing the man had used, an eminently functional and sturdy spell of Wexham, and set his burdens down. He spelled the lamp in the corner into lighting without thinking about it, only then realizing that he hadn't managed to rebury all his magic. Again.

He was beginning to think that hadn't been an accident.

He stood there, wrestling with himself for quite some time. He knew what needed to be done. It should have been a burden to him, that magic in his veins, and getting rid of it a blessing.

He shook his head sharply. He couldn't go any further down that path. If nothing else, his actions in the glade had proven that to him. He was a man in full control of his passions, but he was also Gair of Ceangail's son. Whatever magic he might have inherited from his mother was also tainted with his father's. He leaned back against the stall as again the vision of that river of Fadaire he'd stood in washed over him. Beautiful, almost too beautiful, but running through banks that were corrupted with Olc and Lugham and a half dozen other ugly things his father had been master of.

Perhaps he could have ignored all of that and hoped that he could have overcome his father's legacy, but the absolute rage that had rushed through him in the glade proved that even thinking about it was foolhardy. Better to leave the possibility as something merely to be speculated on when he was in front of his fire with his feet up.

But one more thing first.

He knelt down next to Sarah, sleeping so peacefully, and took her right hand lightly in both his own. He held his breath until he was certain she was still sleeping deeply, then with great care worked on her arm. There were many spells for healing, but the most efficacious were those of Camanaë. He had not only the right to use them, because of his grandmother, but the power to constrain them to work where others might not. Even with only a fraction of his power to hand, they came easily to his tongue and did his bidding without hesitation. He took away the swelling, repaired the damaged tissues, then removed the source of the pain.

But the blackness remained, thin trails where the spell had burned her.

He frowned and tried again, without any more success than his grandfather had had. He sat back on his heels and quickly rifled through his enormous store of spells, ones he had learned in his youth and others he had memorized from the books he'd found in his house, just for the sake of keeping his mind sharp. He tried half a dozen, but with the same result.

Which was no result at all.

Sarah stirred. He didn't release her, but he took a moment and gathered up the rest of his magic, *all* his magic, and buried it again under thick, impenetrable spells of illusion and un-noticing. Should anyone have looked his way to see what he might have possessed, they would have found him not worth a second look. Had they been determined enough to look twice, they would have found only distraction and confusion. He took a deep breath, stepped back figuratively into his familiar and comfortable world of swords and unremarkableness, then waited for the relief he knew he should feel.

Odd that it didn't seem to be coming.

"You have healing hands."

He blinked and realized Sarah was looking up at him. "What?" he asked, feeling unaccountably nervous. If she had any idea who he truly was, or what he was capable of, or what his father had done . . .

"My arm feels better," she said, squeezing his hand and smiling. "Perhaps it was a decent bit of sleep that did it."

"It was," he said without hesitation. "How does the rest of you feel?"

"Starving. Is that supper I smell?"

"Aye, and it's still hot. Care for some?"

"Please."

He pulled a milking stool over, put the basket on it, then sat on the other side of it from her and ignored everything that had just happened in the previous ten minutes. It was a pleasure to simply enjoy a remarkably tasty supper whilst being nothing more than a simple, unremarkable swordsman. It was made all the more enjoyable by pleasant company, to be sure.

And he didn't miss his magic.

Not at all.

"You look better," she said.

He smiled, putting his thoughts behind him. "Sleep and a little axe work do wonders," he agreed. "You look better . . . Rested, I mean."

She smiled. "I've no vanity to wound, trust me. I'm sure I wasn't a pleasant sight."

"Actually, a more pleasant sight I've never woken to," he said honestly.

She blinked, then turned slightly red. She looked at him, blushed a bit more, then threw a hunk of bread at him. He laughed a bit, then gave up any more attempts at compliments and simply watched her as she ate. That seemed to please her even less, but at least what she threw at him was edible, so he helped himself to it and found himself smiling more than he had in years. And whilst he smiled, he considered the lovely woman he had the pleasure of looking at in rather unlikely surroundings. He realized he had completely taken for granted the beauty he'd enjoyed in his youth. Seanagarra was, he had to admit, a spectacular place in which to pass a childhood, especially given that it had been contrasted nicely with profoundly unpleasant fortnights spent at his father's keep in Ceangail, something he had done his damndest to forget. At the time, he hadn't thought anything of Tòrr Dòrainn's forests full of mighty pines and stately oaks. He had no doubt spent more time trampling over flowers that sang and stomping through brooks that laughed for the mere joy of their existence than he had appreciating the incredible gift of enjoying them he'd been given.

His life hadn't been without its share of human beauty as well, of all kinds. Elves in Tòrr Dòrainn, noblewomen in other locales, the stark, harsh beauty of the south where stumbling on a clutch of wildflowers clinging to a sheer rock face was an unexpected reminder that not all the world was full of darkness.

But never in all his years had he looked at something that affected him the way a lovely face framed by hair the color of cognac when held to the fire had. Only it was more than just her visage, or her tenacity, or her willingness to walk into darkness when there was no light to guide her. It wasn't her ability to pick up a weapon that wasn't hers and fight to defend someone weaker than she, or her clear sight, or the reserves of strength and determination he suspected he hadn't seen but a fraction of.

It was her light.

He didn't want to think how badly he needed that light.

There was also the fact that when he complimented her, she threw food at him, but he supposed he should reserve that bit of deliciousness as something to be savored later.

"I'm running out of bread," she said.

He blinked, then smiled at her. "Should I stop complimenting your beauty?"

"Aye," she said shortly. "You're embarrassing me."

"Then you can compliment me."

"Ha," she said with a snort. "And leave you more conceited than you are already? Rather I should point out your flaws, for your edification."

He laughed uneasily. "There is an overabundance of cloth there, I fear. You'll be sewing on my faults all night when you should be sleeping."

"Hmmm," she said, nodding. "Overprotective, overbearing, overskilled . . . Aye, there are faults there enough for the examining." She looked at him, suddenly serious. "Unfortunately, they don't seem like anything but virtues to me, given that you've saved my life with them."

He found himself shifting uncomfortably. He looked hopefully at the basket but found nothing in there to use in his own bit of throwing.

Sarah only smiled and pushed herself to her feet. "Now you know how I feel. I need to walk for a bit. I don't do well in tight spaces."

He rose and picked up the lantern. "Was your mother's house too small for you?"

"I slept in the barn whenever possible," she admitted, "or outside."

He let her out of the stall, then hung the lamp up on a hook and assumed it wouldn't burn the place down. "Why didn't you leave your mother's house sooner?"

She shrugged. "I had to wait until I had earned enough gold to start a new life."

He said nothing, but instead reached for her hand as easily as if he'd been doing it for years. She didn't flinch, or pull away, so he thought he might venture to hold it a bit longer.

"Ruith?"

"Aye."

"Why did the elven princess marry Gair, do you think?"

He stumbled. He hadn't seen that question coming. He took a

deep breath. "I honestly have no idea. She must have loved him at some point, else she wouldn't have wed him, nor had seven children with him. I don't think he was always as he became, though I suppose the seeds were there." He walked out of the barn with her and looked at her by moonlight. "You think about him often, I daresay."

"I don't understand mages," she said simply. "Or at least the ones I've known. I don't understand having the power to do good, but choosing to do evil instead."

"Perhaps they have no choice."

She looked up at him. "Everyone has a choice."

"Perhaps the temptation to be less than what they could be is simply too strong to resist."

"And if you had been Gair of Ceangail?" she asked, stopping and looking at him very seriously. "What would you have done?"

He flinched. His first instinct was to turn and walk away. He'd done it often enough in the past. In fact, he'd done it every last bloody time he'd been faced with something that forced him to come too close to looking at himself, or his memories, or his dreams. He opened his mouth to speak, but found no kind words there. All that was there was the overwhelming urge to tell her it was none of her business what he would have done.

She saw it in his eyes. He knew that because she tilted her head slightly for the briefest of moments, then took a step back, slipping her hand from his.

"I'm sorry," she said simply. "That was a stupid question that deserves no answer." She put on a bright smile. "Are you interested in a little race across the field to that tree and back? Loser has to clean the other's tack."

She didn't wait for him to answer before she turned and bolted. He was so surprised to find his favorite tactic being used by someone else that it took him longer than it should have to even begin to catch her. And then he realized he had truly never given her credit for her speed. He reached the tree after she had, then had to sprint to even reach her before she gained the barn. He bested her by only a step and that only because his legs were longer. He leaned over with his hands on his thighs and gasped for breath.

"Someday you'll outrun me," he managed.

"I almost did today."

"Only because you left me behind, thinking on the glories of watching you do my work for me," he said, straightening with a half laugh.

She scowled at him. "Very well. Go put your feet up and I'll polish your saddle."

He caught her hand before she could walk away. "That isn't what I want."

"What, your boots too?" she asked in astonishment.

He shook his head and tugged her into the barn and along after him down the aisle between rows of stalls. "Something far worse."

"Worse than your boots?" she squeaked.

He smiled and fetched the lamp from off its hook. He led her into the stall and bid her sit on his cloak. He sat down behind her and reached for the brush he'd borrowed from the farmer. He began to unbraid her hair only to fair rip it out of her head when she turned to look at him.

"What are you doing?" she demanded.

"Claiming my winnings, which is you sitting here allowing me to run my grubby fingers through your hair until I'm satisfied. It might take hours, so I'm sure at some point you'll consider it a poor exchange for my having a gleaming saddle."

"You're daft."

"Obsessed."

She laughed softly, then turned her face forward. "Do your worst, then. I'll bear it manfully."

He wasn't sure he would be able to, but he attempted it just the same. He managed probably half an hour of sheer enjoyment before he couldn't fight the thoughts creeping in like water into a boat full of small holes. He rebraided Sarah's hair half a dozen times before he was content with his work, then he simply sat there with his hand on the small of her back.

His path was clear. He was going to have to continue to follow Daniel, and he was going to have to do it without magic. If he'd walked into his father's keep with his magic running through his veins, he would have been immediately identified for who he was. He had no idea who inhabited the keep now, but he had his suspicions and those were unpleasant ones indeed. He didn't imagine Daniel would fare very well there, nor find what he was looking for, but he was a useful idiot so Ruith felt he had no choice but to allow him to continue to freely pursue his course.

The pages of Gair's book were another tale entirely. He had considered destroying each page as he came upon it, but now he felt differently. If his goal was to destroy his father's legacy, it made no sense not to destroy it in its entirety.

He studiously avoided the realization that such had been Connail's plan as well and it had turned out badly for him indeed.

But he was not Connail of Iomadh and Gair was not alive to thwart him. Putting his father's book back together was the only idea that made any sense to him. He had had glimpses of it, of course, and memorized the spells without hesitation, but he hadn't been paying the attention to it that he should have. Perhaps one of his elder brothers could have told him exactly how many pages the book had had, or confirmed his memory of what spells it had contained, but since he had no hope of having that information from them, he would just make do on his own.

And until he was convinced he had the entire bloody thing, he didn't dare destroy the pieces. He wished he had a way to see the pages so Sarah didn't have to be involved. Though he supposed that if his search took him to Ceangail's keep itself, he was most certainly going to find a way to leave Sarah behind—

She turned suddenly and knelt in front of him, looking at him seriously. "Stop."

He blinked in surprise. "Stop what?"

"I can see what you're thinking."

"You cannot," he said, faintly horrified.

"You're planning on running off without me again."

He attempted a look of outrage. "I was not."

"You're a terrible liar."

He closed his eyes and bowed his head. "Sarah . . ."

"Didn't you see what I did with your bow? Can I not be of some service to you?"

He felt the very unwelcome sting of something in his eye. A stray piece of hay, no doubt. He blinked savagely for a moment, then looked at her. "The forest was terrible," he said quietly. "Where I must go now will be worse."

She put her shoulders back. "Magic doesn't trouble me. I can see what you cannot. Is that not worth something?"

The temptation to pull her into his arms and kiss her until neither of them could breathe was almost overwhelming. He wanted to hold her close and let the events in the world march relentlessly past him without his notice.

Unfortunately, he had the feeling that doing either would only make matters an infinite number of degrees worse.

"Your skill, my lady," he said gravely, "is not in question. Nor is your worth to me." He had to take another deep breath and blink to clear more hay out of his eyes, damn the stuff to hell. "It is your safety that I care about. And how am I to guarantee that when I can't guarantee my own?"

She set her jaw. "I don't need you to worry about me. *I'll* worry about me."

He took a deep breath and tried a different tack. "I don't want you to come."

"I don't care what you want."

He dragged his hand through his hair and looked at her in exasperation. "You will be safer here. I will be more efficient if I only have to worry about my own neck."

She lifted her chin. "Can *you* see the pages?"

He opened his mouth, then shut it, against his better judgment. He knew at that moment that he should have told her everything. There was even a little voice inside his head that told him that he should have, that continuing on whilst continuing to hide the truth was going to leave things going very badly for him in the not-so-distant future.

But apparently he was as incapable of putting his foot down with a beautiful, stubborn woman as he was of taking his own very sensible advice. So he cursed, scowled at her, then cursed again.

"This is a very bad idea."

"I'll guard your back."

"I'm afraid you'll have to, and that makes me even more unhappy than just the thought of you being anywhere near that pit of absolute hell."

"Have you been there before?"

"Aye," he managed, but he couldn't say anything else without saying everything else. He rubbed his hands over his face. "This is an extraordinarily bad idea."

"So you've said before. Now, when do we leave?"

He sighed. "We should sleep for a few hours."

"I'll sleep in front of the door, so you'll have to step on me to get over me."

He made no comment simply because that thought had crossed his mind. He spread out his cloak, then lay down. Sarah stretched out a safe, prim distance away, then rolled on her side to look at him. He reached out and took one of her hands in both his own.

"You would be safer here."

"Are we going to argue about this all the way to Ceangail?"

He sighed deeply, then kissed her hand much as she'd kissed his. "Woman, you are going to be the death of me, I fear."

"Not anytime soon," she said, squeezing his hand.

He considered for a moment or two, then spoke again. "The farmer offered us a chamber."

"Did he? Why?"

"He seems to think we're wed. Or at least promised. I think it must have been your tender care of me to convince him of such. Or perhaps you were merely gazing upon my visage with the admiration of a newly made bride."

"Vanity, thy name is Ruith."

He would have laughed at the sudden lightening of his heart, but he didn't think he would manage it without weeping. "I'm just trying to wring a compliment from you." *To distract us both from what lies ahead.*

She smiled. "A futile exercise, for you're well aware of your unwholesome beauty. I shudder to think of the numbers who have fallen victim to it."

"You might be surprised," he muttered.

She only smiled again and squeezed his hand just the slightest bit. He watched her for quite a while before he managed to say the words that burned like a live coal in his mouth.

"If I had been Gair," he said very, very quietly, "I would have kept my family safe."

She opened her eyes and looked at him. "I know."

She closed her eyes again.

That was a good thing, for then she didn't have to watch him weep. Aye, if he'd been his father, he wouldn't have taken his family to that bloody well, he wouldn't have put them in danger. He would have likely walled them up in a castle and only let them out if they'd been accompanied by a full contingent of guardsmen with very sharp swords and brutal spells at their disposal.

Then what did that say about him that he was willing to allow Sarah to accompany him where no sensible soul would wish to go?

He closed his eyes so he wouldn't have to look at the answer.

Twenty-one

❊

Sarah decided that the time would come, hopefully whilst she was still alive, when she would have to sit down and contemplate the consequences of her choices before she made them. She wished she had the time at present, but it was far too late for turning back now.

She wasn't sure she wanted to admit how badly she wished that wasn't the case.

She stood next to Ruith in the shadows of the trees that lined the road leading to that castle and suspected that this time, her choice was going to lead to consequences too terrible to bear. The keep before her was the single most inhospitable place she'd ever seen—and given that she'd grown to womanhood in Shettlestoune, that was saying something.

The grey of the walls was unrelenting, the towers crumbling, the air hanging over those walls and towers full of smoke and stench she could smell from where she stood. There was a profound darkness there, a darkness that permeated the stone, the grounds, even the forest where she stood. It had soaked into the road that led to a bridge stained with it and dripped down from that bridge to pollute the moat below.

She wasn't altogether certain she would manage to cross that bridge, truth be told.

She looked next to her to see if Ruith was equally as affected by it. Unfortunately, he was only staring at the keep as if he studied how best to assault it. His expression was so forbidding, she didn't bother to ask him if he was willing to change course.

He had been grim on the way to that horrible well, true, but his descent into unfathomable depths of it these past two days made his mood before seem cheery by comparison.

It was almost as if he'd known what he would find here.

That was odd, but she supposed it was merely something else to add to the very long list of things about Ruith that were puzzling. She decided there was no better time than the present to examine that list—because it was an excuse to think about something other than what lay in front of her.

It was strange that he had no magic when his family, more particularly his grandfather, seemed to possess quite an enormous amount of it. Sgath had said nothing of Ruith's parents or siblings, but Ruith had said they were all dead. Had they all been slain together? And if so, by whom, and had that slaughter been what had driven him south to Shettlestoune? Surely he wouldn't have traveled there without a desperately compelling reason, not when he had Lake Cladach as another refuge.

And that was perhaps the greatest puzzle of all. If he'd had Sgath's house there simply waiting for him to call it home, why hadn't he gone there instead of continuing on to the wilds of the south?

And how in the world had he managed such a journey at the tender age of ten winters?

Those were answers he obviously didn't want to give, though she supposed the reason for that was likely the most important of all. He had secrets, that lad, that he hadn't even given to Master Franciscus. She couldn't shake the feeling that they led, in a less-than-roundabout way, to the keep standing in front of them.

Gair of Ceangail's keep.

It seemed improbable, but she continued to come back to that name despite its improbability, never mind that Ruith had said nothing at all about the spells of Gair's they had collected, nor had he commented, at least in her hearing, on Gair's having taken Connail's power. And he had certainly said nothing about how he knew his way to the keep standing in front of them. Or to that evil well—

She froze. It had been a well of power that Gair had opened, a well that had spewed its dreadful contents out and slain Gair's entire family. She shook her head. It couldn't have been *that* well, the one they'd left behind them a handful of days earlier.

Could it?

"We should press on."

Sarah looked up at Ruith, fighting to keep her thoughts off her face. Had he suspected it might be Gair's well? Had he listened to one too many tales of black mages and learned many things she wouldn't have expected him to know?

None of which explained how he'd known where that well lay, or why the glade had made him so ill, or why those monsters seemed to be coming for him alone.

Or why, after laying out his plan, he'd stopped speaking two days ago and descended into a silence she hadn't dared break, though perhaps that had been for the best. There had been no reason to discuss their destination—especially her desire to turn tail and run away from it as fast as her legs would carry her.

She took a deep, careful breath. Nay, the choice had been made and there was nothing left to do but keep going and let answers to questions come later. Daniel was quite possibly inside the keep and if not, Ruith wanted to attempt an assault on the library to see if he could find the rest of the pages of that book, or learn what had happened to it. If they found both the book and Daniel together, so much the better.

Though she wasn't precisely sure what either of them would do about it given that Daniel had magic and they did not.

Ruith suddenly pushed off the tree he'd been leaning against, took her by the hand, and started up the road to the keep.

"In the daylight?" she said, wishing her voice had sounded slightly less like a squeak.

"We're travelers seeking refuge from the gathering storm."

"Will they believe that?"

He glanced at her. "If we look desperate enough, they might." He turned back to the keep, no trace of emotion on his face. "We'll look for your brother first."

Sarah took a deep breath, then nodded. She was too terrified to say anything else.

By the time they reached the unguarded bridge that dripped with evil and spanned a moat full of other vile things she didn't want to identify, she was shaking so badly, she could hardly walk. She wasn't afraid of dying; she was terrified of living too long in the tender care of a mage with nefarious intentions.

"I'm a coward." Her teeth were chattering, but she supposed Ruith hadn't noticed.

"Stay behind me," he suggested. He looked at her briefly. "If only you looked more like a lad, I would feel better about your safety."

"I smudged dirt on my cheeks."

He stopped and looked at her. "No amount of dirt, Sarah of Doíre, could possibly hide exactly what you are."

She pulled her hood forward over her face as he had done. "Better?"

"Better would have been leaving you behind," he said grimly, "but as I was fool enough not to tie you up and leave with your howls of outrage ringing in my ears, I have only myself to blame for whatever happens to you."

"I insisted on coming," she pointed out. "To guard your back."

He shook his head slowly. "We are entering a keep, love, where I'm not sure it will matter."

"You needed me to look for the pages."

He sighed. "Aye. Pray we get that far."

He looked at her once more, then nodded toward the keep. She walked across the bridge with him in silence. There was nothing left to say.

Ruith knocked confidently, as if he weren't at all plagued by the terror that raced through her veins. The door creaked open almost immediately and Sarah felt her mouth go dry. She had thought she knew all about darkness, for she had seen it daily with her brother, she had seen it in Ruith's house that first time he'd opened the door to her, and she'd seen enough at that accursed well to last her a lifetime. She had hoped that somehow, those things would have helped her acquire the ability to endure whatever she found in Ceangail.

She had obviously been sorely mistaken.

Ruith kept his hands at his sides, well away from his weapons. He'd left his bow and arrows behind with the horses, along with his sword, but his knives were still down his boots and on his back. Lethal enough still, if the lad looking at him had any sense.

The guardsman opened his mouth to speak, but he was suddenly yanked backward and a fight ensued. Ruith hesitated, then fumbled for her hand.

"Let's go."

She didn't have a chance to answer before he'd pulled her into a passageway full of absolute chaos.

She looked down at her feet. They were almost immediately

reached for by spells and so were Ruith's. She looked around her frantically, then stopped, momentarily overcome by the things she saw.

Spells, innumerable spells, lay in twisting, writhing masses on the floor, put there no doubt to immobilize enemies—or perhaps just those the lord of the keep was unhappy with. Sarah took a deep breath, then looked for escape, ignoring the way the spells had already wrapped themselves around her ankles. In the middle of the passageway the spells were damaged, sliced perhaps with some sort of magical knife. She could see the ends of them waving in a wind that was most certainly not there, as if they'd been noxious vines so virulent that even severing them from their roots couldn't kill them.

"In the middle," she said quickly. "The spells are not so many there."

Ruith wrenched himself away from what tried to bind his feet, then leapt forward, pulling her with him. She went, but almost left one of her boots behind. She drew her knife briefly, slit the spell, then jerked herself away from the ends of it that tried to capture her again. She shoved her knife back down her boot and hurried forward to follow Ruith.

He stopped the first guardsman who looked amenable to it, a man sporting a stitched cut over his eye. The man looked at him with a scowl.

"What d'ye want?" he demanded.

"We be trav'lers lookin' fer a meal," Ruith said in a very decent imitation of the worst of Shettlestoune accents. "Any to be had 'ere?"

"Are ye daft, man?" the guardsman said, scowling. "Can't ye see we're too busy to feed beggars?"

Ruith nodded sympathetically. "What's befallen ye?"

"Some bloody gel and her guardsman came through a pair of days past," the man groused. "A bloody demon with a blade was she, I'll tell ye. The new lord's been raging ever since."

"The new lord?" Ruith asked politely. "Is 'e blond, with a spell—"

The man rolled his eyes. "Hunger's made ye stupid. The lord's Doílain and 'e's dark-haired, of course." He shot Ruith a look of disgust, then stomped off with a curse, apparently oblivious to the spells he was wading through.

Ruith took a deep breath, then turned to his left and strode down the passageway as if he knew exactly where he was going. Sarah would have spared thought for that, but she didn't dare. It was all she could do to keep up with him and ignore the spells she could see lurking in a darkness the torches on the wall couldn't begin to relieve.

They were soon caught up with guardsmen who were running about as if the keep were still under assault. Sarah supposed the confusion provided some anonymity for her and Ruith, but that was little comfort. With every minute that passed, she grew more unnerved. If Ruith felt the same, he didn't show it. She didn't dare press him. She simply followed him as he ducked into a stairwell that led down to what she assumed were the kitchens.

There was no less confusion there. Ruith didn't stop for pleasantries or food; he merely pulled her along with him and wound his way through tables, then back through kegs and barrels and up a tight circular staircase. Sarah found herself now thoroughly unnerved. She would have demanded that he tell her how the hell he knew where he was going, but she didn't have the breath for it, or the desire to sound as panicked as she was.

The place was simply crawling with spells. She could no longer see the walls or the floor for the spells that covered them and continually shifted, leaving her feeling as if the keep didn't truly exist around her. She touched as little of the stone as possible as she climbed what seemed to be an endless set of stairs.

She stumbled out into a chamber behind Ruith, then jumped out of his way as he shut the door and tried to bolt it. The bolt was broken beyond repair and there was no other means to secure it. Ruith cursed, then pushed the hood back from his face.

"We'll hurry."

She nodded. "Please."

He took a deep breath, though that didn't help his color. His face was ashen.

"Do you see anything?" he asked, his voice a harsh croak in the silence. "Any . . . spell?"

Sarah looked around her. It was a library, obviously, and looked as if it had once been in a terrible fire. There were scorch marks on the ceiling still, though someone had apparently made a feeble attempt in the past to clean the floor. It was obvious, however, that the chamber hadn't been used in quite some time. There was a handful of dusty, rickety chairs near the decent-sized hearth but no rug lying on the unforgiving stone floor. She supposed there might have been bookshelves lining the walls at one point, but now the walls were lined with crude wooden things that looked as if they'd been hewn with an axe and nailed together without any care.

"I don't know," she began slowly.

"Look," he insisted. "Hurry."

She shot him a look, but couldn't chasten him for his lack of manners. He was absolutely grey. She nodded, then turned to the nearest wall and looked closely at what lined one of the shelves.

The books bore the marks of the fire that had apparently swept through the library. Blackened spines, wrinkled covers, scorched pages, all covered by copious amounts of dust. She only managed to look at a few books before just the thought of touching more of them made her ill. She turned and looked at Ruith, who had started searching on the other side of the chamber.

"They're covered with spells."

"Aye."

He didn't seem surprised by that, nor troubled by the spells.

Perhaps he was, and he simply refused to show it. She wished she had his control. It was almost all she could do to stay where she was and not bolt from the castle where she might actually breathe clean air again.

She turned back to where she had begun and forced herself to walk slowly along each wall, looking carefully on each shelf to see if she saw anything that burned with that unwholesome light she had come to recognize. She finally knelt down and looked on a bottom shelf. She pulled a book from between its companions and opened it. There was something there, but it turned out to be only a corner of an obviously enspelled page, charred and brittle. She shut the book before that corner could reach out and burn her. Her arm had improved dramatically during that sleep she'd had in the first farmer's barn, though being inside Ceangail's keep had made it ache again.

She completed a circuit of the entire chamber, then decided that if she'd found a corner of Gair's book tucked inside something else, there was no reason not to think other bits of his book might be likewise hidden. She rubbed her arm gingerly and looked at the ruined floor as she walked across the chamber—

And into someone.

She looked up with an apology on her lips, thinking it was Ruith, only to find that it wasn't.

She backed away only to be hauled behind Ruith. He affected a casual pose, but she knew him well enough to know he was anything but that. His arms were folded over his chest, likely to put them closer to his knives if necessary.

"Well," the other man said with a disbelieving half laugh, "I just killed a man downstairs for telling me who he thought he'd seen."

"A waste of your effort, then," Ruith said seriously, "for he was surely mistaken."

Sarah leaned up on her toes slightly so she could see the other man's face. He was dark-haired and tall, handsome enough if she hadn't seen Ruith first, but he was full of the darkness that hung in the passageways downstairs.

"Oh, I don't think he was," the other said softly. "But I wouldn't have believed it if I hadn't seen it for myself."

"Your eyes are deceiving you as well," Ruith said, just as quietly. "Let us be on our way, and we'll trouble you no longer."

"Are you daft?" the other asked with a laugh. "We thought you were dead. Now that I have you here in the flesh, do you think I'm stupid enough to let you go?"

"I don't know," Ruith returned sharply. "How stupid are you?"

The other's face was suddenly quite red. "I imagine you'll find out soon enough."

"Friend," Ruith said tightly, "I've no quarrel with you—"

"Friend?" the other man echoed with a snort. "That seems rather too cold a greeting for—"

Ruith lashed out suddenly, catching the other man under the chin and sending his head snapping back. He fell to the ground with a crash. Ruith turned on her.

"Pages?" he demanded.

"I—I don't know," she stammered.

"Well, look! I can't keep him unconscious forever."

Sarah turned and looked because she was too startled not to. She would have been a little tidier about it, but Ruith was cursing behind her, growing more agitated with every moment that passed. He had to favor his . . . friend . . . twice more with his tender ministrations to keep him senseless, but by then she had long since ceased to be careful about what she was doing. She pulled books off shelves without care, flipping through whatever she dared and shaking the others vigorously to dislodge whatever might have been lurking within the covers.

"Make haste!" Ruith said, his voice very strained.

"I am making haste," she snapped. She started on the last bookcase only to realize that the thumps of books against the stone weren't the only thing she could hear. Before she could point out to Ruith that those were booted feet coming up the stairs, he had taken her hand and jerked her along with him over to another doorway.

"We can't be caught in here," he threw over his shoulder. "Pull the door shut behind you."

She did, though she didn't imagine it would do any good, for again, there was no way to lock it. She stumbled along behind Ruith as he raced with uncanny surety down a passageway that was completely dark. He tried to open the door at what was apparently the end of it, but it wouldn't give way. He pushed her back a bit, then kicked it in. She crawled through the splintered wood after him and out into a great hall.

A hall full of souls waiting for them, apparently.

Ruith stopped so suddenly that she ran full into his back. It should have at least moved him, but it was as if he'd suddenly been turned to stone. She remained on her feet only because she had a decent sense of balance. Ruith was of absolutely no help.

Then again, perhaps he had other things to worry about.

She knew suddenly what a plump rabbit must feel like to find itself caught in an open field by a pack of determined, ravenous wolves. She turned and put her back against Ruith's, but then wished she hadn't. The men she now faced were armed with very sharp swords and vile humors. They looked to be a rather roughed-up bunch, as if that battle they'd recently been in hadn't gone particularly well for them.

She also realized, as she looked about herself a bit more, that those bruised and rumpled lads weren't where the true danger lay. There were other men in the great hall, men who moved suddenly to enclose her and Ruith in a large circle. A spell immediately sprang up between each of them, razor sharp and dripping with an unpleasant sort of magic that made her want to close her eyes so she didn't have to look at it any longer. But if she looked away, she might miss something and Ruith would pay the price.

She would have given much for the chance to simply sit and try to come to terms with what she was seeing, but she knew she wouldn't have that luxury. They were going to be fortunate to escape the hall, much less the keep. For reasons she couldn't understand, the men surrounding her and Ruith were profoundly angry. It was almost as if they had a reason that went far beyond normal annoyance at having one of their doors splintered.

She wondered about the man in the library who had quite obviously known Ruith somehow, but how was that possible? She would have attempted a whispered question to Ruith about that, but before she could decide how best to go about it, she found herself spun around roughly. She started to protest, then she realized who had done the spinning.

It was Ruith.

Not only had he taken her by the arms in a grip that was very painful, he was glaring at her.

"I told you not to follow me here! Can you not obey a simple instruction?"

Sarah blinked in surprise. "What?"

"Shut up," he snarled.

She felt her mouth slide open, but before she had the chance to demand to know if he'd lost his wits completely, he had turned her away from him and shoved her so hard that she went sprawling and slid across the floor.

Under the spell that connected the six men standing in a circle, as it happened.

"Get out of my sight," he ground out. "You disgust me."

She rose to her hands and knees in muck and other things she couldn't bring herself to identify, then turned and looked at Ruith in shock. He wasn't watching her, though. He was looking at a man who had melted through the circle and come to stand alongside him.

"Who is she?" the second man asked, folding his arms over his chest and tilting his head to one side. "A slave girl? Your *leman*?"

"Witch's get," Ruith said with a sneer. "The worst sort, of course."

"Too true, of course," the other man said. He turned to study Ruith. "I must admit I'm surprised to see you here. Actually, I'm quite surprised to see you alive. I was under the impression you were slain during that awful business at the well."

Sarah heard the words, but it took a moment for them to sink in. That *business at the well*?

She felt a chill slide down her spine.

"So what has brought you back to our father's keep," the man continued, watching Ruith with a calculating glance, "or shall I assume by the manner of your entrance that you don't want me to know?"

Sarah watched his mouth continue to move, saw that Ruith was also speaking, but she couldn't hear either of their words.

Their *father's* keep?

Before she could give any of it the thought it deserved, she was interrupted by the sound of very loud and vile curses. The man Ruith had felled in the library came stumbling out of the passageway into the hall, blood dripping down his chin to stain his shirt. He strode through the barbed spell and threw himself at Ruith.

Or at least he attempted to.

Sarah gaped at the spell she could see suddenly glittering in the air around him, binding him in mid-lunge, holding him immobile at a very awkward angle. She wanted to look away, for she had seen enough, but she could not. This was not village wizardry she was witnessing, or the occasional show put on by some traveling mage to delight and astonish, this was hard, unyielding, terribly powerful magic that reeked of evil.

She could hardly breathe.

"Let me go," snarled the man with the bloodied nose.

"I think not, Táir," the man standing next to Ruith said. "I have a question or two for our beloved brother before I take all his magic and kill him."

Sarah felt the floor begin to rock beneath her hands. It troubled her for a moment or two until she realized it wasn't the floor trembling, it was her. She backed away carefully until she felt the wall against her feet, then sat back on her heels against it. The stone wasn't as hard as it should have been—no doubt because of the magic that dripped down it like a noisome drape—but it was preferable to being out in the open where the chamber was so unsteady.

Magic?

Ruith?

Brother?

"I don't care what magic he bloody has, Doílain," the man named Táir ground out. "I have bruises to repay him for."

Doílain lifted his finger and Táir ceased speaking. His mouth was open and his eyes still blazed with hate, but he was, perhaps thankfully, now quite mute. Doílain walked over and pushed Táir back until he became a part of that circular spell.

"Stay there and don't move," Doílain suggested.

Sarah didn't imagine she would want to be anywhere near Táir when he finally managed to get free of what bound him.

Doílain glanced at her as he did so, frowned thoughtfully, then turned to study her.

"You know, Ruithneadh, that's a remarkably pretty wench there, though I suppose I should have expected nothing less from you. Even as a boy, you were a connoisseur of the finer things. But witch's get?"

"A dalliance," Ruith said dismisisvely.

"Of course," Doílain said. "The youngest son of Gair of Ceangail could likely have a princess of any house in any of the Nine Kingdoms, couldn't he? So, if you don't want her any longer, perhaps I—"

"Don't bother," Ruith said shortly. "She talks too much and she has no magic. I imagine you'd want to kill her within half an hour and then where would you be? Look rather in loftier spheres."

Sarah flinched as surely as if he'd slapped her, then she realized exactly what he'd said.

She had no magic? How in the *hell* did he know that?

She shook her head, but that didn't improve matters. She looked at Ruith, but didn't see the man she had eaten with in a barn three days ago, a man who had brushed her hair far beyond the point when she'd assumed he'd tired of it. Instead, there stood a man who looked at her with a hauteur that left her cheeks flaming.

"I have come home and won't need your services any longer," he said. "Get you gone before I'm forced to send you away. I promise you won't like what opens the door to you here."

"Aye, off you go, little rabbit," Doílain said, shooing her off with an indulgent smile.

Sarah realized she was having help with that. Guardsmen took her by both arms and hauled her to her feet. She tripped over bodies that weren't moving—dead perhaps—as she was propelled from the great hall. She looked back only once, but Ruith wasn't looking at her. He was deep in conversation with a man he obviously knew quite well. She realized then that he hadn't needed her help, indeed he had likely never needed her aid. For all she knew, the entire exercise from Doìre to Ceangail had been nothing but a bit of amusing sport for him.

Sport at her expense.

She was dragged across the passageway, then found herself flying out the front door. She landed on gravel that cut her hands and cheeks. She lay there for a moment or two, stunned, and listened to the front doors slamming behind her. She didn't look to see if anyone was on the outside of those doors. She simply heaved herself to her feet and ran, realizing as she did so that she was weeping.

Gair of Ceangail's youngest son?

It should have been impossible, but she could now see how it was all too possible. Hadn't he known things he shouldn't have? Hadn't he been angry with Connail's tales of Gair's evil? Hadn't he been uncommonly interested in the pages from Gair's book that apparently only she could see? Hadn't he been more than willing to accompany her so he could find her brother, who was also quite interested in what Gair had done?

And, the most damning of all, hadn't he known his way around his father's keep, as if he might have lived there at one point?

She tripped and fell to her knees, then staggered back to her feet and stumbled again down the road, feeling the terror she'd been feeling for most of the morning turn suddenly to a clear, clean fury. She might have lost all sense the moment she'd seen Ruithneadh of Ceangail's unnaturally handsome face, but now she was fully recovered.

And furious.

Damn him to hell a thousand times, the liar. He could have, at any point during the past several se'nnights, saved her time and trouble by pulling forth his mighty magic, dusting it off, and using it on her behalf. Instead, he had forced her to spend what little coin she had left on a merry chase that had left her, in the end, without her brother, without her horse-turned-dog, without her purse, and definitely without her pride.

All because of his perverse reasoning, which she was thoroughly convinced would be only understood by another bloody mage.

She had to slow down thanks to a stitch in her side, but that didn't keep her from stomping down the road with as much vigor as she could muster.

Unfortunately, that lasted only a quarter mile before the fine, righteous anger she was feeding began to lose some of its fierceness along the edges. She wasn't afraid of entertaining unpleasant thoughts, though, so she looked at them—albeit with a jaundiced eye.

It was true that he hadn't wanted her to come to Ceangail—likely because he feared she would discover his identity. He also hadn't wanted her to go to that terrible forest with its profoundly evil well, but that was likely so she didn't eat his supplies. There was the difficulty of realizing that the one place he had *wanted* her to come was Lake Cladach, but she rushed quickly by that thought before she became entangled in memories that were too beautiful to think on without weeping.

She realized, with a start, that she was standing still, staring off into nothing at all. She recaptured her fury and started again down the road. That bloody lout could rescue himself, then go on to lead whatever sort of purposeful life sons of black mages led. She washed her hands of him. She had her own quest to see to, one she could obviously not count on anyone but herself to fulfill. The sooner she was about it, the—

She saw a glint of yellow in the trees. She was surprised enough by the sight to leap off the road into a handy clutch of pine trees. She wondered if perhaps she was imagining things, but nay, there it was again: a blond-haired man walking through the trees on the far side of the road, oblivious to anything but his cursing.

Her brother, Daniel.

Sarah cast a baleful glance toward the keep, which was quite obviously Daniel's destination. She supposed she should have followed him, but she had no desire to enter those horrible walls again. She might find her brother, but then she would likely elbow him in the nose and render him senseless. If she saw Ruith again, she would stab him and render him dead.

Perhaps she would simply let all the mages she now knew congregate inside that spell-covered castle, then hope the bloody thing collapsed in on itself. If she could have found the right thread to the spell that covered the stone to accomplish that feat, she would have pulled it without hesitation.

It was tempting.

But so was a life free of magic, enspelled castles, and mages she wanted to see rotting in a hell of their own making.

She stood there for longer than she should have, dithering, before she made a decision, the best decision she'd made in a pair of fortnights.

She turned her back on the keep and walked away.

Twenty-two

※

Ruith knew he was going to die.

    The last time he'd been faced with that knowledge, he'd been a lad of ten winters, standing next to his sister under the boughs of a terrible forest and cursing to give himself courage. He'd watched his father open that well, watched him gape up at its contents shooting toward the heavens, and known that all hope was lost. He remembered letting go of his sister's hand to rush forward and try to stop the madness.

He'd failed.

He'd failed his mother, his brothers, his wee sister who he'd been charged to protect, yet somehow, beyond all reason, he'd been spared—only to find himself standing in a great hall that had once been free of his father's bastards but now was not, waiting to die.

He felt the first spell wrap itself around him even though Doílain's lips didn't move. Doílain was, after all, Gair of Ceangail's eldest son, bastard though he might have been. His power was great, even corrupted as it was by the blood of his mother, the witchwoman of Fás. Then again, she was powerful enough to give the masters at Beinn òrain pause.

The only thing good to come of the day was that Sarah was safe. He regretted how he'd had to bring that about, but perhaps she wouldn't, when she thought about it and could see why he'd done what he'd done. Perhaps she would even forgive him, in time.

He was tempted to release all his power and bring down the hall around his ears, killing everyone inside including himself, but he realized with a start that that was what Doílain was waiting for. He felt the first tentative intrusion inside his soul and knew Doílain was testing him to see just what he had that Doílain might want to take for himself.

"Where have you been?" Doílain asked idly, sending one of his servants off for a chair.

"Away," Ruith said shortly. He sensed others leaning closer, still bound together by magic he couldn't see but could definitely feel, but he paid them no heed. He supposed he knew without asking what *they* wanted.

Doílain put his chair near Táir, shot his brother a sardonic look, then sat and leaned back in that chair, looking for all the world as if he contemplated a fine afternoon behind the chess board.

"I'm surprised you didn't find your way here after Father was murdered. Keir did, you know."

Ruith struggled to mask his surprise. "Is he still here?"

"Unfortunately not," Doílain said with mock regret. "He seems to have slipped out of our . . . protection, shall we say. He has very little power left, of course, so I didn't waste the effort to follow him."

Ruith folded his arms over his chest. "Was my brother an unwilling inhabitant of his own home, then?"

Doílain smiled, but there was no warmth in it. "*His* home? How quickly you forget who lived here for centuries before you were spawned on that pretentious trollop from Tòrr Dòrainn."

Ruith threw himself forward only to realize he hadn't moved. He cursed himself viciously, but quite silently. He had been too long out of the world of mages and their ilk, had spent too many years numbing himself to their machinations and intentions. He had sensed the first spell, but now he realized that whilst he'd been dawdling amongst his memories, his bastard brother had wrapped him in so many spells that he couldn't move.

"If it eases your mind any," Doìlain said, crossing his legs and swinging one foot, "we didn't mistreat Keir. Not overmuch." He smiled. "Just a bit, now and again. Poor lad, he just couldn't fight us. I think Father must have taken most of his magic before he met his very untimely end, wouldn't you agree?"

Ruith didn't want to think on those memories. Aye, Gair had taken quite a bit of power to himself, including most of Keir's, which had rendered him almost unstoppable in the final seconds as he opened the well. Ruith knew that was why his mother hadn't been able to fight him, in the end. Her power had been immense, but Gair's had been more so, augmented as it had been by his sons' bloodright.

He could scarce believe Keir was alive. He had never considered it, but now he wondered why not.

Well, he knew why not. Because he'd hidden himself away in the most unlikely place possible and never intended to come out again, not even to see his family. Or, at least that had been his plan until he'd found a woman with pale green eyes and hair the color of cognac on his doorstep, a woman who wanted nothing more than peace, safety, and a place where she could weave things to make the world more beautiful.

"I wonder what Father left of you?" Doìlain asked.

Ruith didn't have a chance to answer before his soul was ransacked. He felt as if he'd just been kicked in the gut by a young stallion, but he ruthlessly refused to acknowledge it. It would only give Doílain pleasure he didn't deserve. He felt Doílain find the well of magic he'd created inside himself and knew of the other's intense displeasure at its construction.

And imperviousness.

"You won't last," Doílain promised.

"Why did you keep my brother here?" Ruith asked, ignoring the threat. He wished he sounded less affected by both Doílain's torture and the little spells someone—he had no idea who—was tossing at him, painful little spells that stung where they landed and blossomed into raging, invisible fires.

If he escaped, he was going to bring the entire bloody place down on everyone in that circle.

Doílain was smiling, as if he knew exactly what Ruith was thinking. "Amitán, stop tormenting him."

"I never liked him," a voice said from behind Ruith.

"I imagine he feels the same way." Doílain looked back at Ruith. "So, tell me, brother. Why do you think I kept Keir here?"

"My father's spell of Diminishing."

Doílain sat forward suddenly. "*Our* father's spell of Diminishing, boy."

"Perhaps he was *our* father," Ruith conceded, "but you have to wonder why it is he didn't see fit to share that particular spell with you. Could it be that you didn't have the power for it, or was it that he thought you too stupid to use it?"

Doílain was faster than a striking snake, Ruith had to concede that. His bastard brother had backhanded him before he saw the blow coming. He went sprawling only to find himself hauled to his feet and struck again.

Doílain's rage was palpable. "I'll kill you, you little whoreson."

"I suppose you could try—"

Doílain launched himself forward. Ruith felt his head connect with the stone of the floor in an unwholesome and quite abrupt way. He saw stars, but it wasn't the worst thing to happen to him, so he ignored it.

"Can't have what . . . you want . . . if I'm dead," he managed to gurgle.

Doílain heaved himself up, releasing Ruith's throat as he did so. He stood over him, simply shaking with fury. "I'll have your power if it is the very last thing I do on this earth."

Ruith didn't want to lay odds on that happening. He kept that to himself, though, and accepted help to his feet. He thanked his other bastard brothers, who would just as soon have slit his throat as look at him, then concentrated on Doílain. The others were powerful, to be sure, but Doílain was the one to watch. Hadn't he learned that well enough in his youth?

"Give me the spell," Doílain demanded.

"Never," Ruith said politely.

It was then that things began to go badly indeed for him.

He supposed it was prudent not to comment on the quality of Doílain's spells, more of which were being wrapped around him with alarming velocity, but he honestly couldn't help himself. It took his mind off realizations he couldn't help but come to quite abruptly.

He had made a grave miscalculation.

If he had been using his magic all these years, he might have stood a chance of releasing it all, then wiping out the entire collection of his bastard brothers, but his magic was unwieldy and the power too great. He had killed those trolls in the glade successfully, but without any finesse at all. He'd only glanced at them before he'd incinerated them, but they had been a bloody mess, as if a great sledgehammer had fallen upon them. He could only imagine how his other spells might go awry.

And he was in a hall full of mages whose magic might have been black as night, but it was well honed and well used. He wouldn't stand a chance against them.

And whilst Doílain might not have had Gair's spell of Diminishing, he was who he was and his power was not insignificant. Ruith was genuinely afraid that if he released all his power, Doílain might manage somehow to take it—even a fraction of it—and then where would the world be?

Nay, better that it all died with him.

Only he had the feeling his death would not be quick.

At least Sarah would be safe. He regretted to the depths of his soul every word he'd said to her, but what other choice had he had? She was defenseless and he unable to help her. He hoped her fury would carry her at least a few days' south where she would meet up with Franciscus and the two of them would decide, with any luck at all, to go to the schools of wizardry. She could tell the masters her tale, then someone would help her.

And then, with any luck, she would feel his last wish for her, which was that she seek out Sgath and let him build her a little house in that perfect spot on Lake Cladach. He himself would sit down beyond toil or sorrow in the east with his mother, his brothers, and his sister and tell them how much he'd loved her.

A pity he hadn't had a chance to tell her.

"You stubborn git," Doílain panted, "*surrender*!"

Ruith didn't have any strength left to manage even a grunt. He was in his father's hall, surrounded by mages who would as quickly slay him as look at him, and he was quite ill from the memories of living there in the past. It would be easy, so much easier actually, to push Doílain past the point of reason and find himself too dead to be a temptation to them any longer. It would certainly end problems of magic and the pain of knowing he alone of his siblings was left alive to come to . . . well, this. He opened his mouth to spew out the most vile insult he could. Or he did until he caught sight of movement near the window.

A blond man was gingerly crawling through the jagged glass and spells of a window at the back of the hall. He was apparently unhappy with the condition of his hands, judging by the look on his face and the way he was apparently on the verge of letting loose a torrent of curses. But those curses never came. He stiffened, then fell over, senseless.

Sarah crouched behind him in the window well, a rock in her hands.

Ruith focused immediately on Doílain, suppressing his own string of what would have been very impressive curses. He imagined half of them at least would have been directed at Sarah of Doìre. Damn her to hell, what was she thinking? He'd perjured himself to the depths of his soul to send her away, yet there she was back again.

And she would soon be in Doílain's sights if he didn't do something very soon.

He opened his mouth to curse Doílain, then flinched at the streak of lightning that split the great hall from top to bottom.

Sarah.

Her name whispered across his mind as if someone else had said it, though he knew he was the only one in the hall who knew her name. The very thought of her was, as always, a cascade of sunshine pouring down through the trees of a forest. Pure, clear, and enough to drive away the darkness that was in him.

And if he had the chance, he just might shout at her until her ears rang.

He could scarce believe it, but he wondered if he just might have that chance. He couldn't move his head, but he could see if he looked hard enough, a creature of light standing just inside the hall door. Apparently, so could all his bastard siblings. Doílain spun around, curses and spells on his tongue. Six more brothers—which wasn't the full tally, but Ruith didn't spare any thought wondering where the others might be—gathered around Doílain to fight with what magic they had to hand. Táir was left where he'd been frozen in place.

Much as Ruith was himself.

He watched out of the corner of his eye as Sarah walked quickly to where he was, stopping at his side where she might be missed if Doílain turned to look at him.

"Who are you?" she demanded in a harsh whisper.

"What?" he asked in surprise.

"I want your name."

He struggled to breathe. "Just . . . go," he managed. "Please."

"Damn you to hell, I *won't* go until I can take you with me so I can stab you in your sleep. I want your name. Your *entire* name, you pathetic liar."

"I'm a very . . . good . . . liar."

She drew one of the knives from her boot and began to pick at the spells surrounding him.

"Your name."

He supposed there was no point in not giving it to her. "I am Ruithneadh . . . of Ceangail. Or of Tòrr Dòrainn . . . if you'd rather."

Her knife stopped its torture, and she came to stand in front of him. "You're a damned elf!"

"Only three-quarters."

"This isn't amusing and I'm not laughing." And her expression said she was telling the absolute truth. "You lied to me. From the very beginning. Actually, you were lying to me before we even met, living up there on your mountain, pretending to be someone you weren't."

"You weren't exactly . . . forthcoming . . ." He watched the words come out of his mouth and knew—perhaps because his mother seemed to be standing next to him in spirit, shaking her head slightly in that way she'd done when he was starting down a path of bad manners he shouldn't have—that they were the wrong ones.

"I was trying to save my life," she said hotly.

"So . . . was I."

"I wasn't hiding the fact that I had magic powerful enough to undo the world and everything in it!"

She was overestimating his abilities, but he didn't have the strength to tell her so. He could only close his eyes and concentrate on breathing. He didn't even have the energy to pay attention to what was becoming an all-out battle by the hall door.

She took a step closer to him. "Could you have found Daniel without this entire accursed journey? Found him and stopped him?"

There was no use in denying that either. His father had had a spell for everything, from keeping his favorite boots eternally scuff-free to forcing his steward to bring him a delicate infusion of tea every morning without being reminded. Aye, he could have found Daniel. Any other mage with even a rudimentary knowledge of hiding himself might have been more difficult, if not impossible, to locate, but Sarah's brother? Aye, he could have found him easily enough.

"I'm waiting."

He met her eyes. "Aye." If he'd been willing to use magic, which he hadn't been.

She glared at him, then pulled her other knife out of her boot. He wasn't altogether certain she didn't intend to stab him with them both, so he kept his mouth shut and hoped she wouldn't kill him before he'd regained enough strength to apologize.

She scowled at the spells that bound him—spells he couldn't see, as it happened—then from all appearances began to rearrange the strands. The spells were quite unwilling to release him, though, and her tugging was substantially more painful than he'd anticipated it would be. In time, she found something that almost sliced through him as she pulled it out where she could cut it.

And then every last bloody spell he'd been held captive by slithered to the ground like silken threads to pool at his feet.

Go . . .

Ruith found himself on his knees in that mess of spells, but not for long. Sarah hauled him up, then pulled his arm around her shoulders.

"Let's go."

Ruith looked to his right. "We should help whoever that is—"

"Master Franciscus said to go."

He felt his mouth fall open. "That's *Franciscus*? How do you know?"

"I can see him. Can't you? Or does your royal sight not extend to peering inside clouds of sunlight?"

He set his jaw. "You are the one with sight."

"And hearing as well, apparently. He wants us to go." She said it confidently, but she looked rather worried. "I would say I'm surprised to see him here—and even more surprised to see him with magic—but after the day I've had, I think I might have passed being surprised by anything. And I would argue with him, but I imagine we should listen to him and leave before Urchaid decides to detach himself from that darkness he's lingering in on the other side of the hall."

"Urchaid, as well?"

"Apparently, we are surrounded by men with secrets. Actually, I'm surrounded by men with secrets. And unless you're planning on using some of that mighty magic you apparently have to save us all—"

He shook his head sharply. "I will not."

"Somehow, Your Highness," she said flatly, "that is the one thing that doesn't surprise me."

"Don't call me that."

She looked at him in a way that made him flinch. "It's the least of the things I want to call you."

He imagined that was true and decided abruptly that he didn't particularly want the rest of that list. He merely nodded and leaned on her as little as possible. He gave Táir a push that landed him on the floor in the muck, because he couldn't help himself, then stumbled with Sarah across the hall. He forced her to go out the window first, then paused and looked down.

Daniel of Doìre lay on the floor at his feet. He was terribly tempted to just thrust a knife through the whoreson's heart, but he hesitated. He supposed that Daniel would meet his end in some other way, perhaps a more fitting way, if he woke to a hall full of angry bastards. He looked over his shoulder and wondered how it was he hadn't realized how fierce the battle on the other side of the hall was. It was darkness and lightning and terrible noise.

And there was other darkness as well, along the wall as Sarah had said. Urchaid? He didn't imagine she was mistaken, but it was odd just the same.

Go, Ruithneadh. Take Sarah and go.

Ruith hesitated. He couldn't simply flee—

Go. The battle is almost won.

"He wants us to go."

Ruith looked at Sarah, then nodded. "I hear him too." He heaved himself out of the window after her, then reached for her hand. He stopped himself just in time when he realized she was still holding on to her blades—and she had no intention of putting them down.

"Do you have a plan?" he asked, sucking in painful breaths of very cold air.

"Aye, you use your magic and find the pages so we can have this all over with."

"I couldn't see them, even with magic," he said wearily. "That is your gift."

She frowned, then nodded to her right. "Follow me, then. I know where another page is. I think it might be Daniel's, so I've no mind to touch it."

Ruith was so happy to be breathing the putrid air that surrounded his father's keep, he would have crawled over hot coals if

Sarah had wanted him to. He did his best to ignore the expression on her face he had full view of now and again.

Fury didn't begin to describe it.

She led him with unerring exactness to a small pack stuck between two rocks and covered with underbrush. She shoved her knives into her boots, then folded her arms over her chest and looked at him.

"There."

He unearthed from the pack a rolled leather scroll. He undid the leather ties, then slowly unrolled the sheaves.

It was his father's spells of Reconstruction and Diminishing.

Well, half of the latter.

He could hardly believe he was holding both in his hands, but there was no denying it. There was also no denying that there was something, well, odd about those spells. A certain shimmer to the page. He realized, with a start, that the spell of Shapechanging had sported the same thing, as if the spell—

A rumbling started under his feet. He quickly rolled the scroll back up and shoved it down his boot to join the spell of Shapechanging. He would look at them all later, when he had the time to examine them properly. He was also going to have to find a better way to carry them, else he wasn't going to have anywhere to put his feet.

He looked behind him in time to see the castle beginning to tremble.

"Franciscus is inside," Sarah exclaimed. "*Do* something!"

An enormous rumble saved him from having to answer. He watched in absolute astonishment, though without perhaps the regret he should have had, as the keep began to collapse into itself.

Men began to hurl themselves out the windows. Ruith looked for the light, but saw no sign of it. He then turned to Sarah.

"We must run. If they find us, then death will seem a sweet release. Franciscus will see to himself, if seeing is possible."

"Why don't you hide us with a bloody spell of un-noticing?" she demanded. "Surely that isn't beyond your powers."

"I cannot," he said tightly.

She shot him a look of disgust, then turned away. "Very well. We'll run."

And so they did. He wasn't sure how far or how long they ran. It couldn't have been terribly far, for he could still hear the echoes of the keep falling in on itself, apparently piece by enspelled piece. Or perhaps he was hearing with more than his ears. He didn't know and didn't have the energy to attempt to find out. All he could do was continue to stumble along after Sarah.

In time, he realized that her harsh breathing was coming from more than just their flight. He reached for her hand and pulled her back to first a painful walk, then a complete stop. He turned her to him, unsurprised to see fury still burning brightly in her eyes. It was, he supposed, a defense against the tears running down her cheeks.

"I should have told you," he said quietly.

"Why didn't you?" she asked, dragging her free arm across her eyes. It was the arm burned by his father's spell, and the motion left her wincing. She lifted her arm up. "You could have cured this."

"I tried, in the barn."

She froze. "You what?"

"I had a little magic left, after the well," he admitted. "I tried to heal you with it. There is something in the wound that is beyond my skill."

"Then you have used magic," she said, stunned. "Why didn't you say something?"

He looked down at their hands intertwined. "Because I couldn't," he said with a sigh, "but aye, I have used it once or twice. On Seirceil. And at the well, to kill the trolls and burn them to ashes. At the barn, whilst you slept, to try to cure your arm." He looked at her gravely. "But then I took it all and buried it in the well I've been keeping it in these past score of years."

"Why?" she asked, and the fury was gone quite suddenly from her eyes.

"Because I do not want to become my father."

She looked at him for another moment or two, then put her arms around his waist and held him tightly. He returned the favor, holding her close, wishing that neither of them was trembling as badly as they were. Hers wasn't from weariness, he suspected. Then again, neither was his.

"Ruith, you will never be your father."

"I have quite a temper," he said lightly. "You don't know what I could do."

She pulled back where she could look at him. "You're an idiot. Your Highness."

"Don't call me that."

"Again, I have a list that is much worse." She pulled away from him and took a deep breath. "Not that you would care what I called you, I imagine. No doubt there are princesses aplenty who will be vying for your temper's attentions once word gets out, so you'll have no need of my sweet terms of endearment."

"Are you going to be the one to put out that word?"

She shot him a look. "And be the means of subjecting spoiled lassies all over the world to your vile self? You jest, sir."

He smiled in spite of himself, then pulled her close again before she could decide that in his arms was where she didn't particularly want to be. She didn't protest, which he supposed might have been construed as a good sign. He was tempted, whilst she was standing willingly in his embrace, to voice a few more flowery sentiments before she wasted any more thought on gels with useless titles, but before he could compose them in a way he thought wouldn't result in her plunging her knife into his gut, she had gasped and pulled away.

"Run!"

He looked behind them at the wave of darkness approaching,

then turned back and bolted with her. It wasn't comfortable for either of them, he supposed, but he kept hold of her hand as he ran. He had the feeling that if he let go of her, she would be washed away with that tide that was bearing down on them with a relentlessness that was altogether too familiar, though he couldn't credit it with having the same source as the well.

He ran until he couldn't feel his legs any longer, though he realized with a start that the numbness wasn't from the exertion. It was as if he'd run into a lake full of water so cold, his limbs had become completely useless. The particular lake he was standing in, however, was not created by nature. He looked at Sarah to see the realization dawning on her as well.

It was a trap.

"Who?" she gasped.

He would have looked around him to see, but he found he suddenly couldn't. The magic wasn't Doílain's. It was older, somehow, and subtler.

And a thousand times more terrible because of it.

"Use your magic, Ruith," she said, her eyes closing relentlessly. "Open the well . . . inside you . . ."

"I can't," he said, feeling a terrible lassitude seep into him. "He'll take it if I do."

"Who?"

"I've no idea." He struggled for breath. "Powerful."

And then he found he could say no more. He felt Sarah's fingers slip from his grasp, just as Mhorghain's had a score of years ago. He wanted to reach for her, but his arms wouldn't obey and his fingers were numb and useless.

He tried to fight the relentless pull of the spell, but he couldn't. He raged against it, but it was useless. He swore, but even those words slipped away from him before they could warm him.

It couldn't end this way. He had a woman to woo. He had mages to best and the rest of his father's spells to find. There was something about them, that shimmer he'd noticed before but hadn't understood the purpose of until that moment exactly.

The spells were being called.

But by whom?

He felt himself begin to fall. Sarah had been right. He should have at least used a spell of un-noticing. Then perhaps the mage who was attacking them might have passed them by. As it was, he could only suck desperate—and more difficult—breaths of air so thick he could scarce breathe it in. He groped for Sarah, but he felt nothing. He called for her, but his tongue was bound and he had no voice.

He felt the ground suddenly under his cheek and heard the sound of footsteps by his head. He forced his eyes open, but could see very little in the darkness that surrounded him. Boots the color of night. And a piece of lace that fluttered to the ground in front of him.

And then he knew no more.

Twenty-three

❧

Urchaid of truly an exhausting number of places stood over his fallen captives and congratulated himself on a hunt well executed. It had been long and rather tedious, but in the end worth the effort. He had rid the world of Connail of Iomadh and his loose tongue, left that irritating Daniel of Doìre in a ruined keep with angry mages where his enthusiasm for elegant spells would be truly appreciated, and he was now going to very generously take on the task of looking after the only living, legitimate son of Gair of Ceangail.

From afar, of course, and discreetly.

In fact, he suspected the lad would never know. Until, of course, he had collected all the spells of his father's book. And then Ruith-neadh of Ceangail would have no illusions about anything.

Urchaid looked at the leader of the mercenaries he'd hired who was standing under a tree some twenty paces away.

"Take the woman and do something with her. Sell her," he said as an afterthought. "The traders of Malairt should be on their way south soon. She'll fetch a decent price on some farm, I imagine. She's a sturdy-looking gel."

"And what of 'im?" asked the man, chewing on the end of a pipe. "Sell him too?"

"Oh, nay," Urchaid said softly. "He's a lord's son, you see, and requires special care. I'll see to him myself. But he has a temper, unfortunately. Best you bind him, perhaps to that tree over there, using very strong ropes. The spell might wear off him and I wouldn't want any unpleasantness if he wakes."

The man shrugged, then shoved his pipe into a shirt pocket before he went to work with his fellows. Within moments, Ruith and his companion were off, as it were, on their respective journeys, never to be reunited again.

Urchaid studied his new undertaking a bit longer in the darkness. It was odd that Ruithneadh's magic was so . . . inaccessible. Urchaid's command of all sorts of spells from many unique libraries and private solars was impressive, but he'd never seen something that took a mage's power and hid it so thoroughly.

A mystery.

He was almost as fond of a mystery as he was a decently fitting overcoat.

But he was even more fond of a good meal and lively conversation, which he would seek out posthaste. He threw a spell of protection over Ruith, even though it galled him a little to utter the words. The rest of it he would see to on the morrow. It wasn't as if any of the players in the drama he was conducting were going anywhere. Not until he told them to, that was.

He adjusted the lace on his cuffs, then strode off into the rather pleasant afternoon. The witchwoman of Fás set a very fine table in spite of herself and it had been far too long since he'd invited himself to tea.

Too long, indeed.

For more adventures set in the world of the
Nine Kingdoms be sure to look for

Star of the Morning

by Lynn Kurland.
Here's a special preview.

Available in paperback from Berkley Sensation!

I t was a splendid day to be dealing out death.

Adhémar, king of Neroche, nodded to himself over the thought, though he suspected that nothing so exciting would actually come to pass. He was out for a simple jaunt along his northern borders, not a pitched battle. Indeed, it had been so long since he'd encountered any trouble that it seemed that the only thing he did with his sword these days was prop it up at his elbow at supper.

It was a pity, truly. He came from a long line of superior warriors. And he had to admit, quite modestly, that he had inherited more than his fair share of prowess. It wasn't something he made mention of overmuch; his reign spoke for itself. No disasters since he'd taken the crown fourteen years earlier, no wars with neighboring kingdoms, no real trouble with the menace in the north. That sort of peace was a fine accomplishment, though it had robbed him of as many exploits to brag of as he would have liked. At least there

was nothing of a disastrous nature for some bold-tongued bard to
use to entertain those less respectful of a king's burden.

Aye, it was a good life. Adhémar looked about him in satis-
faction. He was surrounded by his most elite guardsmen, each of
them equal to an entire garrison of a lesser king. His castle, Tor
Neroche, hovered on the sheer side of a mountain behind him like
a fearsome bird of prey. Even kings of other lands shivered a bit
when they rode beneath the shadows of those battlements. And
who could blame them? It was impressive in the extreme.

And there were the more personal particulars to consider.
Adhémar turned to those with a decent amount of enthusiasm. He
examined himself, looking for flaws. It was difficult to find many,
though he was surely more critical of himself than he was of anyone else. He was young, for a king of Neroche; he was handsome,
based on reports by others he knew to be perfectly impartial; and
his entire life had been full of might, magic, and many other kings
wishing they could be him.

And now to be out and about, savoring the first days of what
promised to be a glorious autumn, knowing that the seasons would
stretch out ahead of him in as fine a manner as they trailed off
behind him. He listened to the jingle of tack and the low convers-
ings of his men and knew deep in his heart that today would be
yet another day that would pass peacefully and quietly into the
splendor that was his reign.

And then, quite suddenly, things changed.

There was the sound of a slap. Adhémar turned around in his
saddle to find the man behind him looking quite surprised to see
an arrow sticking out of his chest. The man met Adhémar's eyes.

"My liege," he said before he slid off his horse and fell to the
ground. He did not move again.

Adhémar turned to face the assault. It came, somewhat surprisingly, from a bit of forest to the north of the road. Adhémar
cursed as he spurred his horse forward. Surely someone could have

warned him about this. There were mages aplenty in his kingdom and one in particular whose duty it was to see that their northern borders were secure. There would be words later, to be sure.

But for now he would do what he did best, and that would be to intimidate and terrify his foes with his sheer presence alone. That and the Sword of Neroche, the king's sword that had struck fear into the hearts of innumerable enemies in the past. Adhémar drew his sword with a flourish. It blazed with a bloodred magelight that sent his enemies scattering.

Adhémar bellowed his war cry and followed, with his men hard on his heels. They cut through the enemy easily, soon leaving the ground littered with the bodies of the fallen. Adhémar paused on the far side of the glade and examined the corpses from his vantage point atop his horse. The lads before him weren't precisely of the sort he was accustomed to encountering. Indeed, he suspected that they weren't precisely human. He found himself hoping, with a desperation that never found home in his breast, that he was imagining what he was seeing.

He watched his men finish up their work, then resheathed his sword and nodded to his captain to move on. The men made their way up the small hillock to the road, looking over their shoulders uneasily. Adhémar normally wouldn't have admitted that he understood such looks, but he could not lie and say he did not. There was something fell about these creatures, fell and foul and not of this world. And here he'd thought that pesky black mage to the north had been contained.

Obviously not.

He looked over his shoulder for one last quick count of the dead. He counted two score.

But apparently that wasn't all.

Adhémar watched, openmouthed, as from those trees stepped one last something that was definitely not a man.

Adhémar's captain checked his horse and started back toward

the creature. Adhémar called him off. If this spoil belonged to anyone, it was to the king. Adhémar wheeled his horse around and
urged it forward, but despite its training, the horse reared with
fear. Adhémar, despite his training, lost his seat and landed on the
ground in an undignified sprawl. He scrambled back up to his feet
with a curse. He twitched aside his finely wrought cloak and drew
his sword. The magelight shone forth brilliantly.

Then it went out.

A blinding headache struck him at the same time. Adhémar
reeled, but managed to shake his head hard enough to clear it.
He took a minute to look at his sword in astonishment. This was
beginning to smell like a disaster. He drew his sleeve across his
eyes, trying to wipe away the sudden sweat. Damnation, would
the indignities never end this day? He resheathed the sword with a
curse, then drew it forth again with a flourish.

Nothing. Not even a flicker.

He took the sword and banged it with enthusiasm against its
scabbard.

Dull as stone.

He spat out a spell or two, but before he could wait to see if they
were going to take effect, his enemy had taken him by a gnarled,
four-fingered hand and flung him across the clearing.

Adhémar narrowly missed landing in a very unyielding clutch
of rocks. He sat up, looked around blearily, then realized that he
was no longer holding on to his sword. He looked around frantically for it, then saw a shadow fall over him. The creature who had
thrown him across the clearing was standing above him with its
sword raised, preparing to plunge it through Adhémar's chest.

Then the creature paused. His face, gnarled in the same manner as his hands, wore what might have been termed a look of surprise. Then he slowly began to tip forward. Adhémar rolled out of
the way before the creature crashed to the ground. There was a
sword hilt sticking out of his back.

A hand pulled him to his feet and shoved his blade back at him. Adhémar nodded his thanks and resheathed his useless sword. The headache and that unsettling weakness were receding so quickly, he almost wondered if he'd imagined both. It was with an unwholesome sense of relief that he put the whole episode behind him.

Well, except for the discovery that his sword was now apparently quite useless for anything more than carving enemies in twain.

He walked swiftly back to his horse. All was not well in the kingdom and he knew just whom to blame.

He swung up onto his horse's back, then nodded for his company to return to the keep. Someone would need to come back to see to the corpses. Perhaps then he would have answers as to what sort of creatures they had been and who had spawned them.

He looked around him to make certain no one was watching him, then drew his sword halfway from its scabbard. Still nothing but a sword. He waited for it to speak to him, to answer to the kingship in his blood.

The sword was silent.

He, on the other hand, was certainly not. He cursed as he led his company swiftly back to the castle. He swore as he thundered through the gates, dismounted at the front doors, and strode angrily through the hallways, up and down flights of stairs, and finally up the long circular stairway that led to the tower chamber where his youngest brother was supposed to be diligently working on affairs of the realm.

Adhémar suspected that he might instead be working his way through the king's collection of fine, sour wine.

Adhémar burst into the chamber without knocking. He allowed himself a cursory glance about for piles of empty wine bottles, but to his disappointment found none. What he did find, though, was the sort of semi-organized clutter he'd come to expect from his brother. There was an enormous hearth to Adhémar's right with two chairs in front of it, straining to bear up under the weight of books and clothing they'd been burdened with. Straight ahead was a long table, likewise littered with other kinds of wizardly things: papers, scrolls, pots of unidentifiable substances. Adhémar supposed they couldn't be helped, but it seemed all foolishness to him.

He found his brother standing behind the table, looking out the window. Adhémar cleared his throat loudly as he crossed the chamber, then slapped his hands on the table. His younger brother, Miach, turned around.

"Aye?"

Adhémar frowned. His brother looked enough like him that he should have been handsome. He had the same dark hair, the same enviable form, even the same flawless facial features. Today, however, Miach was just not attractive. His hair looked as if he'd been trying to pull it out by the roots, he hadn't shaved, and his eyes were almost crossed. And they were red. Adhémar scowled. "Miach, your eyes are so bloodshot, I can scarce determine their color. What have you been doing, perfecting a new spell to cause painful rashes on annoying ambassadors?"

"Nay," Miach said gravely. "Just the usual business."

Adhémar grunted. He had, quite honestly, little idea what the usual business was. Spells, puttering, muttering; who knew? His brother was archmage of the realm, which Adhémar had always suspected was something of a courtesy title. Indeed, if he were to be completely honest, he had begun to suspect that quite a few things were merely courtesy.

Or at least he had until that morning.

Adhémar drew his sword and threw it down upon Miach's worktable. "Fix that."

"I beg your pardon?"

"It doesn't work anymore," Adhémar said, irritated. He glared at his brother. "Did you see nothing of the battle this morning? Don't you have some sort of glass you peep in to see what transpires in the realm?"

"I might," Miach said, "but I was concentrating on other things."

Adhémar thrust out his finger and pointed at his sword. "Then perhaps you might take a moment and concentrate on this."

Miach looked at the sword, clearly puzzled. "Is there something amiss with it?"

"The magelight vanished!" Adhémar exclaimed. "Bloody hell, Miach, are you up here napping? Well, obviously not because you look terrible. But since you weren't watching me as you should have been, let me tell you what happened. We were assaulted by something. Many somethings, of a kind I've never seen before. My sword worked for a moment or two, then ceased."

"Ceased?" Miach echoed in surprise.

"It was as if it had never had any magic in it at all."

"Indeed?" Miach reached out to pick up the sword. "How did that—"

Adhémar snatched up the sword before his brother could touch it. "I'll keep it, thank you just the same."

Miach frowned. "Adhémar, I don't want your sword. I only wanted to see if it would speak to me."

"Well, it's not going to, so don't bother."

"I think—"

"Don't think," Adhémar said briskly. "Remedy. I can't guide the bloody realm without the power of this sword, and I can tell you with certainty that there is no power left in it."

"Adhémar," Miach said evenly, "let me see the damned sword. You can hold on to it, if you don't trust me."

"A king can never be too careful," Adhémar muttered as he held his sword out to his brother. Point first, of course. There were limits to his trust.

Miach looked at it, ran his fingers along the flat of the blade, then frowned. "I sense nothing."

"I told you so."

Miach raised his eyebrows briefly. "So you did." He looked at his brother. "What of you? Have you lost your magic as well?"

Adhémar thought back to the spells he'd cast as the creature had attacked him. He'd left the scene of battle too quickly to determine if they'd taken effect or not, but he wasn't about to admit as much. Who knew how closely and with what relish Miach might want to examine that? "I'm having an off day," Adhémar said stiffly. "Nothing more."

"Here," Miach said, taking a taper and putting it on his table. "Light that."

Adhémar drew himself up. "Too simple."

"Then it shouldn't be too hard for you."

Adhémar glared at his brother briefly, then spat out a spell.

He waited.

There was nothing.

"Try it a different way," Miach suggested. "Call the fire instead."

Adhémar hadn't done the like since his sixth year, when his mother had taken him aside and begun to teach him the rudiments of magic. It had come easily to him, but that was to be expected. He had been the chosen heir to the throne, after all.

He now closed his eyes and blocked out the faint sounds of castle life, his brother's breathing, his own heartbeat. There, in the deepest, stillest part of his being, he called the fire. It came, a single flicker that he let grow until it filled his entire mind. He opened his eyes and willed it to come forth around the wick.

Nothing, not even a puff of smoke.

"An aberration," Adhémar said, but even he had to admit that this did not bode well.

"Let me understand this," Miach said slowly. "Your sword has no magic, you apparently have no magic, and you have no idea why either has happened."

"That would sum it up quite nicely," Adhémar said curtly. "Now, fix it all and come to me in the hall when you've managed it. I'm going to find a mug of ale." He turned, walked through the doorway, slammed the door behind him, and stomped down the steps.

Actually he suspected it might take several mugs of ale to erase the memories of the day he'd just had. Best to be about it before things became worse.

Miach looked at the closed door for a moment or two before he bowed his head and blew out his breath. This was an unexpected turn of events, but not an unanticipated one. He had been archmage of the realm for fourteen years now, having taken on those duties the same moment Adhémar had taken the throne, upon the deaths of their parents. In that fourteen years, he had constantly maintained the less visible defenses against the north, passing a great deal of his time and spending a great deal of his strength to keep Lothar, the black mage of Wychweald, at bay. Those defenses had been constantly tested, constantly under siege of one kind or another.

Until the previous year.

It was as if the world outside the realm of Neroche had suddenly fallen asleep. His spells of protection and defense had gone untouched, untested, untroubled. He'd known it could not last and was not meant to last.

Perhaps the assault had begun, and in a way he hadn't foreseen.

But what to do now? He was quite certain Adhémar's sword hadn't given up its magic on its own, and that Adhémar hadn't lost his just as a matter of course. If a spell had been cast upon the king, the king had magic enough to sense it. Or at least he should have.

Miach considered that for a moment or two. Adhémar was the king and as such possessed the mantle that went with such kingship. Yet perhaps he'd spent so many years not using his magic for anything more desperate than to hasten the souring of his favorite wine that he'd lost the ability of it, a bit like a man who lost his strength because he sat upon his backside with his feet up and never lifted anything heavier than a fork.

But to have had the sword lose its power as well?

Miach rose and began to pace. There had been no spell laid upon the blade that he could discern, but perhaps there was more at work than he could see. Perhaps Adhémar had been stripped of his magic in the same way. But why? And by whom? He was very familiar with the smell of Lothar's magic and this had no stench of that kind.

Miach paced until the chamber ceased to provide him with room enough to truly aid him in his thinking. He descended the stairs and began to wander about the castle. He tramped about restlessly until he found himself standing in the great hall. It was a place made to impress, with enormous hearths on three sides and a raised dais at the back. Countless kings of Neroche had sat at that table on that dais, comfortable in the magic they possessed.

In the beginning of the realm, the magic had been the king's and his alone. The first pair of kings of Neroche had guarded the realm by virtue of their own power. In time, the kings had either had enough power in and of themselves, or they had found other means to augment that power. The Sword of Neroche had been endowed with a bit of magic itself, but it had always been dependent on the king.

That had changed eventually. It had been the grandson of King Harold the Brave who had looked upon his posterity, considered the queen who had left him for one of Lothar's sons, and decided that the only way to assure the safety of the kingdom was to imbue his sword with all of his power. He did, chose his least objectionable son as king, and made his magically gifted nephew archmage as a balance. It had been the Sword of Neroche, from that time on, that had carried most of the king's magic, folded into the steel of its blade.

Miach looked down at the floor and rubbed the back of his neck. Of course, he had magic of his own, more than he had ever admitted to his brothers, more than even he had suspected when he'd become the archmage. But he knew, in a deep, uncompromising way that reached down into his bones, that it would take all the magic he could muster, as well as all the king could draw from the Sword of Neroche, to keep Lothar at bay should he mount an all-out attack.

Unless there was another way.

He heard the faint hint of a song. He looked around him, startled, but the great hall was empty. He frowned, then resumed his contemplation of the floor.

Again, he heard the whisper of a song.

He realized, quite suddenly, where the music was coming from. He looked up slowly until his eyes fastened on a sword, hanging above the enormous hearth at the end of the great hall.

The Sword of Angesand.

Miach crossed slowly over to the dais, stepped up, and walked around behind the king's high table. He looked up, finding that it was impossible not to do so. The sword was hanging well out of reach, so he was forced to fetch a chair. He pulled the sword down and looked at it.

The Sword of Angesand, fashioned by Mehar of Angesand, queen of Neroche, and laced with enough magic to make even the most strong-stomached of souls quake. Miach held the sword aloft, but saw nothing but firelight flickering along the polished steel, firelight that revealed the tracery of leaves and flowers along the blade. All the things that Queen Mehar loved . . .

It whispered the echo of the song he'd heard, then it fell silent.

Miach looked at the blade. If the Sword of Neroche was unresponsive, was it possible the Sword of Angesand might not be? Could not a soul be found to awaken its magic? If a wielder could be found, perhaps it would be enough to keep Lothar curbed until Miach could solve the mystery of Adhémar and his sword.

Perhaps.

Miach's hand shook as he replaced the sword—and that wasn't from the exertion. It might work. Indeed, he couldn't see why it wouldn't. He turned and walked out of the great hall, convinced that there was no other path to be taken. Neroche's king had lost his magic and the archmage could not win the battle on his own. The Sword of Angesand had power enough bound into its elegant steel to tip the scales in their favor.

Now, to find someone willing to go off and search for that wielder.

Miach made his way through the castle and back into the private family quarters. He found almost all his brothers gathered in their own, more modest hall, sipping or gulping ale as their particular circumstance warranted. He paused at the doorway to the chamber and looked them over. Was there a man there who might have the clearness of vision to recognize a wielder when he saw one?

Miach looked at Cathar, who sat to the right of the king's chair. He was a serious man of five and thirty winters, a scant year younger than Adhémar, who never would have thought to take an uninvited turn in his brother's seat to see how it felt.

Of course, that kind of testing was nothing to Rigaud, two years Cathar's junior and as light-minded as the rest of them were serious. He lounged comfortably in Adhémar's chair, dressed in his finest clothes. Miach looked pointedly at his green-eyed brother and only received a lazy wink in return. When Adhémar entered, he would be forced to bodily remove Rigaud from his seat, which Rigaud would enjoy immensely, though he would no doubt complain about the damage to his clothing.

Next came Nemed, a lean man of thirty-two years with soft gray eyes and a gentle smile. Miach shook his head. Cathar wouldn't have dared take on the task, Rigaud would have forgotten the task in his pursuit of fame and fortune, and Nemed would have found himself ripped to shreds by anyone with any ambition for power.

That left him with only his twin brothers, Mansourah and Turah. They were canny warriors, but with weaponry was where their allegiance lay. They likely would have spent their time fighting over which of *them* might have been more suited to wielding the Sword of Angesand than searching out someone else to do it.

Miach sighed heavily as he realized what he'd known from the start. There was only one to seek out the wielder, and that soul would not be happy to hear the news.

Adhémar suddenly entered the chamber. All stood except Rigaud, who apparently didn't want to give up his seat any sooner than necessary. Miach suppressed a smile at the squawking that ensued when the preening rooster was unceremoniously removed from his perch.

Adhémar sat, then looked at Miach. "Well?"

Miach shut the door behind him, then leaned back against it. No sense in letting anyone escape unnecessarily. "I believe I have found a solution."

"A solution?" Cathar echoed. "A solution to what?"

Miach folded his arms over his chest. He wasn't about to reveal the details of the king's current condition. Adhémar could do that himself.

Adhémar shot Miach a glare, then turned to Cathar. "I lost my magic," he said bluntly.

There were sounds of amazement from several quarters. Cathar frowned.

"This afternoon?" he asked.

"Aye."

"Is it permanent?" Rigaud asked promptly.

"Don't hope for it overmuch," Adhémar said shortly. "I'm sure it will return soon." He shot Miach a look. "Won't it?"

"I'm still working on that," Miach said. And he would be, no doubt, for quite some time to come.

Adhémar scowled, then looked back at the rest of his brothers. "It isn't permanent," he said confidently. "So, until I regain my magic, I'm sure our clever brother over there has a solution to our problems." He looked at Miach expectantly.

Miach didn't want to look as if he was gearing up for battle, so he tried a pleasant smile. "I do," he said pleasantly. "I suggest the Sword of Angesand."

"The Sword of Angesand," Adhémar mouthed. He choked, looked about in vain for something to drink, then pounded himself upon his chest in desperation. Cathar handed him his own cup of ale. He drank deeply. "The what?" he wheezed.

"You heard me."

"You cannot be serious!"

"Why not?" Miach asked.

"Because it is a woman's sword!" Adhémar exclaimed. "You can*not* expect me to carry a woman's sword!"

Miach suppressed the urge to roll his eyes. "It *isn't* a woman's sword. It was merely fashioned by a woman—"

"It has flowers all over it!"

"Think on them as nightshade, dealing a slow and painful death to those upon whom the sword falls," Miach said. "Many men have carried that sword in battle and been victorious with it, flowers aside." He paused. "Have you ever held it?"

Adhémar scowled at him. "I have and nay, it does not call my name. Fortunately," he muttered, "because I wouldn't carry it even if it did."

"I don't expect *you* to carry it," Miach said. "I expect you to find someone *else* to carry it."

Adhémar gaped at him. Miach noted that the rest of his brothers were wearing similar expressions. Except Rigaud, of course, who was calculatingly eyeing the throne.

"What kind of someone?" Cathar asked cautiously.

"I imagine it will need to be a mage," Miach said slowly. "After Queen Mehar last used it, it has only been wielded by those with magic."

"Why don't you take it up?" Adhémar asked. "Or don't you have the magic necessary to do so?"

Miach looked at his brother coolly. "I daresay I do, but the sword does not call to me."

"Have you asked it?"

"Adhémar, I am no longer a lad of eight summers. Even I can

reach up far enough to pull the blade off the wall—which I have done a time or two while you were napping."

"I've seen him," Rigaud put in helpfully. "And more than twice."

Miach shot Rigaud a glare before he turned back to his king. "We need a sword to replace yours until we can determine what ails you."

Adhémar grunted. "Very well, I can see the sense in it. Where will you go to find this mage?"

Miach considered. He couldn't leave Adhémar guarding the borders without his magic. There were times he suspected it was dangerous to leave Adhémar in charge *with* his magic. But telling him as much was out of the question. This would require diplomacy, tact, and very probably a great deal of unwarranted flattery. Miach cleared his throat and frowned, pretending to give the matter much thought.

"I suppose I could go," he began, "but I have no way of recognizing who the man will be." That wasn't exactly true, but there was no point in telling Adhémar that either. "Unlike you, my liege."

"Bloody hell, Miach, I can't call enough magelight to keep myself from tripping down the stairs! You go find him."

"But no one else sees as clearly as you do," Miach said smoothly. "And it will take a special sort of vision, an eye that discerns far above what most mortal men can see, a sense of judgment that only a man of superior wit and wisdom possesses." He paused dramatically. "In short, my liege, it is a task that only you can possibly be considered equal to."

Adhémar opened his mouth to protest, then shut it suddenly. Miach supposed he was grappling with the unexpected flattery and weighing the potential glory of it being true against the trouble of actually leaving Tor Neroche to traipse over the Nine Kingdoms, looking for someone to wield a sword that wasn't his.

Miach saw Rigaud stir, no doubt to say something about

keeping the throne warm for his brother while he was away. He shot Rigaud a look of warning. Rigaud made a rather rude gesture in return, but grinned as he did it. Miach pursed his lips and turned his attention back to Adhémar. His brother finally cursed.

A very good sign.

"I'll need to be back by mid-winter, at the latest," Adhémar announced.

"Why?" Miach asked carefully.

"I'm getting married."

"Finally," Cathar said, sounding rather relieved. "To whom?"

"Don't know yet," Adhémar said, finishing off Cathar's ale and handing his brother's cup back to him. "I'm still thinking on it."

Miach was set to suggest that perhaps Adhémar choose someone with a decent amount of magic to make up for his lack, but he forbore. For now, it was enough to have time to sort out what was truly going on in the palace without his brother underfoot, bellowing like a stuck pig about his sufferings.

Adhémar scowled. "I've little liking for this idea." He looked at Miach narrowly. "I suspect this is a ruse so you can keep your toes warmed by the fire while I'm off looking for a fool ready to volunteer to take his life in his hands to protect us from the north."

Miach didn't offer any opinion on that.

Adhémar swore for quite some time in a very inventive fashion. Finally, he swept them all with a look. "Well, it appears I am off to find a wielder for the Sword of Angesand."

"Have a lovely journey," Rigaud said, edging closer to the throne.

Adhémar glared at him. "Turah will sit the Throne while I am gone—"

"What?" Rigaud shouted, leaping in front of his brother. "Adhémar, what of me! I know Nemed is worthless—"

Miach was unsurprised by either the volume of the complaints or Adhémar's choice. After all, it was well within Adhémar's right to choose any of his brothers to succeed him.

Adhémar held up his hand. "He is my choice and my choice is final. You will, of course, aid him as you would me."

Miach didn't need to look into the future to know what would happen in the king's absence. Mansourah would shadow Cathar, Nemed would stand unobtrusively behind Turah and steady him should he falter, and Rigaud would rage continuously about the injustice of it all. Adhémar looked at Miach.

"And you will do as you see fit, I suppose."

"As he bloody pleases, you mean," Rigaud grumbled.

"As I usually do," Miach said with a grave smile. "I have quite enough to do to keep me busy."

"You watch your back, Adhémar," Cathar rumbled. He wrapped his hands around his cup of ale. "I've no mind to crown Turah any time soon."

"Heaven preserve us," Rigaud gasped. "My liege, perhaps I should come and defend you."

"With what?" Cathar said, scowling. "One of your brightly colored tunics? Aye, blind the bloody buggers with your garb and hope they don't stick you in spite of it."

Rigaud, for all his preening, wasn't above defending his own honor and he launched himself at his eldest brother with a curse. Adhémar moved his legs out of the fray and helped himself to Rigaud's ale. The king's respite was short. Soon he was pulled into the skirmish. Miach sighed. Things never changed, or so it seemed.

Or perhaps not.

Miach looked over the scene of skirmish and though things seemed the same, they were indeed not. Adhémar was powerless. His remaining brothers, even put together, did not have enough magic to keep the brooding darkness at bay. Nay, a wielder for the Sword of Angesand had to be found, and Adhémar was the one to do it.

"Miach!" Adhémar bellowed from the bottom of the pile. "Any thoughts on where I should go?"

"Probably to the most unlikely place possible," Miach offered.

"Ah, but there are so many choices," Adhémar said sourly. He shoved his brothers off him one by one, then sat up and sighed. "The kingdom of Ainneamh?"

"Only elves there," Miach said. "I wouldn't bother. I would turn my eye to a more humble place." He paused. "Perhaps the Island of Melksham."

"What!" Adhémar exclaimed. "The Island of Melksham? Have you lost all sense?"

"It was but a suggestion."

"And a poor one at that." He shook his head in disgust as he crawled to his feet. "Melksham. Ha! That will be the very *last* place I'll look." He glared at Miach one last time, then he strode from the room, his curses floating in the air behind him.

Miach watched as his remaining bothers untangled themselves, collected their empty cups, and made their way singly and with a good deal of commenting on the vagaries of the monarchy from the chamber.

Miach was left there, alone, staring at the empty place where his brothers had been. Unbidden, a vision came to him of the chamber before him, only it was abandoned, desolate, ruined, uninhabitable—

He shook his head sharply. That was no vision; it was a lie spawned by his own unease. All would be well. He was doing all he could. No doubt this was the worst of the disasters.

He reflected again on the places Adhémar might possibly go to find the wielder. Melksham Island was certainly the least likely, which would make it the most likely—but he wouldn't tell Adhémar that. With any luck, he would make it there eventually on his own.

Miach turned and left the chamber, leaving the search for the wielder in his brother's hands.

For the moment.